THE DARK SPAWN

A Medieval Romance

By Kathryn Le Veque

KATHRYN LE VEQUE
NOVELS

Author's Note

It's time for the de Velts to have their saga continued!

I can't believe how long it's been since I last wrote about Jax de Velt or his family, but there is a reason for that. Originally, I was going to write about Jax (*The Dark Lord*) and the knights who served him, men known collectively as The Titans, but I became more interested in Jax and Kellington's children than the men who helped Jax conquer the borders. The kids kept popping up in places – Cassian, mostly, because he served Christopher de Lohr (*Rise of the Defender*). Jax even popped up in *Devil's Dominion* and had a fairly meaty part in that book, so my focus really went to the family as opposed to Jax's collection of cutthroats.

And here we are!

Now, we met Coleby de Velt as a baby at the end of *The Dark Lord*… and that's all we've ever seen of him. He's evidently been working behind the scenes and doing all sorts of wild stuff in my universe, much of which we're going to discover now. As we're going to find out, he's been a VERY busy boy. I don't want to give away too much, but you're going to want to find out what he's been up to. Some of it isn't pretty, but that's understandable – he's a de Velt.

And then we have our heroine, Corisande. A very unusual lady from the House of de Bourne, a new series I'll be introducing next year. They are descended from the last King of Northumbria, Eric Bloodaxe, and they carry the ax as their standard. The Warrior Knights of de Bourne will be an exciting series, and Corisande is as darned near as tough as her brothers.

She's certainly tough enough for a de Velt.

Now, there are a LOT of books of mine set between about 1190 to 1220 A.D. – all of the Executioner Knights, of course, plus the de Lohr series. In reviewing some of these books to make sure I stick with the details of Cole that I've already established, I read two of them that were particularly engrossing – *Devil's Dominion* and *Godspeed*. *Godspeed* has a life-changing event happen for the House of de Velt and it just made me detest King John all the more. If you've read this series, and others set in John's reign, then you know I have a particular dislike for John. Ironic, considering he's my 23rd great-grandfather. No kidding.

Let's talk a little about William the Lion, the King of Scotland at this time. He's mentioned in this book as William the Lion, although that's not what he was known by to his contemporaries. He was called William the Rough, among other things, but for the purposes of contemporary identification, I have used the term we are most familiar with. Also, I had to make sure he was identified from William Marshal. So many Williams!

Now, the warnings – this is not only an Executioner Knights tale, but it's a de Velt book, meaning the rules don't apply here. There are some gross things. There are some disturbing things. A de Velt book always has something that's grittier and more brutal than any other book, so be aware that there are some things in the book that will make you laugh out loud and then other things that will make you cringe.

But that's the beauty of de Velt and the Executioner Knights – they're not sugar coated, and I personally love that. It's so much more relatable and "real". But they will never, ever cross that line into something that's going to turn you away from the book. What happens with de Velt stays with de Velt – and it's something that endears the family to readers. The de Velts make no apologies. Add in a touch of the Executioner

Knights (they're really only secondary to this tale), and it makes it an innately edgy story. But I love these guys, all of them. We should all be so ballsy, loyal, and unrestrained.

I want to mention the most prevalent de Velt physical trait – the different-colored eyes. There's more than one de Velt in this book, so it comes up frequently. The trait is called heterochromia and it is indeed hereditary. I have it myself – my green eyes have yellow around the pupils and a darker teal ring around the entire iris, but Jax de Velt, Cole's father, had it to the extreme – two brown eyes, only the right one had a big splash of bright green in it. His sons inherited that condition, only mixed with their mother's golden-brown eyes' The boys have all sorts of interesting color combinations.

Now, let's talk about some Easter eggs in this book!

Northwood Castle plays a role here, but it's the generation before *The Wolfe*, so you're going to meet the Earl of Teviot, Adam de Longley, and his son, John – who is the John de Longley that William was so fond of in *The Wolfe*. Not huge roles, but they're present. This book is all set pre-de Wolfe, so all of the usual locations we're familiar with – Castle Questing, The Lair, etc. don't really exist as they do in the de Wolfe Pack series. In fact, Castle Questing is mentioned in the context of its original owner, Baron Dudworth. There are a few other subtle Easter eggs in the book, so see if you can find them.

Lastly, as I wrote this book, I realized that the Executioner Knights' stable has really grown. There are almost twenty of them now and it seems that more are added with every book, so I've done something for this book that I haven't done for any of the others – I made a list of the Executioner Knights and where they serve. There are a lot of knights in this book because the Executioner Knights stick together, but not all of them are here. We'll assume those that aren't here are off doing their own thing. I love how the Executioner Knights are growing into an enormous brotherhood. The list is so you can refresh your memory about the players and also get acquainted with two new ones. You'll love them!

The usual pronunciation guide:

Corisande – CORA-sond

Gaia – GUY-uh

Ares – AIR-ees (like Aries, the Zodiac sign)

Anteaus – An-TAY-us

Happy Reading!
Hugs,

Coleby de Velt is the firstborn son of the notorious Dark Lord, Ajax de Velt.

Cole grew up idolizing his father – and knowing all about his history – and he has his father's dark streak. That makes him a perfect agent for William Marshal and the Executioner Knights. As William Marshal himself says – *"Tis better to be at the Devil's right hand than in his path…"* And Coleby is definitely the Devil.

He's the spawn of The Dark Lord and everything that goes with it.

When Cole falls for an unusual woman, it's with his whole heart. He doesn't know how to do anything half-measure – and he doesn't know how to protect himself. Lady Corisande "Cori" de Bourne, an accomplished woman of considerable talent, has bewitched him and, for a sweet moment in time, Cole experiences something he's never known before – a blooming love and a calm to his restless soul he can't begin to describe. He believes he has finally found happiness. Perhaps the darkness has finally met with the light.

Until the Scots attack and Cori is captured.

Unfortunately for the Scots, The Dark Spawn is unleashed. Cole will stop at nothing to rescue his beloved Cori. But when he finally regains her with surprising ease, a horrible truth is revealed.

All is not as it seems.

Can Cole forgive the unforgivable? Or will The Dark Spawn's heart turn cold?

de Velt Motto: *Quoniam magnus coram mors*

Death before mercy

List of Executioner Knights and Allies

As of 1210 A.D.

(Note: some later Executioner Knight tales take place years after this story is set, so as of 1210 A.D., this is where these knights serve and/or are in command of)

William Marshal – Earl of Pembroke, Pembroke Castle and Farrington House

Christopher de Lohr – Earl of Hereford and Worcester, Lioncross Abbey Castle

David de Lohr – Earl of Canterbury, Canterbury Castle, Bellham Place

Peter de Lohr – Lioncross Abbey Castle

Gart Forbes – Dunster Castle, Devon

Caius d'Avignon – Richmond Castle, North Yorkshire

Maxton of Loxbeare – Chalford Hill Castle, Gloucester

Kress de Rhydian – Seton Castle, Scotland

Achilles de Dere – Caversham Manor, Berkshire

Susannah de Tiegh de Dere – a Blackchurch-trained knight, wife of Achilles

Alexander de Sherrington – Farringdon House for William Marshal (a year before he becomes Christopher de Lohr's son-in-law)

Bric MacRohan – Narborough Castle, Norwich Castle, Norfolk

Dashiell du Reims – Ramsbury Castle, Wiltshire. Also

Thunderbey Castle, East Anglia.

Sean de Lara – King John's personal bodyguard

Kevin de Lara – Canterbury Castle (in the service of David de Lohr). Also Hyssington, Caradoc, and Trelystan Castles – Welsh Marches

Cullen de Nerra – Rockingham Castle, Northamptonshire

Cole de Velt – formerly William the Lion's personal guard, now Pelinom Castle

Addax al-Kort – service to Ajax de Velt and William Marshal

Essien al-Kort – service to Ajax de Velt and William Marshal

Morgan de Wolfe – in service to Caius d'Avignon, Richmond Castle

Gareth de Llion – in service to William Marshal

Keller de Poyer – in service to William Marshal at Pembroke Castle/Netherworld Castle (Keller is more of a knight for William Marshal than he's actually a spy)

Garren le Mon – technically, he's believed to be dead after 1201 A.D.

PROLOGUE

NOCTEM INTERFECTIS (A DAY OF SLAYING)

The Month of May
Year of Our Lord 1210 A.D.
Farringdon House, London
Property of William Marshal

"WHAT IS HAPPENING?" A battle-scarred knight with a heavy Irish accent spoke softly. "Does anyone know why we've been summoned?"

He was speaking to a group of men, hovering in the same room, standing silently as they waited in the darkness, with only a flickering fire to light the surprisingly ornate solar of one of the greatest knights in England. It was William Marshal's domain, the lair of England's greatest agents.

Spies… killers… gentlemen knights.

They had been summoned.

It smelled like death.

The first floor solar of Farringdon House was a meeting place, one that William Marshal used to summon the great and powerful of England. It covered nearly half of the floor. There was easily room for fifty or more men in the solar with its great stone hearth, exposed beams overhead, and painted walls. The floor was made from thick slats of wood, but pocked from men who had walked upon it with their spurs and heavy boots. It was a spectacular room, meant for men of greatness.

Tonight was no exception.

The knight's question was met with silence, for truthfully, no one had an answer for him. In fact, they all had the very same question.

Why had they been summoned?

Perhaps only one man really had an answer.

"Sit, lads." Christopher de Lohr, Earl of Hereford and Worcester, took his own advice and planted himself in a cushioned chair next to the hearth. The chair groaned under his bulk. "We shall all know soon enough."

Words of wisdom from the great earl. The group of knights began to settle down, waiting for William Marshal to make an appearance.

And what a group it was.

The big Irish knight who had asked the question was a legacy knight from the House of de Winter. Sir Bric MacRohan was the biggest, meanest knight this side of Eire and The Marshal found him a particularly effective intimidation tool. Next to him, and related to him by marriage, was Sir Dashiell du Reims, captain of the army for the Duke of Savernake. They didn't come any more talented than Dash.

Standing over near the enormous and elaborate table that contained wine and refreshments were a few more knights who had decided that drinking their liege's fine wine and eating the sweets provided were a good enough diversion to pass the time. David de Lohr, Earl of Canterbury and Christopher's younger brother, was one of them. In a chamber full of talented warriors, David was the crème de la crème. There was no one faster with a blade in all of England. Next to him stood Kress de Rhydian and Achilles de Dere, men who were known throughout England as the original Executioner Knights.

If there was a dirty job, they would do it.

Their leader, Maxton of Loxbeare, was standing near the window, looking out over the London streets as they quieted down for the night. Maxton was a noble knight with a dark streak in him and he owed a debt to The Marshal, which is why he and Kress and Achilles served the man. At least, it had been a debt in the beginning when The Marshal had secured their release from a French prison, but these days, they served him out of loyalty.

They might have been assassins, but they were also men of honor.

But there were more men, still. Kevin de Lara, a young knight of great skill, came from a fine Marcher family, while next to him stood Alexander de Sherrington, another Executioner Knight. He would do anything, to anyone, with no regrets. And leaning against the wall near him was Caius d'Avignon, an enormously tall and formidable knight known as The Britannia Viper.

His name said it all.

Rounding out the group were two of the youngest members in Peter de Lohr, son of Christopher, and Cullen de Nerra, son of the Itinerant Justice of Hampshire. They were great knights from great families, and much was expected of them. As agents for William Marshal, that meant that they were the most elite of warriors.

The final member of the collection was perhaps the most intimidating and frightening, even more than MacRohan and The Britannia Viper. His name was Gart Forbes, a monster in battle, and a knight who had served the de Lohrs for years before he married the Dowager Baroness of Buckland. Now, he had his own empire in the wilds of Devon, but he was never far from The Marshal should the man have need of him.

All of these great men, waiting for William Marshal to make an appearance.

Fortunately, the wait wasn't an excessive one.

The time and day had already been pre-destined, so they knew that they were expected, but William Marshal was late. Then they heard a door slam down on the floor below, something that had heads lifting, senses attuned. There were footfalls on the great stone staircase that led to the solar, and as the footfalls drew closer, the knights grew more focused. There was more than one set of footsteps. More than one man was approaching.

Something was afoot.

The great double doors to the solar burst open.

"Excellent," William Marshal said, pulling off his cloak. "Is everyone here?"

Christopher stood up from his chair next to the hearth. "Aye," he said, noting that William was quite rushed. "Everyone is here. How may we be of service?"

William heard him but didn't acknowledge him, at least not right away. He was clearly preoccupied. He tossed the cloak aside and moved for the table where the wine was kept, pouring himself a measure without even offering any to anyone else, including the man who had entered the chamber behind him and was now quietly closing the doors.

Sir Sean de Lara, bodyguard to King John and a secret agent for William Marshal, was the last man into the chamber.

Enormous and terrifying, the man known throughout royal and military circles as Lord of the Shadows found Christopher in a chamber full of men, his expression suggesting that something quite serious was about to take place. It put Christopher on edge, and also David, who came to stand next to his brother. Between them, they controlled a massive army and huge swathes of England, so anything that had both de Lohr brothers involved had to be big, indeed. They just didn't know what it was.

Yet.

As the room full of seasoned men waited expectantly, William downed a full cup of wine and poured himself another.

"I sent for all of you weeks ago, so I will not delay my reasons," he said, smacking his lips as he turned to the room. "I have just come from a meeting with the king. It seems that William, the illustrious King of Scotland, is preparing a large and secretive alliance, so secretive that I have had three agents involved in the quest to get to the bottom of what is happening. It has taken time and money and connections to discover what we need to know, but you should be aware at the outset that this is so serious, Ajax de Velt's army is marching into Scotland as we speak. I have turned the man loose and he has orders to massacre. You *know* what that means."

One could have heard a pin drop in the silence that followed, silence so tense and shocking that it was nearly palpable. Ajax de Velt was legendary in the annals of England's history, a man who, in his prime, had the most brutal and barbaric mercenary army in the known world. Jax had conquered a portion of the Welsh Marches by not only defeating armies, but putting all living men who had surrendered or had been captured on stakes for all to see.

A forest of macabre bodies, the legends said. Jax took no prisoners – every man, woman, and even child captured alive had not been spared. Jax's zenith had been five straight years of terror, five straight years of showing no mercy to those he conquered, and all of England, Scotland, and Wales lived in fear of the man.

But that had been thirty years ago. Since then, Jax had been tamed by the love of a good woman and he had become a content and valuable ally on the Scots borders. Everyone was so scared of the man that all anyone wanted to do was be friendly to him, the king included. No one wanted to stir up the embers of that brutal madman who could kill as easily as breathe.

Therefore, William's announcement was a startling one.

De Velt had been turned loose.

Again.

Christopher, in fact, was perhaps the most shocked of all. He was a good friend of Jax de Velt's, kept in fairly regular contact with the man, and this was the first he'd heard about any of this. As he looked at William in astonishment, only one word came to mind.

"Why?"

William fixed on Christopher. Knowing the relationship between him and de Velt, he motioned for the man to sit down. As Christopher did, stiffly, William came to sit across from him as the knights in the chamber began to gather around.

They didn't want to miss a word of what was about to be said.

"It was not something I did lightly, Chris," William said, settling back in his chair. "What I am about to tell you – tell *all* of you – will not be spoken of outside of this chamber. Am I clear?"

Everyone nodded. Of course, given their line of work, no one ever spoke of anything that was discussed with William Marshal, anyway, but the sheer fact that the man had to say that alluded to the seriousness of the situation.

"Then let me start from the beginning," William said, lowering his voice. "As you know, I have many agents all throughout England and Scotland and Wales. I even have them in France and beyond. My eyes and ears are everywhere, men I pay well for information that keeps England safe from her enemies. Unfortunately, some of our most serious enemies are to the north."

"The Scots," David muttered. "That is nothing new."

William's eyes narrowed at Christopher's younger brother. "Nay, it is nothing new," he said, irritated that he was interrupted. "But what if I told you that our good friend William the Lion is trying to convince the Norse princes of the outer isles to help him gain back Northumbria? Unfortunately, it is true. Jon Harraldsson and his brother, David, are the Earls of Orkney and Shetland. I realize that William has had a tumultuous relationship with them, but my agents tell me that William has promised them lands in Northumbria if they'll help him regain what he believes belongs to Scotland – and the Northmen. Harraldsson has gone so far as to send word to his Norse brethren in Hordaland and Danmark that they, too, will be provided lands in Northumberland if they help the Scots. I fear a Norse army is about to move into the north and the results could be devastating."

It was astonishing information. Christopher looked at the man, incredulous. "How long has this been going on?"

William sighed heavily. "More than a year," he said. "I was only informed about it six months ago and that news came down through the House of de Bourne, Lords of Bernicia. Do you know them?"

Christopher, still dazed, nodded. "I do," he said. "I fought in a couple of battles in the north and they served under the Earl of Northumberland. I seem to remember someone telling me that they are direct descendants of the last King of Northumbria."

William nodded. "They are," he said. "That is why the title they hold is Lords of Bernicia, of the ancient kingdom. If you are unaware, their castle is called The Keld – it is a large place that sits on a major road into Scotland. They control most of the southern portion of Northumberland and even parts of

Yorkshire. Their family is an old and distinguished one, but their relationship to the crown of England has historically been… difficult. Our ancestors stole Northumbria from their ancestors."

"But what does all of this have to do with de Velt marching into Scotland to massacre the Scots?" David wanted to know. He was always the impatient one. "*Why* has de Velt amassed his army?"

William held up a hand to be patient, looking at the host of concerned and curious faces around him. "Because loyalists of William the Lion sent word to de Bourne and asked them to be part of the movement to wrest Northumberland from England," he said. "Now, I would think that to the House of de Bourne, such an offer would be most inviting, but they surprised me. Alastor de Bourne is a man with a head on his shoulders because he knows that if he agrees, the rest of his life and probably the lives of his children and grandchildren would be nothing but warfare. He knows he cannot stand against the English armies that would roll into Northumberland to regain it, so he sent me word instead about the offer to warn me. I already had spies in the Scottish court and they have confirmed these plans."

"Who are the agents?" David asked.

A gleam came to William's eyes. "As I said, I have agents all over England," he said. "Of course, the men in this room are my core, the men I utilize the most, but I have agents in the north who are buried so deeply in their covert actions that you would never guess who they are… and *what* they are. It was those men who secured some of what I needed to know. I informed John of the situation and, for once, we agree that we must act. This conspiracy between the Scots and the Norse is so widespread that we must have a Scotsman who is entrenched in the situation, one who knows the details of this unholy conspiracy because I want answers. Therefore, de Velt is taking his army into Scotland to obtain my prize. At any cost."

Christopher glanced at the faces around them. No one seemed to be following William very well. He was still being somewhat vague.

"Be plain, William," he said in a low voice. "We've all come a very long way because you said that this was urgent, so be plain with the situation and what you need from us."

William's gaze fell on Christopher, hearing his mild irritation. His eyes, yellowed with age, studied the man a moment before he downed the contents of his cup.

He set the cup aside.

"Cole de Velt is Jax's eldest son," he said quietly. "He has also been an agent for me for a few years. I know most of you did not know that, but Sean did. You see, Cole has been assuming Sean's role with William the Lion. As Sean is the protector of John, Cole has spent the past few years moving through the Scottish ranks to get close to the king. He is English, that is true, but he mimics a Scotsman perfectly. He's been pretending to be Scots all this time. He is the one who has identified much of what I have told you, but he has also identified something else – someone who knows a great deal of this conspiracy. I've sent Jax and Cole to extract Alpin Canmore from Fountainhall Castle. I want that man. He'll tell me everything I must know."

"How can we assist?"

William fixed on Christopher. "You will take your army into Northumberland," he said. Then, he looked at the rest of the knights. "Those of you in command of armies will go as well, because if Canmore knows as much as I think he does, William the Lion will not take his abduction lightly. He could take half of Scotland and the Norse princes and march into Northumberland to retaliate. Now do you understand?"

The seriousness of the matter settled deep. This wasn't a simple operation William was speaking of; this was war. Massive war between Scotland and England, with the Norse pulled into it.

Something like that could easily tear the north apart and then some.

"I will have to tell Edward, my lord," Dashiell said. "The Duke of Savernake must know this so that he will grant me permission to take his army north."

William nodded. "You have my permission," he said. "The duke's massive army is essential to this operation. Bric?"

The big, Irish knight answered smartly. "My lord?"

William looked at the man with the pale blond hair and eyes so blue that they were silver. "You may tell your liege and request his army," he said. "I have every confidence that Daveigh de Winter will permit you to bring his army to the north because I need the de Winter war machine. Cullen, the same can be said for you – tell your father what I have told you and request his army. Gart, I require yours, as well. Christopher will be in command of the battle, of course, and you will rendezvous with his army at Sheffield. From there, you will go north to The Keld. De Bourne will welcome you. That is where you shall stage the armies and, hopefully, it will be where de Velt brings the hostage he currently seeks." He sobered dramatically. "Good men, this is mayhap the most serious situation we have faced in recent memory. If we do not destroy Scotland's plans, they will surely destroy us."

William didn't say it to exaggerate. He said it because it was the truth. They understood what the stakes were and the consequences, and perhaps Christopher and David most of all. They'd seen more battles than they could count, but this one… this one might prove to be the most serious. If what William said was true, they were facing an invasion from the north.

In fact, Christopher seemed particularly subdued, staring into the fire as he contemplated what was to come. After a moment, he turned his head towards the group.

"Peter, Cullen, Dash, and Bric," he said. "You will go down to the courtyard and wait for me. Kevin, go with them. The rest of you will remain for a moment. I have something more I wish to say to The Marshal."

The five younger knights broke off without another word and cleared the chamber. When the door shut softly behind them, Christopher found himself looking at those who remained. These men were older, men who had seen a great deal of war and strife in their careers. Christopher, David, Sean, Maxton, Kress, Achilles, Caius, Alexander, and Gart had all seen action in The Levant, as they had gone on crusade with King Richard. That bonded them more than most and there was a brotherhood there that could not be shaken.

Christopher's gaze returned to William.

"Did you truly unleash de Velt, William?" he finally hissed.

William nodded slowly. "I did," he said. "I want the Scots to know that we will stop at nothing to destroy this ridiculous conspiracy, including using de Velt as an attack dog. I want to strike fear into their hearts and that is exactly what this move will do. The first strike must be bold and decisive. You know that."

Christopher nodded, though he wasn't entirely sure releasing such death and destruction was the right move. "You must do what you feel is right, of course," he said. "But de Velt… once the Scots are finished being terrified, they will strike back and strike hard. We may find ourselves in a nasty war regardless, even though that is exactly what you are trying to prevent."

William leaned back against his chair, sighing wearily. "That is what de Lara said."

Attention turned to Sean, who had remained silent since

entering the chamber. He wasn't simply a seasoned knight, but also heir to a large lordship. He and his brother, Kevin, hadn't been on speaking terms for years even though they served The Marshal together. They could work well enough together, but that brotherly bond had been badly fractured by Sean's mission as the king's loyal bodyguard and Kevin's disgust in his brother's dedication to his duty over his noble reputation. But every man in that room held Sean in great esteem for his sacrifice.

And his unparalleled knowledge.

"I work in the shadows," Sean said simply, looking at the eyes upon him. "It was my sense that it would be better to send a few men to capture Canmore rather than an army."

"But we *must* make a statement, Sean," William reminded him.

Sean cocked an eyebrow. "And you are with de Velt," he said. "But my suggestion of a few well-trained men to capture Canmore would have been far less destructive. There might be a leak in the dam, but the dam would still hold."

"Meaning what?"

"Meaning that the Scots would not be aware that we knew of their plans," Sean insisted softly. "The situation would be shaken, but not fractured. There would be no sense of urgency to begin their plans in earnest. As it is, de Velt's charge may bring about the execution of the Scot's scheme sooner rather than later because sending The Dark Lord into Scotland is a decisive offensive. It is a clear sign that we know of their plans and, ultimately, it is an act of war."

"I agree with The Marshal," Gart, who had also remained largely silent, spoke up. "What you say is true, Sean, but we must act swiftly and decisively. The Scots and their Norse allies will think twice about invading Northumberland if they know they will have to face armies like de Velt. It is the perfect deterrent."

Sean and Gart had a long and friendly history. There was no nastiness in Gart's counter, simply honesty. Therefore, Sean simply shrugged.

"Indeed, it is," he said. "But it is also highly aggressive. As I said, I work in the shadows. Sometimes things are accomplished better, and more swiftly, that way. Right now, we've got three of the best agents in England serving the house of de Velt and Cole is one of them. He could have taken his men into Fountainhall Castle, captured Canmore, and made it back to England before anyone was the wiser. With a lot less death."

"And no impact," Gart said quietly.

As he and Sean grinned at each other over their differing opinions, Christopher spoke up. "Three agents?" he asked William. "Who are the other two?"

A hint of a smile crept onto William's lips. "You will not believe it," he said. "They have been serving de Velt for the past two years."

Christopher was curious now. "Who has?"

"The Princes of Kitara."

That drew a strong reaction from Christopher and David. In fact, all of the knights reacted in some way, but not in a negative fashion. In fact, there was delight in their expressions at The Marshal's revelation.

"Are you serious?" Christopher gasped. "Addax and Essien al-Kort?"

When William saw the recognition, he snorted. "I knew you would be shocked," he said. "Those young men you took under your wing and helped train on the sands of The Levant those many years ago have never lost their loyalty to England because of you. You gave them a chance when no one else would and they have never forgotten that. At least, that is what they told me when I met with them a couple of years ago, when they first came to England's shores."

As Christopher's jaw dropped with surprise, David spoke up. "But *how*?" he asked. "You never mentioned this to me at all and you knew of my relationship to them. The last I heard, they migrated north with Thuringian knights, but we lost track of them after that. Where did they go?"

William took another gulp of wine before answering. "Nay, I did not mention it, mostly because they were some of the agents working in stealth for me in the north, and the less everyone knows, the better," he said. "But I knew, eventually, that the time would be right to tell you, so now you know – the royal blood of that powerful and mysterious kingdom is now part of my stable of knights, and they have been utterly flawless."

Christopher shook his head, still in disbelief, but there was pleasure there. The pleasure of friends he thought he had lost. "Not even Jax told me that," he said. "I cannot believe they have been in England for two years and I never knew."

William nodded. "As the story goes, they were in the service of a Flemish duke who is allied with Jax de Velt and that is how they came into the man's service. He adores them."

"But how did they get from The Levant to the Flemish lord?"

William held up a hand. "Those Thuringian knights you spoke of," he said. "But that is a story for another time. For now, we must focus on what is happening in the north. Four weeks ago, I sent a missive to Cole and Ajax de Velt and asked them to unleash their army on Fountainhall with the intention of capturing Canmore as a prize. I instructed them to muster their army and march for Scotland on the first of the month, which was more than five days ago. My guess is that they have already arrived and that the siege is progressing in earnest."

Christopher snorted ironically. "If I know Jax, and I do, the siege is probably already over," he said. "Jax de Velt has never laid siege for more than a couple of days in his entire life. I would wager that the battle is finished and Canmore is already heading for England."

William, however, saw no irony in the statement. He was a man who controlled England, and with it, thousands of men, lords, and armies. He never did anything without a specific motive in mind, and his motive in sending Jax de Velt into Scotland was quite plain.

Gart had said it best.

Impact.

With this much at stake, he wanted impact. But things could go wrong and sometimes, they did. William could only hope this was not one of those times. Therefore, he simply nodded coolly to Christopher's suggestion.

"Let's hope so," he muttered quietly. "God, I hope so."

CHAPTER ONE

The siege of Fountainhall Castle
Seat of Alpin Canmore

IT WAS A scene from old.

Jax de Velt and his sons, Cole and Julian, had roused their army and marched on the Scottish fortress of Fountainhall because William Marshal had ordered it for a very specific reason –

They wanted Fountainhall's liege, Alpin Canmore.

Set amongst the gently rolling hills of the Scottish Lowlands, where the rocks and hills and purple heather came together to form a landscape like no other in the known world, Fountainhall was a feather in the cap of Scotland's borders. Stout and strong, built from granite quarried near Edinburgh, it was a statement to the English kings with their eyes on the prize of Edinburgh and points beyond. It was the guard dog at the gateway into the land of the Scots.

Come and get yer pain, lads…

Fountainhall taunted the English.

But not today.

Today, the fortress was taking a beating from the army of the most feared man in England, Scotland, and Wales.

The Dark Lord and his horrific army had returned.

No one had seen death and destruction like this on the border in thirty years. Jax had been tamed by his overlord, the Earl of Northumberland, and he'd sworn to a peace treaty that had worked very well, at least for the English. They left him alone and he left them alone.

But the Scots hadn't been part of that treaty.

Unfortunately for Canmore, Jax's lands were threatened by raiders coming from Canmore lands but, even worse, there was the rumor of a massive and terrible treaty on the wind, one that would more than likely affect Jax before anyone else because his properties were on the Scots side of the border. Jax had learned of the terrible treaty from his own son, perhaps the best spy the world had ever seen.

Aye… Jax de Velt, the darkest knight of all, had raised a spy.

But he'd also raised one of the most fearsome knights of his generation in Coleby de Velt, and when it was determined that the threat against de Velt properties was too great, the prompt from William Marshal was all Jax needed to mobilize that army of killers that he kept within his tall, pale walls. However, it was more than simply moving against Canmore because of the threat, for The Marshal had a very specific purpose in mind.

A hostage.

And the de Velt army rolled into Scotland like a tempest.

It was chaos.

It was a relatively short march to Fountainhall from Pelinom Castle, seat of de Velt. With a swift horse, it would take a full day, but with an army, it took a day and a half. Truth be told, Jax hadn't marched for battle in such a manner in over twenty-five years. Given that his two properties, Pelinom Castle and Foulburn Castle, were on the borders, he'd seen his share of action. Reiver activity surged from time to time, and he'd been called into English disputes throughout the years, but he never fought the battles he used to fight. The blood, the brutality, the senseless death and destruction. Those tactics were a thing of the past.

Until William Marshal asked him to unleash that monster again.

Not strangely, it hadn't been difficult to draw on the beast he used to be. It had never really gone away. Cole and Julian knew what their father was capable of, just like everyone else, but they'd never seen it at that level until their foray into Scotland.

Then they became part of it.

The Scots never stood a chance.

Fountainhall Castle never really stood a chance, either. It was a walled and moated castle, but it wasn't very large and the moat was hardly a deterrent to an English army with siege engines and ladders. Jax had brought everything he had with him and at noon on the day of his arrival, the siege of Fountainhall began in earnest.

Unfortunately for the occupants, it didn't take very long.

Jax's siege engines with iron projectiles blew holes in the yellow granite walls and destroyed the gatehouse. Once they were in the outer bailey, those same engines loaded up bombs of flaming oil and destroyed a second, smaller gatehouse that led into the complex of the castle. At that point, the army started to stream in and grab victims.

No mercy.

That was the order given by Jax who, in his sixth decade, was still an utterly terrifying and formidable knight. He was completely in control of his army and everything around him, and for sons who had never seen the monster their father had once been, they were seeing a new side to him that they didn't recognize. It was startling and, admittedly, intimidating. About half of Jax's forces were men who had been with him back in those days when The Dark Lord terrorized the borders, so they knew what to do when their liege gave the word and, like old times, they were also given permission to take anything of value.

Spoils of war.

Once the interior gatehouse was down, it was Cole and Julian's task to find Alpin Canmore while their father and his army took care of the Scots. As they fought their way into the inner ward, prisoners were taken by the de Velt army all around them. Men who resisted were disabled on the spot. Not killed, but disabled, because a horrible death was planned for them. For the past six hours, Jax had men in the nearby woods, chopping down young trees and preparing the spikes that the Scots would soon be impaled with.

That was Jax de Velt's primary mode of submission when it came to an enemy army. Cole and Julian could hear the screams of the men as the poles were shoved into their bodies and, like Jesus Christ was hung upon the cross for an audience, those impaled bodies began to go up along the road leading to Fountainhall for all to see. It was absolutely horrifying.

A macabre spectacle of dying scarecrows.

But Cole and Julian weren't focused on what was going on around them, only what needed to be done. They were focused on the keep specifically, which was actually built into the walls of the castle. There were multiple doorways and stairs from what they could see, but Cole was confident he would find what they needed.

In fact, he'd already sent men ahead to gather what intelligence they would need to find their target, and he was mostly looking for the pair of brothers he had served with for the past two years, ever since they came to England from having served Count d'Acoz. The story made known to the English was that they were knights from The Levant who served Jax, but that wasn't the truth. They had been sucked into William Marshal's spy ring because Cole had recruited them. From the first, he'd realized their special talents. Men such as Addax and Essien al-Kort weren't meant to be simply knights.

They were meant for greatness.

And he'd been proven right. While Cole had been entrenched in his mission for The Marshal with the Scottish royal court, Addax and Essien went right along with him. The Scots had loved the unique pair, which had only worked to their advantage. They became the darlings of the royal court, invited to every gathering, every exclusive feast. They were not only great warriors, but they could sing and entertain beautifully. The Scots were inviting and trusting with the men from the far-off and mysterious land of Kitara.

Now, as Fountainhall fell all around them, the results of that misplaced trust were evident.

It had been the Princes of Kitara who had made this moment possible.

"Cole!"

Cole heard his name, his head snapping to the right where Addax al-Kort was just emerging from a doorway with a wooden staircase that led into the bailey. Right behind him came his brother, Essien, and between them they were dragging a Scotsman dressed in female garb, a man alternately cursing them and pleading with them.

Cole and Julian headed in their direction.

"Canmore," he said with satisfaction, inspecting the man. After a moment, he looked to Addax. "Excellent work. Where did you find him?"

Addax was an exceptionally muscular man, with features that had made many a maiden swoon. He was from a place of birth far from England, blessed with black hair and eyes the color of onyx.

"Cowering in the kitchens," he said, his speech accented because the language he was speaking was not his native language. "He thought he could dress as a wench and we would pass him over, but his ugly legs gave him away."

"I saw them first," Essien insisted, a gloriously handsome brother a few years younger than Addax. "I've seen women's legs from here to Alexandria, and nothing could convince me that those hairy, skinny limbs belonged to a woman."

Cole looked straight to Alpin's legs, which were pasty, spindly, and covered with a dark matting of hair. He lifted an eyebrow. "How astute of you, Es."

The young knight frowned. "What do you mean by that?"

Cole pointed to the legs. "A blind man could have seen these are not the legs of a woman," he said sarcastically, poking at the man's ego. But he took pity on him quickly because he'd just accomplished a difficult task. "But excellent work, both of you. The Marshal shall hear of your skill. He will be pleased."

Addax grinned as Essien frowned, looking between Cole and his brother, not entirely pleased that he wasn't getting all the credit. He was the younger, more excitable brother when compared to Addax's cool strength or Cole's unflappable demeanor, but he considered himself just as fine a warrior. He was about to say so when he caught sight of what was going on near the gatehouse and the annoyance in his eyes faded. There was virtually no fighting that he could see, but there was a good deal of noise going on.

Howls of pain.

A sense of foreboding crept over him.

"What is happening out there?" he asked. "What is… why all the screaming?"

Cole didn't turn around to see what he meant. He knew. "The Dark Lord is doing what he does best," he said evenly. "I told you what would happen with this siege, Es. That has not changed. My father has been ordered to destroy this castle and that is exactly what he is doing."

Essien could hear that cries of agony. They all could. He was young and emotional, and when he looked at his brother to see what he thought of what was happening, Addax refused to look at him.

"Ad?" he said, sounding concerned. "Did you understand… surely there is some reason why…"

Addax cut him off. "Warfare makes barbarians of us all," he muttered, glancing at Cole. "You have seen enough of it to know that. This is the moment we have worked for and, now, it has begun. We told you this would happen. Everything we have strived for has come to fruition. For complete victory, these actions are necessary."

Essien could see through the gatehouse, watching as four of de Velt's men rammed a post into the rear of a soldier, ramming it all the way in so it emerged from his belly. Then the soldier was propped up on the side of the road, still alive, placed next to his comrades.

Essien had to take a deep breath.

Truth be told, it wasn't the worst thing he'd ever seen, because he'd seen the Muslims with Saladin's army in The Levant do something similar. When he'd been a boy fleeing his own country of Kitara, he'd see things like that and worse still. Even so, the method was shocking in its brutality. It was true that Cole and Addax had told him this would be the result of Jax de Velt's scorched earth campaign, but to see it in practice gave him pause. To a sensitive soul like Horus Essien Mai al-Kort, horrific brutality was sometimes difficult for him to swallow.

He'd seen too much of it.

"Bastards," Alpin snarled, spittle flying from his lips as he distracted the warriors from what was happening around them. "Ye're all bastards. Why are ye doing this tae me?"

He was speaking of the al-Kort brothers. Alpin knew them to be fixtures in royal circles, favorites of the nobles, so the fact that they wrested him from his hiding place was truly perplexing. He had no idea why they were there. As Essien continued to wrestle with the situation outside the gates, Cole appraised Alpin without a hint of emotion.

"Canmore," he said. "You know why we are here, do you not?"

Alpin eyed Cole, shaken and bewildered. "Why do ye speak like that?" he said, referring to the fact that Cole had no Scots accent, something he'd only known from the man from the beginning of their association. "What is happening here? Ye're the king's protector, the man called MacEacharn!"

"Not anymore," Cole said flatly. "My tenure with William is finished. And I am not MacEacharn."

"No' MacEacharn?"

"Nay," Cole said. "I am English and this is my father's army. We've come for you, Alpin. Would you care to guess why?"

Alpin genuinely had no idea. In fact, the entire situation had him baffled. Earlier that day, an army approached from the south, a fairly large army that his men identified as English and, suddenly, he found himself under siege. His men barely had time to secure the outer gatehouse when the army swarmed and siege engines were brought forth. A bombardment worthy of the Crusades took place after that, with flaming projectiles and men scaling walls. When it had become clear that the army would breach the inner ward, Alpin and a few of his men had dressed as women and hid in the kitchens. He didn't even know what had happened to those men.

At the moment, he was only concerned for himself.

Something very bad was happening.

"*Sassenach?*" Alpin spit out. "I dunna understand any of this. *Who* are ye? What have ye done?"

Cole leaned in to him. "My name is Cole de Velt," he said quietly. "My father is Ajax de Velt, Baron Blackadder and lord of Pelinom Castle. Surely you have heard of him."

A gleam of recognition came to Alpin's eye. "De *Velt*?" he repeated. "Not The Dark Lord?"

"The same."

The light of understanding was beginning to flame for Alpin. "God's Teeth, MacEacharn… ye're no' Scots?"

"I am not Scots."

"A de Velt?"

"Aye, I am a de Velt."

Two years of being a spy to the royal Scots court was just revealed and things began to come clear for Alpin Canmore. He looked at Addax and Essien, understanding they were in on it, too. He began to realize just how much trouble he was in and he instinctively stepped back and away from Cole, but he was being held firmly so he had nowhere to go. Then he looked beyond Cole to the gatehouse and he could see his men being put on poles.

Those screams were something that cut him to the bone.

"God," he muttered, looking at Cole with utter fear in his expression. "What do ye want from me? Why are ye doing this?"

Cole didn't answer him. He turned for the gatehouse and jerked his head at Addax and Essien, who followed him from the inner ward, dragging Alpin past his own men who were being impaled. His men, seeing him, screamed for help if they were able, begging Alpin to save them.

But Alpin couldn't even save himself.

In the end, it was too much for him to take. He lowered his head and wept as Addax and Essien dragged him back to the de Velt encampment and tied him to a post. Alpin was certain he was going to be burned alive but, oddly enough, they left him there with Essien as his guard. No flames, no death.

At least, not yet.

As Alpin Canmore listened to the cries of agony from his men, Cole and Addax returned to the bedlam that was happening at Fountainhall. They found Jax standing on the fringe, watching the activity, but not actively participating. He was simply overseeing everything with the ease of a man overseeing something far simpler, like the harvest of his crops or the training of his men. It was all business to him and Jax held an expression that suggested he wasn't troubled by any of it.

He'd done this kind of thing before.

Next to him stood a commander he'd had with him for many years. Atreus le Velle had been at Jax's side during the entire conquest of the Welsh Marches those years ago, and he had been at Jax's side when he conquered Pelinom Castle. He'd known Jax since childhood and had simply never left him, not even to pursue personal gain or adventure. An innate sense of loyalty kept him with Jax, a friendship that was deeper than most.

Atreus was looking at the carnage going on with the same bland expression Jax had.

"We have him, Papa," Cole said as he walked up on the pair. "He's back in camp with Essien as guard. Addax and Essien captured him quite ably."

Jax and Atreus turned to him. "He is unharmed?" Jax asked.

Cole nodded. "Not a scratch," he said. "Shall I take him straight to The Keld?"

Jax pondered that question for a moment. He'd gone through a lot of trouble today simply to rush his captive off to another man's castle. "Tomorrow," he finally said. "I intend to interrogate the man myself tonight. I realize that the Alastor de Bourne is involved in this situation more than I am, but I am still part of it. We are under threat, too, and we are much closer to the Scots army should they decide to march, so I want to know what this Alpin Canmore knows. If I must protect myself, then I want to know when hell is coming before de Bourne and The Marshal have their way with him. There may be nothing left by the time they are finished."

"You know everything I know to this point," Cole said, lowering his voice. "You know everything I've been gathering over the past two years. Unfortunately, my position next to the king only gave me partial information. There were certain things I did not know that Canmore can hopefully provide. But what we know is this – the Scots, supported by the Norse Earls of Orkney and Shetland, intend to invade England and Alpin Canmore has been sending missives to the House of de Bourne on behalf of William the Lion, as the descendants of the Kings of Northumbria, because the Scots want de Bourne to join their rebellion. They need a strong house inside of Northumberland if they are to succeed."

"But de Bourne has refused them."

"He has, but William the Lion does not yet know that," Cole stressed. "As far as I know, de Bourne has not yet sent a reply to his offer. He sent word to The Marshal first. Therefore, if the Scots army comes... *when* they come... Pelinom is in their path."

Jax nodded patiently. "I understand that," he said. "That is why The Marshal gave me permission to send a message to the Scots and the Earls of Orkney on behalf of all of England in the form of my army. I have shown them what will happen should they carry out this scheme. But what I want to know is *when.* When do they plan on coming?"

Cole lifted his eyebrows. "That is why we have captured Alpin," he said. "That is the only thing we do not know – the time for such things. We do not know when and we do not know from where. For all we know, the Norsemen will come in through Berwick tomorrow. They can bring their longships down the River Tweed and destroy a great deal. This is what Alpin must tell us, Papa. I'm sure he knows."

Jax simply nodded, returning his attention to an entirely new row of impaled men going up along the western side of the road. Most were already dead, but they were going up nonetheless. Cole turned to watch the poles go up, his thoughts shifting from the prisoner they'd captured to the dirty deeds his father was engaging in. The Scots weren't going down without a fight. They'd resisted as much as they could, but the de Velt army was too big and quickly overwhelmed any struggle. The Scots were, therefore, being as noisy as they could, bellowing and screaming as they were put on poles.

It made for a loud and disturbing chorus.

"I've not had to use tactics like this since before you were born, Cole," Jax said as if reading Cole's thoughts. "Something that was a means to an end, as this is. Your mother… she is not happy about what I am doing this day. But, as I told her, it is necessary."

Cole looked at him. "Never did I question your tactics," he said. "You need not explain yourself to me. I understand completely why you must do this."

Jax glanced at him. "Then explain it to me," he said, a warm glimmer in his eyes. "Tell me why I have done this, lad."

Jax wanted to see if his son truly understood and Cole was aware of that. It was important for the father-son relationship that Cole understood that his father wasn't being brutal for brutality's sake. He was doing it with an end result in mind, to protect those they loved and lands they'd worked hard for. Therefore, Cole's gaze lingered on his father a moment before turning to the screaming, writhing men.

"They are a threat," he said simply. "Threats against Mother and my sisters, Effie and Addie. If you do not kill them, they may have the chance to kill my mothers and sisters."

"And not you?"

Cole shook his head. "I can defend myself. What you are doing is defending my mother and sisters. It is defending what belongs to you and what you love, the life you have built. Your family."

As Jax mulled over his son's answer, Atreus spoke up. A wise old man, and strangely gentle given the fact that he was as much of a barbarian twenty-five years ago as Jax ever was.

His blue-eyed gaze fixed on Cole.

"Well put, Coleby," he said, perhaps one of the only people who called Cole by his full name, which was his mother's maiden name. "The methods of elimination are the same, but back in the day when your father was bent on conquest, the reasons behind these actions differed."

Cole cocked his head curiously. "How so?"

Atreus gestured to a big, hairy Scotsman who was resisting about a dozen soldiers who were trying to impale him. "See that man there?" he said. "Twenty-five years ago, your father would have destroyed him because he wanted what that man had. It was a method of eliminating a threat to his greed. But now… now he does it to eliminate the threat to what he has. Do you not think that Scots bastard would kill your mother and sisters given the chance? Of course he would. Every man who is part of Fountainhall's army was already preparing to do just that. Therefore, your father is protecting what he has and, in that aspect, this is not a barbaric end for these fools. It is a just ending to the plans they were preparing to follow."

Cole nodded faintly. "I've spent the past two years learning about these men, sitting side by side with them at a feasting table and listening to them," he said. Then, he gestured to Addax. "Ad has heard as much as I have, if not more. Truthfully, when The Marshal tasked me with spying on the Scots royal court, it was with the intention of keeping watch over their activities. I did not have any particular directive other than to observe and report. The alliance with the Earls of Orkney… that was a surprise. I thank God every day that I was in the right place at the right time to learn of something that would directly affect my family."

Jax put a hand on his son's very big shoulder. "As am I," he said. "You have saved us, Cole. I am proud of you. I am proud of you all."

He meant Addax and Essien, something that made Addax smile modestly. "It has been an honor, my lord," he said.

"What will you do now?" Atreus asked. "Now that your days of infiltrating the royal court are finished, surely you must have a plan for your future. It is not as if you can return to William the Lion. He'll hang you both if he sees you."

Cole and Addax grinned. "I do not know," Cole said honestly. "I assumed I would return to my father's army to be used whenever The Marshal had the need."

"And me," Addax said. "I have found my home with Cole and the House of de Velt, and I do not wish to leave it. My brother and I rather like England."

Atreus looked to the man with eyes as black as night. "Someone told me that you had spent some time on the Flemish tournament circuit," he said. "You do not wish to go back to that foolery? It can make you quite rich."

Addax laughed softly. "I have done many things in my life," he said. "Spending a couple of years in the tournament circuit was simply one experience. Since leaving my home many years ago, I have had the opportunity to do a great many things. Talent, and the ability to learn quickly, will open up the world to you providing other men feel the same way. I have been very fortunate that the Christian knights have seen value in who and what I am."

"And what are you?"

"A prince of my people," Addax said with a twinkle to his eyes. "The son of a king who no longer rules, but a son nonetheless. My father was called *Qara Ejder* to our people and that is the name I adopted on the tournament circuit as a way of keeping him alive. I was allowed to compete because of the testimony of Count d'Acoz. He explained to the marshals of my lineage and bloodlines. In fact, d'Acoz knighted me himself. He said no man was more worthy of the knighthood than *Qara Ejder*."

Atreus was listening intently. "What does that mean?"

"The Black Dragon," Cole answered for him. "He was known in the tournament circuit as The Black Dragon. And they called Essien the God of Vengeance."

Atreus' eyebrows lifted. "That seems both bold and embittered," he said. "Why should they call him that? Essien has never struck me as being a vengeful man."

"Because his name, by birth, is Horus," Addax replied. "Horus is the ancient god of vengeance, a symbol of power to my mother's people. So when Essien also competed in tournaments or sport, he was known as the God of Vengeance. It sounds much more impressive than The Little Princeling, which is what I wanted to call him."

Atreus chuckled. "I find your histories fascinating," he said, but quickly sobered. "I would like to hear more of it when this task is finished. I've not had much opportunity to speak with you and I would like to."

Addax dipped his head graciously, but he, too, realized this wasn't the place for such a casual conversation. They were at the culmination of two years' worth of work, a moment of great brutality and great violence.

There would be time enough for introspective conversation

later.

"What more would you have of Addax and me, Papa?" Cole asked, watching his father's men finally gain the upper hand on the big, hairy Scotsman. "Is there something else you would like us to do?"

Jax nodded. "Secure Fountainhall," he said. "This place is deep in Scottish territory and I cannot spare the manpower to try and hold it, so we are going to strip it and burn it. Take everything of value and burn it to the ground so that it is unusable for years to come. Does Canmore have a wife?"

Cole nodded. "He does."

"Have you seen her today?"

Cole shook his head even as he looked at the enemies impaled upon the poles that were lining the road. "I do not believe so," he said. "I have only met her once, a big woman with flaming red hair."

"Find her and bring her to me."

"I will," Cole said. "Anything else?"

Jax nodded. "I will spare one of Canmore's men to tell people what has happened here," he said. "Someone must be witness to this great destruction and who brought it about. Select that man and bring him to me along with the wife."

Cole pulled tight his gauntlets, preparing to carry out his father's directive. "And where will you be?"

Jax turned his head in the direction of his encampment, his eyes glimmering in the light of the midafternoon sun. He had unique eye coloring, something that only served to enhance his diabolical and ruthless reputation. His left eye was muddy-brown and the right eye, while mostly of the same muddy color, had a huge splash of bright green in it. The man had two different-colored eyes, something he'd inherited from his father and his father before him.

Devil eyes, were the whispers.

Jax's sons had all inherited it to a certain degree, including Cole. He had his mother's golden-brown eyes, but they were encircled with a bright green ring. His brother, Julian, had their father's eyes almost exactly, and Cassian, their youngest brother, had it also but it was far less pronounced. Two of the three girls had avoided that trait, but the youngest one, Addington, had a fascinating mix of the muddy-brown and the green, evenly patterned in both eyes.

They were eyes that defined the de Velt family.

And it was the eyes of Jax himself that were pondering the distant encampment and his son's question.

"I will be with our captive," he said after a moment. "Find me there."

Cole and Addax nodded, heading off towards the smoking fortress, leaving Atreus to oversee the dissolution of the Scots army as Jax headed back to the encampment. It was tucked back in the same small forest that gave up its small, younger trees so Jax's army could make pikes. As he approached, he could see one corner of the forest that had been stripped, with the foliage mashed. Men were still pulling saplings out of the undergrowth and several of them were turning the ends into sharp points with great axes.

Just like old times.

Several tents had already been erected in the encampment, including a tent that housed the wounded. Though the battle hadn't been particularly fierce, there were the inevitable wounded in the tent, men being tended to by a surgeon who had come to Jax through his liege, de Vesci. Piers Michelson used to be a knight for de Vesci many years ago, but he'd found his calling in tending the wounded and healing the sick. He could see Piers, his gray hair pulled back to the nape of his neck, bent over a man who had damaged an eye. But that glimpse was fleeting as he entered his own tent.

The first thing he saw was Essien.

Tall and broad-shouldered, Essien immediately bolted to his feet when Jax entered.

"My lord," he said. "Your prisoner is secure."

Jax's gaze lingered on the young man. "Thanks to you, I am told," he said. "Excellent work, Essien."

"Thank you, my lord."

Jax genuinely liked the young knight who had seen so much, and suffered through so much, even at his young age. It had only made him stronger. Jax wasn't usually sympathetic to younger knights, mostly because they looked at him as something either to be feared or challenged, but Essien showed him nothing but respect.

He received that in return.

"It was most fortunate when my old friend d'Acoz sent you to my service," he said. "Of course, he mentioned something about a compromised young woman and an irate father, and sending you to safety in England, but it was nonetheless a fortuitous happening for me. I do not regret it."

Essien struggled not to grin, a faint blush coming to his smooth cheeks. "Nor I, my lord."

Jax fought off a grin at the randy young knight and the real reason he and his brother had come to England, but he was all business as he turned to Alpin, still trussed up on a pole. His expression darkened as he went to stand in front of the man, looking him over.

The tension in the air bloomed, becoming heavy and un-comfortable. Fear was there as well because when dealing with The Dark Lord, there was no telling what the man would do. More than any knight in England, Jax de Velt was a man to be feared because of his past deeds, deeds he was more than willing to resurrect should the need arise.

"You are Alpin Canmore?" he finally asked.

Alpin jumped at the sound of his voice, filled with fear that the enormous warrior with two-colored eyes was addressing him.

"I am," he said, his voice quivering. "Who are ye?"

Jax was looking at him with intense scrutiny. "I am de Velt," he said. "Fountainhall Castle has been destroyed and, by all rights, belongs to me. You are now my prisoner. Do you understand this?"

Alpin swallowed hard. He'd just heard the confirmation of his worst nightmare. "I do," he said. "The man I knew as MacEacharn now tells me his name is de Velt."

Jax nodded. "He is," he said. "He is my son. He infiltrated your royal court. If you do not understand what that means, it means that he was spying on you and your king. Do you understand that I have the power of life and death over you, Canmore?"

Alpin was struggling not to give in to his utter terror. "What do ye want with me?" he demanded. "I've no' done anything tae ye. I've never attacked yer lands or yer kin. Why did ye do this tae me?"

Jax glanced at Essien, tilting his head towards the tent entry and silently inviting the man to leave. Essien took the hint and quickly vacated. When he was gone, Jax pulled up a sturdy three-legged stool and planted his bulk on it. He focused on Alpin, who was shivering and bound.

"Because you are part of a plot against me," he said after a moment. "Do not deny it, for I know it to be true. You are part of your king's plot with the Earls of Orkney to try and regain Northumberland. Now, I do not fault you your greed or ambition. If anyone understands that, it is I. However, your greed and ambition put my land and my family at risk. This, I cannot allow. Do you understand me so far?"

Alpin was staring at him. More like glaring at him. "I've no' plotted against ye, de Velt."

Jax's dark eyebrows lifted. "But you were part of those gatherings," he said. "The gatherings where the scheme to control Northumberland was planned in secret. You were witnessed there, so you cannot deny it. It would be a lie and I do not tolerate liars."

Alpin's gaze lingered on him a moment longer before looking away. "Ye do what ye must tae keep yer country safe and strong," he said. "So do I."

"That is reasonable," Jax said. "But I was told that your plans included sweeping east to Coldstream and the bridge. 'Tis the easiest way into England unless you choose to go through Gretna. Now, there are a dozen other smaller bridges across the River Tweed, but in order for your armies to flood into England from Coldstream, you would have to pass through my lands. Would you bypass my castles when you did so?"

Alpin knew the answer to that question. He still wouldn't look at Jax.

"Ye're Sassenach upon Scot lands," he said. "Ye dinna belong here."

"Mayhap not, but they are mine nonetheless," Jax said. "It would be much easier if we knew the details of William the Lion's invasion plans, Canmore. We would be better able to protect ourselves. When does he expect to execute his intentions?"

The conversation, in truth, was a little strange. Jax was speaking almost pleasantly, as if this were nothing more than a light discourse. But Alpin wasn't fooled.

"I canna help ye," he muttered.

"That's odd," Jax said. "Because you are the one who has been sending missives to Alastor de Bourne, asking him to join the Scots rebellion. As descendants from the Kings of Northumbria, I believe you told him that it was his duty to rebel against the Normans who took his kingdom away. Do not look so surprised; I know everything. As do many other people. Your missives are no secret."

Alpin *did* look surprised because he was. He'd been sending them for months now, but he hadn't received any reply. Now, he evidently had that reply.

De Bourne had betrayed him.

It was a sickening realization.

Jax could see that he had the man off-balance and he planned to continue that interrogation tactic. The more he could rattle Alpin, the better.

"I have a family to protect, Canmore," he said. "You have seen what I am capable of, yet you refuse to tell me what I wish to know? I will stop putting your men on poles this very minute if you tell me what I wish to know. So in a sense, you are responsible for their deaths. Stop killing them, Canmore. The power is yours."

They could hear the distant screams of agony as more of Canmore's men were impaled on spikes. Jax knew that it must have been excruciating for Canmore to hear those ghastly sounds, so he backed off his interrogation. He wanted Canmore to ponder his question, and his statement, with those cries of pain searing into his brain.

In truth, he was waiting for the wife to appear.

Then things would get interesting.

As Alpin sat on the cold ground and shivered, Jax had soldiers bring in a brazier and food. They brought glowing coals for the bronze brazier, heating up the metal and staving off the chill in the tent as Jax sat in a comfortable chair and ate a meal right in front of his prisoner. He drank wine, ate cheese and boiled beef, and generally acted as if he didn't have a care in the world.

But he was biding his time.

More time passed. The screams and cries grew weaker as the afternoon progressed, but in its place grew a silence that was ghastly and deafening. The wind shifted and the smell of blood was on the air. Jax had eaten his fill of is meal, sitting with Alpin in complete silence, listening to the world go on around them outside the tent. Jax had no idea where Essien had gone, but he was thinking about looking outside of the tent flap to see if he could spy Essien, or even Cole or Addax at that point, when the tent flap flew back and knights appeared.

Cole, Addax, and Essien entered the tent with a man and woman between the three of them. Jax stood up as Addax and Essien shoved the pair to their knees.

"Meet Alpin's wife," Cole said. "This is Margit. The man next to her is someone we found cowering in the stables before we burned them to the ground. His name is Baloch, he says."

The woman took one look at Alpin, bound to a pole, and burst into tears. The man next to her was only slightly more composed.

"Mercy, m'laird!" he cried. "Show mercy, please! I take care of my mother and I'm all she has! Please dunna kill me!"

Jax gazed at the pair quite unemotionally before turning to Alpin.

"Do you know this man?" he asked.

Alpin was looking at the two captives as if he were going to become sick. "Aye," he muttered, barely above a whisper.

"Who is he to you?"

"A cousin."

Jax's focus lingered on him a moment before he turned to his son. "Restrain him," he said quietly. "Expose one hand upon the tabletop."

Cole and Addax lifted the pleading man to his feet, dragging him over to the only table in the tent, the one that Jax had eaten his meal from. As the man cried and begged for his life, they slammed him down onto the chair and extended his right arm onto the table, holding it down. When everything was in position, Jax turned to Alpin.

"I am going to ask you a question," he said. "And for every question you refuse to answer, your cousin is going to lose a finger. When all of his fingers are gone, he'll lose a hand. When the hands are gone, he'll lose the lower part of an arm. When those are gone, I will start on his toes and repeat the process. You will slowly watch him hacked to death and when I am finished with him, I will do the same thing to your wife. Do you understand what I am telling you so far?"

Alpin was pale with terror. "Ye wouldna do such a thing," he said. "'Tis barbaric and un-Christian. Ye canna do such a thing tae a man!"

"I can and I will."

"'Tis uncivilized!"

"It is the way of things," Jax said simply. "Now, I asked you a question earlier, one you refused to answer. I shall ask you again, just once. If you do not answer me, your cousin shall have one less finger. Is this in any way unclear?"

"I –!"

"When does William and Orkney expect to execute their intentions?"

Alpin's mouth worked as if he were going to answer swiftly but, ultimately, he groaned and squeezed his eyes shut. "Ye dunna know… I… why would ye ask me such a question?" he stammered. "Do ye think the king himself takes me intae his confidence? I'm no' a great laird!"

Jax looked over at Cole, who took the hint. He gave a short nod to Addax, who produced an enormous dagger with a serrated edge. It was a beautiful weapon, made from Damascus steel. Quicker than the blink of an eye, Addax cut off the captive's smallest finger on his right hand. As the man screamed in agony, Addax picked up the digit and walked it over to Alpin, taking the freshly cut side of it and smearing it on the side of his cheek.

Alpin vomited all down the front of his tunic.

Addax tossed the finger onto his lap.

Between the screaming of the cousin, the shrieking of the wife, and Alpin's gasps of terror, the tent had quickly become a chaotic place. Jax, completely unruffled in the face of such upheaval, continued to face Alpin.

"*When* do William and Orkney expect to execute their intentions?" he asked again.

Alpin was beginning to grow hysterical as his cousin screamed and wept, his arm still stretched out on the table and bleeding profusely. No one was making any attempt to stop the blood flow.

"I dunna know!" Alpin cried.

Jax looked at Addax, who immediately hacked off the next finger. Alpin's wife began screaming at the top of her lungs, wildly, as Alpin's cousin bellowed in agony and begged for mercy. Addax picked up the finger he'd just cut off and dropped it down Alpin's tunic. The man gagged again as the finger got caught up in the folds of his tunic, holding it against the flesh of his belly.

"Their intentions, Canmore," Jax said quite emotionlessly. "I want to know what they are planning. Your cousin only has eight fingers left."

"Tell him!" the wife screamed. "For the love of God, Alpin, tell him!"

Jax looked at Cole and then to the wife, silently relaying the command. Cole went over to the old woman with the red hair and unsheathed his dagger. The wife screamed at the top of her lungs, knowing her death was at hand, and Alpin began to scream as well.

"No more!" he cried. "Dunna touch her! I'll tell ye, ye Sassenach bastards, but dunna touch her. Cut her and I'll take everything ye want tae know tae my grave!"

Jax called off Cole, who immediately moved away from the woman as she collapsed in a dead faint. He then collected a chair and pulled it up in front of Alpin, looking at the man seriously.

"Excellent," he said. "That was a wise decision. When is William planning to execute his plans?"

Alpin glared him, a look of pure hatred, but his hatred was tempered by his sense of self-preservation. "What assurances do I have that ye'll no' kill my wife after I've told ye want ye want tae know?"

Jax shook his head. "You have none," he said. "But I will give you my word. Answer my questions and I will spare you and your wife and your cousin."

"And his hand? Someone needs tae tend his hand."

"Answer my question and I will make sure he is adequately tended."

Alpin looked at his wife, and his cousin, and it was as if all of his bones suddenly disappeared. He seemed to fold in on himself, his chin dropping to his chest, as if every last piece of defiance and courage slipped quietly away along with the bones.

He was a shell.

Pride held out only so long when faced with such destruction.

"Yer question has many answers," he mumbled. "Ask me something specific and I'll tell ye what I can. But if I tell ye I dunna know, then it's the truth. The Rough doesna take me intae his confidence. I know what I do because I'm a border laird and nothing more."

The Rough was another name used for the King of Scotland, a name that reflected his general methodology and manners, and Jax pondered his next question. He had Alpin where he wanted him in a relatively short amount of time. He thought it would take longer, but given the man's wife was under threat, the resistance ended fairly quickly.

And to his advantage.

As he pondered his next move, Cole stepped forward. He'd been privy to some of the more general gatherings purely by virtue of his relationship with the royal court, so he knew some of the information, things he told his father.

As he'd said, it was the smaller details that had escaped him, and one detail in particular.

"When is the invasion coming?" he asked. "When do the Scots plan to move south?"

In the end, Jax got his information.

By morning, the cousin with the missing fingers had been released with a message to take to William the Rough. Jax let Alpin languish for a couple of days with little food and even less sleep before sending Cole, Addax, and Essien to escort the man south to the mighty de Bourne stronghold known as The Keld for further interrogation.

A naturally suspicious man, Jax suspected that the worst was yet to come.

And they had to be ready.

CHAPTER TWO

Edinburgh Castle

L IKE A LION perched upon a rise, it waited.
Edinburgh Castle had the look of a predator waiting to spring. There was a strength about it, and also comfort, as the beacon of Scots power and protection in a country of turmoil.

Never more so in turmoil than at this moment.

Uilliam mac Eanric, or William, son of Henry, sometimes known as William the Rough or William the Lion, had been the king of Scots for over forty years. Forty years of fighting the English, the Northmen, and sometimes fellow Scots had taken its toll on the man, but he was still standing. He was still strong. There was something to be said for a king who had withstood the pressures of his kingdom for forty years. One would have thought that by this time in his reign, he would have been weary. Old and weary, ready for a new king to assume the throne, but that wasn't the case.

He was a king ready to expand his kingdom.

However, the latest visitor to Edinburgh had news to the contrary.

Even now, as William entered the great hall of Edinburgh Castle, he could already feel his rage building. He was being escorted by several of his men, courtiers and knights and retainers, men who carried out his wishes and helped him manage his lands. He'd just been summoned by one of them with news that wasn't particularly good.

Ye must come, yer grace. Something has happened tae Fountainhall Castle.

Fountainhall Castle was a strategic castle on the borders, very close to English properties. William knew of Fountainhall because the lord, Alpin Canmore, was one of his most loyal subjects. An annoying man and a minor player in the grand scheme of things, but loyal nonetheless.

William didn't like the thought of a border skirmish with the English at this time.

He needed all of his border lords at full strength for what was to come.

Seated at one of the enormous scrubbed tables in the great hall, surrounded by both men and wandering dogs, sat a man with his right hand bandaged and bloodied. As William and his entourage approached the table, William took a good look at the man but he didn't recognize him.

He looked as if he'd been through hell.

That brought concern.

"I dunna know ye," he said as he came upon the table. "Who are ye?"

The man was pale and weak, clearly exhausted, but he tried to stand up. "I've come for the king," he said. "I willna speak tae anyone else. I have a message for him."

There were so many men crowded around the table and around the man that William had to shove a couple away in order to get at him.

"Do ye no' know me on sight?" he asked.

The man eyed him before looking at the retinue around him. His gaze returned to the big, strong-looking old man whose hair in his youth had been red and wavy. Now, it was gray and bristly. A little wild, even.

He shook his head.

"Who are ye?"

"I am the one ye seek," William said simply, planting himself in the chair at the end of the table. "What's this about Fountainhall? And what message do ye have?"

The man with the bandaged hand realized the king was sitting next to him and, for some reason, that seemed to bring out his fear. He'd been strong enough until the king appeared, and now he simply felt fearful.

He began to tremble.

"Yer grace," he said. "The message comes from Ajax de Velt."

That brought a reaction from William and most of his entourage. What had been a mildly concerning situation just turned critical.

The mention of Ajax de Velt, The Dark Lord, made any situation critical.

"De Velt?" he repeated in surprise. Then, he looked at the men around him as if to confirm they'd all heard the same thing before returning his focus to the man. "I know that name."

"Ye should, yer grace," the bloodied man said. "Most people know of the Sassenach who burned half the borders and killed entire armies many years ago. 'Tis the same man."

William blinked in surprise. "He's still alive?"

The man sighed heavily. "Still alive and still killing, yer grace," he said. "Fountainhall is gone and everyone is dead because of de Velt. He left me alive because he wanted me tae deliver a message to ye."

William looked at him in disbelief. "Fountainhall is *gone*?" he repeated, aghast. "What of Alpin Canmore?"

The man seemed to slump forward at the mere mention of

Canmore. "I dunna know," he said, running his good hand through his hair wearily. "The last I saw him, de Velt's men were cutting my fingers off tae force him tae answer their questions. Yer grace, de Velt knows about the alliance with the Earls of Orkney and the Northmen. He says tae tell ye if ye try and bring yer alliance intae England, he'll do tae ye what he did tae Fountainhall. He'll rip yer head off and leave it for the birds tae pick yer eyes out. He says tae tell ye that only death awaits ye if ye come tae England."

The silence in the hall was abrupt and deafening as Ajax de Velt's threat settled upon those in the hall like a fog. It was all around them, weighing upon them, filling their eyes, their ears, their noses.

It was everywhere.

Fear was everywhere.

William could feel it, but he wasn't one to show his fear in any case, not even from Ajax de Velt. But he could see that his men were edgy and the man with his hand bandaged was positively ashen. He sat forward, leaning on the table and focusing on the man bearing the message.

"What's yer name, lad?" he asked, not unkindly.

"Baloch, yer grace," he replied.

"Baloch," William repeated. He looked to the man's hand. "How many fingers did ye lose?"

Baloch lifted the bloodied, bandaged appendage. "Two," he said. "Two before Alpin began tae speak of the Earls of Orkney," he said. "Alpin's wife was spared and she was brought tae him, so he answered their questions tae save her life, too. I was taken away once he started tae speak so I dunna know what became of him."

William nodded, pondering the situation, what he'd been told. "Ye dinna see him again?"

"Nay," he said. "But there's something else. The man ye

knew as MacEacharn? He was with de Velt. I dunna know why, but he was there. I've seen that man at yer side more than once, but he was with the English."

William stared at him for a moment before suddenly looking around, realizing the enormous man with the unusual eyes was nowhere to be found among his retainers. He hadn't noticed until that moment because he had so many of them, but he realized quickly that something was amiss. *Very* amiss.

William was many things, but a fool was not among them.

"MacEacharn," he muttered. Then, he snorted as if amused, but there was no such humor in his expression. "MacEacharn a spy? I dinna anticipate that."

Baloch and the others were watching William closely. The revelation of a spy so close to the king was not lost on any of them. William scratched his chin, sighing heavily, before returning his attention to Baloch.

"Fountainhall is really gone?" he asked.

Tears began to form in Baloch's eyes. "Burned until it's nothing but a shell," he said. "And Alpin's men… good men… were all put on poles tae die. They are lining the road as far as I could see. Some were already dead, some weren't. I can still hear them calling tae me, begging me tae put them out of their misery."

William frowned. "On poles? Tied tae the poles?"

Tears spilled down Baloch's face. "Nay," he said. "Do ye no' know how de Velt kills armies, yer grace? His men went intae the forest and cut down young trees, making one end very sharp. They take the end of it and ram it intae a man's body through his buttocks, all the way through his body until the sharp point comes out of his chest or neck or belly. Those who dunna die right away are left tae a slow and terrible death. *That* is what de Velt promises ye and yer men should ye try tae cross intae England."

William already knew about de Velt, but through Baloch's eyes, he got a clearer picture. So did his men. He didn't dare look at them, knowing the fear and rage and disgust he would see in their eyes. In fact, it was a rather brilliant move on de Velt's part – he knew what kind of effect that level of brutality would have on the Scots. He also knew it would do one of two things – it would either be a deterrent for them to forget their plans or it would turn their anger against him and away from the rebellion that was forming.

It would be distracting, in any case.

Brilliant, indeed.

"So the Sassenach knows of our plans," he muttered. "But *how* much does he know? That is the real question."

Baloch shook his head. "This, I wouldna know," he said. "But the attack against Fountainhall wasna only tae destroy it. They left Alpin alive tae tell them what they wanted tae know."

William lifted an eyebrow. "Ah," he said. "They wanted a prisoner, someone tae interrogate. But how did they know that Alpin Canmore would be that man?"

No one had an answer until the man standing next to William spoke softly.

"They have their spies in our court, yer grace," he said. The man was the young Earl of Fife, the Justiciar of Scotia, a powerful hereditary title. Alexander MacDuff was a trusted, and reasonable, man. "Just as we have spies in theirs. There is enough spying tae go around these days. Someone told de Velt tae go tae Fountainhall and capture Alpin because he is a man who was known tae gather in yer court."

"Then ye're saying he was targeted."

"Indeed."

"And the man lives near the border, so de Velt dinna have tae go far tae find his target," William finished. "De Velt's fortress is near Alnwick, is it no'?"

No one seemed to really know. They were looking at each other, shaking their heads, shrugging. But one thing was for certain; Fountainhall never stood a chance against the de Velt war machine.

William's focus returned to Baloch.

"Was that all de Velt told ye tae tell me?" he asked.

Baloch nodded. "Aye, yer grace," he said. "If yer armies cross the border, de Velt will be waiting and he will no' be the only one."

William sat back in his chair, mulling that information over, before motioning to one of his men. "Take Baloch tae the kitchens and feed the man," he said. "Find him a bed so he can sleep. But he's no' tae leave."

The man William had motioned to was a big man, young, with a heavy short sword sheathed at his side. He nodded, pulling Baloch up from the bench and escorting him from the hall. Baloch's movements were slow, weary, like a man who had just been on a flight for his life.

When he was out of the hall, William spoke.

"It would seem our intentions have reached the ears of the English," he said with some irony. "But I suppose I couldna keep it private for much longer. Every Scotsman in the Highlands is heading south, tae Edinburgh. The Northmen are already on their way. Sooner or later, the English would realize we have come tae reclaim Northumbria. It was mine in my youth, ye know it. The earldom of Northumbria was mine until Henry took it from me, the English bastard. But I'll have it again before I die. 'Tis mine."

MacDuff spoke up. "If the English warlords in the north know of our intentions, then Berwick could be in jeopardy," he said. "We hold it, but enough angry warlords could breach it and oust our garrison. It has happened before. And we *need* Berwick."

William nodded faintly, digesting everything, trying to determine what they needed to do at this point. "The Earl of Ross has men stationed there and has for twenty years," he said. "Angus MacHeth's son is in command and the man has his orders. He knows that he is tae admit the Northmen intae the river when they arrive. If MacHeth is ousted, the boats will be kept at sea and we'll no' have the reinforcements we need."

"What do we do?" MacDuff asked with concern. "If we send more men tae reinforce Berwick, the English will catch wind of it. They'll think we're planning our attack from Berwick and it'll draw them tae the town. We dunna need a concentration of English armies in Berwick when the Northmen arrive. It would be much more resistance than they anticipated."

William knew that. He sat back in his chair, putting a boot-ed foot on the tabletop. "We're assuming the English know about Berwick," he said. "Alpin Canmore knew of it. We've had gatherings twice in the past year tae discuss such things and he was present, so he knew of our plans. Did he tell de Velt?"

MacDuff snorted softly. "De Velt was cutting off fingers tae coerce him," he said. "He had the man's wife. Of course Canmore told him what he knew."

William held up a finger as if the thought had just occurred to him. "But we've no' considered something else," he said. "What of the House of de Bourne, the descendants of Bloodaxe? Alpin took it upon himself tae send them missives, asking them tae join our rebellion in exchange for more lands. What do we know of them?"

"Alpin did that tae ingratiate himself tae ye, yer grace," MacDuff said. "The man wanted yer favor. He'd wipe yer arse if ye asked him tae."

William simply lifted a hand to silence the man. "So would ye if I demanded it," he said, listening to the men snort at MacDuff's expense. "Canmore is an ambitious man, 'tis true, but I knew what he had done. In truth, I was curious tae see if the House of de Bourne would respond. They're a powerful family and they hold the Kielder Pass – one of the main roads intae Northumberland. Do we know if de Bourne has responded tae Canmore's missives?"

He looked at the gaggle of men around him as they shook their heads. No one seemed to be certain, but more than that, no one had been particularly close to Alpin Canmore. He was a vassal of the Earl of Dalkeith, who was busy recruiting men in Galloway. He'd been away for a few months, meaning he probably knew nothing about a de Bourne response.

Only Alpin Canmore would know that.

"Yer grace, it's my sense that Alpin would have told ye had he received a response from de Bourne," MacDuff said. "The man couldna keep it tae himself and he'd want tae shout it tae ye from sheer pride, so it's probable that de Borne hasna given his answer yet."

William nodded. "Ye have a point," he said. "I would have known it almost as soon as Canmore did."

"Exactly."

William reclined against the back of the chair, rubbing his hands together because the joints ached. At his age, they ached badly at times. He pondered the Canmore situation quickly.

In his mind, there was only one path to take.

"Then it is possible that de Bourne hasna responded and possibly willna," he said. "And we must further assume that Alpin Canmore is dead. We must also assume that he told de Velt everything he knew and he knew about Berwick, but I dunna want tae send a great army there tae reinforce it. I'll send a few men with a message telling MacHeth that the English know that Berwick will be the place where the Northmen are tae enter England. That way, he'll be prepared."

"But ye'll send him no army?" MacDuff confirmed.

William could hear some disapproval, perhaps disappointment, in MacDuff's tone. "As ye said, it would only draw attention tae Berwick now," he said. "But that doesna mean I willna send an army when the time for the Northmen's arrival draws near. If they're already on their way, they should be here by June and the mists that crop up from the sea that month will cover the arrival of their ships. It will also cover the movement of an army tae support Berwick."

The men around him, including MacDuff, nodded in agreement. But there was still one more item outstanding.

"Let us speak of de Bourne again," MacDuff said. "If Canmore has been sending him missives about joining us, then he knows our plans. If he sends word tae Canmore agreeing tae join us, there is no one there tae accept the missive."

William looked up at him. "'Tis true," he said, "which means we must send someone tae de Bourne to find out just what his intentions are. Tae have the House of de Bourne with us would be a blow tae the Sassenach army."

"Ye mean John's army?" MacDuff ventured.

William shook his head. "No' John," he said. "The man is a fool. He is only concerned with himself and feuding with his own barons. If it was only John tae be concerned with, we could reclaim Northumberland and he wouldna know until it was too late. Nay, lads, 'tis no' John we are concerned with. 'Tis William Marshal. The man has his finger on the pulse of England and the warlords will follow him. If The Marshal knows of our plans, then we will have a fight on our hands. Mark my words."

"The Marshal is no' the king, yer grace."

"Who do ye think controls England, Alexander?"

It was the truth, a snappish bit of reality to the Scots who would doubt The Marshal's involvement in England's affairs. After a moment, MacDuff nodded faintly in agreement. It was absolutely the truth and they all knew it. William Marshal, Earl of Pembroke, *was* England, and if he knew of the Scottish plans, an invasion into Northumberland just became more difficult.

William Marshal wasn't about to let them in without a fight.

"Then mayhap that is why de Velt did what he did," Mac-Duff said quietly. "Think about it – he devastated Fountainhall, but at whose command? Surely the man dinna take the initiative himself."

William turned to look at him, his yellow-eyed gaze intense. "Then ye have yer answer," he muttered "If I was a gambling man, I would bet upon the fact that The Marshal told de Velt tae attack Fountainhall because he knows my plans."

"Then what will ye do?"

William sighed heavily. "We go tae Castle Keld and the House of de Bourne," he said. "We discover if they are with us."

"And if they are no'?" MacDuff pressed. "What if they are the ones who told The Marshal about the missives from Alpin? What if that is where it all started?"

William grunted at the possibility, something he was thinking about but didn't want to voice. "Then we send enough men through the Kielder Pass tae raze Castle Keld if de Bourne goes against us," he said. "De Velt destroyed Fountainhall. I'll take Castle Keld in revenge. It'll be their punishment for telling The Marshal about Alpin's missives. Alexander, the directive is yers. Prepare my army tae depart for Castle Keld in two days."

"Aye, yer grace."

William's gaze lingered on the man for a moment before turning away. "The Marshal wanted tae send me a message through Ajax de Velt?" he mused quietly. "I'm about tae send my reply."

Every man in the hall understood what that meant. The destructive volley of threats and promises had begun. De Velt had fired first.

Uilliam mac Eanric was going to answer… loudly.

A small army of Scots left.

CHAPTER THREE

Castle Keld, or simply The Keld
Northumberland, England
Three Days Later

"CHRIST, CORI!" A big knight with dark hair and big, scarred hands was standing in the doorway, hand to his nose. "What in the hell is that *stench*?"

It was a disgusting scene he had walked in on. The lady of the castle had just lanced an infected boil on a soldier's thigh and the smell from the infection was filling the chamber. It was a smaller room attached to the knight's quarters of Castle Keld, a chamber used for a few purposes, including bathing or surgery if the need arose.

On this particular morning, the lady of the castle was pressing on the boil, making sure all of the poison was draining out of it and into a bowl that a servant was holding, but it was a ghastly sight and an even more ghastly smell, just as the knight had suggested.

It didn't take long for that stench to overwhelm the already squeamish servant.

It all came flying out.

Once the servant vomited, another one puked, followed by

the very man whose boil they were draining. The horrible stench coupled by the weak stomach of the servant had nearly everyone in the chamber retching, including the knight who had just come in the door. He grunted in disgust and fled the chamber as the lady of the castle very calmly finished cleaning out what she could.

She could hear the knight outside the door, cursing because the entire circumstance was so disgusting, but she ignored him. He was her brother, anyway, and he tended to be a bit dramatic sometimes.

The man had no stomach for things she did every day.

"There," she said evenly, certain she'd gotten out all of the poison. "Quickly, hand me the wine."

The servant who had been trying not to retch again took the earthenware phial from a nearby table filled with a solution of wine and vinegar. The patient bit off a scream as the lady rinsed the boil several times, cleaning it out as best she could. Using boiled linen, she swabbed the boil before tossing aside the dirty linens and using fresh wrappings to bandage the leg.

"May I come back in?" the knight called into the chamber.

Lady Corisande de Bourne was focused on her task, a veritable rock as everyone around her was coming apart with weak stomachs. "I never asked you to leave in the first place, Anteaus," she said. "It still smells just as bad, so enter at your own risk."

He stuck his head back in, eyeing her suspiciously. She was still working on the leg and, as she had told him, he could still smell the rot from it, so he remained by the door.

Like a coward.

"Are you almost finished?" he asked.

She pulled tight on the wrapping, causing the soldier to grunt in pain. "Aye, I'm almost finished," she said impatiently. "I'm trying to keep this man from losing his leg to poison, so you can at least show a little concern for him. He *is* one of your soldiers."

Anteaus glanced at the old man, an old soldier who had been around during the time of his grandfather. Anteaus was two years older than his sister, a young woman who had seen twenty years and three. She was the strength and soul of the entire House of de Bourne even though there were three brothers, two sisters, and a father. There was something about Corisande, or Cori as they called her, that made her the pinnacle of everything strong and noble. Ever since their mother had passed away four years earlier, Corisande had made sure the family remained together. That no one fell aside.

That life at The Keld remained the same.

Anteaus had to admire her for that.

They all did.

But that role within the family also meant she healed the sick and injured, as was her duty as chatelaine of The Keld, and there was no finer healer in all of Northumberland. Probably in all of England. Schooled by their mother, a vastly knowledgeable healer in her own right, Corisande excelled in the healing art.

And in cleaning out disgusting boils.

"I apologize," Anteaus said after a moment. "I know you are only doing your best, but Papa has sent me to tell you that we have visitors and one of them requires your assistance. You must come as soon as you are finished."

Corisande glanced up at him curiously. "Visitors?" she repeated. "Who? I did not hear the sentries."

"I know," he said. "These walls are so thick, you probably would not hear the return of Christ if he came down on top of you. In any case, you must come as soon as you are finished."

Corisande was concerned that there were visitors and she was not present to tend them. She turned to the servant beside her.

"Finish tying off this bandage," she said. "Make sure it is nice and tight. Have him lie down for the rest of the day and I will check on the leg tomorrow."

The servant, one who tended the knights and other senior soldiers, nodded sheepishly, embarrassed he had vomited in front of Lady Corisande. As he took over the bandaging, Corisande went to wash her hands of dirt and poison in a bowl containing a mixture of warm water and a type of grain alcohol that was purchased in Carlisle, distilled in Scotland. It cleaned well enough and killed any poison she might have lingering on her hands so that the poison from one man wasn't transmitted to the next. It was something her mother had taught her.

She followed that process religiously.

Quickly, Corisande darted out of the chamber, which was located in an outbuilding built against the massive outer wall, which was over thirty feet high in places. The Keld was, in fact, a place that was meant to impress and intimidate, and it did both of those things quite ably. The castle itself was an enormous complex situated on the gently rolling hills overlooking the River North Tyne.

Because of the hills, the gatehouse was on a lower level than the rest of the castle, so one entered through a massive gatehouse, up a small and vulnerable roadway, and then into the vast bailey. That central courtyard was enormous, with a great hall built against one of the walls, stables against another, and a series of troop houses where the soldiers would lodge because Corisande's mother, Thalassa, didn't like her hall full of men. To appease her when they were first married, her father, Alastor, had built the troop houses.

But Corisande honored all of her mother's traditions and wishes, even years after her death. Nothing had changed in that respect – the soldiers still weren't allowed to sleep in the hall and Corisande carried on her mother's role. Her father was still head of the household and her brothers, Ares, Atlas, and Anteaus, still managed the army and the security of The Keld, and Corisande and her younger sister, Gaia, managed everything else. It was a tight-knit family that loved each other and worked well together.

And they all called The Keld home.

To them, it was heaven.

"Who are the visitors?" Corisande said as she caught up to Anteaus. "Was Papa expecting anyone? He did not tell me."

Anteaus shook his head. "He was not anticipating anyone," he said. "They were… unexpected."

"What does that mean?"

Anteaus paused briefly, turning to her. "You must keep this to yourself, Cori," he said in a low voice. "You cannot repeat what I am going to tell you."

She looked at him seriously. "Of course," she said. "What is wrong?"

Anteaus eyed her before he started to walk again. "The visitors are from Pelinom Castle to the north," he said. "They were engaged in a big battle a few days ago… a very terrible battle, so do not ask about it. All Papa wants you to do is tend the man they've brought with them. He is a prisoner."

Corisande's brow furrowed as she thought on what her brother had told her. "A prisoner?" she said. "Why did they bring him here?"

Anteaus shook his head. "I cannot tell you more than I have," he said. "Please do not ask. If Papa wants you to know, he will tell you, but for now… just make sure the prisoner is well enough. That is all you need do at the moment."

Corisande's brow was still furrowed as she thought on her brother's mysterious words. Walking beside him as they headed towards the massive, square keep on the north side of the bailey, she glanced up at him as if trying to read his thoughts. Anteaus was a seasoned warrior, but he could also be emotional. While older brothers Ares and Atlas were knights with a steely strength about them, serious men who never showed much of what they were feeling, Anteaus was hot-headed and ready to show every emotion that was bubbling forth.

But Corisande couldn't read him at the moment.

Her curiosity grew.

The keep loomed before them, a colossus of stone and iron. There was a forebuilding that protected the steps leading into the entry level and they passed through the massive iron gates that protected the stairs, heading towards the equally massive door at the top. They entered a surprisingly small entry room at the top, one that was secured by one heavy door that led into a larger central foyer. Once they entered the foyer, Anteaus led her into their father's solar.

The private solar of Alastor de Bourne, Lord Bernicia, was a luxuriously appointed chamber that was quite small given the size of the keep. There were hides on the floor, tapestries on the walls, and the entire room smelled of leather and smoke, and of a rare incense her father liked to burn every so often because it reminded him of his wife. It was a resin he had sent all the way from London, called *olibanum*, that was harvested in lands as far away as The Levant from a thorny tree that grew in the deserts. Churches burned it regularly and Lady de Bourne had been a pious woman. Hence, Alastor burned it because it reminded him of his wife.

But it made Corisande sneeze.

In fact, that's what she did the moment she stepped into the solar. A loud, shrill sneeze. Several pairs of eyes turned in her direction, startled, as Alastor came out from behind the table where he had been standing.

He held out his hand to her.

"Ah," he said, taking her arm gently. "My daughter making an entrance into a chamber as only she is capable. Good men, this is Lady Corisande, whom I have told you of. Cori, please greet our guests."

Alastor teased her about the sneeze, but Corisande was mortified. Unfortunately, her nose was still itching but she managed to fight it off as her father pulled her towards a group of men. She was blinking her eyes to clear them of the tears that had formed from her sneezing, so she didn't get a good look at the men until she was nearly standing next to them.

The first thing she realized was that the largest man she had ever seen was positioned directly in front of her.

In fact, she blinked her eyes again, this time because she was startled. Standing in front of the man, at eye level, she was looking at his sternum. Her gaze moved up his body, to his powerful chest and impossibly wide shoulders, to his neck, and finally to his square jaw. He had dark blond hair past his shoulders, and as her gaze moved upward, she could see that he had the crown pulled back and secured behind his head. He had handsome, even features, with arched brows over eyes that could only be called unique.

She'd never seen anything like them.

"Cori, this is Sir Cole de Velt," her father said, indicating the massive knight. "He is the son of Ajax de Velt of Pelinom Castle, a valued ally."

Corisande still wasn't over the sheer size of the man, but she managed to dip into a curtsy. "My lord," she said. "Welcome to Castle Keld. Had I known you were coming, I would have made sure you were met with refreshments and comfort. I fear I have failed miserably in my duties. Please forgive me."

The knight was looking at her with those unusual eyes, a golden-brown ringed in a bright green. Coupled with his arched brows, it almost gave him a sinister appearance. As if the Devil himself had come to England and taken human form. Everything about the man seemed to radiate fear and intimidation because of those eyes and, truth be told, Cori was a little intimidated simply looking at him. His gaze was piercing, unnerving.

But he shook his head to her polite statement.

"No apologies are necessary, my lady," he assured her in a voice that bubbled up from his toes. "We came quite unannounced on business with your father."

He may have looked like a handsome terror, but the words out of his mouth were polite. And that voice… like molten steel, strong and fluid. Corisande wasn't sure what to do other than smile timidly at the man when he turned to indicate two knights standing with him.

"These are my men, Sir Addax al-Kort and Sir Essien al-Kort," he said. "We must impose upon your hospitality for the duration of our visit, but I assure you that we will be no trouble. Anteaus has already told us that we can sleep in the knight's quarters."

Corisande looked to the two knights standing with him, noticing immediately that they didn't look like any pale Englishman she'd ever seen. They were quite handsome, with black hair and dark eyes. She nodded her head at them.

"My lords," she greeted, her gaze returning to Cole. "You are most welcome at Castle Keld. We do have room in the keep if you wish to stay here."

Before Cole could reply, Alastor pulled her over to the hearth where a man she had failed to notice was sitting next to the fire, hunched over. He was older, with stringy, gray hair and a grayish cast to his skin.

He didn't look well.

"See to this man, please," he told her. "He has not fared well and I need him."

Corisande's thoughts moved from the knight with the piercing eyes to the quivering form of humanity in front of her. Concerned, she took a step towards the man and lifted her hand to touch his face to see if he had a fever, but the moment he saw her hand heading in his direction, he lashed out and smacked it away.

"Dunna touch me, Wench," he hissed. "I'll no' have…"

He was cut off when a massive hand suddenly grabbed him by the neck. Startled, Corisande looked up to see Cole as his grip on the man's neck lifted him straight out of the chair. The man began to kick and gasp, and she instinctively put her hand on Cole's forearm in an attempt to defuse the situation.

"Please release him," she said steadily. "I am quite unharmed, truly. He is simply ill and unsteady."

Cole's eyes narrowed dangerously at the man, but he did as she asked. He put him back in his chair.

"Strike her again or touch her in any fashion and I will break your arms," he growled. "Do you understand me, Canmore?"

The man sat there and rubbed his neck, breathing heavily. But he refused to answer and Corisande was a little more assertive about putting herself between the man and that gigantic, and evidently volatile, knight.

She could feel the tension in the air.

"Here, now," she said gently, reaching out again to touch his face. This time, he didn't push her away. "No one is going to hurt you. I am here to help you. What is your name?"

He was exhausted and ill, eyeing her with a baleful glare. "Canmore," he rasped. "'Tis all I'll tell ye, so dunna ask for more."

Corisande was fairly accustomed to being around sick people because it was so much of what she did at Castle Keld and the surrounding village. She had a great deal of compassion and a genuine ability to be gentle and kind. It was simply in her nature.

But she also realized that Canmore was here for some unhappy purpose.

She could feel it.

"Canmore," she said, kneeling in front of the man so that she was looking up at him. "As you have heard, my name is Corisande. I am the chatelaine here at The Keld and part of my duties are to tend to the health and well-being of our visitors. Now, I do not know why you are here, or what your business is with my father, but that is of no matter to me. Clearly, you are ill or injured, and I would like to help you if I can. Will you allow me to?"

Her words were kind and reassuring, throwing Alpin off guard in the slightest. He kept eyeing her, as if unsure what to say, and then his gaze would move over her head, clearly looking at the men standing behind her.

He was as nervous as a cat.

"I… I'm just weary," he finally said. "Nothing is wrong with me that a meal and drink willna cure. I'm no' sick."

Corisande wasn't sure if she believed him, but she didn't dispute him. She rose from her knees. "Then I shall make sure food is brought to you," she said. She turned around to look at the rest of the visitors. "In fact, I shall make sure a meal is prepared for all of you. Would you like to rest before you continue your business with my father? Surely it can wait a few hours."

Her father opened his mouth to reply, but the door to the solar slammed back on its hinges and Corisande's two older brothers appeared.

Ares and Atlas de Bourne were men of remarkable courage, talent, and command ability, but they were also bold, aggressive, and lacked sheer human empathy at times. They were quite involved in the politics of the north because Ares was the Sheriff of Westmorland and Atlas assisted him in his duties, leaving Anteaus and their father to command the vast empire of The Keld. The sheriff appointment, in fact, had been from the king because Ares had been heroic in a battle against the Scots a few years earlier. Having proven himself, the king gave him the title and responsibility of keeping law in the north.

But that meant Ares had a sharper temperament than most, dealing with the worst society had to offer sometimes, but he also had a reputation for fairness. No one had ever said Ares de Bourne was unfair or corrupt. His sense of justice and morality were always intact.

But so was his hatred for the Scots. As he stormed into the solar, his attention went immediately to the man in the chair.

"Is that him?" he demanded, pointing to the Scotsman.

Having left his daughter, Alastor put himself between his enraged son and the Scots prisoner. "It is," he said evenly. "If you wish to remain while we speak to him, then you may do so. But you will let me do the talking, Ares. Do you understand?"

Ares tore his gaze away from the Scotsman long enough to glare at his father. "He is the one threatening us with a Scots vendetta and I am not allowed to question him?"

Alastor shook his head. "I will do the speaking," he repeated. "Will you respect my wishes?"

Ares rolled his eyes and turned away, pulling off his helm and ripping off his gloves as Atlas followed suit. He may have been unhappy, but he did as his father asked. He kept his mouth shut. As he and Atlas began putting their things on a table near the door, Alastor returned to his daughter.

"You are no longer required," he said. "Thank you for coming."

Corisande had been watching everything very closely. There was something strange going on – three big, unfamiliar knights had brought a beaten Scotsman to The Keld, a man who had her older brothers furious for some reason. Anteaus was the calm one of the bunch and even he didn't look too pleased.

That had Corisande concerned.

"Papa?" she said as he took her by the arm. "Mayhap I should remain. He does not look well at all."

Her gaze moved to the Scotsman and Alastor's focus followed. He looked at the man for a moment before shaking his head and firmly directing her towards the door.

"If I need you, I will send for you," he said.

"I shall bring food."

"No food. Not now."

"But…"

He cut her off as he ushered her out of the door. "No food, but please stay near," he said. "If I summon you, then I do not want to have to send the servants out to hunt you down. Understood?"

Corisande stood just outside the door, looking at her father and feeling some fear. She didn't know why, but she did. The man seemed… edgy.

He wasn't the edgy type.

"As you wish," she said.

Corisande's last glimpse into the chamber before her father shut the door was of Cole de Velt, standing over the Scotsman slumped on the chair. For a brief moment, their eyes met and Corisande felt a rush go through her. Something about those unusual eyes made her feel a chill, or quite possibly a thrill.

She wasn't sure which.

All she knew was that when the man looked at her, she could physically feel it.

And then the door shut in her face.

Puzzled, and the least bit concerned, Corisande lingered by the door for a moment before turning away. In spite of what her father said, she intended to go to the kitchens and make sure a meal was prepared for their visitors. Perhaps a bit of sustenance would put everyone in a better humor.

Or perhaps that grim gathering in the solar was a harbinger of things to come.

CHAPTER FOUR

S HE WAS BEAUTIFUL.

Quite beautiful.

Cole had seen a lot of women in his time. He'd even married a few years ago to a d'Umfraville daughter, whose family was an ally of the House of de Velt. Mary had been her name, a lovely girl with soft, red hair and a bright smile. She'd been a little meek, very obedient, and Cole had been happy with her. They'd even had a daughter, Lucy, who had looked a good deal like Cole's mother. But a fever had taken them both, within two days of one another, and shortly thereafter Cole was given the directive by William Marshal to spy on the Scottish court.

Cole was certain he'd been given that directive to distract him from his grief.

But that hadn't worked too well. It had taken time for him to recover, throwing himself into his work, ignoring the pain until it became a dull ache. Then, on a visit home, he'd met Lady Audrie de Longley, daughter of the Earl of Teviot. She was petite and pretty, with golden-red hair and a charming manner, and he'd shown enough interest in her to help him move on after Mary's death. He hadn't asked for Audrie's hand yet, but both families assumed that would come at some point. Even

Cole assumed he would do it at some point, but he wasn't in any hurry.

He wasn't in any hurry to take on another wife and open himself up to more heartbreak.

Now, he'd just met a woman whose green eyes seemed to throw lightning bolts at him. Every time their gazes met, he felt a jolt. Lady Corisande de Bourne was a serene, elegant beauty with lips like a rosebud and blonde hair that tumbled in voluminous curls down her back. She was seemingly kind and well spoken, a gracious and well-trained young woman that made her family proud. Not that he hadn't met plenty of women like that, but he'd never had such a reaction to them.

It was most curious.

And perhaps even quite intriguing.

But he couldn't focus on that now.

"My lord," he said, lowering his voice as he took Alastor by the arm and led him over into a corner for privacy. "I know we've only arrived, and I have not yet had the chance to tell you anything in-depth about my father's discussion with Canmore, but that is by design."

Alastor looked at him curiously. "What do you mean?"

"I mean that I want to see what Alpin Canmore tells you before I fill you in on what he told my father," he said. "I want to do it now while he's weary from travel because his exhaustion will make him more vulnerable. May I make a suggestion to you?"

Alastor was listening intently. "Please do."

Cole turned his back to Alpin and the room completely so that no one could read his lips or even hear him before continuing.

"Get the man drunk," he muttered. "I've seen him when he's drunk and he becomes one of those men who cannot keep his mouth shut. He'll argue, scream, laugh, tell stories… all of it when he's drunk, so if you ply him with ale, I have a suspicion you will learn what you want to know."

Alastor was intrigued by the suggestion. "Did your father do this?"

Cole shook his head. "My father has his own ways of doing things and getting a man drunk is not one of them," he said. "He would rather use intimidation than try an easier way. But that is the way of Jax de Velt and the man's methods are his own."

Alastor's eyebrows lifted. "Indeed, they are," he said. "And they work for him. I would not presume to question The Dark Lord's methods. But I like your suggestion. Did Canmore say anything on the journey here?"

"Nay," Cole said. "Not a word. The man had just seen all of his men killed and his home burned, so he was not exactly in a talkative mood."

Alastor understood. He sent a servant for wine – copious amounts, as he put it – and went to the hearth to throw more peat upon it. The moors of Northumberland and North Yorkshire were full of peat bogs, so there was quite a bit of it. Soon enough, the hearth was flaring with fuel and the chamber began to warm up considerably.

Alastor could see from the corner of his eye that Alpin leaned into the heat, holding out his hands and closing his eyes. At least, he could see the man until Ares and Atlas began to crowd around him and blocked his view.

"Well?" Ares demanded. "What are you waiting for, Papa?"

Alastor eyed his sons. Ares looked much like he did in his youth, big and muscular, but also quite handsome with brown eyes and light brown hair. Ares de Bourne had no shortage of female admirers and as Sheriff of Westmorland, he was quite sought after by rich lords for their eligible daughters. Atlas, on the other hand, looked like his mother's father – enormous and bald was the best way to describe him. He was more of a follower than a leader, but there was no finer warrior in the land.

Alastor paused a moment before answering.

"I want you two to listen to me carefully," he said quietly. "Ares, I realize your position in life is bringing justice to the north on a regular basis and you are well aware that I am proud of you for your fair and just judgment, but I will tell you again that I am in control of this situation. It is extraordinarily delicate and has nothing to do with judging a crime or dispensing justice. We are speaking about the potential of a terrible war, so you will allow me to deal with this man in my own way. You will keep silent, both of you, unless I ask for your help or opinion. Do you understand me?"

Ares wasn't happy; that much was clear. He looked at Atlas, who wasn't particularly thrilled by their father's directive, either, but they knew better than to argue. At least, Atlas did. Ares tried and Alastor simply pointed a finger at him, but it was a finger that shut the man's mouth.

For a moment, anyway.

"Can you at least tell me what you are planning?" Ares hissed in frustration.

Alastor's gaze drifted over to Canmore, laboring to warm himself after a day and a night of no heat and little food. After a moment, he rubbed his chin, a move that was meant to shield his mouth a little so there was less chance of anyone other than his sons hearing what he had to say.

"That man over there is the one who has been sending missives demanding we side with the Scots and their Northman allies," he muttered. "According to Cole, Canmore has just seen his castle burned to the ground and his men butchered, courtesy of Ajax de Velt."

Ares' brow furrowed. "Is *that* how he became de Velt's

prisoner?" he said, aghast. "Ajax de Velt declared war on him?"

Alastor nodded. "You were not here when Cole and his men first arrived," he said. "Cole told me that The Marshal ordered Ajax de Velt to raze Canmore's castle of Fountainhall and take Canmore a prisoner, and raze it he did. He butchered every man and woman in that castle. The Dark Lord of old was unleashed on the Scots to send a very specific message, lads – that we are aware of their plans and that any attempts to roll into Northumberland will be met with similar force. Ajax was able to glean some information out of him, but now it is my turn. I am going to find out everything I can and in order to do that, I am going to ply a man who has seen little food in the past two days with a goodly amount of drink. I've sent a servant for it."

Ares looked at him as if he were expecting more. His eyebrows lifted. "You are going to get him drunk?"

"At Cole's suggestion. He says it loosens the man's tongue."

"*In vino veritas*, is that it?"

"Exactly."

Ares glanced over at Cole de Velt, standing near the hearth. He was an absolutely enormous knight, with dark blond hair and eyes that almost had a reptilian appearance because of the strange coloring. Ares knew the of the man's family, of course. Everyone in the north did. Cole had distinguished himself in a some of the baron's wars against the king a few years ago, but he hadn't heard of the man for the past couple of years. Still, here he was, in the middle of a serious situation. He'd captured a prisoner that was important to the de Bourne cause, and the cause of all of northern England.

Because the directives to his father were coming from a de Velt, Ares shut his mouth. The family's reputation was beyond contestation and he wasn't going to argue about it.

In fact, he wanted to see where it went.

Backing off, Ares and Atlas headed over to a corner of the chamber where Anteaus was leaning against the wall.

Watching... and waiting...

They were willing to see just how far a little drink would take them.

"MY FATHER ASKED for *what*?"

The question came from Corisande as she faced the servant her father had sent to the kitchens. The servant was the man who shadowed her father at The Keld, an older man with missing teeth and a round form, but humbly obedient.

"Drink, my lady," the servant said. "He asked for the frost wine from Saxony."

She frowned. "That is our most expensive wine," she said. "It will also get a man drunk after only one cup. It is very strong."

"He asked for it, my lady.

Corisande had come to the kitchens to make sure food was prepared for their visitors and she thought the servant's request for the very sweet, very strong "frost" wine was a strange one. They didn't have very much of it because it was expensive, and when there was a gathering, her father and brothers favored apple ale from York that had been brewed by the same family for two hundred years. They bought it by the wagon loads.

But her father wasn't asking for the apple cider ale this time.

He was asking for the strong wine.

"Is someone ill and needs reviving?" she asked curiously. "That wine is so strong that I have given it to my father and my brothers when they do not feel well. It is medicinal."

The servant shook his head, his jowls quivering. "No one is ill that I am aware of, my lady," he said. "Although… although one of the men does not look very well."

"The man sitting by the hearth?"

"Aye. Mayhap it is for him."

That only made her more curious. Her father had specifically sent her away, telling her that the Scotsman didn't need assistance, but perhaps that wasn't the case. Her dedication to duty demanded she return to that room – and the ill visitor.

"I will bring it," she said. "Go about your business."

The servant obeyed. Corisande went to the vault beneath the kitchens where they stored things like meat and butter and anything that did well in cold storage, including the frost wine, which was made from frozen grapes and prized for its sweetness. She found three dusty earthenware bottles, sealed with wax, and brought them up to the kitchens.

Between her and the cook, they managed to dislodge the wax on all three bottles and pour the contents into two big pitchers. With the pitchers and cups on a tray, Corisande headed for her father's solar once again, grimly determined to be of help. When she reached the chamber door, she didn't bother to knock.

She walked right in.

The men in the room turned to her, surprised she had made a reappearance, but she ignored them. Anteaus, always the good brother, rushed to help her set the heavy tray upon the table that contained the things their father needed to manage the de Bourne empire. Vellum, quill, and maps were pushed away to make room. A cup with a little ale left at the bottom, old, spilled when Anteaus accidentally knocked it over in his haste.

He wiped it off with his hand.

"My thanks, Cori," Alastor said, though he didn't sound pleased. "You did not have to bring this yourself.

Corisande brushed off her hands after having wiped up the remnants of Anteaus' spill. "I know," she said, her focus drifting over to the man seated before the hearth. "But this wine is quite… strong. Mayhap our guest should be aware."

Alastor suspected that she knew it was for the Scotsman. She was obvious about that, and he knew she only wanted to help a man that was clearly in distress, but her presence was starting to annoy him.

"Go, now," he said. "You may leave us."

Corisande ignored him. She poured a full measure of the wine into the cup and went to the man on the chair before her father could stop her.

"Here," she said. "Drink this. It will make you feel better."

Canmore eyed her, eyed the drink, and his thirst won out over his stubborn pride. Refusal had been written all over his face, but he wanted the drink. He needed it. He snatched it from her with quivering hands and downed nearly half the cup in two big swallows. Licking his lips, he eyed her again.

"There's no poison in this, is there?" he asked suspiciously.

Corisande cocked an eyebrow. "'Tis a little late to be asking," she said wryly. "But I will answer your question – of course there is no poison in it. That is a very fine wine from Saxony. It is quite strong, so be cautious."

Canmore's gaze lingered on her and took another gulp. "It is a woman's drink."

He said it as if that were a bad thing. "I notice that has not stopped you from drinking it," she said. "Drink it all down. It will help warm and calm you."

He obeyed and downed the rest of the sweet, tart wine. He seemed quite normal about it until Corisande reached out to take the empty cup. Instead of handing it to her, he grabbed her hand and yanked her hard against him. The cup clattered to the ground and, in an instant, his hairy arm was across her neck.

In an instant, the tables turned. The captive was now in control and the sounds of swords being unsheathed echoed against the walls.

But Canmore was prepared.

"I'll kill the lass if ye dunna drop yer weapons!" he growled, backing up against the wall next to the hearth and dragging Corisande with him. "Do ye hear me, ye bloody Sassenachs? I'll kill her if ye dunna do as I say!"

Corisande yelped as he gave her neck a good squeeze and she grasped his arm, trying to keep him from strangling her. All she could see was her father and brothers in front of her, various stages of outrage on their faces and weapons in their hands. Ares was positively red with fury. But her father forced them to back away and she found herself looking at Cole de Velt.

He moved to stand right in front of her, absolutely fearless.

"I did not think you were this stupid, Canmore," he said in that deep, grumbling tone. "You disappoint me. My father still holds your wife. If you release Lady Corisande, I will not tell him of this, but if you refuse, I will send word to my father about your behavior. It will not go well for your wife."

Canmore was trembling all over, his edgy gaze glaring at the man with the unusual eyes. "Ye'll send word tae yer father tae release her or I'll snap this lass' neck and ye'll no' be able tae do a thing about it. Do as I say!"

Cole didn't move. His gaze was fixed on Canmore like a hunter sighting prey – unblinking, unmoving. After a moment, he smiled, but it was humorless.

And terrifying.

"Give her to me and I will not tell my father what you have done," he repeated. "If you do not, do you want me to describe what my father will do to your wife? And do you wish for me to describe what will happen to you? I hope pain is something you enjoy because you will have your fill of it. And so will your wife."

Canmore's trembling seemed to grow worse and his grip on Corisande tightened. "Ye dirty, lying bastard," he said. Then, he looked around the chamber at the faces gazing back at him, but he mostly focused on Alastor. "All of ye are dirty bastards. De Bourne, I made ye a fair offer and this is how ye repay me? Do ye no' realize that the Northmen are coming tae reclaim their lands? If ye dunna stand with them, ye'll die. All of ye will die."

"You first," Alastor growled.

Canmore sighed heavily, his nasty breath on Corisande's neck. "Ye're the descendants of the Bloodaxe," he said as if the man were a dolt. "These lands belong tae ye. How can ye no' want what is yer due? We're offering tae help ye. Can ye no' see that, ye fool?"

Alastor stepped forward, standing next to Cole. "'Tis you who are the fool, Canmore," he said. "I do not know who has been feeding you tales of victory, but this is a battle you cannot win. There is a whole massive country to the south with thousands of men who will come north and drive you and your Northmen allies back into Scotland. They'll drive you all back into the sea."

"'Tis our right!"

"'Tis madness."

Canmore's mouth was working furiously. "This was once the land of the Picts, long ago," he said. "The Northmen came and took Lindisfarne and Berwick, and they ruled for many years in the north. They are willing tae share this land with us – and ye. Yer bloodlines come from the last King of Northumbria. Eric Bloodaxe was a bloody ruler, a strong ruler. Would he no' want ye tae reclaim yer right?"

They were arguing the contents of Alpin's missives to Alastor for all to hear. This was everything he'd sent to Alastor in those hastily scribbled missives he'd been sending over the past year. But Alastor was grateful for the opportunity to discuss them because he wanted to make it clear to Alpin, as well as his allies, where he stood.

He had no time for delusions of conquest.

"Do you know where our family name comes from?" he said. "A *bourne* is a stream, a brook that runs through the land. An ancestor took the name de Bourne because it was said that Eric Bloodaxe killed so many, and was such a vicious and evil ruler, that there were streams of blood running all throughout his land. I have no desire to continue his legacy as such. There will be no blood on my lands as long as I am head of the House of de Bourne, and I shall not rebel against the English, of which I am one. We are united, and the north is peaceful for the most part. I will not engage in a war I know I cannot win."

Canmore shook his head as if the man were a complete idiot, but his trembling was growing worse. That wine he'd sucked down so rapidly was already filling his veins and going to his head, making him unsteady.

"Then ye'll die a fool's death," he said. "There are others that dunna feel as ye do. They are prepared tae join us."

Alastor was careful in his reply. "Other Englishmen?"

Canmore snorted, pulling tighter with his grip on Corisande, who had thus far remained silent and still. But she winced when he squeezed tighter, something that made Ares and Atlas lurch in her direction as Alastor held up a hand to stop them.

Not yet, lads…

"Answer me," Alastor said. "There are other English? They must not be very powerful. There is no one in the north that I know of who would join you. The Normans rule here, Canmore."

Canmore made a noise that sounded suspiciously like a

chuckle. "Ye know nothing," he muttered. "*Tha an fhìrinn ann am Bearaig.*"

Alastor didn't speak Gaelic, but he was coming to the end of his patience. He wanted his daughter back and it was clear that the wine Canmore had ingested was making him tipsy. The frost wine had that effect on even the strongest of men.

"De Velt," he said to Cole, still looking at Canmore. "Send word to your father. If he holds this fool's wife, tell him to do what he wishes with her. Hang her from the battlements if he chooses. Canmore is no longer of any value to us."

He was trying to force Canmore into more of a confession, but it had the opposite effect. As the man began to tense, Corisande could feel what the men in the room couldn't. She could feel the arm around her neck tightening and she was starting to see stars because of it. But there was one problem to Canmore's grip. He had her at an awkward angle, his arm partially covering her chin, which was probably the only thing preventing him from genuinely strangling her. She had been listening to the odd conversation, coming to realize he was no ordinary visitor. In fact, he was a prisoner from what she could gather, obviously someone who had been trying to coerce her father into doing… something. She had no idea what it was and she didn't care. All she knew was that she didn't want to die.

Fear had her planning her own escape.

She wasn't going to let the man break her neck.

Lowering her chin, she managed to get her mouth on the fleshy part of his arm without him really noticing because he was too focused on de Velt. Quick as a flash, she bit him, digging her teeth into his flesh as hard as she could.

The results were as she had hoped.

Canmore screamed and loosened his grip as Cole shot out a giant hand and grabbed her, pulling her away from Canmore as the man staggered sideways. It was just enough for Addax to step in and grab the man by the throat, but Canmore panicked and ended up pitching himself backwards as Addax lost his grip. His momentum took him straight into that roaring fire.

In seconds, he was consumed with flame.

Cole still had Corisande, but Alastor quickly reached out and pulled her against him, throwing her into a protective embrace as Addax and Ares tried to pull Canmore out of the hearth. But it was too late. His hair and clothing had gone up in an instant and he was already fully engulfed. His cries of agony filled the chamber as Alastor quickly ushered his daughter out while Anteaus and Atlas ran for buckets of water, their shouts to the servants echoing through the keep.

The entire situation disintegrated into chaos.

Alastor had taken Corisande out of the chamber, but only to the door before he released her and ran back into his solar as a man burned to death before his very eyes. Corisande stood in the entry, watching in utter horror as Canmore's squirming lessened. He was mostly in the hearth except for his legs, but he was kicking so much that he was scattering big logs of burning wood onto the floor. He was risking burning down the entire chamber, so she watched as Cole and the knights who had come with him shoved Canmore back into the hearth and used a shovel and a fire poker to keep him there.

Gradually, he stopped moving.

After that, Corisande couldn't watch anymore. She wandered over to the mural stairs as her brothers and several soldiers rushed back into the keep, into the solar to extinguish the burning body. She made it as far as the third step before plopping down and watching the activity, shocked and horrified by what she had just witnessed.

She'd never seen anything like it.

Even though Alastor had tried to remove her from the scene, she could still see what was happening. The door to the chamber was open and she could see men moving about, tossing water into the hearth and moving anything flammable away from the mess. Servants brought some of the chairs out of the solar along with the vellum that had been on the nearby table to keep it safe from the flames and water now being thrown around.

Corisande began to think that she had somehow contributed to the man's horrible death by biting him. If she was honest with herself, this whole situation had started when she entered the chamber with the wine. Her father had told her to stay away, but she hadn't listened. She'd wanted to help the Scotsman in defiance of her father, but she'd ended up making herself a target when the man grabbed her.

And now this.

Arms wrapped around her torso, she hung her head and tried not to weep.

"My lady?"

A deep voice startled her and she lifted her head to see Cole standing there. He was looking at her with concern.

"Is he dead?" she asked hoarsely.

He nodded. "Aye," he said. "There was nothing we could do. Are you well? He did not injure you?"

She shook her head. "He did not injure me," she said. "But… but I fear I killed him."

His brows flickered with confusion. "How did you kill him?"

She opened her mouth to explain, but the tears started to come. "I let him grab me," she said, trying not to openly weep. "I did not mean to, but I did. Had I not given him that wine, he would not have grabbed me. I would not have bitten him and he would not have fallen into the hearth."

She sniffed and lowered her head, wiping at the tears that were trickling down her cheeks. Cole's gaze lingered on her a moment before he took a seat on the step below where she was sitting. Since the stairs were wide, they were a few feet apart, a proper distance, as he faced her.

"I think you are looking at this the wrong way," he said with a surprising amount of compassion. "Alpin Canmore was a man with free will. He made the choice to grab you. He was not coerced. Everything that happened was by his choice. You did nothing wrong."

Her shaking hand continued to wipe away the tears that were falling. "You are kind to say so, but it is not the truth," she said. "It would not have happened had I not been there. I did not mean to cause trouble."

"You did not," Cole said. "Any trouble was caused by Canmore alone. You were simply a victim of his bad decision, so you must not blame yourself for any of this, my lady, truly."

Corisande could see that he was trying to comfort her, making sure she was tended to as her father and brothers dealt with the madness in the solar. Realizing that Cole had made a special effort to come to her when everyone else was occupied made her take a second look at the man. It was an inordinately kind gesture on his part and certainly not expected from a man who bore the name of the most brutal warlord in England.

"I… I do not think I have seen you here before," she said after a moment. "Have we never met before now?"

Cole shook his head. "Never," he said. "I have known your father and brothers for years, of course, because they are allies with my father, but I have never been to The Keld. And I am sure you have never been to my home."

"Where is your home?"

"Pelinom Castle. It is to the north, on the Scots border."

"You serve there with your father?"

He nodded. "I do."

For such a terrifying-looking man, in both size and manner,

he had an unusual gentleness as he spoke to her. In fact, he had succeeded in calming her down, and Corisande wiped the last of her tears as Cole managed to make her feel a little less shaken. In fact, she felt better with his reassurance.

"You have been very kind, my lord," she said. "You did not have to take the time to speak with me after… after what happened, but I am grateful that you did."

The corners of his mouth twitched. "It was my pleasure," he said. "You see, I have three sisters, only one of which is a calm, rational female. The other two are flighty and a bit dramatic at times, but they are sweet and lovable. They are my sisters, after all. Should they become upset over something, I would hope that someone would speak kindly to them and calm them."

Corisande grinned, revealing lovely teeth. "Then you are well-versed in handling hysterical woman."

He snorted. "Hardly," he said. "Effie is a handful even in the best of times, but Addie is more manageable. There was a time when she would not leave me alone, sitting in my lap and holding my hand everywhere I went, the little goose. I could not shake her no matter what I did."

Corisande eyed him dubiously. "You probably did not even try."

"Of course I did," he insisted. "But then she would cry and my mother would become angry, so I was forced to endure."

"And you loved it."

He lifted his chin defiantly. "I did not and you cannot make me say otherwise."

Corisande giggled at him because she could see that he was jesting. There was a lightness to the mood that hadn't been there before and after the horrors of the day, it did her heart good. The man had a comforting manner about him, at least with her, and it intrigued her immensely. She liked it. In fact, she thought he was rather sweet and was about to taunt him again about his annoying little sister when the door to the solar suddenly slammed back on its hinges.

Ares and Addax appeared, dragging the charred, smoldering corpse out into the entry. The stench of burned human flesh began to seep into the air, that sickening sweet smell, and Corisande had a quick, sickening glimpse of the body before Cole abruptly stood up and blocked her view.

"Where is your chamber, my lady?" he asked steadily. "Mayhap it is time to retire until this mess is cleaned up."

Corisande was unable to see anything with that big body in her field of vision. "I do not think that is necessary," she said. "My father's will surely need my assistance now and…"

He interrupted her, though he was not harsh. "Someone will attend to your father," he said, standing on the bottom step so she had no choice but to stand up and move up a stair or two. "He has several knights at his disposal and hundreds of soldiers, so you needn't worry. I realize you are the chatelaine and this is your domain, but let the men handle this. You do not need to sully your delicate senses with this unsavory task, my lady."

There was that kindness again, so unexpected from a man so fierce. Corisande found herself looking into those eyes, this time at close range, and seeing that they were truly remarkable. A golden-brown band circled the pupil and a bright green band encircled the golden-brown. They were looking at her pleasantly, but she had seen them turn hard when dealing with the Scotsman.

They were quite remarkable as, she suspected, was he.

"Your concern is most appreciated, my lord," she said, smiling timidly. "But I do not need to retire to my chamber. I should be part of this. As you said, the keep is my domain. I cannot shirk my responsibilities, no matter how distasteful."

Cole opened his mouth to politely argue with her, but a

shout from Alastor interrupted him.

"Cori!" he boomed. "To your chamber!"

Corisande caught sight of her father as he pushed past the men and servants hauling debris out his solar. "But –!"

Alastor cut her off. "Argue with me and I will authorize de Velt to pick you up and bodily carry you to your chamber," he said unhappily. "Get out of here. I will not tell you again."

By that time, he was almost to the stairs, and Corisande thought it would be best to obey the man. When he was angry, which was rare, it would do no good to argue. With a glance at Cole, and a grateful dip of her head for the concern he showed her, she gathered her skirts and rushed up the stairs, disappearing into the level above.

Cole tried not to be too obvious about watching her as Alastor huffed and puffed beside him.

"What did he say?" he demanded. "Canmore, I mean. He spoke Gaelic. What did he say?"

Cole was distracted from his thoughts of the lovely Corisande by Alastor's question. He knew Gaelic fluently because he had been raised on the borders, but also because of his position in the Scottish royal court. That was their primary language so if he wanted to understand anything, and convince them that he was Scots, then he had to know it flawlessly. Scratching his head, he turned to Alastor.

"He said the truth lies in Berwick," he said.

Alastor was still worked up over the entire incident, the usually placid man twitching nervously. "Berwick?" he repeated. "That seems odd. Did he say the same thing to your father?"

Cole shook his head. "He told my father that the Earls of Orkney had sent a request to their Northmen brethren last year, explaining this rebellion and asking for their assistance," he said. "My father did what he had to do in order to encourage the truth from Canmore, as I told you when I arrived. He burned the man's home and impaled his army. He spent an entire night interrogating Canmore, but the gist of what Canmore told him was this – the Northmen have had a year to prepare for this onslaught. Canmore knows that they are preparing to come to the shores of England in the summer, but he does not know exactly when. My father asked him twenty different ways and Canmore's answers were consistent."

"And he is certain it was the truth?"

"As certain as he can be," Cole said. "All Canmore knows is that he is waiting for word from William the Lion as to when and where to move his army, but he doesn't know anything more than that. In my two years in Scotland, I was unable to discover little more than what Canmore told my father, so the words *tha an fhìrinn ann am Bearaig* – the truth lies in Berwick – is something new. I've not heard it before."

Alastor was watching his soldiers enter the keep with a litter to put the burned corpse upon. "Then mayhap he had enough of that wine to loosen his tongue just a little."

"Possibly."

"In all of your time at the side of William, you never heard the mention of Berwick?"

Cole shook his head. "My directive was not to become an advisor or close confidant," he said. "My directive from The Marshal was to observe. That meant I only heard certain things. There were times William called a special council, but I was excluded like the rest of his guard. But Alpin had been part of those gatherings, which was why we thought he could supply any information I missed."

It made sense. The life of a spy meant to blend in. Alastor rubbed a hand over his face, struggling to think.

"Berwick has a river," he muttered. "A river that flows deep into England, the border between England and Scotland."

Cole nodded. "That is true," he said. He paused before continuing, his tone ominous. "A river that is deep."

"How deep?"

"Deep enough to accommodate longships."

Alastor looked at him, surprised. "God's Bones," he said. "Do you suppose that was what he meant?"

Cole lifted his shoulders. "It is possible," he said. "My father's methods were brutal, so it is a tribute to Canmore's self-control that he didn't mention Berwick to him, but the wine… he must have had just enough of it, as you said. Enough that he let Berwick slip. That was something I did not know."

Alastor sighed heavily. "Then it *must* be Berwick," he said. "Sometime in the summer, those longships will come to Berwick."

That realization wasn't lost on Cole. In fact, he felt a sense of urgency about it because it made perfect sense. If there was to be an invasion by the Northmen, the River Tweed would be a perfect vessel for their onslaught. It would cut England and Scotland in half and they could bombard and attack from the river. They could even bring Scotsmen on those longships and launch them into England that way.

The possibilities were endless.

"I must send word not only to my father, but to William Marshal," he said. "He will want to know."

"Who does Berwick Castle belong to these days?" Alastor asked. "Do you suppose the garrison commander is in league with the Scots?"

Cole cast him a long look. "You do not know?"

Alastor shook his head. "Berwick is a far enough away that I do not normally concern myself with the town," he said. "Carlisle is the largest city nearest to me and that is where I focus my attention. Why? What is happening with Berwick?"

Cole lifted his eyebrows. "You are not going to like the

answer," he said. "King Richard sold Berwick to the Scots right before he went on crusade to raise money for his armies. It has belonged to the Scots ever since."

Alastor shook his head with regret. "I knew of that," he said. "But that was twenty years ago. I suppose I was hoping against hope that it was again an English garrison after all these years."

"It is not."

"Then the Scots at the garrison will make it easy for the longships to enter the river."

"And straight into the heart of England."

That was the truth of it. Even as Cole spoke the words, he felt as if he'd just been hit by a hammer. Everything they'd wanted to know had just become clear.

Unless, of course, it was a diversion to throw them off the path of the true plans.

But Cole didn't think Canmore was that smart.

"I must tell my father," he repeated. "And unless we want the Scots at Berwick to openly welcome the Northmen, we are going to have to gain control of that castle before the summer months arrive."

Alastor looked at him. "I will pledge my army for that purpose," he said. "Tell me what more you need, Cole. I will do what I can to support the efforts."

"I will," Cole said. "I will send word to my father tonight. I would not be surprised if he came to The Keld to discuss the situation with you."

"I would be honored by his visit."

There wasn't much more to say at that point. They both knew the implications. What Ajax de Velt's army couldn't accomplish, some strong wine could. As Alastor went after his sons to inform them of his discussion with Cole about Berwick, Cole headed out to find Addax and Essien to tell them the same thing. There was a great deal at stake and no time to waste.

Alpin Canmore's death wouldn't be in vain.

He told the English what they wanted to know, and they would be ready.

Or die trying.

CHAPTER FIVE

T HAT EVENING'S FEAST wasn't like any other.

Tonight, it was different.

At least, that's how Corisande felt as she gazed out over the packed great hall. It was full of men, feasting and laughing and drinking, and the enormous hearth was spitting more smoke into the room than was probably going up the chimney, so a fine haze of blue smoke hung up near the ceiling.

In spite of what had happened that afternoon, the mood of the hall was one of gaiety. As if a man hadn't burned to death in Alastor's hearth, a man who had been key to much of the political winds that were blowing in their direction. As Corisande looked out over the hall, it was as if the men of The Keld hadn't a care in the world.

At least, that was the attitude of the rank and file. On the dais, however, the mood was a quite different. Those men knew what had transpired earlier in the day because they'd been part of it, so they were a bit more subdued.

Perhaps reflecting on what the future would bring.

"Who are those men with Papa?"

The question came from Corisande's younger sister, and the youngest de Bourne sibling, Gaia. She had seen ten years and eight and was newly returned from fostering at Prudhoe Castle. Corisande had only seen her youngest sister intermittently over the past seven years until her return home a few months ago, so the sisters were still coming to know one another as grown women. But Corisande knew one thing for certain –

Her sister was man-crazy.

She was a pretty little thing, too, petite and blonde as their mother had been. Already, she was giving Alastor and her older brothers fits because she would flirt and tease, and then her father and brothers would have to rush in to fend off the men she had been toying with. There was one squire in particular, one who had served with distinction for a few years, who Gaia would not leave alone. The poor young man had been the object of her attention since her return to The Keld and three weeks ago, Alastor finally sent the lad south to an ally's home simply to get him away from his man-eating daughter.

Now, Gaia was already eyeing the visitors to The Keld, Cole de Velt included, and Corisande knew there was going to be trouble.

Gaia had little restraint when she saw a man she found attractive.

"Those men are important allies," she said. "They are here on serious business with Papa and you will not embarrass him. No winking, smiling, or pinching, Gaia. Do you understand?"

Gaia looked at her sister, frowning. "What has happened to you?" she said. "You used to be much more fun when we were younger. When did you become so serious?"

Corisande had limited patience for her sister's antics these days. "I have grown up but, evidently, you have not," she said. "Do not behave like a trollop. Papa has warned you against such things. Now, where is Gratiana?"

She was asking about the female ward they'd had at The Keld for three years now, a young woman from a good family that had a small castle on the Welsh Marches. Lady Gratiana de Allington was a mature young woman of good character and, fortunately, didn't subscribe to Gaia's foolery. In fact, Gaia frightened her, so she didn't usually solicit her company.

And Gaia knew it.

Therefore, she lifted her slender shoulders in a careless gesture.

"Who knows?" she said. "More importantly, who cares? Gratiana is as bad as you are when it comes to fun. The woman does not have a frivolous bone in her entire body."

Corisande eyed her little sister, wondering for the hundredth time about the company she must have kept at Prudhoe that gave her such an attitude. Little Gaia was quite worldly, and not in a good way, and Corisande found herself wondering just how her sister would embarrass herself tonight in front of the visitors.

Keeping her busy was the only solution.

"Return to the kitchens and make sure the cook has more bread being prepared," she said. "Your help in the kitchens is invaluable to me. I appreciate it."

Gaia rolled her eyes, clearly displeased. "But I should be sitting at the table with Papa and the others," she said. "So should you. Why are we serving the meal? We are not servants."

Corisande looked at her. "Nay, we are not," she said, "but we are the daughters of the Lord of The Keld, and that means we ensure that everything is perfect for his men and his guests. They taught you that at Prudhoe, didn't they?"

Gaia's expression suggested they had, but she'd hated every minute of it. "I have learned everything I need to know," she said, turning her nose up at anything that involved management or domestic responsibilities. "I want to sit with Papa and his guests. Who are they, anyway? Do you know them?"

Corisande's gaze moved to the table where her father and

brothers were sitting with Cole and his men. Specifically, her focus lingered on Cole, seated between Ares and her father, listening to Alastor as he went on about something. As she looked at him, she couldn't help but remember how kind he'd been to her earlier and her sister's question stirred something odd in her…

Jealousy.

She didn't like the idea of her sister paying attention to Cole and she had no idea why except she'd rather liked his attention on *her*. She didn't want that same kindness turned to her lascivious sister, where it would be wasted. Corisande was rather old not to have been married yet, and it had been a long time since she's given any regard to a man who showed her attention. It wasn't as if she'd had a lack of attention from suitors, but the only man she'd ever considered marrying had gone off to France three years ago.

Sir Auden de Stroude had been his name. He was the last of his family, an old family from Cornwall, and she'd met him when he served the Earl of Hexham, her father's close ally. Auden was sweet and handsome, and he'd paid her a great deal of attention, so much so that her father demanded to know the man's intentions.

Before they'd been able to discuss it, however, Auden had been sent to properties in France owned by Hexham. There were disputes there and Auden was supposed to defend the properties, and negotiate a truce, but he never returned. Hexham told Alastor that the knight had married a local noblewoman to secure peace, and that was the last time Corisande had really thought about a man in romantic terms.

But the introduction of Cole de Velt had awakened something.

"I know who they are," she said after a moment. "The man seated next to Papa is Sir Cole de Velt. His father is Ajax de

Velt, a great and terrible warlord from the north. The men with him are his knights, Sir Addax and Sir Essien. They are brothers."

Gaia was fixed on the al-Kort siblings. "I have never seen men like them before," she said. "They are not English."

"I do not believe so."

"Where are they from?"

Corisande shook her head. "I do not know," she said. "I did not ask."

Gaia grinned as she looked them over from a distance. "They must be from someplace far away," she said. "Mayhap they are from Rome or Athens, great warriors like those in Papa's books. Don't they look like that to you? Like the gods of old?"

Corisande nodded faintly. "I can see them with wings on their shoulders, shooting bolts of fire from the heights of Olympus," she said, grinning at her sister when the woman looked at her. "Surely, they are great warriors if they are with a de Velt and if you by chance speak to them, do not wink at them or pinch them. I will not have them returning to Olympus with tales of Alastor de Bourne's bold daughter."

The smile on Gaia's face turned to a frown as Corisande winked at her and turned away, heading back towards the kitchens. She hadn't taken two steps when the scruffy servant who had helped her tend the soldier with the infected boil approached her from the shadows.

"My lady," he said nervously. "The man whose leg you lanced today is in great pain. The boil seems to be very red and angry. You should come and see him."

Corisande was distracted from her kitchen duties. "Of course," she said. "Has a fever sparked?"

"Not yet, my lady."

"Where is he?"

"I took him back to the knight's quarters, my lady. He waits for you there."

She paused a moment, thinking. "Then bring hot water and boiled linen," she said. "I will send someone for my medicament bag. Gather those things and meet me in the knight's quarters."

The servant nodded and ran off as Corisande turned to her sister. "Gaia, you must manage the kitchens," she said. "I may not return for some time, so please make sure Papa and his guests are well-supplied. Will you do this?"

Gaia nodded. "Aye," she said. "Where are you going?"

Corisande gestured in the general direction of the bailey. "To tend a man with an inflamed wound," she said. "I shall return as soon as I can."

With that, she dashed off, staying to the recesses of the hall as she made her way towards the main entry. Gaia watched her sister until the woman departed and instead of going to the kitchens as she'd been asked, she headed straight to the dais where those fascinating men were. She wasn't going to spend her evening in the kitchens when there were handsome males to be entertained.

That night, Essien was the first one to be pinched by a naughty blonde with an impish grin.

IT WAS COLD on this evening, a dusting of brilliant stars spread across the heavens as Corisande moved quickly beneath that dark sky, heading towards the stables.

She had a particular purpose in mind.

The stables of The Keld were quite old. In fact, a portion of them belonged to the bones of an even older building, for there had been Romans in this location at one time and Castle Keld had been built over the ruins.

Someone told her once that the stalls where the horses were housed had, at one time, been small sleeping cells for the Roman soldiers. When the castle was built by a de Bourne ancestor, the building that contained the cells was incorporated into the stables. There were also two enormous stone troughs left by the Romans that were used by the livestock.

One particular trough was Corisande's destination.

This trough was nestled deep in the earth near the stalls and was fed by a natural spring. There was a type of moss that grew on the north side of the trough and it was that growth that Corisande was looking for. It was a very old moss and it had some kind of medicinal quality to it because she had used it many times to help alleviate swelling and poison in wounds. It was hairy, and had a sort of bluish-green cast to it, but whatever it was worked very well in helping heal the sick.

As Corisande entered the stables, she paused to light an oil lamp. It was quite dark in the stables at this time of night and she needed some light by which to see, so she collected an oil lamp used by the stable servants that had the flame mostly covered. An open flame in a stable was a recipe for disaster, so she lit it carefully.

With a little lamp burning weakly against the darkness, Corisande made her way to the end of the stone stable where the old, chipped trough was half-buried in the ground. Holding the lamp aloft so she could get a better view, she knelt down to inspect the northern part of the trough where the bluish-green moss grew. There was quite a bit of it and she began pulling it off, collecting a goodly handful of it.

"So this is where you went."

Startled by the voice, Corisande looked up to see Cole entering the stable. On her knees, bent over the mossy trough, she straightened up to face him.

"Were you looking for me?" she asked. "I apologize if you had to hunt me down, but there is a soldier with an infected boil and as strange as it sounds, the moss on this trough is known to cure skin wounds. I must tend to the man."

He put up his hands because she sounded apologetic that she'd left the hall to do what was clearly a more important duty.

"There is no need for apologies, my lady, truly," he said, coming closer. "I was not looking for you. I came to see to my horse, who seemed to have an odd gait today. I wanted to see if he has developed a lameness, so the fact that you are here is purely coincidental."

That was a lie. An utter, complete lie. Cole had seen her leave the hall and he'd followed. He'd spent the entire evening listening to Alastor when his mind was really on the man's daughter as she hovered on the fringes of the great hall, making sure the meal ran smoothly. He kept wishing she would come and sit at the dais, but she didn't. Instead, she had departed the hall and a younger girl with similar features joined the table, but she seemed to be quite interested in Essien, much to the man's horror.

But Cole didn't have time to laugh about it.

He was focused on the lovely Lady Corisande.

When she left, he left, using the same excuse he'd just given her to relief himself of the table. God only knew why he had followed her. He still didn't know. All he knew was that after their brief conversation earlier that day, she was lingering in his thoughts, subtly but unmistakably.

Curiosity, more than anything, had brought him into the stable.

He was wondering why she fascinated him so.

But Corisande didn't seem to suspect anything was amiss

with his weak excuse. At least, he thought it was weak. To make it appear stronger, he headed over to the stall where his fat, black stallion was tethered, contentedly dozing.

"I am sorry to hear about your horse," she said as he went to the stall. "I could make a mustard plaster for the leg if you think it would help."

Cole slapped the beast on the rump, pretending to eye the hind legs. "That is kind of you," he said. "Is healing animals among your talents, too?"

Moss in one hand and lamp in the other, Corisande wandered over to the stall. "My mother was a great healer," she said. "Her knowledge in herbs and medicines was unsurpassed. She taught me what she could, so I know a little something about healing men and animals."

"And you enjoy it?"

She looked at him as if surprised by the question. "I do," she said. "There is something satisfying about helping a man regain his health. Or helping a horse with a lame leg."

She smiled as she said it and Cole smiled in return. "And it will be greatly appreciated," he said, thinking he should probably look like he was examining the legs, so he bent over and began feeling carefully around the fetlocks. "I've not met many women with a talent for healing. In fact, I cannot recall one. Usually it is a man's profession unless the woman is a midwife. I assume you do that, too?"

Corisande watched him gently squeeze the legs of the horse. "I have delivered two babies in my life," she said. "Midwifery is an exacting profession and, frankly, not something I prefer. For an unmarried young woman, it is a little unseemly."

He glanced at her. "That is the most shocking statement I have heard today, in a day of many shocking events."

"What do you mean?"

"That you are unmarried."

"Why?"

He stood up and looked at her. "Because you are beautiful and clearly accomplished," he said. "You should have a line of men outside the gatehouse, waiting for their turn to woo you. But given you have older brothers, I would wager to say that they have scattered that line of men before it gathers. Protective brothers do that."

Corisande laughed softly. "Is that because you have chased away your sisters' suitors?" she asked. "It takes one to know one, as it were?"

He shook his head firmly. "Christ, they can have them," he said dismissively, moving to the other side of the horse. "In fact, I go from village to village trying to pay men to take my sisters away, although the eldest one is already married. Allaston married a Welsh warlord a few years ago."

"Allaston," she repeated. "That is a lovely name. And you mentioned the other two were Effie and Addie?"

He bent over another leg. "Allaston, Effington, and Addington," he said, grunting as he lifted the hoof. "My mother's name is Kellington, so those were the names she insisted on naming my sisters. But we call them Allie, Effie, and Addie."

Corisande leaned against the stone wall of the stall, watching him inspect the hoof. "You speak fondly of them," she said. "Not many brothers do that. I am fortunate that my brothers and I get on well. I do not know what I would do without them."

He dropped the hoof and stood up. "To get on well with siblings says something about one's character, I think," he said. "It speaks of the capacity to be tolerant, to consider others, and to appreciate the strength of family bonds. I am sure your brothers would kill for you, just as I would kill for my sisters. I consider myself fortunate to have such a family."

She cocked her head as she listened to him. "Most men do

not speak that way of their families," she said. "That is a rare trait."

"What trait?"

"That you love your family."

He frowned, but it was all for show. "Bah," he said. "They are pests, all of them, although my brothers are good lads. And my father is the greatest knight in the realm."

"And your mother?"

He looked at her. "She is my rock."

"That is very sweet."

"And your mother?"

"She died a few years ago. I miss her every day."

His voice softened. "I am sorry," he said. "I can only imagine what a great loss it was. But she has a fine daughter to be proud of."

It took Corisande a moment to realize that he meant her. "Me?"

He burst into soft laughter, displaying big, white teeth with canines that protruded just a little. It was a dashing smile. "Aye, *you*," he said. "Who did you think I meant?"

She grinned, embarrassed. "I have a sister, you know."

His brow furrowed thoughtfully. "The little blonde lass who joined us in the hall?"

Corisande's smile vanished. "She joined you?"

He nodded. "When you left, she came to the table," he said. "She sat with Essien. She seemed quite interested in him."

Corisande rolled her eyes. "Because he is handsome and new," she said. "Gaia has an eye for a handsome man. I'm afraid your knight may not be rid of her easily."

His eyebrows lifted. "Ah," he said. "Well, we shall be leaving on the morrow and she will not be able to follow him."

Corisande felt a distinct sense of disappointment to realize he was leaving so soon. "Tomorrow?" she said. "So soon? We thought you would be our guests for a few days, at least. I am sure my father would like to come to know his ally better."

Cole wondered if he heard a hint of hope in her voice, if by saying her father she really meant her. Personally.

He leaned against his horse.

"I must return to Pelinom and tell my father what transpired here today," he said. "But I should like to return soon, with your permission, and spend time coming to know an ally better."

There was a spark there, something they could both feel, something burning low in the belly as if something between them had been kindled. A hint of interest, a shadow of attraction.

It was there.

Corisande began to feel the least bit giddy because of it.

"You are always welcome at The Keld," she said. "I do hope we see more of you. And your men, too, although your knight may not wish to return if my sister makes herself a terrible nuisance."

Cole fought off a grin. "I will leave him home."

"Where is home for him? I mean, where is he from? My sister asked and I did not know."

Cole gestured in a general southerly direction. "A land very far away," he said. "Addax and Essien are princes to their people, from a kingdom called Kitara."

Corisande was interested. "Truly?" she said. "Where is it?"

"Far away," he said. "In a land of ancient kings. There is an enormous river that runs through that desert land and Kitara is on that river. It would take you years to reach it."

"If it is so far away, what are they doing in England?"

"They were young when there was an insurrection in their country," he said, moving to the end of his horse where she was standing. "Their father was killed, so they were forced to flee.

Truly, their life story is something quite amazing. They made their way to The Levant and ended up under the care of Christian knights. When the wars were over, they traveled to Ghent where they were trained, and knighted, and then they came into the service of my father. They are brilliant men and fine warriors."

"They are *princes*," Corisande said. "They should be treated as such. God's Bones, they should not be sleeping in the knight's quarters. They should be in the keep, in a fine chamber with a soft bed."

She seemed a little panicked that she had royalty in her house and had not given them proper treatment. But Cole smiled and put a big hand on the fingers that were holding the moss.

"They are knights," he stressed, a twinkle in his eyes. "The knight's quarters suit them quite well."

"Are you certain?"

"I am."

He removed his hand from her fingers, which had only really lingered there for a brief moment, but Corisande felt his flesh against hers like a brand. It was difficult to think of anything other than the feel of his hand against hers, something she'd not experienced in a very long time.

"If you say so, then I will not worry," she said, trying not to appear distracted. "When you return, I hope you bring them. I should like to hear of their travels and of the land of Kitara. It is a beautiful name."

"Sounds like a woman's name, doesn't it?"

She nodded. "Indeed," she said. Then, she paused a moment. "My lord, may I ask you a question?"

He nodded. "You may," he said. "But I would be honored if you would call me Cole."

Corisande smiled bashfully. "Thank you," she said. "But

only if my family is not around. They may not like it if I become too familiar. It will sound disrespectful."

He chuckled. "I will assure them that you have my permission," he said. "What is your question?"

Her smile faded. "I am not quite sure how to ask this," she said. "I have not yet seen my father since the events of the afternoon, and I am not sure he would answer me truthfully. I sense that you would not lie to me."

"I would not lie in any case. What is it?"

"The man… the Scotsman from today," she said. "I have been wondering… was he a prisoner?"

Cole wondered what brought on the change in subject, but he answered truthfully. "Aye."

"Was he trying to lure my father into a war?"

Cole shook his head. "If you wish to know more, then you must ask your father. I have told you all I can."

She understood. "Thank you for being honest with me," she said. "But I do hope he was not trying to lure my father into a war. We have seen enough of that."

He peered at her strangely. "Here?" he said. "At The Keld?"

She shook her head. "Not here," she said. "But my father trots out his army every time there is an action against the king in the north. He does not like the man very much. There are a few barons this far north who support the king and there are others who do not. Disputes arise. In fact, there was one a few months ago and my father went to support Prudhoe Castle against Lord Lanchester. It seemed that Lanchester wanted Prudhoe for the king and d'Umfraville called upon my father for assistance to chase him away. That was a rather… messy battle."

Cole hadn't heard of that particular skirmish, but he wasn't surprised. John's loyal barons were generally unscrupulous and targeted major castles from time to time with the intention of holding them for the king.

"The men of The Keld were fortunate to have you," he said. "I am sure you tended to them quite ably once they reached home."

She looked at him oddly. "I tended to them at the battle," she said. "I am my father's surgeon."

Cole stared at her a moment before his eyebrows slowly lifted. "*You* went on a battle march?"

She nodded. "Of course," she said. "Anytime my father's army is called out, I go with them. The men have a much better chance of surviving if I am able to tend to them quickly."

It took him a moment to digest that. Women weren't surgeons and they certainly didn't go on battle marches. At least, he'd never heard of anything like that in his life. But at The Keld, that was evidently the situation – the chatelaine healer was also the surgeon. Her practice of tending the ill and sick crossed over into battlefield.

He wasn't sure he liked that at all.

"I see," he said. "That is a very difficult life for a woman. I am surprised your father permits it."

Corisande shrugged. "As I said, I am their best chance for survival," she said. "My mother used to go with the army, too."

"*Two* women surgeons?"

"Indeed."

Cole had never heard of such a thing. To think of Corisande de Bourne in the midst of a battle… nay, he didn't like that at all. A battle was no place for a woman, but he refrained from voicing his opinion. She clearly didn't see anything wrong with it and he didn't want to interject his position when he really had no place to. But it occurred to him that if de Bourne sent his army to Berwick, as he had pledged, then Corisande might be going along as the surgeon.

… and he had a distinct problem with that.

He'd known the woman a matter of hours and, already, he didn't like the idea of her in danger.

It was a most interesting situation.

"Hopefully, there will never be another cause for you to venture out with the army," he said, smiling weakly. "The Keld seems to be at peace for the moment. So we shall hope it remains that way."

"And you'll still come back and visit us?"

"I said I would. I meant it."

The way he said it caused her cheeks to flush. He could see it in the dim light of the lamp. But she lowered her gaze, and the lamp, and his glimpse of those pretty cheeks was dimmed.

"Then I shall be in the stables before dawn with some food for your journey," she said. "I hope that is agreeable."

"I am grateful, my lady."

"If I am to call you Cole, then you are to call me Cori."

"It would be my greatest honor."

"But do not let my brothers hear you. They might think you are being too forward."

He laughed low in his throat. "I can handle the de Bourne brothers."

"And they think they can handle you."

He burst out laughing. Corisande smiled broadly, a big dimple in her right cheek, as she handed him the lamp.

"As much as I would like to continue this conversation, I am afraid that I must tend a soldier with an infected wound," she said, holding up the growth in her hand. "That is why I came to collect the moss. But it was most agreeable speaking with you, Cole. I am glad we had the opportunity."

His gaze lingered on her. "As am I," he said. "And it will not be the last time."

"I hope not."

With a bashful smile, she turned and headed out of the

stable, leaving Cole standing there with the lamp in his hand and a big grin on his face.

Nay, it wouldn't be the last time he talked to her.

Not in the least.

CHAPTER SIX

"WHAT IS THE matter with you?"

The words were mumbled. Cole thought he was the only one awake, but he was mistaken.

Cole, Addax, and Essien were all sleeping in the same chamber in the knight's quarters of The Keld. It was the largest room in the block, with three beds crammed into it simply because all of the other chambers were full. It wasn't that The Keld had so many knights, because the de Bourne brothers slept in the keep, but it was the simply the fact that the space was needed for the soldiers, so the knight's quarters really wasn't full of knights.

It was full of soldiers.

But Cole didn't realize that until it was time to go to bed and the servant who attended the men in the knight's quarters was apologetic and offered to kick some of the soldiers out of their smaller chambers, but Cole waved the man off. They were only going to be there for the night, so it really didn't matter. He went to bed along with Essien and Addax in the same chamber, but he had ended up lying awake most of the night listening to their snores.

Or, so he thought.

Addax was awake, too.

"What makes you think anything is wrong?" Cole muttered softly, turning to see Addax laying on his belly, looking at him. "Why are you awake?"

Addax lifted his head. "Because you have been laying there, sighing all night," he said. He sighed heavily a few times just for effect. "By the Gods, Cole, you sound like someone is punching you in the belly every few minutes and your breath is being expelled at an alarming rate. What is the matter with you?"

Cole looked at the man for a moment before returning his focus to the ceiling. He'd been staring at it for hours as he lay flat on his back. Staring, thinking… after a moment, he sighed heavily, realizing for the first time that he was doing it.

"You see?" Addax said. "There you go again. Are you ill?"

Cole pursed his lips wryly. "Nay," he said. "I am not ill."

"Are you in pain?"

"Nay."

Addax rolled his eyes. "You will be the next time you sigh like that and do not tell me what the issue is."

Cole grinned, lopsided. "I do not even know where to start."

"Then there *is* a problem?"

Cole didn't say anything for a moment. "Ad, let me ask you a question."

"Ask, my friend."

"What do you think of Audie?"

Addax looked at him curiously. "Audie? Lady Audrie?"

"Aye. You know her nickname is Audie."

"She is a pretty girl, well-educated. Why?"

"Do you like her?"

"I've not had a great chance to know her, but what I have seen, I like."

"You know that our families are expecting me to marry her."

"I know."

"Let me ask you another question."

"Go ahead."

"What do you think of Lady Corisande?"

Addax's head came up, the dark eyes glittering. "Ah," he said after a moment. "I understand now."

Cole looked at him. "You do? Then explain it to me."

Addax pushed himself up, swinging his legs over the side of the mattress. "What do you want me to explain?" he said. "Lady Corisande is beautiful and she is a fresh face. She is simply new and interesting. You've found a pretty new girl to look at."

Cole rolled onto his side to look at him. "I have seen plenty of beautiful, fresh faces in my life, but not one of them has made me feel like I've been struck by lightning when I look at her."

"Not even Mary?"

Cole shrugged, reflecting on the wife he'd lost. "I do not know," he admitted. "With Mary, my feelings for her were a calm and comfortable thing. But with Corisande… all I know is that I feel bolts of lightning rush through my veins when she looks at me and we had a nice conversation earlier this evening when I left the hall. It is difficult to describe, but talking to her… it is so easy. The words simply flowed and I do not converse easily, Ad. You know this."

"She makes you feel comfortable."

Cole nodded. "I look at her and all I want to do is smile," he said. "Christ, that sounds like madness even as I say it. But the way she handled herself when Canmore took her a prisoner speaks of her inner strength. I have never seen a woman handle herself so well in the face of danger."

"And that impresses you?"

"It does."

Addax scratched his head. "Then mayhap you should keep

away from Audrie de Longley until you can figure out if the attraction to Corisande de Bourne is something more than simple infatuation. But you do have a commitment of sorts with Audrie, Cole. This could get… tricky."

Cole sat up. "There *is* no commitment," he said. "Simply an expectation that has never been spoken aloud. I have never asked to formally court her. Audie is charming and witty, but there is also a superficialness to her. When I speak to her about my life, about my interests, she listens politely and immediately starts talking about herself again. It would be nice to have a wife who was interested in my likes and wants again. Mary was."

"And you think that Lady Corisande can replace Mary?"

Cole shrugged. "Not replace her," he said. "It is not my intention to replace her at all. But if I could find an intelligent woman who showed interest in me, that would mean something. With Audie, everything you need to know about her is right there in front of you. There's nothing deeper with her. No wants, no dreams, no desires."

Addax regarded him in the dim light. "And you sense something deeper in Lady Corisande?"

Cole half-nodded, half-shrugged. "I don't know what I sense," he said. "All I know is that she makes me sit up and take notice in a way Audie never has. She's like a goddess on the mountaintop and I am but a lowly servant at her feet. The woman is far too good for me and I know it, but that does not stop my interest in her."

Addax was grinning at him. "Then mayhap you should explore that," he said. "Es and I can return to Pelinom and tell your father what has occurred here with Canmore. Why not remain here under some pretext? Get to know Lady Corisande and see if she's really the goddess on the mountaintop that you think she is."

Cole shook his head. "I would like to, but I cannot," he said.

"I must tell my father personally what we have discovered, but when that is finished, I will return here if I can. I have promised myself that. And I have promised Corisande, too."

"She knows of your interest?"

"Nay," Cole said. "But it is quite possible that she will at some point soon."

Addax grinned, his white teeth flashing in the dim light, as Essien suddenly rolled onto his back.

"By all that is holy," he muttered, putting his hands over his face. "Will you two shut your bloody mouths? How is a man supposed to sleep?"

Cole started laughing as Addax used his blanket to beat his brother, who yelped and ended up grabbing the blanket. A full-scale brawl was about to erupt but Cole stood up, putting himself between coiled Essien and snickering Addax.

"Enough, you idiots," he said. "I get that enough from my own brothers. I do not need it from you two."

Essien cooled down, but only a little. He fell back on his bed, his arms over his eyes. "Cole, if I were you, I would stay away from Lady Corisande," he said.

Cole was heading over to the basin of freezing water to wash his face in the pre-dawn darkness. He struck flint and stone to light the oil lamp on the table before glancing at Essien.

"Why?" he asked.

Essien grunted. "Because if she is anything like her sister, she is an annoying monstrosity."

Cole grinned as he turned back to the basin of water, collecting a bar of lumpy, white soap next to it that smelled of pine and rosemary.

"I saw that she was paying you an inordinate amount of attention last night," he said as he splashed water on his face. "She is a pretty little thing."

Essien's arms came away from his face. "She is pretty, but

she pinches," he said, making pinching gestures. "She's got crab claws and she uses them. I swear to you that my entire left side is bruised from her pinching."

Cole lathered up his stubble with the soap and picked up the razor that was next to the basin, one belonging to Addax.

"The bruises are badges of honor," he said as he carefully shaved his left cheek, using a small bronze mirror on the table. "Since when do you complain if a pretty girl leaves marks on your body? That has never bothered you before."

Essien yawned. "Normally, it would not," he said. "But the youngest de Bourne sister is far too much of a child for me. I like my women older. And less pinchy."

Cole washed off the razor in the water. "With your ugly looks, you are lucky she finds you handsome enough to pinch," he said. "Speaking of ugly, what was done with Canmore's body?"

Addax answered as he pulled his tunic over his head. "Ares sent it to the priests at St. Oswald's," he said. "It was a terrible way to die, but mayhap better than the way the rest of his men died. I suppose the man should be grateful for small mercies."

Cole finished with the right side of his face, ignoring the comment about Canmore's army. He knew that Essien and Addax had been somewhat sensitive to what his father had done at Fountainhall and Cole wouldn't be put in a position where he had to defend his father's tactics to them, Essien in particular.

Ajax de Velt was beyond reproach, in his opinion.

"My father will be very interested in the mention of Berwick," he said, changing the subject slightly. "Canmore never mentioned Berwick to him, so that is a new and curious bit of information."

"Will he move troops there?" Essien asked.

Both Cole an Addax nodded, but it was Cole who answered.

"If that is where the Northman ships intend to enter England, then he'll have to," he said. "My suspicion is that we shall all be going to war very soon and William Marshal will be heading north, if he is not already."

Addax was pulling on another tunic to protect against the cold morning, but his movements were slowing. "Cole," he said after a moment. "I have been thinking… your father left a survivor from Fountainhall to deliver a message to King William."

"He did."

"Was that wise?"

Cole had just finished shaving his chin. "What do you mean?"

Addax straightened out the tunic. "I mean that sending a survivor back to William the Lion means that the king will know that we are aware of his plans," he said. "Do you not think he will adjust for that? He may change his plans altogether."

Cole wiped off the remaining froth from his face. "I am certain that my father considered that," he said. "On one hand, we capture Canmore and glean what we can from the man and we kill any witnesses to our activities. No one knows what happened, or where Canmore is, and the Scots continue with their plans to charge into England. On the other hand, we raze Fountainhall, capture Canmore, and let William know that we are well aware of his plans and we have demonstrated what we will do to him should he try to enter England. It gives William pause, of course. But does it make him amend his plans? I think they are already in motion. He cannot change them. We are going to Berwick and he will probably go there, also. We will try to prevent the Northmen from entering the River Tweed and he will try to prevent us from stopping them."

Addax could see the logic. "Assuming King William realizes we know of Berwick."

"If I were the king, I would assume that."

Addax conceded the point. "Then we shall tell Lord de Velt what has transpired here, and then we're off to Berwick," he said. Then, he scratched his head wearily. "I do not think I have had a day's rest since coming to England, Cole. Between The Marshal and your father, it has been quite eventful. Has it always been like this?"

Cole smiled weakly as he reached for his own clothing. "Pelinom and my father are usually quiet for the most part," he said. "That is why I chose to serve William Marshal, why I have followed the man's directives for the past ten years. I feel as if I am accomplishing something."

"And what have you accomplished?"

Cole's smile grew. "I shall be instrumental in helping prevent a Scottish invasion, for one," he said. "In truth, the vast majority of my work for The Marshal has been in Scotland and on the borders. I speak Scots, without sounding like an Englishman, so I am perfect for the task. I have found it rewarding. Haven't you?"

Addax nodded. "Indeed, I have," he said. "Who knew that two skinny lads from a faraway land could find such adventure in England. And such friends."

Cole slapped him affectionately on the shoulder. "Such friends, indeed," he said. "Now, why don't you seek out Lord Alastor and tell him that we are departing. I told him last night that we would be leaving before dawn, but it would be polite to bid him a farewell. I shall meet you in the stables when you are finished."

Addax, fully dressed, headed out into the common room where their mail and protection were stored on frames. There hadn't been enough room in their small chamber to keep everything with them, so Cole finished dressing and headed out into the common room himself, donning his mail and the black and red tunic bearing the great-fanged boar's head of Ajax de Velt.

Even as Cole headed out into the icy morning, his thoughts were not on his journey ahead, but on the young lady sleeping safe and sound in the keep off to his left. He thought fondly of those pale green eyes and silky blonde hair he'd like to run his hands through someday. Someday when her brothers weren't around. It was true that he could handle them, mostly, but it would be easier if he had his brothers, Julian and Cassian, with him. No one would tangle with the de Velt brothers, not even the overly confident Sheriff of Westmorland.

The thought brought a smile to his lips.

He'd return to The Keld, for certain. And he would bring reinforcements with him.

The faint light emitting from the stable caught his attention up ahead and he headed for it.

CHAPTER SEVEN

"W HERE ARE YOU going?"

Corisande froze midway through pulling a heavy robe over the shift and woolen dress she was wearing. It was a very cold morning, before sunrise, and there was frost on the windowsills so she was dressing warmly.

But a hissing voice had her pausing.

"Go back to sleep, Gratiana," she whispered. "I have duties to attend to."

Gratiana de Allington lifted her dark, messy head. "At this hour?"

Corisande waved at her, a gesture that suggested she lay back down. "We have visitors departing this morning, if you must know," she said. "I also have an ill soldier and I wish to see how he fared through the night. Is there anything else you wish to know?"

Gratiana shook her head and lay back down. She was a curious girl, but that only went so far in the early hours of the morning. Thankful that she didn't have to deal with more of Gratiana's questions, Corisande pulled the fur-lined robe tight and headed from the dark, warm chamber.

The keep of Castle Keld was a big, cold block of ice on

mornings like this. The stone it was built from literally turned to ice when the temperatures dipped, making the walls slick and the floors slippery. It was mostly dark in the stairwell except for a few intermittent torches and Corisande could see her breath hanging in the air as she carefully made her way down to the entry.

She was a woman on a mission.

She was fairly certain that she hadn't slept all night, afraid she was going to miss the dawn and miss seeing Cole off. She had told the man that she would bring him food and she intended to do just that, although she knew deep down that it was really just an excuse to see him before he left. Certainly, they'd had visitors before. There had been many visitors over the years and she had never personally met any of them in the stable with a bag of food for the coming journey.

But Cole was different.

He wasn't just *any* visitor.

Truth be told, she had lain awake all night thinking about the enormous knight with uniquely colored eyes. When she had first met him, she had thought he had a rather sinister appearance. He had a square jaw and sharply angled features. There was nothing soft about his face at all, and the way his eyebrows arched over those eyes was something almost reptilian. At least, that's what she'd first thought. But the more she looked at him and the more she came to know him, the more she realized that all of those elements came together for a fantastically handsome man.

His size was truly something impressive. He was quite tall, but the sheer breadth of his shoulders and the circumference of his arms were things to be admired. She'd seen him use that strength against the Scotsman in her father's solar, lifting the man as if he'd weighed no more than a child, and she found that strangely alluring when it should have been wholly intimidating.

Maybe that made her strange, but she didn't really care.

She was coming to like what she saw of the frightening Cole de Velt.

They'd had two significant conversations yesterday and both of them had shown a gentle side to the knight who looked as if he did not even know the meaning of the word. He had been kind and compassionate with her, something so unexpected but something she had found endearing.

Something that, down deep, had healed something in her, something that had shattered in Auden's wake.

In truth, when Auden had left her, she had put thoughts of men out of her mind. That incident had made her hate men in general for quite some time and she was only now just starting to overcome that. Men had no honor, in her opinion, and she was only now starting to look at men without the usual apathy until Cole had shown her a kindness that she had forgotten existed outside of her own family. Her brothers had always shown her an inordinate amount of kindness, and she loved them very much, but that was the only kindness she had trusted up until yesterday.

Cole was quickly causing her to change her mind.

Therefore, she was determined to see him again before he left. Maybe there was a part of her that didn't believe he really would return to her as he said he would, so perhaps this would be her last glimpse of him. But then again, it was wrong of her to distrust the man before he'd given her a reason to.

She just didn't know what to think.

All she knew was the way he made her feel.

The kitchens of Castle Keld were already working at full capacity at this time in the morning. The cook baked bread every morning, bread that would be eaten throughout the day, so the kitchens smelled like yeast with delicious aromas.

Corisande collected a few smaller bread loaves along with cheese, small apples, and leftover meat pies from the night before.

All of it ended up in a canvas sack that was used to haul grain up from the vault. They had enormous stores down in the sublevels beneath the keep, and the servants used the sacks to bring the grain up to the kitchens. She walked around the kitchens twice, looking for anything else she could stuff in the sack before finally locating a stash of little round dough balls that had been basted in honey. Those had been on the menu the night before and there were just a few left, so she threw those into the sack.

The sack was nearly overflowing at this point, so she scurried out of the kitchens and headed towards the stables. The eastern sky was just starting to show hints of pink and orange as the sun begin to rise over a land that was crunchy with icy dew. Corisande knew that Cole was going to be leaving at dawn and she hoped she wouldn't be too late. Rushing into the stables, she saw that it was still mostly dark, so the activity for the day hadn't yet started. However, the horses heard her and thought they were about to be fed, so they began to stir and make noise.

Quietly, she made her way over to Cole's fat, black stallion.

Round, black eyes were looking back at her.

Corisande had been around warhorses enough to know that they weren't the most docile of creatures. In fact, her brothers owned horses that she swore breathed fire. Therefore, she had a healthy respect for the beasts that were trained to kill men, but the eyes gazing back at her didn't look like a killer.

He had an enormous, beautiful face.

"I know you're hungry," she whispered. "I am sorry, but I did not come to feed you."

The horse lifted his head, curled its lips, and showed her big horse teeth. It wasn't a vicious move, but a rather humorous one. Such humor should be rewarded, so she pulled out a dough ball and carefully held it up to the horse on her flat palm. She was prepared to yank her hand back at any moment, but one sniff from those big horse nostrils and the horse gladly sucked up the sweet treat.

With a grin, Corisande went to sit next to the trough with the healing moss to wait for Cole to make an appearance.

It wasn't long in coming.

Cole entered the stable, followed by a pair of servants who quickly went to light lamps so they could move about feeding the animals. She heard Cole ask one of the men if the horses had been fed yet, but they hadn't, so Cole shook his head with disappointment and went to his horse. He petted the beast as he assured him that he would soon have a full belly. The servants were already bringing grain for the animal as Cole stepped aside so the beast could be fed.

"What's his name?" Corisande asked.

Cole turned sharply to see her sitting in the shadows near the trough and a smile creased his lips.

"Who?" he asked.

"The horse."

"His name is Drago."

"He is very nice."

He gave her an odd look. "He is *not* nice," he said. "He is a vicious war animal, so guard your fingers when you are around him. What are you doing sitting in the dark like that, anyway? If one didn't know better, one might assume you were an assassin lying in wait."

Corisande laughed softly. "If I was an assassin, you would already be dead," she said. Then, she lifted the sack. "I have brought you the food I told you I was going to bring. You may as well eat some while you are waiting for your horse to be fed."

Cole came over to her and eyed her with some amusement,

before taking the sack from her hand. He peered into it, made difficult because the stable was still dark. But he inhaled deeply.

"I can smell the bread," he said. "What else did you bring me?"

"Cheese and apples," she said. "There are also little meat pies in there along with sweet dough balls. Your horse had one and he heartily approves."

Cole turned to frown at the horse. "Glutton," he muttered. But he returned his attention to the sack as he walked over to the very last stall next to Corisande. It was empty and he sat down on the dirt floor, leaning back against the wall. "You have gone through the trouble of bringing this to me. Will you join me?"

Fighting off a smile, one of pure delight, Corisande went into the stall and sat across from him, a proper distance, but a good position from which to watch him. She realized that she liked to watch the man. He told a thousand tales with those eyes, that face, and that big body conveyed the life of a man of experience.

Everything about him spoke to her.

"Thank you," she said. "It is kind to share your meal with me."

He snorted. "You brought it," he said, pulling out a still-warm loaf of bread and tearing it in half, handing her a chunk. "I do not usually eat in the morning but, more importantly, I do not usually break my fast with a beautiful young lady when I do. I am honored."

His flattery brought that giddy feeling she was coming to associate with him, as if her cheeks were about to burst into flames. She took the warm, fresh bread and tore off a piece of it, popping it in her mouth.

"I remember back in the time when I fostered, the knights would yell at the squires and pages and tell them they were old women if they ate anything until the day was nearly over," she said, hoping he couldn't see the flush on her face. "That was difficult on some of the younger boys. The women were allowed to eat, but the boys were forced to work instead. There was one little boy – he was quite young – who was so hungry and would weep because he would not be fed. We used to take him food when the knights were not looking."

Cole was watching her in the darkness. "Do you know why they refused him food?"

"Because they were cruel?"

He chuckled. "Nay," he said. "They did it for a very good reason. When one is on a battle march, or in battle itself, there is no telling when food will be available or even feasible. When a man is traveling for his lord, it is his dedication to duty that will carry him through, not the lure of comfort and food. They do not feed the young men to toughen them, to make them focus on things they can control and not the things they cannot. It is a discipline tactic."

She eyed him dubiously. "Withholding food from a child is a discipline tactic?" she asked. "It seems to me that there are better ways to accomplish such a thing."

"Like what?"

She shrugged. "Like reason," she said. "Most children are bright and willing to learn. Reason with the child, explain the way things are, help them to understand."

Cole took a big bite of his bread. "All true," he said. "But nothing leaves a mark more than physical distress or pain. That is why children are beaten when they are naughty. Remembering the pain will teach them not to be naughty again."

"And you advocate beating a child?"

"Nay," he said. "Unless the child is incorrigible, I do not see the need. I agree that reasoning can sometimes do more good than beating or starvation, but these have been discipline tactics for hundreds of years. They were used on me and I did not turn out too bad."

Corisande laughed softly. "I suppose not," she said. "Where did you foster?"

"Kenilworth and Norwich," he said. "And you?"

"Prudhoe."

"That is not far from here," he said. "Have you remained in the north your entire life?"

"Mostly," she said. "I have been to London twice with my family but, mostly, we remain in the north, where our family has lived here for many generations. Our ancestors were the Kings of Northumbria, so I am sure we will remain here for many generations to come. This land is in our blood. And you? Have you ever lived anywhere else?"

"I did when I was fostering," he said. "But my father is the first generation of our family to live in the north. Our family is from Colchester, as an ancestor of mine was the *dapifer* for Eudo FitzHerbert."

Corisande cocked her head curiously. "What is a dapifer?"

"A steward," Cole said. "In this case, he was more of a military governor for FitzHerbert, but my family settled in what is known as the Roman River Valley, just south of Colchester. There are many people, even now, who display the de Velt eyes. I think that my ancestor had several wives, to be truthful."

"De Velt eyes?" Corisande cocked her head curiously. "You mean the colors?"

He nodded. "Surely it cannot have escaped you that my eyes are different," he said. "Our entire family line has eyes that are variations of two colors – my father has it most pronouncedly."

"What do his eyes look like?"

"One is brown and the other is brown with a big splash of green," he said. "My eyes were brown when I was an infant, but they developed the green in them as I grew older. My brothers have similar traits, as does my youngest sister."

"Interesting," she said. "Interesting and beautiful, I think. You say that half of Colchester has these two-colored eyes?"

He laughed softly. "Practically," he said. "I have an uncle who lives at our ancestral home of Abberton Castle, but it's known as Purgatory to the locals."

"Why do they call it that?"

Cole swallowed the bite in his mouth and went for the meat pies. "Because my ancestor, in order to enforce military rule in Colchester, did some unsavory things," he said. "My family has a history of that. Undoubtedly, you know of my father's reputation."

Corisande nodded. "A little," she said. "I know that your father waged war on the borders many years ago."

Cole looked at her. "Be under no illusions," he said. "He did not wage war. He waged conquest and he did it the way our ancestors did it. It is the de Velt way."

"How did your ancestors do it?"

His gaze lingered on her for a moment. "Blood and gore, my lady," he said, unwilling to tell her the truth of it if she did not already know. "That seems sufficient. The de Velts are more brutal than most."

Corisande watched him dig a meat pie out of the sack and take a big bite. "You do not seem brutal to me."

"That is because we are not fighting one another."

"True," she said. "And I am thankful."

She grinned as she said it, causing him to smile. He handed her part of the meat pie and she took it gratefully. When their fingers brushed, her heart leapt, just a little. She bit into the pie, noticing that he was watching her as she did so. His smile broadened when their eyes met.

"Let us speak no more of war and brutality," he said. "I have enough of it in my life. I want to talk about you."

"Me?" she said, surprised. "Why me? I am uninteresting."

He frowned. "That is a lie," he said flatly. "You are very interesting."

"Then what do you want to know?"

He thought on the question. "Other than heal the sick and tend to your chatelaine duties, what else do you do? Surely you have something to do with your leisure time. Painting, mayhap?"

Corisande wiped some pie goo off her cheek. "I have a garden," she said. "To be truthful, it was my mother's garden and I grow a variety of herbs and flowers, many of them used in healing. I love to dig around in the garden and watch things grow."

"That is commendable."

"And you? What do you do when you are not fighting?"

He paused as he thought on his own leisure pursuits, something that seemed very foreign to him. "I like to hunt," he said. "It has been a long time since I last went on a hunt with my father and brothers, but the hunts always go the same way – four dominate knights fighting for the right to claim the prize. I am the eldest, so it is my right, but Julian and Cassian do not think so. The last time, we were hunting boar, I had it in my sight, but Julian scared the boar away while Cassian caught me off guard and tried to tie me to a tree."

Corisande giggled. "And your father?"

"He chased off my brothers' horses so they could not ride," he said, snorting at the memory. "My father and I chased down the boar and killed it while my brothers had to walk all the way home. My mother was livid when they told her how my father and I had beat them, preventing them from capturing the game. Those liars."

Corisande laughed into her hand. "That sounds like my brothers," she said. "They would kill or die for one another, but

Ares and Atlas mostly side against Anteaus, who is a genuinely kind man. He's quiet and the other two are not, but he is smarter than both Ares and Atlas combined. They taunt each other, wrestle each other, trick each other… but I love to watch it. It is truly hilarious sometimes."

"And your younger sister?" he said, finishing the last of the meat pie. "Do you get on with her?"

Corisande shrugged. "Mostly," she said. "I will tell you a secret – Gaia has just come home from fostering and she is a changed girl."

"How?"

"Let us say that she likes… men. Pinching your knight last evening was only the beginning."

Cole bit his lip to keep from grinning at the cheeky young woman. "Why do you say that?"

She lifted her shoulders in exasperation. "Because she will pursue him relentlessly," she said. "Pinching, winking, demanding kisses. Aye, she demands kisses. She denies it, but Gratiana has heard her."

"Who is Gratiana?"

"A ward," she said. "Gratiana is a fine, mannerly young woman and Gaia views that as a curse. But my sister has changed. My father does not know what he is going to do with her because she flirts with men who try to warm to her, but my brothers end up chasing them away. I fear for Gaia, truthfully. One day, my brothers will not be around to save her from the wrong man."

Cole brushed off his hands, finished with his meal. "How old is she?"

"She has seen ten years and eight."

"Then she is old enough to know better," he said. "Mayhap she will outgrow this behavior when she realizes that decent men do not like women who are too forward. She'll only attract the dregs with her behavior."

Corisande nodded in resignation. "I hope she realizes it soon because trying to manage her behavior is exhausting."

His eyes glittered at her across the dim stall. "You seem to be doing a good job of it," he said. "Your show of concern is touching. It seems that you have great compassion and caring for everyone."

There was that flattery again, making her feel bashful and giddy. "She is my sister," she said simply. "I do not wish to see her come to harm."

"Of course you don't. Not many people are so considering, even of family members."

Corisande didn't know what to say to that, so she simply smiled and lowered her head. The sun was starting to rise, faint rays peeking in through the ventilation holes in the stable that faced east, and Cole managed to tear his gaze away from Corisande long enough to see that his horse had finished his meal and was in the process of tearing up the bucket his food had come in. He had it in his mouth, tossing it around.

Cole stood up and brushed off his breeches.

"Drago, *arête*," he commanded quietly, tugging on the bucket until the horse released it. "*Jij stoute jongen.*"

Corisande was still sitting on the opposite side of the stall wall, unable to see what Cole was doing but grinning because he was talking to his horse as if it could understand him. "What language are you scolding your horse in?" she asked.

Cole laughed softly. "Dutch," he said. "He was raised in Antwerp, so he only understands the language of his people."

"What did you tell him?"

"That he is a naughty lad."

"And he understands you?"

"Of course he does. We have great philosophical discussions, Drago and I."

He could hear her laugh. Grinning at the horse, he petted the beast on the head affectionately as he tossed the bucket aside, only to notice Essien and Anteaus entering the stable. They were heading for their animals as more sunlight began to stream in through the ventilation holes.

Morning was upon them.

"Where is your brother?" Cole asked Essien. "Is he finished with Lord Alastor yet?"

Essien began to check over his spotted stallion. "Nay," he replied. "But he should be here soon. By the way, I was just speaking to Anteaus and he was telling me that he fostered at Northwood. I am sure he knows many of the same people you know."

Cole looked over at Anteaus, whose horse was next to Essien's. Anteaus de Bourne was young and handsome, but muscular to the point of being bulky. He remembered briefly what Corisande had said about her older brothers siding up against the younger one.

Cole suspected that was an interesting match-up, given Anteaus' size.

"Is that so?" he said. "When were you there, Anteaus?"

Anteaus picked up a nearby horsehair brush and began brushing the dust from his brown animal. "From the time I was nine years of age until I had seen ten years and eight," he said. "I was knighted there by the Earl of Teviot and I remember that Northwood was a strong ally of Pelinom and de Velt. We helped your father fend off a couple of raids while I was there."

"How long ago was that?"

Anteaus cocked his head in thought. "Six years ago was the last time I was there," he said. "Mayhap eight or ten years ago. That was a period in time when the reivers seemed to be very active. I do not think you were at Pelinom at that time, but I remember your brothers."

Cole shook his head. "I have spent a good deal of time at Norwich and also Pembroke Castle," he said. "I only came home to Pelinom a few years ago. Home to stay, that is."

Anteaus turned back to the horse. "So I heard."

Cole looked at him curiously. "Heard what?"

Anteaus gestured to Essien with the hand that held the brush. "Essien says you are going to marry Audrie de Longley," he said. "That will keep you in the north. Her father will not let her out of his sight. He was always very protective over her, you know. Lady Audrie was a sickly child, like her brother. John de Longley is not much of a warrior because of it, but he is a great statesman. I grew up with him."

Cole was frozen with surprise. He hadn't expected his association with Audrie de Longley to come out of Anteaus' mouth. With Corisande sitting on the other side of the stall wall, she must have heard it. He was momentarily speechless, unsure where to go from there, wanting to explain away Anteaus' comment for Corisande's benefit but not wanting to make it obvious that he was trying to distance himself.

But he had to say something.

He wanted Corisande to hear him dispute what was more or less the truth.

He'd never in his life been in such a position.

"John is a good man," he said steadily. "But Lady Audrie and I…"

Corisande was suddenly standing next to him, the sack of food in her hand. "Do not forget this," she said, all but shoving it at him. "I wish you a pleasant journey, my lord, and God-speed wherever your path in life takes you."

She sounded so… hard. Cole took the sack, clutching it against his chest because she'd very nearly threw it at him. Their eyes met and the warmth he'd seen there just a few moments earlier was gone. The pale green eyes weren't glowing anymore.

They were like stone.

Before he could say anything, Corisande pushed past him, heading from the stable, but Anteaus stopped her.

"Where did you come from?" he asked, surprised. "Why were you hiding?"

Corisande paused. "I was not hiding," she said, sounding irritated. *Hurt.* "I brought Sir Cole some food for him and his companions to take on their journey. It is all part of my duties, as a good chatelaine."

She didn't really answer his question as to why she had just emerged from a darkened stall, but he didn't press her. He let her go, turning back to his horse as she headed from the stable.

But Cole couldn't let her go. God help him, he couldn't. There was absolutely nothing spoken between them – no implication, no hint, no inferred intentions – but even so, he hadn't wanted her to hear about Audrie. He kept telling himself there was nothing to hear, that it wasn't anything of consequence, but the truth was that there was. He knew it. He knew that his family and her family expected them to marry. Everybody but Cole expected them to marry.

But it was quite possible he had other ideas about marriage.

He set the sack down and headed out of the stable.

He could see that Corisande was nearly out of the stable yard by the time he got outside. The sun was just peeking over the eastern horizon and the sky was shades of pink and blue and purple, with puffy gray clouds scattering in the gentle breeze. Cole could see her up ahead and he picked up the pace. He ended up running up behind her and the sound of his rapid footfalls startled her. She turned around with a gasp when she heard the commotion, nearly tripping on her own feet.

"I am sorry," he said quickly, reaching out to steady her. "I did not mean to frighten you."

When Corisande realized who it was, she straightened up

and pulled her arm from his grasp. "You didn't," she lied. Her gaze upon him was guarded. "What do you want? Do you require something else?"

He just looked at her, feeling an odd sense of desperation. He'd never experienced anything like it and he wasn't quite sure how to answer her. He just ended up staring at her for several long seconds before sighing heavily.

"Aye, I do," he said. "I require your attention, just for a moment. I am not entirely sure how to say this, or even if it is important to say, but I should like to explain something to you."

Her brow furrowed, but not from curiosity. She appeared decidedly displeased and it was apparent that her guard was up. "Explain what?"

Cole was trying to think of a pleasant, believable way to explain away what she'd just heard, part of which involved calling Essien a liar, but he couldn't quite bring himself to do it. As he had told her once, he didn't lie.

He wasn't going to start now.

But he wasn't sure how he was going to explain something that even he didn't quite understand.

"Just a moment of your time, my lady, and if you do not like what you hear, you are free to walk away," he said quietly. "I will not stop you. I am not sure where to start, but I will start with what happened yesterday with the Scotsman. I told my men this, but now I shall tell you. The way you handled yourself when he took you hostage greatly impressed me. You showed calm and reason in a situation that would have made most women hysterical. That speaks strongly of your character. And in speaking with you yesterday and even this morning, I am coming to know a witty, humorous, kind, and caring woman. I was so enchanted by you that I did not sleep last night because I could not stop thinking about you."

Corisande's eyes were wide at him. "But… Cole, I…"

He put up a hand to silence her. "Please let me finish," he said. "If you do not feel the same way, I shall not trouble you further, but I want you to know what is on my mind. I know I am the son of Ajax de Velt and that does not make me a worthy suitor, and I am resigned to that. But you, my lady, are a very special woman and I wanted you to know that. My thoughts and feelings towards you will always be those of the greatest admiration."

By the time he was finished, Corisande had lost some of the hardness in her expression, but she was looking at him with some doubt. Even so, no amount of doubt could stop the faint flush in her cheeks from his kind words.

"That is… kind of you to say so," she said. "I have enjoyed coming to know you, also. But since this is a moment for honesty, I will tell you that for a betrothed man, you have been paying me an inordinate amount of attention and I do not appreciate that in the least. It is not fair to me and, most of all, it is not fair to your betrothed. It is…"

Again, he held up a hand, more firmly this time. "Stop right there," he said. "I am not betrothed. Essien misspoke and your brother misunderstood. But I would be lying if I did not tell you the complete truth – that my family has expected me to marry Lady Audrie de Longley for some time now. I will be further honest with you by telling you that I have considered it, but I am in no hurry to do so. You see, I was married before, but I lost my wife and child a few years ago. Audrie is simply a prospect, I suppose. I am not in love with her, but she is pleasant enough. The marriage would be a political one, mostly, and not a love match."

Corisande had an expression suggesting sorrow. "I am sorry about your family," she said softly. "That must be a difficult burden to bear."

"It was," he admitted. "But I am moving forward with my life. There is no use dwelling in the past. Audrie has helped me do that in a sense, but then… then, I met you."

"But we have only just met," she said, sounding perplexed. "How can you know anything about me?"

He shook his head. "I do not," he said. "It is a feeling more than anything, an instinct. My lady, I am not a charming man by nature and I certainly do not toy with women's feelings and emotions, but there is something about you that is different from any woman I have ever met. That is why I told you I would return to visit you. I… I would be honored if you would allow me to get to know you better, Corisande. I could think of no greater privilege."

Her cheeks were full-blown red by this point, flattered beyond measure by his calm, quiet words. "What about Lady Audrie?"

He lifted his wide shoulders. "We are not betrothed."

"But was it implied?"

"It was, by everyone else but me."

Corisande thought on that a moment. Perhaps it was foolish of her, but she believed him. She'd seen enough men, and had been suspicious of them, to suspect when she was being lied to and she didn't sense it from Cole. She could only sense his sincerity. Even so, the not-so-small issue of Lady Audrie stood between them. She wasn't going to discount it.

In fact, she felt some pity for Lady Audrie.

"In the spirit of great honesty that seems to have overtaken us both, I would like to get to know you better, too," she said. "But I want to tell you of something I have not spoken of since it happened. A few years ago, there was a knight from an ally whom I shared a fondness for. He made it clear he was fond of me and, much like you and Lady Audrie, a future betrothal was implied. But before anything could take place, however, he was sent away by his liege to settle a dispute. He was gone for some time and I was eventually told that in order to settle the dispute, he had married the daughter of an enemy. I've not thought of him since, nor have I entertained the thought of another suitor. Until you."

His eyes glittered at her in the early morning light. "And?"

She met his gaze, without reservation. "And I would be very flattered to come to know you better," she said. "However – you must make it clear to Lady Audrie that there is no betrothal between the two of you. This must be resolved before you and I can keep company. I will not be happy at another's expense, Cole. Someone did that to me and I will not do that to another."

Cole gazed at her a moment before a smile spread across his lips. "This is why I admire you so much," he said. "It takes an extraordinary woman to think of others before herself. I will make things plain to my family, and to Audrie's, so that they understand a marriage between us is not possible. It would be greatly unfair to her if my thoughts were with another woman."

"Indeed, it would."

Corisande's smile mirrored his. It was an important moment between them, as thoughts as well as intentions were established. It was something Cole had never done with Audrie, but within a day of knowing Corisande, he was doing it with her.

It just felt right.

Reaching out, he took her hand and kissed it gently. He liked it so much that he kissed it again before releasing it.

"I shall return as soon as I can," he said softly. "Have more of those meat pies waiting for me when I do."

Corisande burst out in quiet laughter. "A romantic sort, are you?"

He grinned, full-on. "Pies *are* very romantic," he said. But his smile faded as he looked at her. "Anything would be romantic with you, I suspect. I am looking forward to discovering that for myself."

Corisande's face was so red that she thought it might burst into flames any moment. Cole didn't think he was very good with women, but the truth was that she was butter and he was the hot knife. All he had to do was look at her and she was melting. After years of closing herself off, it was a wonderful feeling.

"Then I will see you when you return," she said. "Godspeed on your journey, Cole. And take care."

Corisande thought she might have seen a little blush in his cheeks, too, before he turned away.

The realization made her laugh.

But, *oh*… what a joyous laugh!

CHAPTER EIGHT

The village of Otterburn
The Queen's Head Tavern

IT WAS A loud, boisterous establishment that Cole, Addax, and Essien found themselves in.

Situated in the middle of a bustling village in the wilds of Northumberland, the tavern was the only place in town and given that night had fallen, the place was packed with travelers and diners and those that just wanted to get drunk and have a good time.

The three of them fit into those categories.

They managed to commandeer an excellent table next to the window so that they could watch the comings and goings of the tavern. Cole pushed the table away from the door, angling it so that all three of them could sit with their backs to the wall, facing the entry. No one wanted to sit with his back facing the door, especially on a busy night like tonight.

A group of traveling minstrels were also in the tavern on this night and they sat near the hearth, playing lively tunes as the patrons danced with some of the serving wenches. In fact, a couple of the serving wenches were in high demand as partners, so much so that the owner of the tavern and his wife ended up serving food to some of the tables. Happy patrons were happy spenders, so they let the girls dance.

The weather outside was starting to cloud over and rain could be smelled upon the air, and that meant bodies were crammed into the tavern because no one wanted to stand outside and drink, as they so often did. But Cole, Addax, and Essien had the best seats in the house and when anyone would drift near, they would kick them away. They didn't want to be crowded on, especially when many of the tavern guests were armed.

And they weren't all English.

Otterburn was near the Scots border, although that particular stretch of the border was somewhat barren. However, there was a major road that ran between England and Scotland nearby, and that meant Scots traveling south. It was fairly common here. When the three of them had entered the tavern, they'd already seen at least two small parties of Scots, men who were keeping to themselves, but they certainly eyed Cole and Addax and Essien as they entered the tavern.

There were suspicious glances all around.

But the truth was that Addax and Essien were used to be stared at, given their family roots were not in the northern hemisphere, so that wasn't unusual for them. Once the three of them assumed their seats, the staring was interrupted as the owner and his wife brought out beef and ale stew along with warmed wine against the cold night. There was bread, peas, and stewed fruit, and the hungry knights ate their fill with their eyes on the Scots over on the other side of the common room.

Since the inn was so crowded, they were certain there would be no sleeping accommodations, but Cole made the attempt to secure at least one room. The only thing the tavern owner had left was his largest room, and it was costly, but Cole gave him the money without hesitation. There was only one bed, he was told, but the wife went upstairs to fashion two pallets for the floor.

Comfortable beds awaited and, hopefully, a peaceful evening.

"Well, lads," Addax said. "One night in this ghastly place and we should be at Pelinom by tomorrow evening if the weather holds."

Essien was elbow-deep in his meat stew. "Did you see the announcement as we came into town?" he said. "The ones that were nailed to the buildings on the outskirts?"

Cole was shoveling stew into his mouth as fast as Essien was. "Don't even think about it," he said.

Essien's head came up from his meal. "Think about what?" he said. "The tournament? And why not?"

Addax looked between the two of them. "What tournament?"

"It was posted on the bills as we entered town," Cole said, mouth full. "They were huge bills, Ad. You truly did not see them?"

Addax shook his head. "I was looking for the tavern," he said. "Where is the tournament?"

"Morpeth," Essien said. "Lord Ashlington is sponsoring them. It has been a long time since we have competed for sport and prize money, Ad."

Addax looked at his brother as if the man had gone mad. "Now?" he demanded. "You want to compete *now*?"

Essien didn't back down. "It would only be for a few days," he said. "The tournament does not start until next month, anyway. All I am saying is that it would be fun to compete if we are not committed elsewhere at the time."

"You mean if we are not fighting off a Scots invasion," Cole said quietly. "Essien, we have responsibilities elsewhere. There will be time enough for a tournament when this is over. The one in Morpeth will not be the last."

Essien returned to his food, but he wasn't happy. And he wasn't ready to give up, either. "Those were the days," he said with fondness, trying to coerce his brother into agreeing with him. "Weren't they, Ad? Destroying our competition in Ghent and Brussels and Roubaix? You should have seen us, Cole. The Black Dragon was unbeatable in the joust and the God of Vengeance dominated in the mass competition. We were unstoppable."

Cole could hear the excitement in Essien's voice as he reveled in the memories of his tournament days. "You were unstoppable because I was not there," he said, lifting his cup of wine to his lips. "Had I been there, you would not have won."

Essien's dark eyes twinkled. "Would you care to put that boast to the test?"

Cole took a long drink of wine, belching loudly when he was done. "Of course I would," he said. "But not at Morpeth. We have more important things to do, Es. The tournament will have to wait."

Essien returned to his food, none too happy yet again. "I will hold you to that."

"I hope you do."

Essien took another bite of his food, his mind still lingering on the tournaments of his past. "It's strange," he said. "When I look back on my life, and all of the things I have done in that short time, I think it was the tournaments that I liked the best. The excitement, the money, the women…"

"It was the women who got you in trouble," Addax reminded him.

But Essien waved him off. "I have always loved competition," he said. "When I was a very young boy, I was always fascinated with games. We had games in Kitara, long ago. Remember, Ad? They were called *Qurucu*."

As Addax nodded, Cole spoke. "What does that mean?"

"It means The Founding," Addax said. "It was a festival to honor our ancestors, the ancient Kings of Kitara. There were horse races, music, games of strength and skill. Es and I were too young to compete, but our father did. I swear that I remember him winning every game. Our father could do no wrong."

Cole had slowed his eating, watching the brothers as they reflected on their homeland, which was rare. They had been very young when they'd been forced to flee, something neither of them liked to remember, and Cole was aware of that. But it seemed that this reflection wasn't filled with angst, but of admiration.

It was a rare good memory of home.

"What was his name?" he asked. "I do not think I have ever asked you that."

"Amare," Addax said. "He was a man of great vision and great honor, something that threatened some people."

Cole sat back with his warmed wine, interested in a rare glimpse into their past. "And these people are the ones who started the rebellion against him?"

Addax nodded. "Mostly," he said. "My father had a younger brother, Ekon, who coveted his power. It was Ekon who started the rebellion against my father and stole his throne."

Cole nodded faintly. "Surely he would have wanted you dead, too, Ad. You are your father's heir."

"That is true, but we had the loyalty of my father's servants," he said. "When the rebellion started, they took Essien and I away, dressing us as servant children. We had a sister, you know. Adanya was her name. I do not know what became of her and that will always haunt me. I am the eldest son, after all. I should have made sure she was protected."

Cole had never heard that before. As the music blared and

the roar of conversation filled that stuffy tavern, he found himself in a serious conversation with Addax and Essien on a taboo subject. Perhaps it was the wine causing them to speak of things they kept well-buried, but Cole had seen them both drunk before.

This was something else.

Perhaps it was simply time to speak on it.

"You were a child," he said. "You cannot blame yourself for not being able to help her. It sounds as if you were lucky to escape with your lives as it was."

Addax looked at him. "Would you feel the same way if we were speaking about your sisters?" he asked. "Allie and Effie and Addie? How would you feel then?"

Cole conceded the point. "Guilty as hell," he said. "I did not mean to diminish your feelings, Ad. I apologize."

Addax held up a hand. "You did not," he said. "I did not mean to be confrontational, but Adanya's fate has always been with me, like a shadow."

"Hopefully, she was helped to escape just like you were," he said. "Mayhap she is safe just as you are, living a good life."

But Addax shook his head. "Do you know what I think?" he said. "I think my uncle spared her to marry her. What better way to assume the throne of Kitara by marrying his niece, the king's daughter? I do not think she is dead. She is a queen. But it makes me sick to think on it."

Cole felt a good deal of sympathy for him. "Do you ever think of returning?"

A smile flickered across Addax's lips. "I do," he said. "I think of it often. I think of the money Es and I earned from the tournaments we competed in and the money your father and William Marshal pays us. I am saving my money so I can buy an army to take with me back to Kitara. An army of the most brutal mercenaries the world has ever seen. I will return to

Kitara and I will retake it, someday. At least, that has always been my intention, but since leaving Kitara those years ago, my life has gone in directions I could never have dreamed of. Mayhap I shall return to Kitara, but not now. I still have much more to do here in the land of people who seem to fight so much against one another."

Cole chuckled. "And more knights to defeat in the joust."

"Exactly."

Cole sat forward, looking Addax in the eyes. "You have become my closest friend, Ad," he said. "The past two years have seen you and I go through a great deal together. We have faced life and death together. I hope you will not return to Kitara without me by your side."

Addax smiled warmly at him. "I would not have it any other way, Cole," he said. "You are my brother even if you do not look like me."

"But I think like you. And my heart is the same. That is enough."

Addax held up his cup to them and they shared a toast to their friendship. It was a genuine moment between them, the misplaced prince and the spawn of the man many considered the prince of darkness. In a sense, they were both misplaced, both trying to find where they belonged.

And *who* they belonged to.

"But until I accompany you back to Kitara, the world we live in is here and now," Cole said after a moment. "I feel like my world has changed. Everything I thought it would be doesn't seem so certain any longer."

Addax leaned forward on the table, looking at him closely. "Lady Corisande?"

Cole nodded slowly. "Lady Corisande," he said. Then, he snorted. "Odd, isn't it? Feeling that way about a woman I have only just met."

Before Addax could reply, Essien suddenly leapt up from the table and grabbed a serving wench who had just lost her dance partner. Handsome, young Essien could charm even the most frigid heart and the serving wench, once she got over her shock of being grabbed by a strange man, wholeheartedly jumped into the dance with him.

Cole and Addax watched Essien swing the woman around as she squealed with delight.

"There he goes," Addax sighed. "I swear to you, we are going to have to flee England at some point because he will have gotten another girl in trouble. If I could only find him a wife."

Cole chuckled. "You would only make them both miserable," he said. "Essien is not ready for a wife yet."

"Are you? Again?"

Cole looked at him, knowing he meant Corisande. "I do not know," he said honestly. "All I know is that I am away from Corisande and I do not like it. I want to return to her so badly that I can almost taste it."

"Are you going to tell your father?"

Cole nodded. "I must," he said. "I promised Corisande that I would settle the marital expectations with Audie before I pursued her in earnest. She says she does not want to be the reason for another woman's unhappiness."

"She sounds like a wise woman."

"She is," Cole agreed. "Far wiser than I am. Do I want to marry her? I do not know yet. I hardly know her. But my instincts tell me that she will be the woman at my side for the rest of my life and that thought does not distress me at all."

"Then I wish you luck," Addax said. "You deserve happiness, Cole. I know you do not think so, but you do. What happened with Mary was very tragic, but the sun will shine again for you. Mayhap it will shine with Corisande."

Cole lifted his big shoulders. Since it seemed to be a night for confessions, he felt less restraint than usual to confess his own.

"Mayhap," he said. "I suppose I have always had the feeling of being cursed because of who my father is. After Mary and Lucy died, I remember hearing my father tell my mother that I was being punished for his sins. I do not think that, but I do feel as if I've been cursed by the de Velt name in some ways. But with Corisande… oddly enough, I do not feel any judgment from her. She does not seem to care that I am a de Velt. I feel comfortable with her, more at ease than I have ever felt with anyone."

Addax's eyes twinkled. "Good," he said. "I am happy for you. In fact, I…"

He was cut off when the music suddenly stopped and something caught his eye. Both Addax and Cole looked over to where Essien had been dancing with the serving wench only to see that the woman had been yanked away from him and there were now three or four soldiers between the wench and Essien.

The implication was obvious.

Cole and Addax were on their feet.

"Who are ye?" one of the soldiers stepped forward, shoving Essien back by the chest. "Where do ye come from? I've never seen the likes of ye around here before."

Essien was volatile. He didn't take kindly to be shoved around, but Addax grabbed his brother before he could take a swing at the soldier.

Cole put himself between them.

"That was unwise," he rumbled to the soldier. "He was minding his own affairs, as should you. Go sit down and I will pretend I did not see you shove my friend."

The soldier looked Cole over. In fact, his companions did, too. They could see how big and fierce he was and those eyes… they were terrifying. The soldier stepped back but he didn't leave.

"This doesn't involve ye," he said. "Yer friend was being rough with Matilde."

"He was dancing with her," Cole said. "He was not being rough with her and you had no reason to intervene, so sit back down. I will not tell you again."

The soldier snorted, but it was all for show. He had companions that needed to see how brave he was.

"And just who are ye to tell me what to do?"

Cole didn't take his eyes off the soldier. "I am de Velt," he said. "Ajax de Velt is my father. If you've not heard of my family, then you are either stupid or daft. But if you have, then you know what we are capable of. Now, do you wish to continue this challenge?"

That brought a reaction from all four of the men. A couple of them reached out to pull the soldier back, away from Cole.

"De Velt?" the soldier repeated, sounding far less confident than he had only moments earlier. He was an older man and, suddenly, fear flickered across his face. "He's the one who stormed the borders years ago."

"He did."

"I remember White Crag Castle," he said, remembering those horrors from long ago and without the wherewithal to keep his mouth shut. "I remember what your father did to those men. I was serving at Etal Castle at the time and I remember how… God's bones, what he did to those men. Your father is a monster!"

He realized too late he probably shouldn't have said that and his companions pulled him away even further, out of the range of the enormous knight. He had drink in his veins, as they all did, which fed both courage and stupidity.

But Cole had seen that same fear in the soldier's eyes too many times to count. He didn't really care that the man called his father a monster because it was the truth. Ajax de Velt had done some monstrous things.

He was used to hearing his father called such things.

And he used it to his advantage.

"Then you will get out of my sight or I may do to you what my father did to his enemies those years ago," he said. "Leave now or suffer the de Velt wrath."

The soldier turned around and nearly plowed his comrades over in his haste to leave. As the men began to scramble, Addax turned to the musicians and quietly commanded them to start playing again as he dragged his brother back over to their table. Cole remained in place, watching the soldiers leave through the back door of the tavern. When they were gone, he headed back to their table. The buzz of conversation and the music gradually returned to the room.

Things slowly went back to normal.

"Well," Cole said as he sat heavily in his chair. "That was disappointing. I think I was hoping for a fight."

Addax grinned but Essien was still angry he hadn't been allowed to retaliate. Frowning, he poured himself more wine as Addax noticed movement on the far side of the tavern.

"Cole," he said quietly. "Look."

Cole glanced over his shoulder to see several Scots also leaving through the rear entrance, the one that opened into the stable yard. It was where the soldiers had gone, but it seemed strange that the Scots should follow. They were leaving in the dead of night, heading into a village that had shut down at sunset. The only thing for miles was uninhabited landscape.

It was most curious.

"Did you get a good look at them?" he asked Addax.

"Nay," Addax replied. "Did you?"

Cole shook his head. "I did not," he said. "I am concerned that mayhap there was a man among them who recognized us from our days in William's royal entourage. It's not as if you and your brother are not recognizable."

Addax conceded the point. "Even if they did recognize us, why would they leave? For what purpose?"

Cole shook his head. "I do not know," he said thoughtfully. "But if there was a man among them who recognized us, he heard me give my name as de Velt to the soldier and without a Scots brogue. I've been pretending to be MacEacharn for the past two years."

That thought hadn't occurred to Addax. "Then mayhap we should retire for the evening. Or leave altogether. Mayhap they've gone to warn others."

"They have no reason to, but you may be correct," he said. "Mayhap we should find lodgings in the stables this night, just to be safe."

The decision was made. Cole's saddlebags were underneath the table along with Addax and Essien's, and as he bent over to pull them out, the tavern owner approached them.

The man seemed to be rather nervous.

"M'lords?" he said, looking at all three of them but mostly looking at Cole. "Forgive me, m'lord, but I heard you say that you are de Velt?"

Cole looked at the man, feeling intolerant of any nonsense or judgment this night. "Everyone within earshot tonight heard the same thing," he said, unfriendly. "What do you want?"

The tavern owner was wringing his chapped, scarred hands. "I thought you should know," he said. "You must warn the other warlords."

"Warn them about what?"

The tavern owner jabbed a finger at the rear door. "The Scots," he said. "I did not want to say anything while they were still here, but now that they are gone, I will tell you. I heard them speaking of an army moving south, through the Kielder

Pass."

That caught Cole's attention. "A Scots army moving through Kielder Pass?" he repeated. "Are you certain of this?"

The tavern owner nodded emphatically. "I've lived my entire life here," he said. "I understand the Gaelic. The Scots spoke of it openly, probably thinking I would not know their language, but they spoke of meeting up with the army coming through Kielder Pass. They did not say why, or when, but I thought you should know."

Cole was stunned by what he was hearing. "Did they say anything else to that regard?"

The man shook his head. "Nay," he said. "But I'm English. If I hear something from those damnable Scots, I am not going to keep it a secret."

Cole looked at Addax and Essien, shocked, before digging into his purse and handing over a silver coin to the tavern owner to thank him for the information. As the man scurried away, Essien hissed.

"What do we do?" he demanded. "They are already coming into England!"

Cole pulled his saddlebags from underneath the table. "We leave," he said. "That is what we do. If they are coming through Kielder Pass, they are going to run headlong into The Keld. Es, you ride for Pelinom. Ride hard and tell my father everything. Ad, you and I will return to The Keld and warn them of what is coming. Mayhap William the Rough is moving swifter than we thought."

It was a horrifying thought. It had been their understanding that nothing would happen until the summer months, but that was evidently incorrect.

The time was now.

On a cold, clear night with a bright moon hanging in the sky and scattered clouds blown around by an icy wind, Essien headed north to Pelinom Castle as Cole and Addax headed back for The Keld, trying to avoid the Scots they knew to be on the same road. They had to ride through forests and across streams, which slowed them down. And when the moon began to sink low in the sky, they were hindered by the threat of complete darkness but, still, they pushed on.

They had no choice.

They had to get to The Keld before the Scots did.

CHAPTER NINE

The Keld

"**Y**OU MUST BE mad. Scots? *Here?*"

It was about an hour before dawn, with the moon hanging low in the sky and the hint of light on the eastern horizon. Alastor had been awoken out of a dead sleep by Anteaus and Atlas standing in his doorway. Anteaus had the night watch, so he was in full protection, but Atlas was only half-dressed. He'd been sleeping until his youngest brother yanked him and Ares from their warm beds.

Scots are on the approach.

Now, they were pulling Alastor out of bed.

"They are at the gate, Papa," Anteaus said grimly. "They are demanding to speak with you."

Alastor was climbing out of bed, but he was in complete disbelief. "Christ," he muttered. "They've come for Canmore."

"How would they know he was here?" Atlas asked. "They have no way of knowing he was brought here. For all they know, he's with de Velt or he's dead. There is no connection to us."

That was true, but Alastor was still half-asleep and his mind was mulling over the worst-case scenarios. He went to the basin of water near the hearth and splashed it on his face before going in search of his breeches.

"Possibly," he muttered. "Where is Ares?"

"Keeping them company," Atlas said. "They are outside the gatehouse. He has not admitted them."

"Good," Alastor said with relief. "And they've only asked to speak with me? Nothing else?"

Atlas shook his head as he watched his father pull on his breeches. Anteaus found his father's boots and handed them over.

"Nothing else," he said. "But the man leading the army identified himself as Alexander MacDuff, Earl of Fife and the Justiciar of Scotia."

Alastor's head shot up, his eyes wide with surprise. "He said that?"

"He did."

That seemed to muddle Alastor as Anteaus began to help the man dress by putting his arms in the sleeves of a heavy leather robe that went from his neck all the way down to his feet. Alastor was so lost in thought that his sons had to help him dress.

"The Justiciar of Scotia," he repeated, almost in awe. "That is a powerful position, lads. It is not usual for a man like that to come on a mission such as this. Do you know what I think?"

"What?" Atlas demanded.

Alastor's thought processes began to clear. "I think he's here to get an answer to the missives that Canmore has been sending," he said. "I never answered, so they've come for an answer in person."

"Do you really think so?"

Alastor lifted his hands. "Why else would the Justiciar of Scotia come to call?" he asked. "The man holds tremendous power in Scotland. Now, if we could capture him…"

Both Atlas and Anteaus looked at their father in shock. Then they looked at each other as if considering the very possibility. "If we could capture him, it's possible we could know more than we've possibly dreamed of," Atlas said, his face alight. "And William the Rough would think twice before marching into England if we held his justiciar as a hostage."

Alastor was warming to that idea. "Indeed, he would," he said. "If MacDuff is foolish enough to come here, then he is taking a big chance. How many men did he bring with him?"

Anteaus appeared a little pained. "Hundreds, Papa," he said. "It could be thousands, but it is dark so we cannot see how many with great accuracy. But we know there is an army with the man. If we take him hostage, they'll not take kindly to it. We'll find ourselves in a war."

That brought Alastor pause. He pulled tight the robe that Anteaus had placed on him, fastening the ties at his chest in a thoughtful manner.

"If MacDuff has come to find out why I've not replied to Canmore's missive, he brought an army for only two reasons that I can see," he said. "If I agree, he will want to harbor his army inside The Keld. If I do not agree, he'll use it to attack us. It seems to me that one way or the other, the Scots intend to use that army."

That seemed to be the most logical conclusion. Atlas and Anteaus looked at their father, waiting for orders.

"Papa?" Anteaus finally said. "What will you have of us?"

Alastor drew in a long, thoughtful breath before replying. "Atlas," he said softly. "You will make sure the army is well-prepared. If you have not done so already, I want men on the battlements, archers at the ready, and the entire army ready to defend The Keld to the last stone. Is that clear?"

Atlas nodded firmly. "It is, Papa."

"Anteaus," Alastor said, turning to his youngest son. "You

will tell your sisters to close up the keep. All doors, all windows are to be shut and reinforced. The kitchens are to be sealed. Move the horses, and especially the chargers, down into the vault through the kitchen yard entrance. The vault will hold twenty or thirty horses, so move in as many as you can."

"And the rest of the animals?"

"Keep them in the kitchen yard and away from the stables," he said. "They should be safe in the fortified yard. But make sure the keep is secure and then join us at the gatehouse."

Anteaus nodded. Alastor put his hand on his youngest son's cheek, a gesture of reassurance, and sent both of his sons out to go about their tasks. He then waited a nominal amount of time before leaving his chamber and heading out to the bailey.

He had a man to speak with.

THE ENORMOUS GATEHOUSE of Castle Keld was lit by a dozen torches, all of them burning heavy with black smoke that gathered in the barrel-vaulted ceiling of the passageway. The soldiers were keeping their distance from the enormous portcullis, which had thankfully been lowered when the Scots appeared. The iron fangs dug deep into the ground, anchoring it, so there was no chance of loosening it or charging it. On one side stood Ares, and on the other side…

Dozens of dark figures.

Squaring his shoulders, Alastor stepped into the passage-way, moving slowly for the portcullis.

Ares caught sight of him.

"This is my father, Sir Alastor de Bourne," he said formally. "My lord, this is Sir Alexander MacDuff, Earl of Fife. He has asked to speak with you."

He was indicating a man on the other side of the portcullis, wrapped heavily in woolen garments and leather shoes. Alastor could see that MacDuff was surprisingly young for a man with so much responsibility, with a head of dark hair and a dark beard that he kept neatly trimmed.

Alastor had expected a much older man.

He met the man's gaze curiously, but cautiously.

"One wonders if you only wished to speak with me, then why did you bring an army?" he said casually. "That could be interpreted as threatening."

MacDuff forced a smile, without humor. "I brought the army tae support ye, of course," he said. "I've brought reinforcements for yer ranks."

"Reinforcements for what?"

MacDuff blinked as if surprised by the question. "For our alliance."

"There is no alliance."

"But Alpin Canmore has sent ye missives tae that regard," he said. "Did ye no' receive them?"

"I've received them. And I've given no answer to that regard." Alastor peered at him through the grate. "Why are you really here, MacDuff? Who has sent you to force this alliance upon me?"

MacDuff paused a moment, looking at Alastor and trying to read him. He was fairly certain that de Bourne wasn't happy to see him. No man liked to be pressured into a life-changing decision by a stranger. But the resistance he was meeting was obvious and he could see that there was a reason why de Bourne hadn't replied. He'd either ignored the missives or he wasn't yet ready to respond. In any case, the time was upon him to make a choice.

MacDuff had come a long way for an answer.

"M'laird, I would be pleased tae discuss this with ye in private," he said. "Do ye truly wish for yer men tae hear of yer private affairs? Will ye no' invite guests into yer home?"

Alastor ended up standing close to the portcullis, looking at the young earl in the torchlight.

"You have brought a Scots army into England," he said, lowering his voice. "That does not speak of a friendly visit to me, nor does it speak of a negotiation. You brought men to force me into making a decision. You brought your army to intimidate me. You are not guests; I did not invite you. Let us come to the point of this, MacDuff – you have come here to force me to answer Canmore's missives."

MacDuff moved towards him, motioning for the men standing near him to stay back. He went to meet Alastor at the portcullis, an iron grate and hundreds of years of hostilities between them.

"I have," he said honestly. "But I was hoping we might speak civilly before we came tae business. I dinna come tae bully ye intae responding, m'laird. I came tae see if we could come tae an agreement."

Alastor still wasn't convinced even though MacDuff's delivery had been polite for the most part. He found himself looking beyond MacDuff, at the dozens of dark silhouettes behind him.

"How many men did you bring?" he asked.

Macduff studied him a moment before answering. "Enough," he said. "We've been traveling for three very long days and require shelter. Will ye no' let us in?"

Alastor lifted his eyebrows as if it were a foolish request. "I will not," he said flatly. "Scots and English confined within these walls is an invitation for disaster, so I will not let you in. If you truly wish to stay, then your men must set up camp outside of the walls."

Something in MacDuff's expression changed at that moment.

He no longer found himself looking at a potential ally.

"As ye wish," he said, coolly. "But I've come a long way at the direction of the king. I would appreciate a moment of yer time tae discuss what I've come tae discuss."

Alastor looked him in the eyes. "You have come to ask me what my response is to Alpin Canmore's many missives," he said. "Therefore, I will tell you. You can return to your king and tell him that I refuse any alliance with the Scots. I will not enter into a battle that I cannot win. *You* cannot win. There are greater armies in England than there are in Scotland and the north lands, and you are entering into something that will assure your destruction. But it will not be mine. Make sure you tell William that."

MacDuff's eyes glittered in the weak light. "William is the rightful Earl of Northumbria," he said. "That title was taken from him by Henry. He wants it back and he shall have it."

Alastor cocked an eyebrow. "You dare to tell me that?" he asked. "My family descends from the Kings of Northumbria. This land was mine before it was ever William's. The man is arrogant beyond measure to presume the land is his because it *is* mine and it will remain mine. If he comes to take it, I will fight him for it. I will not align with him simply to gain a piece of the pie of something that already belongs to me. Northumbria is mine, it will *always* be mine, and any man who thinks otherwise is my enemy. Now, get off my lands before I turn my army loose on you. I do not want to see your face again."

With that, he turned away from MacDuff and headed out of the gatehouse, but MacDuff wasn't finished with him yet.

"Ye're making a mistake," he called after him. "William will come and when he does, he will bring hell with him. Ye can be burned by the flame or ye can align yerself with the Devil. Dunna be foolish, de Bourne. *Think!*"

He was shouting by the time he was finished. But Alastor kept walking, unmoved and unimpressed. He grabbed Ares as he went.

There were plans to make.

"Reinforced the walls," he commanded quietly. "Drop the second portcullis and secure the gatehouse. I fear we will have an onslaught when the day fully breaks."

Ares nodded sharply and headed off as Alastor continued towards the keep. He'd just made a decision that was going to affect the health and welfare of his people, but he'd never felt better about anything in his life. Hell was indeed coming, but it wasn't coming for him.

MacDuff would find that out soon enough.

And so would The Rough.

Unfortunately, MacDuff had other ideas.

"Pssst! *You!* Open this gate!"

Addax was trying desperately to get the attention of a soldier inside the kitchen yard as he and Cole stood at the postern gate of Castle Keld.

They were trying to get inside before the Scots saw them. Because of the low-setting moon and the near complete darkness, they had been extremely fortunate to have made it to the castle without being discovered. But it had been more fortunate that they had discover the Scots at all.

Shadows moving in the darkness had tipped them off.

Castle Keld was on a rise overlooking a small village of the same name, and the area around the village was lush with growth and trees. That growth only disappeared at the base of the hill Castle Keld was perched upon, and Cole and Addax had come in from the northeast, losing themselves in that growth as they made their way towards the castle.

But there were phantoms on the hill surrounding The Keld, phantoms that trickled down the road, seemingly clustering around the western edge of the village. It didn't take a great intellect to realize that the Scots had beat them to Castle Keld, so they carefully made their way through the dark trees, finally emerging on the northeast side of the castle and making their way up the hill via the postern path.

Now, they stood at the gate.

Addax was trying desperately to catch the attention of someone while Cole held on to the horses and watched their backs. Drago, the happy glutton, ripped at the fat, juicy grass on the hillside as Addax did everything but shout as he tried to get someone's attention. The postern gate was in two parts, with an outer gate that led to a small, enclosed yard before another gate was opened into the kitchen yard. Therefore, Addax had to work hard to make his presence known.

But finally, it worked.

The cook happened to be in the yard gathering eggs when she saw Addax at the outer gate. She had a torch with her and she went to the inner gate, curious as she peered towards the outer gate. Recognizing the prince from Kitara, she threw the bolt on the inner gate and quickly went to open the outer one, swiftly admitting Addax and Cole and their horses.

Cole slammed the gate behind him and locked it securely.

"Did the Scots see you?" the cook, a round woman with a knot of hair on top of her head, asked eagerly. "They're at the gatehouse, you know."

Cole nodded wearily. "We know," he said. "Where is Lord Alastor?"

The cook shook her head as they passed through the second

gate and bolted that one securely behind them. "I've not seen him," she said. "But Anteaus told us to secure the keep. I'm gathering my chickens and moving them into the kitchens."

They were moving quickly through the kitchen yard. "Where is Anteaus?" Cole asked.

"The last I saw, he was in the keep."

Cole thanked her, leaving her with her chickens as he and Addax headed into the main bailey. They could see men on the battlements, battlements that ran all the way around the castle walls but, unfortunately, they all seemed to be bunched up towards the gatehouse, undoubtedly watching the Scots.

He shook his head.

"Idiots," he muttered. "Thank God we were able to come in through the postern gate, but no wonder we were able to come that way. No one is watching it."

Addax shook his head in disapproval. "If the Scots want to breach this place, they'll find any opening or any area that is not well protected," he said. Then, he reached out and took Cole's horse. "Go – find Lord Alastor and tell him his postern gate is poorly guarded."

Cole handed over Drago, who still had big pieces of green grass sticking out of his bridle. "Find me when you are finished," he said. "If the Scots are here, that can only mean that we are going to find ourselves in a battle when the sun rises and that is not far off."

Addax took the horses quickly as Cole continued towards the gatehouse where there seemed to be an inordinate amount of activity. He was just passing the keep, albeit at a distance, when he heard someone call his name. Coming to a halt, he could see Corisande and Anteaus standing at the bottom of the forebuilding that led into the keep.

Cole headed in their direction.

"I came to warn you that the Scots were traveling down

Kielder Pass," he said as he came near. "It looks as if I am too late."

Anteaus was in full battle protection. "They arrived less than an hour ago," he said. "They want to speak with my father."

"Where is your father?"

"At the gatehouse."

Cole turned in the direction of the gatehouse, seeing the dozens of torches and men milling about. There was a sense of urgency in the air and a current of uncertainty, but no one seemed to be panicking. At least, not yet.

He returned his attention to Anteaus.

"This cannot be good," he said. "An army of Scots does not simply travel into England to socialize."

Anteaus' gaze was also fixed on the gatehouse. "My father thought they may have come looking for Canmore," he said. "But there is no way anyone would know Canmore is here. It is more than likely they are here to discover if my father is going to side with them or not."

Cole couldn't disagree. "More than likely," he said. Then he returned his attention to Anteaus. "Addax and I came in through the postern gate. It is without a guard, so I would strongly suggest moving men to protect it. If the Scots figure it out, you will have an onslaught trying to come in through the rear."

Anteaus stepped away from the forebuilding, looking at the wall walk, which was lit with men and torches as well.

He grunted unhappily.

"There *were* men there," he said. "I placed them myself, but it looks as if they have all moved forward to watch what is happening at the gatehouse."

"My thoughts as well."

Anteaus turned to him. "Cole, would it be too much to ask

for you to secure the keep?" he said. "It looks as if I am needed elsewhere."

Cole nodded before he even finished speaking. "I would be honored," he said. "Do what you must. I will make sure the keep is secure."

Anteaus raced off. Cole watched him for a moment before finally turning to Corisande.

It was the first time he'd really looked at her since the conversation with Anteaus had started and that first glimpse of her in the early morning darkness did not disappoint. Dressed in a heavy robe, her blonde hair braided over one shoulder, she looked like an angel.

"Inside, lady," he said, a smile on his lips. "We must get you and the other ladies to safety."

Corisande smiled and all of the stress and concern Cole had experienced on his harried ride back to Castle Keld seemed to melt away.

"I am glad to see that you are safe," she said as he took her elbow and turned her for the steps. "Have you been traveling all night?"

He nodded as he escorted her up the stairs. "All night," he said. "We were in Otterburn when were told that a Scots army was moving south through the Kielder Pass. I knew we had to warn you but, evidently, we were too late."

Corisande was watching her feet as they headed up the stairs, careful not to trip on her robe. "But you came," she said softly. "That is all that matters. And I'm glad you're back, Cole."

He watched her lowered head. "May I tell you a secret?"

"Of course."

"I came to warn your father and brothers, of course, but my main concern was you."

Her head popped up, looking at him with surprise. "It was?"

His eyes glimmered warmly. "It was," he said. "It *is*. That is why I am going to make sure you and your sister and the women are locked up safely in this keep before I return to see what your father would have of me. If I did not know you were tucked away safely, I do not think I could go about my business properly."

They paused at the top of the stairs, facing one another. "That is a very sweet thing to say," Corisande said, clearly touched. But the warmth in her eyes faded. "Cole… if there is a battle, I am my father's surgeon, so I cannot remain locked up in the keep. I will need to move to the great hall so that I may tend the wounded."

He had a feeling she might say that and his first reaction was to insist that she retreat into the keep and remain there, but he knew he couldn't. He had no right. In fact, he had no right at all to make any demands of her, but it was difficult to restrain himself.

Difficult, indeed.

Cole was a man who did everything wholeheartedly. He never did anything only haphazardly, whether it was his profession or personal relationships. He just didn't have it in him not to give all of himself to something he was passionate about, which was difficult when navigating his fledgling feelings for Corisande. He didn't want to overstep his bounds.

But he wanted to make sure she was completely safe.

"I understand," he said, reaching out to discreetly take her hand in an electrifying gesture. "If you will retreat into the keep for now, I will come for you if there are wounded and escort you to the hall personally. There really isn't any reason for you to be out here at the moment, so it would be better if…"

Shouts caught his attention. He couldn't see what was happening because he was in an enclosed forebuilding, but he could hear men shouting.

Something was happening.

Still holding Corisande's hand, he began pulling her back down the steps.

"Bolt these doors when I am gone," he told her swiftly but calmly. "Then you will retreat into the keep and bolt every exterior door, every shutter. Do you understand?"

Corisande was trying very hard not to trip on her robe as she struggled to keep up with him. "Aye," she said. "But if there are wounded…"

"If there are wounded, I will come for you," Cole said. They had reached the forebuilding entry and he helped her shut the enormous oak and iron doors. "Bolt these!"

The doors slammed in his face and he could hear Corisande throwing the heavy bolts. Whirling around, he caught sight of men dashing to and fro. Now he was seeing the panic he hadn't seen earlier. He could see Alastor running in his direction.

"My lord?" he shouted. "What is amiss?"

Alastor was breathless. "Damned Scots," he said. "They wanted to seek shelter here for the night, but I turned them away. They've gone after the village."

"They are trying to draw out your army so that you will open your gates."

Alastor shook his head grimly. "I know," he said. "But the village is vulnerable. I cannot deny them protection, Cole."

Cole turned in the direction of the postern gate. It gave him an idea.

"Addax and I just came in through the postern gate," he said. "I do not know if the Scots are even aware of it, but we can take a contingent out through the gate without opening the gatehouse. How many Scots are there?"

Alastor lifted a hand helplessly. "I could not tell in the darkness," he said. "Hundreds, at least."

"Then let us move a few hundred men through that postern gate immediately and protect the village," he said. "I will go and so will Addax."

Alastor put a grateful hand on his shoulder. "Thank you," he said sincerely. "I will find Ares and send him and Atlas with you."

Cole was already on the move, heading for the stables. "I will find Addax and meet them at the postern gate."

Everyone was running for their respective destinations. The Scots, spurned by Alastor's refusal, had set their sights on the little village next to the castle. It was an invitation for the men of The Keld, an invitation that was about to be decisively answered but not in the way the Scots had hoped.

The spawn of the darkest lord of all had been unleashed.

CHAPTER TEN

THE WOUNDED HAD been trickling in all day.

Corisande had emerged from the keep shortly after dawn, shortly after her brothers and Cole took three hundred men and charged into the village to defend it from the rampaging Scots. Alastor had remained in command of the castle and he assured his daughters that a battle like this couldn't last long, but he had been wrong.

So very wrong.

The Scots were angry. That much was clear. Offended by Alastor's refusal and exhausted from their swift and long march from Edinburgh, they had attacked the village with mindless zeal. As Cole and the others realized once they reached the village, it wasn't that the Scots were bent on raiding the town. That didn't seem to be their purpose.

Their purpose seemed to be destruction.

Because the Scots had been traveling in the dark, they had a good many torches available and they used them. They started at the edge of the town, nearest the castle, and begin lighting the cottages on fire. In fact, they lit anything worth burning. All Alastor and the troops remaining in the castle could do was watch from the sealed portcullis as the village began to go up in flames. They certainly couldn't open the portcullis, which was exactly what the Scots wanted them to do. What the Scots didn't know was that a heavily armed contingent from the castle was coming in from the northwest.

They realized that too late.

The plan was to box the Scots up against the burning section of the village and trap them between the flames and the castle. There was no real concern that the castle would catch fire because it was made of stone and iron. There wasn't much that could catch fire on the exterior. The Scots realized too late that there was an incoming force from the fortress, charging in and forcing them back against the flames. But even the charge of the English was slowed by the villagers that were fleeing for their very lives. The incoming army was met with a tide of humanity that was running from the Scots.

Even so, the army pushed through and the Scots found themselves under attack. However, Cole and the others realized very early on that Alastor had underestimated the number of Scots. He had guessed a few hundred when, in fact, there seemed to be more like six or seven hundred. The contingent of men from The Keld were outmanned, but there was no comparison between a Scots warrior and a heavily armed English soldier. Better still, they were no match for the elite English knights.

Cole was in his element in a battle. He was quite large, quite strong, and exceptionally skilled. He had inherited his father's talent with a sword and that was never more evident than it was at that moment as he used his enormous broadsword to dispatch Scotsman after Scotsman.

Cole had been taught long ago by a master knight at Norwich Castle to use every part of his body in a fight, not simply his sword hand, so watching him fight was like watching a well-choreographed dance. He could multitask with the best of them, fighting with his broadsword in one hand but also using his legs and feet to kick and shove. His left hand usually held his shield, but since they were mostly dealing with foot soldiers, his shield was slung over his left knee and his left fist was creating devastation for any Scotsman who came too close.

His skill in battle was also a testament to his relationship with Drago. He and Drago had been together at least fifteen years, ever since his father had given him the warhorse when he had been a squire. He had learned to fight while riding the big horse and, in battle, the two of them could move as one. Cole would give the horse his head, secure the reins to the saddle, and let Drago fight his own battles.

It was truly something to watch.

A battle that Alastor had predicted would not take long, unfortunately took most of the day. The Scots were not inclined to retreat and the English were forced to beat up on them more viciously than usual. Cole had personally cut down several mounted Scots and at least a dozen foot soldiers, and he was hardly winded. Much like his father, he had the love of battle in his veins. The longer and more vicious the fighting, the better Cole liked it.

He hadn't endured a battle like this in a very long time.

As the afternoon began to wane, the Scots seemed to be retreating. There were many dead and many wounded, and the English began to form a line to push them back onto the road heading north. Several were already heading up the road, carrying or dragging their wounded, but the bulk of the Scots were still fighting to the death.

Cole thought it was rather a wasted effort on the part of the Scots because they were in an enemy land with no real directive, yet they were fighting rabidly. It wasn't as if they were fighting to overtake a castle or to confiscate something of value. They were fighting because they were offended by Alastor's refusal and they were fighting to punish the offender.

But that wasted effort would work to their advantage because those who survived the fight would return to William and tell him that the English were not going to be easy victims to his plan. Certainly, Alastor de Bourne wouldn't be an easy victim, nor would he be an ally. Much like the battle at Fountainhall Castle, the battle at Castle Keld was also sending a message.

And Cole was helping send it.

But the English weren't without their casualties, too. There had been a few. Throughout the battle, Cole had kept his eye on Addax as the man did battle against the Scots. Addax hadn't trained in the English way of fighting his entire life like most knights had, as he hadn't met his first English knight until he was about twelve years of age. But he had learned quickly, and even now as he fought on horseback, no one would have ever known that he hadn't grown up with a sword in his hand. He was one of the best natural warriors Cole had ever seen, but that didn't stop Cole from keeping an eye on him.

A brotherly eye, so to speak.

In all of the skirmishes Cole had ever fought with him, Addax had never once failed in anything he'd ever attempted. The man was an elite warrior. Cole was about to turn his attention to the battle once more when he caught sight of Addax being pitched off his horse.

In a flash, Cole was heading in his direction.

A big Scotsman with a big club had managed to catch Addax on the back of the neck. As Cole reached Addax, he was just in time to see the Scotsman hit Addax again on the head. In a flash, Cole swung his broadsword in the direction of the Scotsman, expecting to hit him somewhere between the middle of his back and the top of his head. At this point, he wasn't going for accuracy as much as he was simply going for a death blow, wherever it may fall. The Scotsman, catching a flash of the sword, managed to put up his hand to block the strike, but he only managed to get his hand cut off along with his head.

Both went rolling to the ground.

Cole leapt off his horse and pulled a dazed Addax to his feet, slinging him over Drago's broad back and leaping on behind him. Digging his spurs in, he headed for Castle Keld.

Truthfully, Cole didn't even know how badly Addax was injured. He was simply trying to get him away from the heat of the battle so he could recover his wits. But as he slowed Drago, he happened to look down at Addax and he could see blood all over the man's hands and arms. The blood was coming from somewhere, so he pushed forward and took the path back around to the postern gate.

All he knew was that he had to get his friend to safety, battle be damned.

"Is THE WATER boiling?"

"Aye, my lady."

"The linens are being steamed and kept clean?"

"Aye, my lady."

"Then bring me more bandages because one of the men came in with a big gash on his head. I'll need something to stop the bleeding."

Corisande was interrogating the cook as the woman followed her around the great hall. Already, they'd had several wounded from the skirmish in the village, but certainly nothing that was overwhelming. It seemed as if the Scots were getting the worst of it, so Corisande had about twenty or thirty of her father's soldiers to tend to.

There were the usual gashes, slashes, and missing fingers. One soldier even had missing toes because a Scotsman had used an ax on his foot. All of the injuries to that point weren't life threatening providing they received the proper care, which Corisande efficiently provided.

In fact, she'd left the keep shortly after Cole had instructed her to barricade it. She and Gaia and Gratiana, along with several servants, managed to shutter more than half the windows before the progress came to a halt. Corisande watched the fight from her bower window, realizing the Scots weren't trying to come into the castle at all. They were quite focused on the town itself. Therefore, she made the decision to leave the keep and prepare the great hall to receive any wounded.

The wounded had come early. Gratiana and Gaia had accompanied her to the great hall, but Gaia began to cry the moment the first bloody injury arrived, so Corisande sent her to the kitchens to make sure there was a steady supply of hot water. It was really the only thing Gaia was capable of because she not only hated mundane chores, the sight of blood made her ill. She didn't want to be around it at all, and about an hour into the battle, the cook reported that Gaia had retreated to her chamber and refused to come out.

Therefore, the burden was left to Corisande.

But she didn't mind, really. She was in her element tending the sick and wounded. In fact, it was better not to have to worry about Gaia, the sister she was still coming to know. But she had Gratiana's help and the help of several servants, so the men were well-tended. As the cook left her and headed back to the kitchens to collect some of the boiled bandages, drying out over the heat and flame of the hearth, Corisande made her way over to a young soldier who had received a fairly nasty gash to the head. It covered most of his forehead and ended near his left eye.

The servant tending him was the same servant who tended to the knight's quarters, the one who had helped her when she'd lanced the infected boil a couple of days ago. The servant took good initiative trying to stop the bleeding on the gash, but the only thing that would really stop it would be stitching it up, which Corisande intended to do. As she came upon the wounded man, she spoke quietly but firmly to the servant tending him.

"They are bringing more bandages," she said. "Now, we need to lay him perfectly flat and you must hold his head still so he does not move it while I stitch."

The servant nodded, moving to the opposite side of the young soldier, who was looking at Corisande fearfully. Her father had over a thousand soldiers at Castle Keld and she didn't know every one of them, but she had seen most. However, she didn't recognize this slender young man. He looked very young and very scared.

She smiled reassuringly.

"Just a few stitches and you'll be as good as new," she told him. "You must lay down. All the way down; that's right."

The servant was pulling him back, his head eventually resting on a folded blanket. But the young man was still looking at Corisande with terror in his eyes.

"Are you going to stick a needle in me?" he asked, his voice quivering.

Another servant appeared with a tray containing a jug of the wine and vinegar mixture Corisande favored. There were also a few bandages as well as a needle and catgut, which had been soaked in a salt solution. Corisande had learned everything she knew from her mother, including how to treat the catgut and how to keep her needles and bandages clean by soaking them in the wine and vinegar solution. Her mother believed that people had a better chance of survival if the items touching them had been cleaned of any poison from the previous patient, and Corisande had seen that belief in action.

It worked.

She smiled at the terrified young man.

"I will tell you what I am going to do so that you are not afraid," she said steadily. "What is your name?"

"Dunne, my lady."

"You have not been at The Keld long, have you?"

He tried to shake his head a little, held still by the servant. "Nay," he said. "My mother and father have a farm to the west. I came to Castle Keld to earn money to send to them. Lord Alastor is our liege. My father says he is a fair man. But I've never been in a battle before."

"I see," Corisande said. "Then you're really a farmer."

"I am, my lady."

"It is noble of you to want to earn money for your family."

"Will I be sent home because I was hurt?"

Corisande shook her head. "Of course not," she said. "But I must stitch your gash. I am going to put something on it to cleanse it, and it will sting a little, but I know you are brave. Then I will quickly stitch it up so you will only have the smallest scar. You can tell your mother and father that you were very courageous in battle."

The young man nodded briefly, unsteadily, and Corisande silently motioned to the servant to hold the young man's head steady. As the servant clamped down on the young soldier's head, Corisande quickly swabbed the wound in the wine and vinegar solution. The young man made a pained face but, to his credit, he didn't cry out.

Quickly, Corisande stitched up the gash. Unfortunately, it was a jagged cut and it took thirteen fine, careful stitches. But when she was done, she swabbed the wound with the solution again and made sure she removed all of the dirt and sweat she could see. By this time, the cook had sent out more clean bandages and she left the male servant to carefully wrap the young soldier's head.

But the young soldier smiled gratefully at her.

Standing up, she turned to the hall to see who needed her help next and was startled to see Cole standing a few feet away.

He was watching her closely.

"Cole?" she said with concern, moving towards him. "Are you injured?"

He shook his head. "Nay," he said. "But Addax was hit in the head, twice, by a very big Scotsman with a club, so I brought him here. He has a bloody nose and ears."

"Where is he?"

Cole pointed to the opposite side of the hall, near the hearth, and they could both see Addax there, propped up against the wall.

Corisande went over to him.

"Someone tried to bash your brains in, did they?" she said as she knelt down beside him. "I hope you punished him severely."

Addax's dark eyes glimmered with mirth. "I did not," he said wearily. "But Cole did."

"He did?"

Addax sat still as she inspected his face to see where the blood was coming from. "He cut his head off," he said "I saw it rolling off into the grass along with his hand. I am certain Cole would have chopped the man to pieces had I not been bleeding all over myself. He chose to seek help for me rather than continue his revenge."

Corisande lost some of her humor as she looked up at Cole, who gazed back at her neutrally. As if he hadn't just partially hacked a man to death. Truth be told, she wasn't surprised to hear that given Cole's size and skill, but that same man spoke to her sweetly and with vulnerability… to think of him cutting off a head jarred her, just a little.

She had to remember that he was a de Velt.

He was a killer.

"He made the right choice," Corisande said, returning her attention to Addax. "Now, let me take a look at you. May we remove your helm?"

Between her and Cole, they managed to get the dented helm off and Corisande went to work. Standing at Addax' feet, holding on to the man's damaged helm, Cole simply watched her.

All he could seem to do was watch her.

Corisande had been with the young soldier with the gash on his head when he'd arrived with Addax, lugging the man over to the spot where he was now. It hadn't taken him long to find her in the hall, bent over a young man and reassuring him that everything would be well in the end.

Dressed in a brown broadcloth dress with a linen apron, stained, her long hair was pulled into a braid that trailed down her back and she wore a kerchief over her head to keep it away from her face. Cole had been struck by her confidence, her kindness, and her fluid beauty as she tended to the young soldier and deftly stitched up his head. There was something about Corisande that made him feel reassured and comforted, something he'd never experienced before.

Not even with Mary.

Mary had been a sweet woman who had been obedient to a fault, and at the time they were married, that was what Cole needed. He hadn't been eager to marry as it was, so a wife who somewhat blended in with the house and hold and never gave him any trouble was perfect for him. He didn't exactly ignore Mary, but he wasn't as attentive as he could have been. He knew that. Little Lucy came and he'd found himself being more thoughtful of his little family, enjoying it more than he thought he would have. Then the fever struck.

He'd been away at the time, at Alnwick Castle on an errand for his father. He'd been gone five days and in those days, his wife and child had succumbed to the same fever. It had been vicious and fast and overwhelming, and he well recalled returning home to find his mother and father waiting for him in the bailey. He didn't believe anything they told him until he saw the bodies for himself.

Sometimes, that episode of his life seemed like a bad dream and he had regrets about it. Regrets that he wasn't the father and husband he could have been. Regrets that he'd never once told his wife that he loved her.

Perhaps that was why Corisande gave him hope.

He was older now, and wiser, and he understood the value of a good woman. There was part of him that always wanted to marry a woman who was like his own mother – smart, focused, determined, loving. He found that he required more than a pretty girl who made herself scarce. He wanted a wife he could be proud of and in watching Corisande, it struck him that she was exactly that – someone he could be proud of. Someone he could boast of to other men, telling them that he had a wife who was strong, brilliant, beautiful, and loving.

Wasn't that what all men wanted?

Cole watched Corisande examine Addax, looking at both eyes, inspecting the split scalp on the back of his head, the one that bled so profusely that when bent over as he had been, blood had streamed into his ears and nose and mouth. It was all from that gash to the back of the head, as Corisande determined, and she went through the same process with Addax that she'd gone through with the soldier. She cleaned, she rinsed, she stitched, and she bandaged, and Addax was well-tended.

Corisande wanted him to rest, however, so Cole escorted

the man back to the knight's quarters and watched him as he climbed into his borrowed bed. Addax didn't want to stay in the hall with everyone else, but simply be alone to recover. Cole left him alone, sprawled out on his bed, and returned to the great hall.

He found Corisande supervising a young, dark-haired woman as she cleaned up an eye injury. Cole seemed to remember seeing the lass when he'd feasted with Alastor and the de Bourne brother and he was told that she was a ward. It was the Gratiana Corisande had spoken of. When Corisande looked up and saw him standing behind her, she left her post and went to him.

"Is Addax lying down?" she asked.

He nodded. "He is," he said. "But I always thought that men with head injuries should not sleep. Should we send a servant to keep him awake?"

She shook her head. "I do not think there is anything to worry over," she said. "He is exhausted from battle and some blood loss, but I did not see anything else that was concerning. It is right that he should rest now. No more fighting for him."

Cole took her word for it. "As you say," he said. "But there is more for me. I should return to the battle and help your brothers."

She grew serious. "Must you?"

"I must, unfortunately."

"Did you really cut that man's head and hand off?"

"I did."

"But why his hand?"

He gestured, lifting his left hand to his face. "Because he raised his hand to stop me and it got in the way," he said, watching her features ripple with distress. "Would you rather I did not and let him kill Addax?"

"Of course not," she said, growing frustrated. "I simply

meant… I do not know what I meant. I've seen battle before. I know what happens. That does not mean I like it or understand it. The next injured man they bring in here could be you and I would not like that at all, Cole. I think it would make me sick."

The corners of his mouth twitched. "This is our first real test of coming to know one another," he said. "I can see that you are a competent, knowledgeable healer, and you can see that I am a knight who will fight to the last man. You have your vocation and I have mine."

She eyed him. "I know what you are," she said. "My father and brothers are the same. But with you…"

She stopped herself and turned away, but he reached out and grasped her by the arm, preventing her from moving away. "But with me *what*?"

Corisande shook her head and tried, weakly, to pull her arm away. "It does not matter," she said. "I have already said too much. If you really do intend to return to battle, please be careful."

He didn't let her go, but his grip wasn't crushing. It was firm, strong. She finally stopped trying to pull away and just stood there, turned away from him.

"Cori," he said in a soft, seductive purr. "Look at me."

Slowly, she did. He smiled faintly at her when their eyes met. "It is my duty to return," he murmured. "But for you, I will be especially careful. Only for you."

Corisande returned his smile, however reluctantly. "You must think I am a terrible bother," she said. "I have no right to even suggest that you should be careful. I am no one to make such a request."

His smile faded. "That is not true," he said. "You *are* someone to me and, God willing, you will become more important by the day. As I said, this is all part of coming to know each other and, unfortunately, we are doing it under strained circumstances. But this will pass."

She gave him a long look. "It will not be the last battle you ever attend."

His grin was back. "Nay, it will not be," he said. "But I've done fairly well until now. It is my intention to keep my limbs and body intact because I do not want you sticking needles in me like you did to Addax and that young soldier. You would probably do it excessively hard simply to punish me."

Corisande started giggling. "Are you telling me that you are not afraid of a broadsword, but you are afraid of a little needle?"

He finally let her go, chuckling because she was. "Do not laugh at me," he said, pretending to be wounded. "I have had my share of stitches and they hurt like the blazes, so if I can avoid them, I will."

Corisande found that quite funny. "You are an immoveable object, a knight of the highest order," she said. "But if I come at you with a needle, will you faint?"

"I might."

She burst out into gales of laughter that were cut short when Alastor entered the hall. Seeing Corisande and Cole, he rushed in their direction.

"They are leaving," he said to Cole. "The Scots, I mean. They're finally leaving. We've got more wounded, so I am going to open the portcullis to admit my army."

Cole was already on the move, unsheathing his broadsword. "I'll come with you," he said. "In case the Scots decide to turn around, I'll be standing at the mouth of the gatehouse to discourage them."

Alastor turned around and rushed out, preceding Cole from the hall. Cole may have been focused, but he hadn't forgotten Corisande. He paused at the hall entry long enough to turn around and wink at her.

And then he was gone.

Corisande stood there for a moment, replaying that wink over in her mind a few times before returning to her duties. Not strangely, she couldn't keep the smile from her face or the giddiness from her heart.

Not strangely, she was coming to like the man who so badly wanted to court her.

CHAPTER ELEVEN

Berwick
One month later

THE TAVERN WAS called *Blankenship* and it sat in the wharf area of Berwick's seedier side, a district called Hide Hill. This lower section of society contained all of the dregs, thieves, pickpockets, robbers, and thugs that one could imagine, all of them using the dingy buildings as hovels and lairs during the day. When night came, like vermin, they would wander out to find their victims.

Berwick had been through a great deal of turmoil over the past hundred years or so, with the English in charge of mighty Berwick Castle, then the Scots, then the English again until Richard the Lionheart sold Berwick to the Scots to raise funds for his foray into The Levant.

The Scots didn't seem to have much interest in law and order. The castle at Berwick, an enormous bastion with a massive keep, had become no better than a stable with all of the Scots living there like animals. A man named Shaw MacHeth was in command of the garrison, so Addax and Essien had discovered.

In fact, that had been their task – to discover what they

could about Berwick.

After MacDuff's attack on The Keld, Cole and Addax had returned to Pelinom Castle to tell Jax everything that had happened, from Canmore's gruesome death to the Justiciar of Scotia coming to demand de Bourne's allegiance. The key of Jax's focus, and everyone else's, seemed to be Berwick.

That locale was the only nugget of information they had to go on for a coming invasion, the only thing of interest that had come up in their interrogation of Canmore, so Jax sent Addax and Essien to Berwick to discover what they could while Cole went to Alnwick to relay everything to the Earl of Northumberland, Yves de Vesci. Once Cole was finished at Alnwick, he was supposed to return to Pelinom, but he'd returned to The Keld instead.

A month later, that's where he remained.

Cole's presence at The Keld wasn't entirely unnecessary, as a liaison between his father and Alastor de Bourne, since de Bourne seemed to be such a target for the Scots, but Addax and Essien knew why he'd really gone there.

There was a pretty little blonde who had his attention.

And Jax knew nothing about it… yet.

In fact, it was probably best if Cole stayed away from Berwick considering he was a de Velt and they were known in these parts. Addax and Essien made the perfect spies because they blended in with the rabble that came off the cogs anchored along the river's shoreline. Berwick was a fairly cosmopolitan port, with ships coming in from France, Spain, Lisbon, and several of the Baltic countries. There was a blend of many nationalities here, so the two brothers from the lands beyond The Levant blended in quite well.

But it had been a long month. Mostly, they were focused on Berwick Castle and the comings and goings, but they also spent their time in the taverns and hovels, pretending to be sailors looking for a job, but also pretending to be drunk the entire time so no one would hire them and no one would take them seriously.

Addax had even taken to letting his hair grow on his face and, a month later, had a seriously bushy beard growing, while Essien had taken to shaving his head and wearing jewelry he received from women in exchange for what he termed as "services". Addax knew what he meant, and Essien had bedded several women who were either concubines or even wives of the Scots at Berwick Castle, so he had learned a great deal from the local women. As he'd told Addax, a woman never spoke more loudly or more freely when he was withholding a climax from them. Addax had to shake his head at his brothers rather bawdy way of doing things, but it worked.

A month into their mission, they had more information than they could have hoped for.

With Addax and his bushy beard and Essien with his gold earrings and jewels around his neck, they made quite a pair on the dirty, smelly streets of Berwick, but they were tolerated and completely overlooked in most cases. Scots from the castle would drift into the taverns and speak rather freely in front of them. Sometimes, they would speak freely *to* them after they'd had a few drinks purchased for them.

One of the more important things they had learned while trolling in Berwick was the fact that MacHeth didn't keep his fortress very secure. The gatehouse was always open, and any number of gates down to the river were also always open and often without a guard. There was one particular gate down at the river's edge they didn't even lock any more. It remained open all the time, day and night, although if someone wandered into it and ended up at the castle, there was usually a guard at the mouth of the passage to stop them.

MacHeth himself wasn't at the castle all of the time. He

came and he went, and although he had a wife at the castle and a few children, it was common knowledge that he also had a mistress who lived to the north in Coldingham. When he left, it was usually by himself, as he apparently didn't see the need to travel with a contingent of men.

However, they noticed something over the past week that had their interest. MacHeth had been present more than usual and there had been an inordinate amount of activity at the castle. Men were coming and going, but mostly coming. There was some kind of a buzz going on that neither Addax nor Essien could quite get the pulse of. Something seemed to be happening, but they didn't know what it was.

Given that MacDuff had ample time to return to Edinburgh after the battle at The Keld, it was quite possible that William the Lion was sending men to shore up Berwick's defenses because he suspected the English knew that Berwick would be the entry point for the Northmen. The only flaw in that theory was the fact that the castle still had loose security and men came and went at all hours in any case. If William knew that the English were on to him, keeping the castle open didn't make much sense.

Unless, of course, they were expecting reinforcements from the sea.

On exactly the one-month mark since their venture into Berwick, Addax and Essien found themselves in the tavern called *Blankenship* because this was the tavern frequented by so many Scotsmen. There had seemed to be a particular buzz about the castle today because a group of Scots had arrived from the north the day before, and Addax and Essien wanted to know why.

They had a plan to put into motion.

Essien had been watching the tavern most of the day and he knew that several Scots from the castle had visited, but he wasn't watching them so much as he was watching the women they kept company with. Like most taverns, Blankenship had its share of local ladies. Addax had been inside the tavern, pretending to be drunk, also watching to see which men found company with which women. That would be key when Essien joined him, because Essien would then go after the women who had spent the afternoon with MacHeth's men.

He wanted information.

At dusk, Essien entered the establishment, grabbing the first woman he came to and laughing seductively. The serving wench had seen him in the place many times, and he was a favorite, so she laughed right along with him and give him a big kiss. Essien asked her to bring him some ale as he left her and made his way across the crowded common room until he came to his brother, sitting at a leaning table with his back against the wall.

There was a half-filled cup of ale in his hand.

"Greetings, my drunken friend," he said, slapping Addax on the shoulder so hard that drink splashed out of the cup. "The night is young and so are the women. It will be a good evening!"

He was being boisterous and loud, as he usually was, but the regulars at Blankenship were used to him. In fact, he was so obnoxious sometimes that they tended to shut him out, which was exactly what he wanted. He plopped down next to Addax, who was using his fingers to wipe up the spilled ale and then lick them. He portrayed the perfect drunk, unwilling to lose even a drop.

"No one else has a chance with you on the prowl, you alley cat," he said. "The evening will be good for you, I think, but not me."

He put the cup to his lips as Essien leaned back against the wall. "What do you have for me?" he muttered, his gaze on the room.

Addax still had the cup to his lips. "Celandine," he whispered. "MacHeth's man has just left her."

Essien's attention went to the wench named Celandine who was over near the kitchens. She was busty, dark-haired, and pretty. Essien had spent time with her before and it was never wasted because she chattered like a magpie. He kept his eyes on her as he spoke to Addax.

"We have been here for a solid month," he mumbled. "We've learned what we could, we've made nuisances of ourselves to every tavern in town, and everyone thinks we are drunken fools. I will glean what I can from Celandine, but regardless of what she tells me, we must return to Pelinom tomorrow. We have enough to tell de Velt."

"We have everything except when the longships are coming," Addax said, his lips still on the rim of his cup. "That is what we need, Es. We estimated a summer arrival, but summer is nearly upon us. De Velt must have time to rouse armies and move them to Berwick."

Essien's nostrils flared. "We are men of many talents, but I am tired of pretending to be a drunkard with a flair for jewels," he said. "I have more jewels than I know what to do with. Who am I going to give them to, anyway?"

Addax sighed heavily. "That is the least of our worries."

"Untrue," Essien countered. "This entire month has been beneath us. I do not want to do this any longer."

"You will do as you are told."

Essien looked at him. "We are knights, not fools," he said. "I want to be at the tournament in Morpeth where I belong."

Essien often showed distain for things he felt were beneath him, as a man of royal blood. Addax had been dealing with that since Essien had been a child, and in moments like this, pretending to be men they were not so they could glean information against the coming invasion was when Essien strained against orders. It was true that he was excellent at what he did, and he made a splendid spy, but there were times he had resented the position he found himself in.

Like a wild stallion, sometimes Essien had to be reined in.

It was the powerful nature in him.

Addax understood because he had much that same nature, but he had more discipline than Essien did. He drained the last of the watered ale in his cup.

"Go to Celandine," he said. "Get what you can from her, if anything, and we shall depart for Pelinom on the morrow."

"Swear it?"

"Follow your orders, Es. Do as you are told."

Essien grunted unhappily but when Celandine appeared again, carrying drink, he smiled brightly and got up from the table, heading in her direction. As Addax watched, Essien gave her his very best seductive expression, took the tray from her, and sat it on the nearest table. Then he snaked his arm around her waist and pulled her off towards the rear of the tavern, which had a yard that contained a small livery. That was Essien's destination.

Literally, a roll in the hay.

Addax waited for him.

And waited.

The tavern filled up as the night deepened. A cog from Copenhagen had moored along the dark river shore and the tavern was overrun with big, blond sailors who were loud and happy. Addax pretended to be mostly passed out, awakening only to pretend to drink more ale when what he was really doing was spitting it out in the corner. Still, he had managed to imbibe enough that he was fairly drunk and as he sat with his chair tipped against the wall, his head back as he struggled not to fall asleep, Essien reappeared from the rear of the tavern.

The expression on Essien's face had Addax up and moving.

The Princes of Kitara didn't wait until morning to depart.

By the light of a full moon, they headed back to Pelinom.

CHAPTER TWELVE

Edinburgh
One week later

"DAMN THE MAN," William hissed. "And he started a battle because of it?"

MacDuff stood before William as the man warmed himself in front of a hearth that was taller than he was. The biggest hearth in Scotland, he liked to say. It warmed his old bones and brought him comfort in a world where there was little to be found.

At the moment, comfort had eluded him once again.

The comfort of an English ally.

"Aye, yer grace," MacDuff said. He had a big gash on his neck and a bandaged arm, evidence of the nasty battle he'd been a part of. It all played into his role as a victim to Alastor de Bourne's rage, which was his intention. He didn't want his king to know that he had actually failed. "I was polite. I tried tae negotiate with the man. 'Tis no' the first time I've dealt with a warlord and I know how tae handle such a man, but de Bourne is without reason. He sent his army out tae attack us. I lost many men."

William sighed heavily and came away from the fire, rubbing his hands together because his joints pained him. He eyed his young justiciar, hearing defeat in the man's voice. He certainly looked beaten and so did his men. There were several who had accompanied him to meet with the king and every one of them looked as if he'd been on the wrong side of a nasty row.

"Then the fact that he dinna reply tae Canmore's missives meant he dinna want tae be part of it," he said. "His silence *was* his answer. And no sign of Canmore on yer travels? Ye heard nothing?"

MacDuff shook his head. "Nothing," he said. "We can only assume that Canmore is still with de Velt."

William simply nodded, pondering a situation that had taken a bad turn. Not that he wasn't prepared for it, because he always prepared himself for the worst. That was how he had been able to rule for so long. Expect the worst, hope for this best.

In this case, the worst had happened.

"Then we must move forward without Alastor de Bourne," he said, looking to MacDuff and the other men in the hall. "Alpin Canmore is a prisoner of Ajax de Velt and we must assume he's told him everything he knows. That means the English are going tae be casting their eyes on Berwick and we canna allow them tae control the town or the river. If they do, our allies from the north will have nowhere tae go when they arrive."

"They can go tae Newcastle," MacDuff said. "They can go tae Humberside. There are other rivers."

William held up a finger. "True," he said. "But there are no other rivers that are the border between England and Scotland. If they go tae another river further tae the south, the chances of our armies uniting wouldna be good. And it is imperative that we unite if this is tae succeed."

He had a point. Every man in the hall knew it. William

turned back to the hearth, wringing his hands, considering his options when the truth was that he already knew what he was going to do.

He had already planned it in his mind a hundred times over.

"We go tae Berwick," he said quietly. "Whatever army we have now will go tae Berwick. We'll send word tae the allies who've no' yet arrived in Edinburgh tae hold until they receive word from me. We'll keep Berwick free, and the River Tweed free, and once the longships head down the river, we can bring the rest of the armies south. We'll converge in Kelso and head south, through the Kielder Pass. It would have been better for de Bourne had he allied himself with us, but no matter. We'll take the pass *and* his castle. From there, we'll go east and take Alnwick, seat of the Earl of Northumberland. Once we have Alnwick, we'll launch north again tae Bamburgh. If we can hold those four castles – Bamburgh, Berwick, The Keld, and Alnwick, we can anchor intae Northumberland and the English will never get us out."

He spoke with great passion, a gift he had, something that had rallied men to his side for forty years. This moment was no different. Alexander MacDuff may have entered the hall defeated, but William made him feel as if it was only a setback.

"We're with ye, yer grace," MacDuff said. "Give the word and we'll head tae Berwick."

William looked at him. "The word is given," he said. "Rally the army. We depart for Berwick in two days. We must get there before the English do."

MacDuff nodded firmly as several of William's military advisors headed out of the hall to carry out his command. There were three thousand men in and around Edinburgh, all of them waiting for their king to give the command that would send them south, into England, to reclaim what rightfully belonged to The Rough.

Now, the time had come.

The Scots were on the move.

CHAPTER THIRTEEN

Castle Keld

"E XCELLENT, MY LADY," Cole said with approval. "You have an excellent aim on the target."

Corisande grinned.

Beneath sunny skies and mild breezes on a fine spring day, she was having another lesson in archery along with Gratiana and Gaia. Somehow, Gaia got it into her head that they all needed to know how to shoot arrows, known as bolts, given the attack from the Scots the previous month, and Cole volunteered to teach them.

But it wasn't just Cole. Ares, Atlas, and Anteaus were also in attendance, each one helping the woman in their own way, but it was so overwhelming that Gaia had been in tears early in the lessons. They all wanted to help and show the women how much of an expert they were, but Atlas and Ares ganged up on Gaia and she dissolved in tears because of it.

Then came Cole.

He was surprisingly patient with the ladies, kind and gentle, and they loved him for it. Now, it was Cole teaching Gaia and Corisande, while the three de Bourne brothers helped Gratiana, who was less fragile than Gaia was when it came to her confidence. Moreover, she had her eye on Anteaus, so she liked his attention.

On this lovely day, Cole was standing over Corisande's left shoulder, peering over her head, as she fired off arrows into the targets the men had set up in the stable yard. He was watching her aim, that was true, but he was standing closer than he should have in the hopes that he might feel her body heat near his.

He just wanted to be close to her.

"Do you really think so?" Corisande asked, turning to look at him as a pair of soldiers removed the bolts from the targets and rushed back to the women with them.

Cole nodded. "Indeed," he said. "You have the de Bourne gift of accuracy. I would not be surprised if you were more skilled than your brothers."

Ares heard him. He and Cole had become friends over the past month, men who had always known of one another but who had never had the chance to get to know each other. Cole's month at The Keld had seen that situation between them change and, in fact, they liked each other very much. They thought alike and had much the same work ethic. Therefore, Ares made a face at Cole, one of distinct displeasure, when he heard the comment.

"There is no possibility she has become as skilled as I am with you as her teacher," he said flatly.

Cole cocked an eyebrow. "Is that so?"

"It is."

"Shall I prove just how much more skilled I am than you?"

Ares was always up for a challenge. That's what Cole liked about him, something he found utterly amusing. Any challenge and Ares was pawing the ground to accept it, ready to charge like a bull. He disarmed Gaia as Cole took the bow that Corisande had been holding and when the soldiers brought the bolts back, Cole and Ares loaded them.

"My lady, give the word and we shall fire," Cole said to Corisande.

"But what is the prize for the winner?" Gaia asked, clapping her hands excitedly. "The winner should have a prize! A jewel? A coin? A kiss from the lady of his choice?"

Cole heard the hope in her voice and he knew she meant him. In fact, young Gaia had been making a nuisance of herself with him for the past couple of weeks, much to Corisande's distress. While she and Cole drew closer, Gaia set her sights on the enormous de Velt knight and it was all Corisande could do to keep from throttling her sister.

But still, Gaia persisted.

The young woman couldn't take the hint.

"A word of congratulations should be sufficient," Cole said steadily. "Lady Corisande, if you will."

Corisande was standing just a couple of feet away from him and she complied. When she cried "mark", Cole and Ares let the bolts fly straight to the targets. Gaia and Anteaus were running for the targets before Cole had even lowered his bow, and with Corisande at his side, he walked over to where Atlas and Anteaus were examining who came closest to the center of the target.

The targets were drawn with charcoal onto a piece of canvas with a tight bale of hay behind it. Even the soldiers were hovering over the targets, looking to see who had fired with the most accuracy.

"You both hit the center of the target," Atlas said. "But I do believe Cole is closer to the center of the center than Ares is."

Ares frowned deeply and yanked his brother out of the way to get a closer look. Even he could see that Cole's bolt was directly in the center of the center, but he was unable to admit it.

"I had something in my eye," he said. "I could not see the target clearly."

Cole fought off a grin. "Would you like to do it again?"

"Nay," Ares said, turning away. "You would only cheat and have someone move the target at the very last second."

"I do not need to cheat to best you, de Bourne," Cole said. "In fact, your sister could best you. Why not challenge her?"

Corisande grinned at Ares, who brushed her off. "She cheats, too."

Corisande started laughing. "So we all cheat, Ares? Or is it possible that you could lose?"

Ares refused to indulge in any conversation about the possibility of him not being the absolute most skilled man among them as Gaia grabbed him by the hand and tugged on him.

"Please do it again against Cole," she begged. "I want to see you compete again!"

Ares looked at his youngest sister. "You vixen, you do not want to see *me* at all," he said, inferring she only wanted to see Cole perform again. "Go away from me, now. You give me a rash."

Gaia giggled but she didn't let go of him as everyone else laughed at his comment. She was irritating enough to indeed give someone a rash. They were all heading back to their starting marks when a soldier approached Anteaus and muttered in his ear.

Anteaus' smile faded.

"What is it?" Atlas asked.

Anteaus thanked the soldier and as the man ran off towards the gatehouse, Anteaus turned to the group.

"Our scouts have seen an enormous army pass through Hexham," he said. "They are heading north along the road that will eventually lead them to us."

The frivolity of the past several minutes was doused in one

swift statement.

"An army from the south?" Ares said, baffled. "It would not be the Scots."

"Mayhap the Northmen?" Atlas said. "Mayhap Berwick wasn't the point of entry at all. Mayhap it was further south and now they are moving north, into Northumberland."

"What about your scouts to the north?" Cole asked. "Have they reported anything?"

Anteaus shook his head. "Nothing," he said. "At least, nothing today, but I do not think it is the Northmen. The scouts said they were flying banners."

That brought curiosity. "What banners?" Cole asked. "What were the colors and the emblem?"

"Yellow and blue," Anteaus said. "The emblem was a lion's head, but I do not recognize it."

A smile began to spread across Cole's lips. "I do," he said. "That is de Lohr. The Earl of Hereford and Worcester."

That brought surprise. "Are you certain?" Ares asked.

Cole nodded. "I know it is not as recognizable in the north as some, but in the midlands and south, it is one of the most recognizable standards in all of England. My father is allied with de Lohr and we have fought with him several times. In fact, my youngest brother even serves de Lohr. So, aye… I am sure."

Realization that one of England's most powerful warlords was heading their way was sinking in. "But what about The Marshal?" Ares said. "Surely he is coming, too?"

Cole nodded. "I am certain he is," he said. "De Lohr is simply the first. There are several more, I am certain. My father and The Marshal have been in contact about William the Lion's plans. I told your father on the day I arrived with Canmore that it was The Marshal who ordered my father to raze Fountainhall to send a message to William. I also think it was a stalling tactic so The Marshal could move armies north while William was still stunned from my father's attack. Don't you see? The Marshal has sent de Lohr. He's come to help us defend the north and the first thing we shall do is move them straight into Berwick."

That bit of news brought hope and excitement. Anteaus ran for the keep where his father was, while Ares and Atlas headed to the gatehouse to make preparations. Everyone was moving with a purpose except for Cole, who was left with the women.

He looked at the three of them.

"Well," he said. "It looks as if you are going to have thousands of men on your doorstep very soon."

"*How* soon?" Gaia asked, already thinking about the numerous new knights to pinch.

In fact, Cole could hear her eagerness.

"Armies do not move very quickly," he said. "If they are in Hexham, I would say that they should arrive here by this evening. It is just a few hours' ride for a man on a swift horse."

Corisande's eyes widened. "This evening?" she gasped. "God's Bones, I must get organized. I will need lodgings for the knights and the commanders. Gratiana, go to the knight's quarters and remove all of the soldiers who are sleeping there and have the entire place scrubbed. It smells as if pigs have been living there. Gaia, you will help me with the keep. I cannot have the Earl of Hereford and Worcester sleeping on anything other than a clean and comfortable bed. Run ahead and tell the servants of his impending arrival and have them boil water and vinegar so they can start scrubbing the floors. Hurry, ladies!"

With that, she suddenly turned for the kitchen yard, rushing to tell the cook of the meal that would be needed for the evening. Cole watched her run off as Gratiana and Gaia lingered.

"I do not know what she is so excited about," Gaia said.

"The keep is clean enough."

Cole looked at her. "The state of the keep reflects directly on the chatelaine," he said. "She wants to make a good impression, which is something you should be concerned with also. Do as she says and see to the servants."

Gaia turned those big, blue eyes to him and latched on to his arm. "I am much better when I am entertaining guests, not preparing for them," she said. "I am excellent with conversation and I know how to make guests laugh. Cori can deal with the servants. That's what she is good at."

There was something condescending in that remark that Cole didn't like. Gaia had a high opinion of herself, a spoiled little lass who firmly believed the world should fall at her feet.

He unwound her hand from his arm.

"Go," he said, firmly and quietly. "You have been given a task. Do not disappoint me and ignore it. There are great knights arriving tonight and I do not wish to be embarrassed because you have not done as your sister asked and they are faced with slovenly quarters."

Gaia wasn't at all deterred by him removing her from his arm. She grinned up at him, impishly.

"As you wish," she said, turning for the keep. "I should not want to embarrass you."

Cole felt it, then; a sharp sting on his left buttock right where it met his thigh. He was wearing fine leather breeches today, thin and comfortable, and Gaia had managed to pinch him right through the leather. She wasn't quite out of arm's length, so he lashed out a trencher-sized hand and spanked her right on the buttocks. It sounded like the crack of the whip and Gaia yelped as she put a hand to her arse, looking at him accusingly.

Cole smiled thinly.

"My apologies," he said. "My hand slipped."

Outraged, Gaia stormed off towards the keep. Cole watched her go, a real smile playing on his lips, as he heard giggling behind him. He turned to see Gratiana standing there.

"I am sorry," she said, putting a hand over her mouth. "I should not have laughed, but… but she has deserved that for a very long time."

Cole fought off the smile that threatened to broaden. "As I said, my hand slipped."

"So did hers when it pinched you."

He looked at her a moment before finally breaking down into a snort. "She'll think twice before letting her hand slip again," he said. "And you, my lady? You have duties, too."

Gratiana nodded, looking off to the knight's quarters. "I know," she said. "But I was wondering… this army that is coming? Does this mean we will see more fighting here?"

"Do you mean to ask if they will attract trouble?"

"Aye."

Cole shook his head. "I do not think so," he said. "I would not worry about it, my lady. Whatever happens, we will keep you safe."

She was reassured, but not too terribly. There was still worry on her face. "My home is very peaceful," she said. "Until the battle last month, I had never even seen a siege. It has given me new respect for men who see battle after battle. That kind of carnage and destruction must do something to your soul."

Cole looked at her. Gratiana was a dutiful girl from a lesser noble family and, truth be told, her goal was to marry very well to help her family's circumstances. Cole suspected that was why she had her eyes on Anteaus, but the man was out of her reach simply for the fact that he was a de Bourne, a descendant of the Kings of Northumberland. Undoubtedly, all three de Bourne brothers would be expected to marry very well.

He wondered if she knew that. It was a pity, really. Gratiana was a nice girl and she was compassionate, like Corisande.

It was a pity she might never get what she wanted out of life.

"It does," he said after a moment. "Maybe you will understand why some men are so terribly hard. Sometimes it is what life has done to them. It is difficult facing death like that on a regular basis and not be affected by it."

Gratiana looked up at him, lifting a hand to shield her eyes from the sunlight. "You face it, yet you are not hard," she said. "In fact, you bear the name of England's most notorious warlord, yet you are nothing like the name would imply."

He smiled faintly. "You've not seen me yet in battle," he said. "I am hard enough. Harder than most. Now, you have duties to attend to and I shall not keep you. You did well today with your target practice."

Gratiana smiled gratefully and headed off towards the knight's quarters. Cole didn't give her a second thought as he turned for the kitchen yard.

The last place he had seen Corisande.

The kitchen yard seemed to be devoid of servants. Cole suspected they were all inside the kitchens listening to Corisande tell them what glorious guests they were to have that evening.

One thing he'd learned about Corisande over the past month, among many, was the fact that she was a perfectionist. She liked everything perfect and she wanted to make each and every visitor feel as if they were the most important visitor The Keld had ever known. It was an enormously impressive skill, this woman who could make people feel very special, and he hovered outside of the kitchen door, listening.

He could hear her voice inside.

Something about the dulcet tones of her sweet voice filled him with more joy and contentment than he had ever known. There was satisfaction in his heart that he'd never had before.

As he leaned against the wall next to the door, listening, he knew he could have listened to her forever. He'd never known a life like this.

He'd never known a woman like this before.

That's why he'd come back to The Keld after the incident with Alexander MacDuff. His father had sent him to Alnwick to tell Yves de Vesci everything, but the entire time he was away from The Keld, he missed Corisande something fierce.

A yearning that tore his guts out and then some.

So, he returned to The Keld when he was supposed to return to Pelinom. He told Alastor that his father wanted him there in case something more happened with the Scots, so he was there as the eyes and ears of de Velt and William Marshal, which made sense to Alastor even if Cole thought it was a rather weak premise. But he served both masters so, in reality, it *was* the truth.

But his truth was that he couldn't spend one moment more away from Corisande.

It had been an unconventional month of courting her, although it really wasn't courting because he'd not spoken to her father, nor had he even told his father. The issue of Audrie de Longley still hovered over them, but there was no opportunity for Cole to get back to his father and tell him about the situation and there was certainly no opportunity for him to get to Northwood Castle to speak with Audrie.

Therefore, the situation was a little uncertain as far as asking Alastor to court his daughter, but he knew he'd have to ask the man sooner or later. He was certain that people weren't oblivious to the fact that he was quite attentive to Corisande. Surely something like that hadn't escaped the notice of Alastor, Ares, Atlas, and Anteaus. The person who hadn't noticed was Gaia, but that was because she was wrapped up in her own little world. Gaia only saw what was important to her, not the blossoming romance between her sister and the big de Velt son.

But Cole had never been so aware of something in his entire life.

So, he stood there and waited for the chance to speak to Corisande alone. Perhaps he'd even steal a kiss. He'd done that several times over the past couple of weeks. In fact, he saw an opportunity now as servants began to leave the kitchens, spilling out into the yard and not seeing him because he was pressed back against the wall next to the door. He could hear Corisande's voice growing closer as she told the cook to make one of her specialty pies for the evening's guests. She walked out of the door, passed right by him without seeing him, and headed in the direction of the buttery.

The buttery was its own stone building built against the kitchen wall, cold and perfect for butter and cheese and milk. There were no servants in that direction, so Cole followed Corisande. His movements were stealth and silent, surprising for a man of his bulk, but the moment she opened the door and peered inside, he wrapped her up in his arms from behind and carried her into the buttery, shutting the door behind them.

Corisande had yelped at first, startled by someone grabbing her, but she immediately knew that it was Cole. In fact, she started to giggle as he nuzzled her neck, her shoulder, the back of her head, before spinning her around and slanting his mouth over hers. Any resistance she had, however weak, fled as her arms went around his neck.

These kisses were becoming something that Cole's days revolved around. The urge to taste her overwhelmed him until it was no longer something he could ignore. She tasted as good as she looked and the feel of her in his arms was well worth the risk of being discovered.

He wanted more with every breath he took.

Pulling Corisande tightly against him, his kisses became

more insistent. His tongue licked at her, gently prying her lips apart and snaking into her mouth. Against him, Corisande collapsed completely, overwhelmed by his strength and his power. She was coming to crave his touch, though she wasn't apt to let him know it. Pretending to be resistant to him, even ignoring him, had lit a fire under the man until it exploded in moments like this.

And she loved it.

"Well?" he said, his lips against her cheek. "Do you want me to stop, you little minx?"

Corisande was breathless and flushed. "Nay," she whispered. "But if my brothers catch us, they will not take kindly to you."

His response was to kiss her again, suckling the life from her. Corisande couldn't catch her breath and her entire body was hot and tingling. Cole's touch lit a fire under her, too, and perhaps that was why she was inclined to ignore him, to not fall into his arms every time he looked at her. His touch made her want to do things with him that only naughty women did. She knew about the ways of men and women and she'd seen enough servant women being groped by soldiers to know that men liked to touch parts of a woman's body that even a woman didn't touch very often, so she well understood how men and women could behave with each other.

Cole made her want to behave like a wanton.

"I have not had the chance to speak to my father about Audrie," Cole said as he nibbled her jaw. "I have wanted to do this properly, Cori, but the more that time passes, the more I am not sure if that is even possible. I do not know when I will see my father again to speak on something other than warfare and it is something I wish to do personally, but I may not be able to. Would you object to my sending him a missive and telling him of the situation?"

Corisande's hands were on his big shoulders as he had his way with her. "Nay," she said. "The sooner you do it, the better."

"Then I shall," Cole said, pulling back to look her in the eyes. "But I want to ask your father's permission to marry you before the situation with Audrie is resolved. I will be truthful with him and explain everything, but I wish to do it now. I do not want to wait another moment, Cori. May I?"

Corisande hesitated and he saw it. He gave her a pained expression and she hastened to reassure him. "I am not sure how he will react if he knows you are betrothed to another woman."

"I am *not* betrothed to her."

She put her fingers over his mouth to shush him but he ended up kissing them, softly and gently, which only caused her resolve to weaken further. "I know," she murmured. "But mayhap you had better not tell him, not unless you have to."

"I have to," he told her. "Thanks to Essien, Anteaus already knows there was something between Audrie and me, and he will undoubtedly tell your father, so I have no choice. I do not want your father to think the man who wants to marry his daughter is a liar."

Corisande cupped his big face. "My strong and noble knight," she said softly. "Truth is important to you."

"It is the only thing that makes a man truly honorable."

She smiled faintly, stroking his stubbled face. "You have always been honest with me and I appreciate it more than you know," she said. "You know that you will always have my honesty as well. I cannot imagine not having that between us. It is the foundation upon which everything else is built."

He leaned forward to kiss her again, this time with more emotion than lust. It was a kiss that shook him from his head to his toes, something that consumed his entire being.

"I never knew I could feel this way about someone," he murmured. "You are strong and admirable and brilliant, Cori. How is it that a woman like you could even consider a man like me?"

Her hands were still on his face. "Because you are kind and gentle, strong and wise," she said. "I am the one who is unworthy, Cole. You are from a great family and as your father's heir, you should marry the daughter of an earl."

"I do not want to marry the daughter of an earl," he said. "I thought I made that plain. I want to marry the daughter of the man who would be the King of Northumbria if there was such a kingdom. I want to marry Princess Corisande."

She grinned. "I am *not* a princess."

"You will always be my queen."

Her smile faded as his sweet words touched her deeply. Leaning forward, she kissed his cheek, his chin, before pausing to look him in the eyes.

"Speak to my father before the day is through," she whispered. "I will tell my brothers so they know what you are about to do. I am sure they will support you. They like you a great deal."

Cole shook his head. "I appreciate the offer, but I shall speak with them," he said. "This must come from me. You will tell your sister and make sure to tell her not to pinch me anymore. If anyone is going to pinch me, it will be you."

Corisande's eyes narrowed. "Did she pinch you again?"

"She did. And I swatted her for it."

Corisande's eyes widened and then she began to laugh. "God's Bones, that little goat deserved it," she said. "Well done, my darling. I applaud you."

His smile faded. "Say it again."

"Say what? Well done?"

"My darling."

She put her arms around his neck, pulling him against her tightly. "My darling," she murmured. "You are my dearest darling."

He held her close in a moment that was ever so pivotal for him. "And you are mine," he said. "I have never had anyone call me by a term of endearment. There is something about it that makes me feel as if I belong to someone, a bond that cannot be broken."

"It cannot," she assured him. "It will not. But you must speak to my father."

He released her, setting her to her feet. "I will do it now," he said. "I want to do it before de Lohr arrives and I will be occupied with other things."

"What other things?" she asked.

He looked at her a moment. In the past month, he had never told her about his work for William Marshal. All she knew was that he called Pelinom Castle home, so she went on the assumption that he served his father. He did, that was true, but the higher power in his life was William Marshal. It was quite possible that The Marshal would send him on another mission once the threat of the Scots invasion was over because when one served in the stable of England's greatest spies, one did not simply walk away from it.

Truth be told, Cole wasn't entirely sure he wanted to walk away.

He could see now that he was going to have to tell Corisande the extent of his service for William Marshal, but not now. There would be time for it later. She was a reasonable woman and he was certain she would understand.

Perhaps she would even be proud of him.

Pride in a husband who served with the most elite knights in England.

Odd how he'd never thought about someone being proud of

him for doing his duty, but he very much wanted that approval from Corisande.

It meant everything to him.

"My father is involved in this crisis with the Scots," he said after a moment, avoiding a heavy explanation until they had the proper time to discuss his service for The Marshal. "I will be as involved in this situation as your own father and brothers, so that means I will be involved with de Lohr and the other warlords who are coming north. I fear I may not see you as often as I wish, but know that I will be thinking of you. You are the queen of my heart, Cori, and I worship every moment with you."

He gently cupped her face, kissing her on the soft cheek, as she flushed madly with his sweet words. She still hadn't gotten over the frantic blushing she did when he was kind and complimentary with her.

She never wanted to get over it.

"I understand," she said. "You are an important man. And I will be thinking of you, too."

He winked at her and gave her one last kiss. "I yearn for the day when the threat of war is over and we can get on with our lives," he said. "Normal things, like traveling to Paris so I can purchase my wife some finery. That reminds me – I saw a post for a tournament in Morpeth that is taking place this month. I yearn for the day when you can watch me from the lists as I destroy the competition in a tournament. Everyday things like that have never meant so much to me as they do now."

She smiled faintly. "I would very much like to see you," she said. "You must be very good."

He snorted. "Good?" he said, incredulous. "I am the best you have ever seen. Those whelps Addax and Essien think they are the best because it was their profession for a couple of years, but they've never gone up against me. I will show them who is the best on the field. And off."

Corisande laughed softly. "My brothers think that they are the best," she said. "They have competed in local tournaments, but it has been a while. I am looking forward to the day when you can unseat them all."

He scratched his head. "It may take some doing, in truth," he said. "That lot is rather skilled but, in the end, I shall not fail. Not with my queen's favor feeding my courage."

"And you shall always have it."

He gazed at her warmly, his mind wandering to a year or two or three in the future, when he had her by his side permanently. With Corisande's support, nothing could stand in his way.

"Thank you," he said softly. Then, he drew in a heavy breath. "As much as I do not want to leave you, I must go about my business and so must you. But I will see you tonight."

"You most certainly will."

He turned for the buttery door, but she remained where she was. He stuck his head out, making sure no one was around to see them, before turning to her one last time.

"We are clear," he said quietly. "And, Cori?"

"Aye?"

"If you are wondering if I love you, wonder no more. It is safe to say that I do."

With that, he was through the door, heading out into the kitchen yard, as Corisande stood there with her mouth open and her eyes wide. But her shock was momentary; it was followed by a smile so bright that tears came to her eyes.

It was safe to say that she loved him, too.

CHAPTER FOURTEEN

COLE FOUND ALASTOR in his solar.

That dusty, cold room that still smelled of seared human flesh. He was burning something in a pewter bowl, incense to cover up the fact that a man had burned to death in that chamber and the stench still hadn't left. The incense was an earthy scent, something he could smell far back in his nose, like cold dirt. It almost smelled like a grave. He stood at the door, seeing Alastor as the man sat with his back to him, gazing out over the bailey in a rare quiet moment.

Quietly, he rapped on the panel.

"Who is it?" Alastor asked without turning around.

"Cole, my lord," Cole replied. "May I enter?"

Alastor turned his chair around, facing him. "How may I be of service, Cole?"

He sounded weary and Cole thought that it was a rather direct question, one that he didn't want to answer right away. He thought that he might need to gently ease Alastor into the true purpose for his visit, so he started out with something unrelated to his real reason. As he'd told Corisande, he wasn't a liar by nature, but that didn't mean he couldn't dance around the subject a little.

Besides… he had to build up his courage.

"I was curious if you've heard from my father," he said. "Addax and Essien have been in Berwick for at least a month. We have no word?"

Alastor shook his head. "None," he said. "It takes time to produce results sometimes, but I do not have to tell you that. You know it all too well."

Cole nodded. "That is true," he said. When the conversation threatened to die, he pointed to the smoking bowl. "What is that? I have smelled it before, I think."

Alastor's attention moved to the bowl and its ribbons of blue smoke. "It is called *olibanum*," he said. "It is harvested in lands as far away as The Levant from a thorny tree that grows in the deserts. My wife loved the smell and it reminds me of her, so I burn it."

Cole understood. "I see," he said. "It must be precious and rare."

"It is. Like my wife – precious and rare."

He said it like a prayer, reverent and wistful. Cole thought it might be a good time to lead into the real reason for his visit.

"What was her name?" he asked.

Alastor fanned the smoke a little, inhaling it when it blew in his direction. "Thalassa," he said. "Thalassa de Ryes. Very old family, south in Hampshire. It has been a few years since I last saw my wife and this resin reminds me so much of her. My children hate it, but I do not care. I suppose we all have our own ways of remembering. But I digress; forgive me. Is there anything else you need from me, Cole?"

Cole didn't give him a straight answer. "It is true we all have our own ways of remembering," he said, sticking to the subject of dead wives. "Whenever I see a thistle, I remember my wife. She loved them."

Alastor's brow furrowed. "You were married?" he said,

surprised. "I did not know that, Cole. When were you married?"

Cole smiled weakly. "Years ago," he said. "I was very young, newly knighted. Her name was Mary and she was from a fine family also. As my father's heir, my parents were most anxious to find me a good wife. Truthfully, I'm not sure I had a choice. They chose her for me."

Alastor was warming to something they had in common. "As did mine," he said. "As the descendent of the Bloodaxe, I had no choice in the matter. What was an arranged marriage turned out to be a love match, however. I was fortunate. Yours was not a love match?"

Cole shrugged. "I would not say that it wasn't," he said. "Mary was sweet and obedient, but I simply did not want a wife. I was young and there were things I wanted to do with my life. But the situation improved when she bore my daughter, Lucy. I think that was when I realized what it means to be a husband and father. I was just coming to like it when she and my daughter passed away suddenly from a fever."

"Oh, Cole," Alastor said, grieved. "I am so sorry, lad. What a tragedy."

"It was."

"How long ago?"

"Two years now."

Alastor reached out and grasped Cole around the wrist, giving him a supportive squeeze before releasing him. "You have my sympathy," he said. "But you are young still. Any lady would be lucky to have you as a husband, I am sure."

Cole was hoping the conversation might reach this point. Now, he had a perfect opportunity to bring up Corisande.

He took a deep breath.

"Would you consider me for your daughter, then?" he said. "Corisande, I mean. I would make her an excellent husband and

I swear upon my oath that I would love her for the rest of my life. My lord… I would like to ask your permission to marry her."

Alastor looked at Cole in shock. In fact, his mouth even popped open. "Cori?" he asked, incredulous. "*My* Cori?"

Cole nodded. "Aye," he said, unsure if Alastor was appalled or pleased with the request. "As I said, I learned a great deal about being a husband in those years that I was married. I would be devoted and true, I swear it. Cori would never want for anything. I realize the de Velt name is either feared or hated in England, and mayhap not the most prestigious, but I promise you that I would make a worthy husband. She would have a good life."

He sounded like he was begging and Alastor put up a hand to ease him. "Cole, I do not doubt your character," he said. "But…"

He was cut off when Ares suddenly appeared in the doorway. "Papa," he said, interrupting. "The army from the south is growing closer. You must come."

Alastor was on his feet, but he wasn't so preoccupied that he didn't realize that Cole was expecting an answer. He put a hand on the man's shoulder as he walked past him.

"I am sorry, Cole," he said. "We shall continue this conversation later."

"Cole, you come as well," Ares said. "If it is The Marshal, I am sure he will want to see you."

So much for a most opportune discussion. Cole could have throttled Ares for coming when he did. With a heavy sigh, he stood up, slowly dying on the inside because Alastor had been cut off mid-thought. Was the man opposed to a marriage and simply wanted to let him down easy? If he had been agreeable, surely he would have said so right away.

But he hadn't.

Or he hadn't been *able* to.

Feeling frustrated and disappointed, Cole followed Alastor and Ares from the keep.

"THERE WAS A battle here," Bric said in his heavy Irish brogue. "Look at how half of the village as been burned. They're only now rebuilding. I wonder what happened?"

No one had an answer, least of all Christopher de Lohr.

Riding at the head of a contingent of six thousand men, he was focused on Castle Keld in the distance, rising like a jewel above the darkening landscape as the sun sank low in the west. In fact, the pale-stoned castle was bathed in pink, giving it an ethereal appearance.

They'd arrive at their destination.

Unfortunately, the village surrounding their destination had clearly seen some destructive activity. The village hugged the hill that the castle sat upon, with cottages stacked about a quarter of the way up the rise and then again dotting the surrounding countryside. There was a business district in the village that surrounded the communal well, and those cottages as well as some on the north side of the village had been damaged or burned.

"Something has happened, indeed," Christopher said, looking around. "Had it been a fire that had spread from one house to the next, there would have been continuity in the damage, but there's none at all. It's in clusters, which tells me someone took a torch to the village."

"Does de Bourne have enemies we did not know about?" Dashiell asked.

"None that I am aware of."

The reply came from William Marshal.

Riding behind Christopher, his the three-point shield was slung over his left knee, perhaps the most recognizable standard in England – the Scarlet Lion.

The Marshal was fairly old to be going on a battle march, but he was determined. If there was a war to be managed, he intended to do the managing first-hand, and in a case like this with the Scots threatening to invade Northumberland, he wasn't going to stay home and leave the heavy fighting to men like Christopher and David de Lohr, Alexander de Sherrington, Bric MacRohan, Dashiell du Reims, Maxton of Loxbeare, Kress de Rhydian, or even Achilles de Dere.

He was going to come personally.

These were the men whose armies had been gathered the fastest, armies ready to move on short order. Christopher and Maxton had moved their armies from the Welsh Marches with the help of Alexander, Peter, Kress, and Achilles, while Bric brought the de Winter war machine from Norfolk and Dashiell came up from Wiltshire.

David was riding with his brother and he was still expecting his army from Canterbury to catch up with them at some point, but that was at least a week away, as were the de Nerra and Forbes armies. They were far to the west and in Gart Forbes' case, nearly to Cornwall, so there were still pieces of the mighty army moving to rendezvous at The Keld, including The Marshal's own army from Pembroke Castle in Wales. Pembroke's army was to join with the de Lara army at Welshpool and then they would make their way north.

Lastly, they were still expecting troops from Richmond Castle, led by Caius d'Avignon, and those troops should be arriving in a day or two. Caius was under orders to go straight to The Keld, so it was only a matter of time before they appeared on the horizon. The six thousand men that were arriving today wasn't nearly the end of all of the men that would eventually join.

And The Marshal was counting on it.

"Bric, Dash," The Marshal said as he turned to the men closest to him. "We must set up an encampment for the night, so send out men to find the best ground before it gets too dark. Somewhere near the castle. Be quick about it."

Bric and Dashiell reined their horses around, breaking off men to go on the hunt for a suitable piece of land to park a massive army on, as The Marshal spurred his horse forward until he was riding next to Christopher.

"I am very curious to know what has been happening here," he muttered, looking around the damaged village. "*Who* has de Bourne been fighting?"

Christopher shook his head in reply even though he knew it was a rhetorical question.

But it was a very good one.

Coming to the north end of the village, The Marshal called a halt to the army. Leaving Kress in charge, he took Dashiell, Maxton, Alexander, and Achilles with him and along with Christopher and David and Peter, they made their way towards the gatehouse of Castle Keld.

It was a great collection of knights that approached.

"It has been a long time since I have been here," The Marshal said. "I had forgotten what an imposing place it is."

"Impressive," Christopher said. "I have never been here."

"William," David said, gesturing to the gatehouse. "We are being met."

They looked to the gatehouse to see a couple of men heading out in the darkness on foot, holding torches. The first man that came into view was older, with a crown of silver hair, and William came to within ten feet of him before reining his steed to a halt.

"Lord Bernicia?" he said hesitantly. "Alastor de Bourne?"

The man looked him over before replying. "And you are?"

"William Marshal."

That brought tremendous relief and the man visibly re-laxed. "My lord," he said. "Welcome to Castle Keld. Cole told me that it was you, but I wanted to make sure. I wanted to see your face."

"And so you have," William said, looking over Alastor's head to features he recognized. A smile tugged at his lips. "Cole, you are to be commended. Your work on behalf of England has been flawless."

"Thank you, my lord," Cole said as he stepped forward, smiling as he held the torch up to get a look at the men accompanying The Marshal.

He recognized them in an instant.

For some reason, everyone accompanying William began to chuckle. Looking at a smiling Cole had them laughing. The man never smiled and even when he did, there was something sinister about it, like the cat who was about to swallow the canary. Or already had. In fact, it was Peter who dismounted his steed first to go and greet Cole as one would a long-lost brother. Since their father's were great friends, the men knew each other well.

He embraced Cole fondly.

"Cole," Peter said, squeezing him. "You ugly fool. How long has it been?"

Cole snorted. "Not long enough, Peter," he said. "I would insult you in return, but your father is within earshot and he might not take kindly to it. Suffice it to say you are no uglier than usual."

Peter grinned, patting him on the cheek, as Cole turned his attention to the rest of the knights. "Max," he greeted Maxton, looking to the man behind him. "Achilles. I thought I smelled you the moment the army entered the village."

Maxton laughed. He had a sense of humor. Achilles, however, did not. He frowned. "You nasty cuss," he said. "Come and say that to my face. I dare you."

That made Maxton laugh harder, slapping an arm across Achilles' chest to prevent him from dismounting. "You would never survive," he said. "He is a de Velt, remember?"

As Achilles conceded the point, Alexander dismounted his steed and headed in Cole's direction. Alexander was known as Sherry to his friends and he turned his black eyes on Cole, studying him for a moment.

There was warmth there.

"I've not seen you in four years," he said, smiling and extending his hand. "I heard you had infiltrated the Scots. Quite a task, de Velt. A lesser man would not have handled it so well."

Alexander was more sedate than the others, perhaps more introspective, a man who preferred working alone than in a group, but he was a deeply loyal friend to those he loved and admired. Cole was one; they'd met several years ago when Alexander had first returned from The Levant and The Marshal was recruiting more knights for his stable of spies. Since Cole had the de Velt legacy, he'd made a perfect candidate and it had been Alexander's task to seek him out, at Norwich Castle during that time, and essentially interview him. He liked what he had seen.

He still did.

Cole, too, considered Alexander a loyal and true friend. He took his extended hand and held fast.

"It is good to see you, Sherry," he said. "I've missed that face, always looking at me as if expecting more from me than my own father does."

Alexander laughed softly. "Because I do," he said. "You are

greatness, Cole, as proven by your most recent task."

"Speaking of tasks," The Marshal said as he dismounted his horse stiffly. "What has happened to this village? Have you suffered a recent attack, Bernicia?"

He was addressing Alastor by his formal title and Alastor sighed heavily. "Aye," he said. "In fact, there is a great deal to tell and little time to act, so come inside and let us discuss the situation. Much has changed since you received de Velt's missive."

The Marshal nodded, handing over his reins to Dashiell, but his focus moved to Cole. "Did your father raze Fountainhall as I commanded?" he asked.

All eyes were on Cole has he nodded. "Aye, my lord," he said. "Fountainhall is no more."

"And her army?"

"Still on poles, as far as I know," he said. "It was my father's habit to leave them up until they were nothing left but leather and bone."

That was an impactful statement. The Dark Lord had indeed razed a castle and destroyed an army as only he was capable of. It was eerie and terrifying. The Marshal looked at Christopher, who lifted his eyebrows as if to emphasize the scope of the horror that had undoubtedly occurred.

"Good," The Marshal said simply. "And Canmore? Was he captured?"

"Aye, my lord."

"Where is he?"

"That is what we must discuss, my lord."

The Marshal didn't ask anymore questions. He had what he wanted, mostly, but he was intensely curious about the rest. He could see by the expressions on Cole and Alastor's faces that a good deal more must have happened.

Perhaps the abduction of Alpin Canmore had only been the

beginning.

Without another word, he followed Alastor into the vast bailey of Castle Keld.

"HE BURNED TO death?" Christopher repeated, shocked. "Christ. The man fell into the hearth and burned to death?"

Alastor nodded. "Of his own accord, I might add," he said. "In fact, that hearth right there. You can still smell the burned flesh. The stench is in everything."

He was pointing to the enormous hearth against the wall, the one blazing with a friendly fire that hadn't been so friendly when Alpin had fallen into it. Everyone turned to look at it, as if there were something different about it than other hearths, but the truth was that it looked normal enough.

Normal enough and deadly enough under the right circumstances.

Alastor's solar was crowded with the men who had accompanied The Marshal north, as well as his own sons and Cole de Velt. All of them now looking at the hearth after hearing a rather horrifying story about Alpin Canmore's death.

In fact, The Marshal took a good look at the black-stoned fireback before turning away with a grimace.

"Astonishing," he muttered, returning his attention to Alastor. "And he spoke of Berwick before he fell into the hearth? That is not something I have heard before."

"Nor I," Alastor replied. "It was Cole who translated what he said, for he spoke it in the Scot's tongue. Mayhap to tease us, since I do not speak the Gaelic. Mayhap he knew that."

The Marshal looked at Cole. "What did he say, exactly?"

Cole didn't hesitate. "*Tha an fhìrinn ann am Bearaig.*"

The Marshal lifted his eyebrows, curious. "I see," he said. "So the man said that the truth lies in Berwick. And that was all?"

"That was all, my lord," Cole replied.

The door to the solar opened at that moment and a beautiful woman with blond hair and a green velvet gown entered. Cole almost didn't recognize Corisande because she was dressed in finery and jewels, her hair elaborately styled, which was something he'd never seen on her before. She was exquisite.

She looked like a queen.

His heart did a little leap at the sight of her as she carried a tray with cups and a pitcher. She smiled politely at the men in the room and they parted ways, allowing her to reach her father's table. Corisande set the tray down and behind her, Gaia entered carrying two more pitchers of drink, but whereas Corisande had been demure and polite, Gaia smiled boldly at every man who met her eyes.

Cole had to fight off a grin at the cheeky little wench.

"Excuse me, my lords," Alastor said. "These are my daughters, Corisande and Gaia."

Most of the men were polite in greeting except for Peter de Lohr. He seemed to go out of his way to greet Corisande, which immediately set Cole's blood to boiling. He adored Peter, but that adoration didn't extend to tolerating the man's attention on Corisande. She didn't seem to notice, or really care, as she curtsied politely to the room.

"My apologies for the interruption, my lords," she said. "Welcome to Castle Keld. A meal to celebrate your arrival will be served in the great hall when you are ready."

She curtsied again and swiftly departed, but not before she caught sight of Cole and smiled faintly. His gaze was warm upon her, his expression rather soft, but Gaia was slower to move. As Peter was staring at her sister, Gaia was staring at Peter and dragging her feet until Ares grabbed her by the arm and all but shoved her out of the chamber. She gasped in outrage as he slammed the door on her, smiling wanly to those who had noticed as if to apologize for his sister's nosey behavior.

But The Marshal wasn't paying attention. He was still focused on Alastor.

"I want to start this conversation from the beginning so there is no misunderstanding," he said as Anteaus began to pour the wine into cups. "Jax de Velt razed Fountainhall as only de Velt can and left Canmore to interrogate."

Alastor nodded. "Aye, my lord."

"And after he was finished with Canmore, after discovering that The Rough's time for invasion into Northumberland was summer, he sent Canmore to you for further interrogation."

"Aye, my lord."

"Canmore told you that the truth lies in Berwick, which leads us to believe that the longships will enter through the River Tweed to reinforce the Scot's invasion into the north."

"Aye, my lord."

"And the Justiciar of Scotia, Alexander MacDuff, came all the way to The Keld to demand an answer to the missives Canmore sent you, an invitation to join their rebellion."

"Aye, my lord."

"He tried to destroy the village when you refused to join."

"That is what happened, my lord."

William took a cup of wine offered by Anteaus, drinking deeply as he pondered what he'd been told so far. Alastor was looking at Cole, silently suggesting he tell the man about Addax and Essien.

Cole took the hint.

"There is more beyond that, my lord," Cole said. "After

learning of Berwick, and after the attack on the village, I returned to Pelinom with Addax and Essien al-Kort. They have been with me since the beginning of this situation and they are invaluable."

Across the chamber, Christopher smiled wearily. "The Princes of Kitara," he said, accepting a cup of wine that was offered to him. "I have not seen them in many years. When The Marshal told me that they were involved, I wasn't surprised. I knew them as young lads, you know. I was the first English knight they had contact with in The Levant. Were it not for me and Marcus Burton, my old and close friend, those two might have wandered into trouble and gotten themselves killed. Mayhap you already know this, Cole, but when I found them, they had just escaped from a merchant caravan."

Cole looked at him curiously. "I did not know," he said. "What were they doing with a merchant caravan?"

Christopher made his way over to a big, cushioned chair in front of the hearth, pushing Achilles away when he tried to steal it away from him. He lowered his bulk down carefully.

"When they had escaped the revolution in their father's kingdom, a merchant caravan took them in," he said. "Addax, Essien, and the servants who smuggled them out of Kitara were given shelter and protection with this caravan, but by the time they reached Acre, they'd starved and beaten Addax and Essien nearly to death. When they escaped, I found them."

Cole nodded in understanding. "They had not told me their circumstances," he said. "I knew that they were acquainted with you in The Levant, but not how they came to know you. You saved them, my lord."

"They were good lads," Christopher said. "They were smart, eager to learn. When the crusade was over, I headed home but they went to Thuringia with a group of Thuringian knights. They were good men; I knew them. I had my own problems with Richard and John, and I simply did not have time to worry over two young men who needed more attention than I could give them."

"They speak of you most fondly, my lord," Cole said. "They will be happy to see you."

"Where are they?"

The warmth in Cole's eyes faded and he looked to The Marshal. "That is what I was about to tell you," he said. "When we returned to Pelinom and told my father what we knew, he sent Addax and Essien to Berwick to discover what they could and report back to him. The Scots hold the castle, as you know."

The Marshal nodded. "I know," he said. "That has long been my regret that Richard sold Berwick to raise money for his foolish campaign to The Levant. The last I heard, the Earl of Ross was in command."

Cole nodded. "Angus MacHeth has control of it, but it is his son who is the garrison commander," he said. "It makes perfect sense that Berwick would be the point of entry for the Northmen, my lord. With MacHeth in command of the garrison, there will be no one to stop them unless…"

The Marshal was listening closely. "Unless *what*?"

"Unless we lay siege and wrest control from the Scots. I believe my father thinks we should."

"That is *exactly* what I think."

The voice came from the chamber door. Startled by the voice that was deep and raspy, everyone turned to see Jax standing in the opening flanked by Addax and Essien.

A smile spread across Cole's face.

"Greetings, Papa," he said. "I did not know you were coming. Why did you not send word?"

Jax stepped into the chamber and the first person to physically greet him was Christopher. From one old friend to another, Christopher embraced the man, happy to see him. He and Jax smiled at each other for a moment before Jax turned to his son, to the men in the chamber.

"I did not send word of my arrival because it was faster to simply come here myself rather than send a messenger," he said, his gaze moving from Cole to The Marshal. "It is a two-day ride from Pelinom, but I thought it important to come personally to see Lord Bernicia. What I did not expect was to see the Scarlet Lion standards flying over an encampment to the west. My lord, it is agreeable to see you again."

He was addressing The Marshal at that point, and William was thrilled to see his most fearsome warlord. Even more than The Marshal himself, Ajax de Velt was legendary. The modest solar of Alastor de Bourne, at the moment, was filled with legends. Moreover, there weren't many men The Marshal was so terribly excited to see, but Jax was one of them. He approached the man, reaching out a hand to him.

Jax took it.

"De Velt," The Marshal said with satisfaction. "I am pleased. I was told of your success with Fountainhall. Excellent work, as always."

Jax held The Marshal's hand for a moment before releasing it. "Laying siege and sowing destruction is much like riding a horse," he said. "One never forgets, even if one has not ridden in twenty-five years or more. I am pleased with the outcome as well. It was… fruitful."

"Fruitful, indeed," The Marshal said. "We were just discussing the fall of Fountainhall and the death of Canmore."

Jax nodded his head before The Marshal even finished speaking. "Aye, that was most unexpected," he said. "But I believe we received the information we needed from him, and after Addax and Essien spent the past month in Berwick, we have even more. Thank God you are here, William, because you need to hear this."

The mood took a serious turn as everyone looked over at Addax and Essien. Since Essien was the one who had actually gotten the information first-hand, Addax gave his brother a gentle shove, encouraging him to speak. Everyone was looking at him expectantly.

Essien took the hint.

"My brother and I spent the past several weeks in Berwick, pretending to be sailors looking for a job aboard one of the many cogs that come into the city," he said. Essien was an excellent orator, comfortable in a group of men. "We also pretended to be drunk every day so jobs were not forthcoming because no one wants to hire a drunken sailor, but pretending to be in that state afforded us the ability to glean information any way we could."

"What did you hear?" The Marshal wanted to know.

Essien fixed on him. "We left Berwick four days ago," he said. "On the last day we were there, I spent time with a woman who was known to keep company with men from the garrison at Berwick Castle. I will not tell you how I received the information from her, but suffice it to say that I did and I believe it reliable. The woman had told me things before that had come to pass, so her information has been proven. She told me that according to her lover, who is one of the commanders at Berwick, the Scots are already moving south. They are already heading for Berwick."

That was the information they had all been looking for and every man was listening intently. The Marshal, hearing what he had hoped not to hear, at least not yet, sighed heavily.

"When?"

"Now, my lord," Essien said. "She told me that they were coming to Berwick to join their Northman allies and that the entire city was to celebrate the arrival of the Northmen soon."

The Marshal's eyebrows rose. "The Northmen are *already*

moving for Berwick?" he asked, trying not to appear too surprised. "When are the they coming?"

"Any day, my lord," Essien said quietly. "Everything is happening now. I do not know when her lover received this information, but I know she was with him the afternoon that she told me all of this. It is possible he told her then, which means William the Rough's army has been heading south from Edinburgh for days."

"Christ," Cole muttered. "They could be there right now for all we know. That means the Northmen's arrival must be imminent. If they take those longships into the River Tweed, we may never get them out."

For a moment, everyone froze, looking at each other in surprise. They had expected to have weeks, even months, before the Scots and the Northmen converged, but according to Essien's source, that event was imminent.

The unholy alliance was coming together imminently.

With that realization, The Marshal took his empty cup and poured himself another measure of Alastor's fine French wine. He downed nearly half the cup before turning to the group.

"The time for action, good knights, is now," he said calmly. "We cannot wait for the rest of the armies to join us. We must move and we must do it tomorrow. Essien, did the woman tell you how many men the Scots are bringing?"

Essien didn't look happy. In fact, he glanced at the men around him, at his brother, before answering.

"According to her lover, there will be two Scotsmen for every Englishman," he said. "He boasted this to her, evidently. As far as numbers, I do not know what that means, but I can only imagine there will be a great many of them."

"Thousands, at least," Cole said, a quiet rumble. "Lest you forget, I've spent the past two years with The Rough and the past year or so listening to men speak of this invasion. I know he had Highlanders coming to Edinburgh by the thousands, plus men under the rule of the Earls of Orkney. Longships carry anywhere from fifty to eighty men, depending on the size of the ship, and if we even have ten of those arrive at Berwick, we are talking about almost a thousand men or more. If there are twenty ships, double that. Add that to the thousands of Scots and there more than likely really will be two Scotsmen for every Englishman. Or more."

So there it was, out for all to hear. The reality of the situation, bigger than they had expected. Sooner than they had expected. It was up to The Marshal and his armies to stop them.

They were out of time.

Therefore, The Marshal didn't waste any.

"Then all roads lead to Berwick," The Marshal said calmly. "Who knew that seaside village would determine the fate of northern England."

It was a rhetorical statement, but not an untrue one. "It looks that way, my lord," Cole replied.

William wasn't one to panic in any case. Panicking never solved anything; he'd learned that long ago. He was an old warhorse with hundreds of battles in his vast experience and he would have to draw on that knowledge.

He gestured to the group.

"All of you will go and eat now," he said. "Bernicia's daughter said there is a meal being served in the hall, so partake of it and rest for a few hours. Make sure your men rest and eat. I must speak with de Bourne and de Lohr and de Velt and we must come up with a plan of attack for Berwick. Maxton, you and Sherry will remain. I will send for the rest of you when we are ready to discuss our battle plans."

The men understood that there was nothing more to do, at least for a few hours, so they turned for the door and began funneling out, but not before Addax and Essien went to

Christopher and David and embraced them warmly.

It was the first time they'd all seen each other in a long time, a most pleasant reunion. Christopher smiled wearily at the pair, as proud of them as if they were his own sons. But there was no time for conversation, or for reminiscing, so Addax and Essien followed the others out of the hall. There would be time enough for pleasantries later.

When everyone had gone and the door shut quietly, The Marshal sat down in a chair next to a large table that held maps and the like.

He looked at those left in the room.

Christopher and David de Lohr, Ajax and Cole de Velt, Maxton of Loxbeare and Alexander de Sherrington. Of all of the men at his disposal, these were some of the best. He puffed out his cheeks, trying to determine where to begin.

He looked at Alastor.

"Do you have a map of Northumberland that we can examine?" he asked.

Alastor nodded wearily, a man resigned to the fact that they really were going to war. Perhaps some part of him hoped it would never come to that, but the threat had come to fruition. As the men crowded around his table, he spread out a well-used map that covered the area from the River Tyne to the River Tweed. It was smudged and torn in places, but it gave a good overview.

The Marshal bent over it.

"Now," he said. "If what Essien's friend says is true, and The Rough is moving an army out of Edinburgh for Berwick, they should arrive in the next day or two. That is before we can get there. That means we cannot use the element of surprise and their armies will see us coming. Jax, you have fought the Scots longer than I have. Give me your thoughts."

Jax folded his big arms across his chest, looking at the map before him. He could see just how close Pelinom was to Berwick and that did not give him any comfort in the least.

It put him right on the edge of the battle.

"Before I left Pelinom, I instructed my son, Julian, to take his mother and sisters away from Pelinom," he said. "Something told me to remove them. Call it a hunch, I suppose, but Julian and about a hundred men are taking my wife and daughters south to Alnwick Castle. Pelinom is strong, but it cannot stand against thousands of Scots and Northmen, so they are heading south as we speak. As for Berwick, it is my sense that it is a three-pronged attack, meaning we will have three objectives."

The Marshal was looking at him with interest. "And that would be?"

Jax thumped on the map, next to Berwick. "We have Scots coming from the north," he said. "We have Berwick Castle, and we have the arriving Northmen. Part of the army needs to engage the Scots to drive them away from Berwick while another part of the army shall go for the castle itself. The remains of the army will sit at the mouth of the River Tweed and prevent the Northmen from entering the river by any means necessary."

It made perfect sense and The Marshal sighed heavily. "That will take a good many men," he said. "We have six thousand with us now with an addition five or six thousand still coming north. Maxton, can you send word to Caius to take Richmond's army directly to Berwick?"

Maxton, standing behind David, nodded. "Aye," he said. "In fact, I will ride to meet him and come north with him. May I suggest something?"

"Please do."

"If the Northmen haven't arrived yet by the time this army reaches Berwick, then you can divide your army into two groups to go after the Scots and after the castle," he said. "Richmond is big enough to take the mouth of the River Tweed and wait for the Northmen."

The Marshal cocked an eyebrow. "Providing they move fast enough," he said. "He is at least two days behind us."

"We will move faster," Maxton assured him. "What about Northwood Castle? Are they sending men?"

"I have sent a messenger to Lord Teviot telling him what is happening," Jax said. "He is sending men to join with Pelinom's troops. We will have at least fifteen hundred men between the two of us."

"Excellent," The Marshal said with some enthusiasm. "That reinforces our numbers greatly. What about Castle Questing? Baron Dudforth has a small army, though the man hasn't been right in the head since returning from The Levant. Something about a sword he lost on crusade. He's apparently always looking for it. Jax, do you know the man?"

Jax nodded. "I do," he said. "He has a fifty-man army, and that's being generous. Dudforth has one of the largest castles in the north and a tiny army to staff it because no one in their right mind would attack that place. I can say with some certainty that asking him for men would not be to our advantage. He does not have enough to make a difference. There are several other castles in the area, like Wark and Roxburgh, but they belong to the Scots right now."

The Marshal looked back to the map. "Then we'll have to make do with what we have," he said. "But every army that is set to join us must be told to go directly to Berwick. Sherry, can you make sure that happens?"

Alexander nodded. "I will have the missives drawn out within the hour."

The Marshal glanced up at him. "De Lara, Forbes, de Nerra. They must be told."

"I will make sure of it."

The wheels were in motion, everything focusing on Berwick. Alastor stepped away from the table, rubbing his eyes wearily. "Then it is settled," he said. "I must make sure my army is ready to depart on the morrow, so you will excuse me. I must ensure the provision wagons and quartermaster and surgeon are prepared."

The Marshal waved him on. "Do what you must," he said. "I plan to eat and then sleep for a few hours. We shall regroup here two hours before dawn to go over the plan with everyone before departing."

The group began to fracture, breaking into little clusters of conversation, but Cole remained by the hearth, thinking about the last few words Alastor had spoken.

Provision wagons and quartermaster and surgeon…

That meant Corisande.

He wasn't going to mention that to Alastor, not in front of everyone, but the more he thought about it, the more opposed he was to her going on a battle march, and possibly into one of the nastiest battles the north had ever seen. He didn't want her involved in that.

He didn't want her involved at all.

Over to his left, Christopher and his father were in conversation. He could hear his father ask about Cassian, his youngest son, who had been serving at Lioncross Abbey for a few years. Jax wanted to know if he'd come with Christopher only to be told he'd been left at Lioncross because Christopher had pulled so many of his senior officers with him when the army moved out. Someone had to stay behind and protect Lioncross, he said, and Jax seemed glad. It was bad enough that he had one, and possibly two, sons involved in the battle at Berwick, so leaving his third son behind to be bored but safe… he seemed quite agreeable to that.

He wanted at least one son safe.

And Cole wanted Corisande safe.

Without another word to the men in the solar, he quit the keep in search of a certain blonde he was very much in love with.

CHAPTER FIFTEEN

S HE KNEW HE wasn't happy.

In fact, he was bloody well furious.

Corisande knew Cole was deeply upset that she was riding with the wagons at the rear of her father's army, but it couldn't be helped.

She had a job to do.

The past two days had been a whirlwind. The armies of William Marshal had descended on The Keld and within the space of one night, the army of Castle Keld had been mustered and that included the surgeon's wagon.

Knowing how Cole felt about her accompanying the army, Corisande had struggled to focus on properly supplying what she needed as a field surgeon. She had been her father's surgeon for quite some time, as she had told him, and she knew what to do. She knew what she needed and she knew how to organize. But this time was different.

Cole was watching her.

He hadn't said anything to her about her father's command to muster the army so quickly. He hadn't said anything to her about the surgeon's wagon going along to Berwick with her in it. In fact, he hadn't said anything at all, but he had watched her as she went about her business. She had been moving between the keep and the kitchens and the stable yard where the surgeon's wagon was located, and everywhere she went, she caught a glimpse of him watching her from afar.

Lingering.

Corisande suspected that he wanted to say something to her, to tell her how much he disapproved of her going along with the army but, to his credit, he didn't make the attempt to actually speak. He pretended to be busy, too, but in his case, he really was. His father had arrived from Pelinom Castle and he spent a good deal of time with his father as they helped William Marshal in the duties leading to the departure of the armies for Berwick.

But the truth was that Corisande was watching out for him, too.

Every time she went outside with an armload of boiled linen or the sewing kits that she used to stitch up the wounded, she would look around for him. Mostly, she had seen him with his father and she didn't want to interrupt, so she put her head down and continued to go about her own business, although she was acutely aware of his.

She hadn't talked to Cole since their rendezvous in the buttery and what he had told her then held true – his duties took him away from her and there was no time to speak. There was a great chaos going on at The Keld with multiple armies and multiple commanders, and although Corisande didn't know the exact details, she had caught wind a few things from her brothers in passing. Anteaus had told her that the Northmen were already at Berwick and they were taking a massive army to essentially chase them away, so she knew whatever battle they were facing was going to be a serious one.

The anticipation in the air was a palpable thing.

But there was something else on her mind as she went

about her business.

She wondered if Cole had asked her father for permission to marry. When he had left her in the buttery, it had been with the intention of going straight to her father and speaking with him. There was a large part of her that had been waiting for him to tell her what had transpired, but because of the arrival of The Marshal's armies, all of that seemed to have become a lesser priority.

She understood, but it was still disappointing.

An entire night of preparations and little sleep had translated into a completely assembled army just after sunrise. Corisande had been exhausted from being up all night, but the surgeon's wagon was ready and it pulled out of the stable yard along with the quartermaster's wagons and the provisions wagons about two hours after dawn. Because there were so many men to move, the army from The Keld was the last one to move out at the rear of The Marshal's procession.

And just like that, they were going to war.

There was some added drama before they left, however. Because Corisande was going, Alastor forced Gaia to go as well. There was a tradition of women surgeons in the House of de Bourne, so tearful Gaia was forced into the surgeon's wagon, too.

Corisande sat in the rear of the wagon with her sister as it lumbered along the road, driven by one of her father's soldiers. Behind them was a division of her father's army to protect their rear, and Corisande remained awake and alert throughout the morning, but by the time the nooning hour passed, she was becoming drowsy for lack of sleep and the constant roll of the wagon. She ended up curling up underneath the wagon bench and falling asleep to the sound of Gaia's unhappy sniffles.

She didn't awaken until sunset, when the army halted so that the men could be fed. Because they had spent all night preparing to depart, many of the men had not slept, either, so a complete halt was called so that the men could eat and sleep for a couple of hours. They were traveling during a full moon, so there was plenty of light at night to travel by.

It was clear to Corisande that the army was desperate to get to Berwick because there was very little rest for the men. The knights were pushing the foot soldiers, and her brothers would charge up and down the column, shouting encouragement to the men to keep them moving. That tension she had felt back at The Keld followed them, driving the army north. Corisande may have had it easy sitting in the back of the wagon and sleeping on occasion like she was, but she knew that would end as soon as they entered into the battle.

She would be lucky to have any rest at all after that.

Because there were so many men and the army was so big, travel was somewhat slow, which is why they chose to travel most of the night to make up for lost time. On the second night of travel, they stopped out of pure necessity on the outskirts of a small village and set up camp on a meadow to the southeast. A brook ran through the camp and men washed their faces and rested while the cooks from the different armies prepared meals for their men. Tomorrow, they would be in Berwick and the madness of war would begin in earnest.

It was a final night of peace before the chaos.

With nothing much to do, Corisande helped the cooks with the de Bourne army. There were four cooks, in fact, and they pulled out a side of pork and began to boil it with beans and celery, creating a rich and inviting stew. Bread was baked in portable ovens, which were nothing more than clay kilns set on the edge of the fire. As Gaia remained in the surgeon's wagon, unwilling to help in a domestic chore and feeling sorry for herself, Corisande was busy helping the cooks by stirring the enormous pots of boiling beans and pork when she heard a voice behind her.

"My lady, you have been summoned."

Corisande stopped stirring, turning to see Cole standing behind her. He was armed to the teeth, dressed for battle, and sporting a growth of beard on his chin from travel and no rest.

"Who has summoned me?" she asked.

Cole simply beckoned her with a crooked finger and, frustrated that he wouldn't even answer a simple question, she turned back to the stew.

"Whoever it is, you may tell them that I am busy," she said. "I've no time for your foolery, Cole."

"It is not foolery, I assure you," he said. "Please stop what you are doing and come with me. Your father has asked me to bring him to you."

She stopped stirring, then, and wiped her hands off on the apron she was wearing. She was wearing a brown broadcloth garment, durable, with long sleeves and a heavy skirt. The apron was part of the outfit and although she had washed it, there were faded bloodstains on it. She always swore it when she went to battle with her father's army. Leaving the bubbling pots, she brushed a stray piece of hair from her forehead with the back of her hand and followed Cole.

Clouds had drifted in from the sea to the east, scattered across the sky beneath the moonlight. Every once in a while, one would cross in front of the moon and darken the landscape. As Corisande walked next to Cole, feeling his silence to the bone, a cloud passed in front of the moon and she missed a small hole that was right in front of her. As she tripped over it, Cole reached out to keep her from falling, but she yanked her arm away angrily.

"Stop it," she said. "Leave me alone. If you cannot be civil enough to speak to me, then you need not worry over my health."

She heard him sigh sharply. "I am not being uncivil," he said. "I simply haven't had the opportunity to speak with you. We have been traveling for two days."

She hissed at him. "That is a lie and you know it," she said. "I have been sitting in the surgeon's wagon ever since we left The Keld. There has been ample opportunity to speak to me, but you will not do it because you are punishing me for obeying my father's order and coming on the battle march. Well, I will not tolerate your behavior. If you want to be angry, be angry at my father. Better still, be angry at the Scots for starting this stupid mess. But instead, you'd rather be angry at me for doing my duty. It is a shallow man who would do such a thing."

"I am not going to apologize for being concerned for you."

Her response was to stick her tongue out and make a rude sound. "Pish," she said. "Save your insincere sorrows. I am not interested."

Cole came to an abrupt halt, grabbing her by the arm so she was forced to stop right along with him. Beneath the silver moon, he faced her.

"I *am* sorry if I have upset you," he said, his voice low. "Truly sorry, Cori. I am. But this will be a brutal battle and I will not apologize for not wanting you near it. Battle is no place for a woman and especially not *my* woman."

She pulled her arm out of his grip. "So you do not speak to me for two days to convey that concern? That is very petty, Cole."

He was trying not to look too contrite. "Mayhap," he said after a moment. "Mayhap I am petty and shallow, just as you have said. But I also happen to love you and if something happened to you, I would want to die. I lost one wife, Cori. I could not lose another, not before our life together even started. I am not displaying that concern well enough and, for that, I will again apologize, but this is all new to me. I am doing my best."

Corisande was starting to soften, just a little. When he put it that way, perhaps she wasn't all that angry with him, after all.

"It is new to me, too," she said. "But becoming angry at me will not solve the problem."

"I am not angry with you."

"They why have you not talked to me for the past two days? Why have you simply lurked and stared at me, as if I am doing something wrong?"

He made a face, looking at his feet. "Because I was afraid to say what I was thinking, knowing you did not wish to hear it," he said. "It was wrong of me, I know, but I did not know what else to do. I still don't."

He sounded a little lost. Corisande took pity on him and put her hands on his, squeezing them tightly.

"I will be safe with the wounded," she assured him softly. "I know how to use a bow and arrow, and I know how to use a dagger. I can protect myself, I promise. I'm more concerned with how Gaia is going to do on a battle march than I am with any threat from the Scots. Truly, Gaia is going to be the biggest problem I have."

Cole relented completely, looking around to make sure they weren't being watched before pulling her into his arms and kissing her deeply. But it was a quick kiss because he didn't want anyone to see them, so he released her almost as fast as he grabbed her.

"I do not envy you the situation with your sister," he said. "You should have brought Gratiana. She seems more willing to help."

Corisande nodded. "She is, but my father has sent her home," he said. "She is only a ward, after all, and with these battles, he did not want her in such a volatile situation. I will miss her, but it is better for her to return to her home and be safe."

"It is better for *you* to return to your home and be safe."

She shook her head in resignation. "Cole…"

He put up his hands in surrender. "I know," he said. "But I had to say it. Come along, now, before your father sends your brothers out to look for us. I think they are already getting suspicious."

They started to walk again, heading for the big de Bourne tent that had been pitched in the distance. Corisande could see the red and yellow striping of the tent, even beneath the moonlight.

"What does my father want to talk to me about?" she asked.

Cole shook his head. "I do not know," he said. "But you should know I did have a few words with him about permission to marry you before The Marshal arrived."

She looked at him with some excitement. "And?"

"And I barely got it out of my mouth when we were interrupted. He's not yet given me an answer."

"I see," she said, disappointed. "Did he seem receptive?"

"He didn't instantly deny me. I think that's a good sign."

She smiled, but she wasn't entirely enthusiastic. She was disappointed that her father hadn't instantly approved. Discreetly, she slipped her hand into the crook of his big elbow as she collected her skirt with the other hand, using him to steady herself as she crossed a particularly muddy part of the ground. At least, that was her excuse.

It just felt good to hold him.

"There's a tavern in town," he said quietly as they drew closer to the tent. "I was thinking about securing a room there."

She looked at him. "Why?" she asked. "You have a tent and a bed, do you not?"

He looked at her. "Do you?"

"Nay."

"The room would be for you."

She thought that was a rather sweet gesture. "I would like that."

"I thought so," he said. "Speak to your father while I go into town and see about a room for you."

Corisande thought that was a smashingly good idea. She thought about suggesting bringing Gaia but thought better of it. Her lazy sister could sleep in the wagon. Perhaps she and Cole could spend a few quiet moments together if she had a room all her own.

With that thought on her mind, they drew near the de Bourne tent and Ares suddenly appeared. Before Corisande realized what was happening, he reached out and took her hand off Cole's arm. In fact, he separated them quite obviously.

"Inside, Cori," he said, speaking to her but keeping his eyes on Cole. "Father has something to say to you."

He was posturing as if he wanted to throw a punch at Cole. There was an expression of hostility on his face and Cole simply backed away, turning to leave without another word. Corisande thought her brother had been exceptionally rude, glaring at him before stepping into the tent where her father and brothers were.

It was warm in the tent because of a brazier, but it smelled of dampness because of the tent being wet when packed away for travel. Mold grew in the seams, scrubbed away by servants, but the smell still lingered. Her father was seated next to the brass brazier, sharing some wine with her brothers.

Corisande looked at them curiously.

"What do you want?" she asked. "I am helping the cooks prepare the meal for the men but Gaia is sulking in the wagon and she is completely useless. Really, Papa, you should not have forced her to come. She is miserable and when the fighting starts, I fear how she will react."

Alastor lifted his eyebrows in resignation. "She is a de Bourne and much is expected of her," he said. "I'm only sorry I sent her away to foster at Prudhoe, although you went to the same place and you did not acquire the bad traits that Gaia has. She is a pretty lass, and a smart one, but she's as empty-headed as a piglet. Finding a husband for her will be a challenge. But for you…"

He trailed off, looking at her as he sipped his wine, and her brow furrowed.

"What *about* me?" she asked.

Alastor looked away as he set his wine down on a nearby table. "I was telling your brothers that Cole has asked permission to marry you," he said. "I have asked them what they think of him and his request."

Corisande wasn't surprised that her father had spoken to her brothers about it, but she was miffed. This wasn't a group decision as far as she was concerned.

"This is not their choice, Papa," she said. "It is yours. Cole is a fine man and I would be honored to be his wife."

"He's already betrothed," Anteaus blurted out. He seemed agitated, an unusual state for the usually sedate brother. "Essien told me that he's betrothed to Audrie de Longley."

Corisande went on the defensive. "Essien misspoke," she said flatly. "If you had asked Cole, he would have told you the truth. Did you know that he was married before? His wife and child died of a fever two years ago. He has been completely honest with me about everything, including Audrie de Longley. He never asked to court her, but he has visited her and her brother at Northwood. Any betrothal is simply expectations from the de Longley family – there has never been a formal contract."

Anteaus frowned as Alastor spoke up. "He should have told me that from the beginning," he said. "It would have been the honorable thing to do."

Corisande threw up her hands. "He barely had a minute of your time before The Marshal's army arrived," she said, exasperated. "He did not have the time to tell you that."

Alastor conceded the point. "Mayhap," he said. "Our conversation was barely started before it was over. But these expectations you speak of with Audrie de Longley concern me. I do not want to be viewed as having taken a prospective husband away from an earl's daughter."

Corisande looked at him, trying not to let her emotions get the better of her. "He was never hers to begin with, Papa," she said. "And he will make that clear to them as soon as he is able. As soon as the Scots and the Northmen settle their troubles. He will not shirk that duty, Papa. He is an honorable man in every way and… and I love him. I want to marry him, Papa. Please do not deny us."

Her lower lip was quivering by the time she was finished and Alastor, having a soft spot for his daughter, put up a hand.

"Do not fret so," he said. "I have no intention of denying him, for the general consensus is that Cole is a good man and your brothers approve of him. But he must settle the issue with Audrie de Longley before I will give him my permission."

Hope filled Corisande. "But you *will* give it?"

"I will."

With a shriek of delight, Corisande ran at her father to embrace the man, nearly tipping his chair over in the process. She was so happy that she hugged Anteaus and Atlas and finally Ares, who still didn't look convinced. She grinned at him.

"Be truthful," she said, pinching his chin. "You do like Cole. I know you do."

Reluctantly, Ares nodded. "I do," he said. "He will make you a fine husband. But you are too good for him, Cori. He does not deserve you."

She laughed. "Spoken like a true brother," she said. Then, she turned excitedly to her father. "Papa, Cole is going to secure a room in town for me so I am not sleeping in the wagon bed. He thought it would be more comfortable for me. I… I thought I would take Gaia with me so we can both sleep in a warm bed for tonight. May we?"

The last part was totally a lie, but she added her sister into the mix so her father might more readily agree. It wasn't as if she were going to sneak off into town with the man who would soon be her husband if Gaia was along as a chaperone.

As she hoped, Alastor nodded.

"I do not see why you cannot," he said. "Which tavern?"

She shook her head. "I do not know," she said. "But I will send word. And I will be back with the army well before dawn."

"See that you are," he said. "We will depart well before sunrise for Berwick, although I'm fairly certain they know of our approach. Any army worth their weight in gold would have scouts combing the area, so I think it is safe to say that we will be met. That being said, your instructions will be to go with the other surgeons and provisions wagons and remain far to the rear of the battle."

Corisande nodded. "I know," she said. "I have been here before. But tomorrow… all of you will be very careful, won't you? You are my family and I love you. I do not want anything to happen to any of you."

She was looking to her brothers as she spoke, seasoned knights, scarred and filled with the experience of dozens of battles. But it only took one to be fatal and they all knew it.

Especially Corisande. As thrilled as she was about Cole, it was such a sweet moment on the precipice of something brutal and deadly. Her brothers had seen battle, but so had she and she knew how fragile life was. The human body did not react well to being violated by swords and spears.

She didn't want to lose a beloved brother to something so tragic.

"You needn't worry," Ares said, giving her a weak smile. "We have been through this before. It is the Scots you should worry over."

"I do not care about the Scots. I care about you."

Ares went to her, kissing her on the cheek before fixing her in the eyes. "And I worry about *you*," he said. "And Cole. My eyes will be on him from now on. If he makes a misstep, he will have to answer to me."

The focus of the conversation shifted back to Cole and Corisande, giving her brother a wry expression.

"Do not be nasty to him," she said. "He has done nothing to deserve it. You were rude to him a few moments ago and that was not necessary."

Ares thrust his chin up defiantly at her and turned away as Anteaus took his place. He looked at his sister closely. In fact, she was two years than he was, her having seen twenty years and three and him having seen twenty years and one. But he didn't feel like simply a brother at the moment.

He felt like a protective one.

"I know the de Longley family," he said quietly. "I like them; they are good people. I do not want to see them hurt by Cole, nor do I want to see you hurt by him."

"I know, Tay."

"You must make sure he makes it clear about Audrie. There must not be any hard feelings."

Corisande nodded patiently, patting him on the cheek. "I know, my darling," she said. "I promise he will make it right. He is a man of honor and he will make it clear to them. Everything will be well; you'll see."

Anteaus didn't seem too sure about that but, to his credit, he didn't say anything further. As he stepped away, Atlas came to stand in front of her.

The rather emotionless, apathetic de Bourne brother was looking at her appraisingly. Corisande lifted her eyebrows expectantly.

"Well?" she said. "Did you have something to say to me?"

Atlas shrugged. "Cole is passable," he said. "He'll do."

Corisande began to laugh. "God's Bones," she said sarcastically. "That is high praise coming from you, Atlas. What glowing words of adulation."

Atlas fought off a grin as he went to find his cup of wine. With all of the brothers having spoken their minds, Corisande turned to her father.

"May I go now?" she asked. "I want to make sure everything is ready for tomorrow before I go to the tavern."

Alastor waved her off. "Go," he said. "And, Cori?"

"Aye, Papa?"

"Tomorrow, you will force Gaia to help you when the battle begins," he said. "Do not let her shirk her duties. Tending the wounded will do wonders for her character."

Corisande nodded, wondering if what he said was true. She wasn't entirely sure Gaia had any character but, at the moment, her sister was the last thing she wanted to think of. She wanted to think about Cole and the evening to come.

She'd have to deal with Gaia soon enough.

"I will try," she said, turning for the tent opening. "And I will see all of you on the morrow."

"Wait," Ares said. "I will escort you."

Corisande let her eldest brother take her by the arm and lead her out of the tent. They turned in the direction of the surgeon's wagon, across the muddy meadow that she'd traversed with Cole. She had a feeling Ares had more to say about the situation with Cole, out of earshot of his father and brothers, so she eyed the man as the crossed the moonlit grass.

"Well?" she said softly. "What is it?"

Ares grunted at his perceptive sister. There wasn't much he could keep from her, one way or the other.

"Are you sure this is what you want, Cori?" he asked. "With Cole, I mean. He is a de Velt and there are those who will always look at that family with distain and fear."

Corisande looked up at him. "Do you?"

Ares shook his head. "Nay," he said. "I understand Jax de Velt. I understand why he did what he did and I do not judge him for it. I've no intention of holding one man to another's sensibilities, but not everyone thinks the way I do. Be aware that bearing the name de Velt may cause some… obstacles."

Corisande could sense that he was genuinely trying to be helpful. "Not that the name de Bourne and being descended from the Bloodaxe haven't been obstacles enough, eh?" she said, giving him a smirk. "I appreciate your concern, Ares, you know I do. I respect your opinion in all things. But Cole is a decent and honorable man, and I am very fortunate that he wishes to marry me. I believe we will have a good life together, no matter what his name may mean to some people."

Ares could see that she wouldn't be discouraged. Not that he expected she would be, but he had to make sure she understood. Therefore, he simply smiled at her.

"I hope so," he said. "And if you thought I was rude to Cole, I will apologize to him. But until you two are legal wed, it is my duty, as your beloved older brother, to ensure you are kept safe from an amorous suitor."

She laughed softly. "So you do not think I can smack him on the nose if he becomes too bold?"

"I would hope you would kick him somewhere else instead."

Her laughter grew. "He is rather big," she said. "I might have to kick terribly hard and I do not want to ruin our chances of having children."

Ares rolled his eyes. "You should not speak on such things, you sassy wench," he said. "God's Bones, you are unrestrained."

She sneered at him. "*You* started it."

"I did."

He started to laugh because she was. They were just passing by some de Lohr tents when a figure appeared, walking in their direction. Peter de Lohr came into view, smiling at the pair beneath the moonlight, but his gaze eventually moved to Corisande.

"I thought I heard chatter back here," he said. "Good eve to you, my lady."

Corisande looked up at the blond, handsome young knight with the bright blue eyes. "And to you, my lord," she said. "I am sorry if our conversation disturbed you."

He shook his head. "It did not," he said. "But confidentially, I am bored to tears sitting with my father and uncle."

"Then go entertain yourself elsewhere," Ares said. "You are bright and inventive, de Lohr. Think of something."

Peter sighed sadly. "Alas, they will not let me out of their sight," he said. "All they want to speak on are battle stories I have heard a thousand times. They are old men and have no idea how to have a good time."

"Just what good time did you have in mind?"

Neither Corisande nor Ares had asked the question. It came from Cole as he suddenly appeared from behind a de Bourne tent. He headed towards them, like a panther stalking prey. Only he wasn't stalking Corisande or Ares, but the rather oblivious Peter.

The man had no idea just how close he was to a de Velt beating.

"Greetings, Cole," Corisande said. "Ares was escorting me back to the cooking area."

Cole smiled faintly at her, but his attention swiftly turned to Peter, who had no idea why Cole was looking at him as if he wanted to throttle him.

"Good eve, Cole," he said, puzzled. "I was just telling Lady Corisande that sitting with my father and uncle has me bored to tears. I was going to hang myself simply for something to do."

"Nay," Cole rumbled, taking a step towards him. "Let *me* hang you."

"Peter," Ares said as he let go of Corisande and put himself between Cole and Peter. "I shall take pity on your boredom. My brothers and I were about to start a game of chance, so you can join us. Bring the de Lohr millions with you. I want your money and I want it tonight."

He began to drag Peter away, who literally had no idea why he was being manhandled or why Cole looked as if he wanted to kill him until Ares explained the situation to him later, for his own safety. As Cole stood there and watched him go, he felt a gentle hand on his arm.

"He was perfectly polite," she said, sensing why Cole was up in arms. "You truly have nothing to worry about."

Cole still wouldn't look at her, watching Ares and Peter disappear into the de Bourne tent. "You are correct – I do not," he said, turning to face her. "But *he* does. I must have a talk with Peter to ensure he does not enter another man's territory."

Corisande fought off a grin. "Am I your territory?"

He lifted an eyebrow. "If he takes another step in your direction, he is going to find out the hard way."

She couldn't hold back the laughter anymore. Wrapping her hands around his big forearm, she began to pull him towards the surgeon's wagon.

"You have nothing to worry about," she assured him again before changing the subject. "My father wanted to tell me that he will give permission for our marriage provided you settle the situation with Audrie de Longley. We happen to have my brothers' approvals as well. Therefore, we are practically betrothed."

As she had hoped, her diversion worked. Cole looked down his nose at her, a smile playing on his lips. "Then this is already the best day of my life."

"Truly?"

"Truly."

She smiled up at him before laying her cheek against his arm affectionately. "Mine, too," she said. "My father also says that I can sleep in town tonight. But I told him a little lie."

"What lie?"

"That I was going to bring Gaia with me," she said. "Let me be clear – I am *not* going to bring her. But I told him that so he would not think I was sleeping alone."

Cole almost said what he was thinking, but he refrained. *You will not be sleeping alone.* But he didn't mean it in the lewd sense, that he'd only rented a room for her simply to take advantage of her. He didn't mean that at all. But he wasn't going to leave her alone in a town surrounded by over seven thousand men. He intended to stay with her and watch her sleep simply to make sure she was safe.

Truth be told, it was the night before battle.

He wanted to spend what might be his last remaining moments with her.

"I see," he said after a moment. "Then collect your bag, or whatever you wish to bring, and make your excuses to your sister. While the men are eating boiled pig, you shall dine on the finest the tavern has to offer and sleep in the most comfortable bed I could procure. My future wife shall have only the best."

She smiled at his determination to take great care of her. In truth, she liked it very much. "There's one more thing," she said.

"What?"

"I've not even met your father yet and I have been on a battle march with him for two days."

He chuckled, low in his throat. "Not to worry," he said. "Who do you think I have invited to sup with us?"

The thought of meeting Jax de Velt was thrilling. A little intimidating, but thrilling. Corisande gripped his hand, her eyes alight with the possibility.

"Wait here," she said. "Let me grab my satchel. If Gaia happens to see me, I do not want her to see us together. She might become suspicious."

"I'll wait."

Flashing him a smile, she scurried off across the dark meadow, heading for the surgeon's wagon in the distance, and Cole watched her like there was nothing else on earth worth watching. Wholeheartedly, with his entire being.

She consumed him.

As he'd told her, it was already the best day of his life.

A life that he prayed was only going to get better.

CHAPTER SIXTEEN

THE NORTHWOOD CASTLE banners were flying high as they joined William Marshal's encampment. The dark green banners with the black, clawed serpent announcing the Earl of Teviot made its way into camp, but only to the edge. The soldiers guarding the camp perimeters had Teviot's army settle at the edge of camp because, logistically, that was the easiest thing to do.

Teviot's men began to set up their base.

Directly behind them came the red and black de Velt army from Pelinom, led by Atreus and Julian, who had escorted his mother and sisters to Alnwick Castle and then made it back in time to join up with his father's army. Pelinom's army was positioned next to Northwood's, and Jax joined his men as their encampment was established.

An encampment that was attracting some attention.

Truth be told, all of the armies under the command of William Marshal knew what de Velt's army had done to Fountainhall Castle, so everyone was eager to catch a glimpse of the legendary army that put their enemies on poles. Most agreed that they had never been so glad to be allied with someone and especially Jax de Velt.

Jax was due to meet up with Cole at the only tavern in town, called The Falcon and the Flower, but he wanted to check in with his men and have Julian and Atreus join him. Both knights were in the process of making sure the men were settling down for the night, but to Jax, Julian looked particularly exhausted. He came up behind his son, eighteen months younger than Cole, and put his arms around him to give him a hug.

Julian grinned.

"Greetings, Papa," he said, waiting for Jax to step back before he lifted an enormous sledgehammer and drove a stake halfway into the earth. "Where is Cole?"

"Over in the de Bourne camp," he said. "He is going to join us in town for a meal, so let someone else do that and come with me."

Julian looked at his father as he leaned on the hammer. "It will take them twice as long," he said. "I am the only man in northern England who can drive these stakes into the ground in a reasonable amount of time. Do you not know that about me?"

Jax chuckled. While Cole was enormous and powerful, both in height and breadth, Julian was shorter but had the strength of Samson. As his brothers would tease him, even his muscles had muscles. He was a physical specimen of perfection, a knight of the highest order who had worked hard for that physical perfection, and he was obedient to a fault. His resemblance to his father was uncanny, feature for feature, but he was a fair, much like Cole. They both had dark blond hair, only Julian shaved the sides of his head to velvety numbs while leaving the top a little longer. He preferred it that way.

But the eyes…

That was where Julian stood out. He had the two-colored eyes that all of the males in his family had, and almost the exact same splash pattern that his father had, only instead of having a muddy-brown left eye and a half-brown right eye, the brown color was pale, very nearly the color of a topaz. That bright green burst was still very prevalent in his right eye, so big that it nearly covered the entire eye. Looking at the man, a first glimpse would make it seem as if he had one topaz-colored eye and one green eye.

It was an interesting look on an uncommonly handsome young knight who was, unfortunately, quite self-conscious about it. For that very reason, Julian had always had difficulty looking men in the eyes. Not because he was shifty or ill-mannered, but simply because he knew how he looked.

Unthoughtful men and women had commented on it enough times.

And Jax knew it, too.

"All I know is that you are a pain in my arse and a light in my heart," he said after a moment. "Finish what you are doing, then, and seek me when you are done. I am going to find Teviot and pay my respects."

As Julian waved him off and began swinging the sledge-hammer again, Jax headed over to the Earl of Teviot's encampment. It had been a while since he'd seen his old friend and ally, and as he wandered into camp, he was recognized by Teviot's knight, John Winebald. A tall man with a premature crown of gray hair, he dropped what he was doing to escort Jax to the earl's tent and ushered him inside.

Adam de Longley, the third Earl of Teviot, was a handsome man with dreamy blue eyes. His hair, quite red in his youth, was now streaked with gray. He was sitting at a table with his son, John, but the moment he saw Jax enter, he bolted to his feet and rushed to the man, embracing him as one would a brother.

"Jax," he said happily. "My dear friend, how long has it been?"

Jax smiled at the man he genuinely liked. "At least six months," he said. "It has been a while."

"A while, indeed," Adam scoffed. "Too long. I was hoping we would see you when your army came to Northwood to join us, but they said you were with William Marshal."

Jax nodded. "I was," he said. "There is much happening, Adam. We'll gather with the other commanders before sunrise and go over the situation."

Adam's smile faded somewhat. "I assumed as much," he said. "I was not told what the trouble was, only that we were needed at Berwick. I committed my men without question, you know that. I assume it is with the Scots."

Jax lifted an ironic eyebrow. "When it is *not* with the Scots this far north?"

"Good point."

There was a moment of wry humor between them before Adam led Jax into the tent, towards the table, where his son, John, stood up to greet him.

"My lord," John said. "It is an honor to see you again."

Jax looked at the short, rather round knight who was a fierce fighter and a just commander. "And you," he said. "I did not mean to interrupt your sup. Please continue. I simply wanted to pay my respects."

"You'll stay," Adam said decisively. "We were just finishing. John has duties to attend to, anyway."

He was all but throwing his son out of the tent, but John obeyed his father like a good lad. He moved away from the table, excusing himself, as Adam demanded Jax sit and join him in some wine. From Tuscany, he said, pouring some for Jax as the man sat down. Sitting opposite him, he collected his own cup and lifted it to Jax.

"To our friendship," he said. "And our alliance. Both are very valuable to me."

Jax lifted his cup before drinking deeply of the rich, red wine. He smacked his lips. "Excellent," he said. "But, then again, everything you have is excellent. You are a man of taste."

Adam flashed his big, if not slightly yellowed, teeth. "Everything I am came from my father, Alexander," he said. "You never knew him, did you?"

Jax shook his head. "Nay," he said. "But I would have many years ago had I laid siege to Northwood like I planned. Fortunately for your father, I was stopped at White Crag and then I married my wife, who made me promise not to continue my dreams of conquest. Alas, Northwood was spared."

Adam chuckled. "Thank God," he said, his smile fading. "I was very young at the time, when you were active on the borders, shall we say. I am glad you gave it up. I like you much better as an ally than as an enemy."

Jax grinned, drinking from his cup. The wine was quite tasty. "I would not worry about our association changing anytime soon," he said. "I, too, like you better as an ally."

Adam's gaze lingered on him a moment before sitting back in his chair. "That is good," he said. "And I hope it holds true for always because there is a reason why I wanted to see you so badly, Jax. There is something I must tell you."

"What is it?"

Adam scratched his head. "It is difficult to know where to start," he said. "I have two children, John and Audrie, and I am proud of both of them. But women… Jax, you have three daughters. Do you understand them? The way they think?"

Jax snorted. "God, no," he said. "I wish I did. It would make my life much easier. Allaston was the obedient one, a good girl. I suppose I never had to worry about her, but Effie and Addie can drive a man to drink. My wife tells me to be patient with them, but there are times I want to run from my home screaming and tearing my hair out."

Adam laughed softly. "I understand completely," he said. "Dealing with Audie sometimes has me contemplating throwing myself from the battlements. But the truth is that I would do anything for her, to ensure her happiness. And I know you would do the same for your daughters."

"Unfortunate, but true," Jax said. "We only want to see them happy."

Adam drew in a deep, contemplative breath. "And that is what I must speak to you about," he said. "Audie wants to marry."

"I know. To Cole."

Adam shook his head. "Nay, *not* to Cole," he said. "To be honest, she has hardly seen Cole over the past couple of years and when he did visit, it was only for a day and then he was gone again. You know what they say, Jax – out of sight, out of mind. Audie has found love with the Earl of Sunderland's son, Ren. They wish to marry but I told them I had to speak to you first, to make sure there would be no hard feelings if Audie did not marry Cole."

Jax didn't seem overly upset by it. "If she has found love elsewhere, they would only both be miserable if we forced them to wed, and I do not wish to see Cole miserable," he said. "He has had enough misery losing Mary and Lucy. He is fond of Audie, but if we are being honest, I never believed he was in love with her. Fond, aye. Love, no."

Adam seemed very relieved. "Then you do not think this will upset him?"

"He is not an emotional man, Adam. He will wish her well, of course, but I do not think he will be heartbroken."

"Then you will speak to him?"

"I will. Do not be troubled."

Adam puffed out his cheeks and wiped a hand over his face. "Thank you, Jax," he said. "I have been anxious for this moment. You have eased my mind considerably. I very much wish for our families to be joined in marriage, but not with Cole and Audie. One of your daughters does not wish to marry John, do they?"

Jax grinned as Adam laughed. "Allie and Effie are spoken for," he said. "Addie is… well, she is young. Mayhap too young for John. Why? Has he shown any interest in my daughters?"

"Nay," Adam said. "But I thought I'd ask. There's a young woman he has shown some interest in over in Carlisle. Helena is her name, the daughter of a rich merchant, but John is to inherit my titles and lands, so I was hoping for a better match than that."

"He is getting older, Adam. Mayhap you'd better let him settle for the merchant's daughter."

"Mayhap."

They sat a moment in silence, downing the rest of their wine as Jax thought on how he would break the news to Cole that Audrie de Longley was to marry another. That reminded him that he was to meet his son at the tavern in town, so he finished his wine and stood up.

"I am sorry to cut this short, but I have an appointment to keep," he said. "Thank you for the wine and the conversation. We should not let so much time pass between visits."

Adam stood up. "It is my fault," he said. "I will make more of an effort to visit you and your lovely wife. I know my own wife would like that. She thinks highly of Kellington."

Jax smiled gratefully. "As do I," he said. "I will see you on the morrow."

"We'll teach the Scots a thing or two, won't we?"

"Indeed, we will."

Quitting the tent, Jax headed out into the night, in the direction of the gently glowing town in the distance.

"You were very thoughtful to do this," Corisande said as she stood in the door of her newly rented room. "I almost feel guilty that I left Gaia back in the encampment. *Almost.*"

Cole was standing in the doorway, too, grinning as the tavernkeeper's wife finished with the last details of the room, making sure the fire was banked and the bed had enough warm covers on it. She looked anxiously at Corisande.

"Will ye be wanting a bath?" she asked.

Corisande hesitated, not wanting to sound demanding, but Cole spoke up for her.

"Bring her one," he said. "Quickly, now."

Before Corisande could stop the woman, she fled the chamber and left Corisande standing there in uncertainty.

"You did not have to do that," she said. "I do not require a bath. Truly, Cole, the bed is quite enough."

He leaned against the doorjamb, a smile playing on his lips. "For what you are about to face for the next few days, let me provide what comfort I can for you," he said. "Please. I want to."

Corisande set her satchel on the bed. "You are very thoughtful," she said. "But I have told you that I have faced battle before, Cole. I know what is coming. I am under no illusions that it will be pleasant."

He simply nodded his head, averting his gaze because he didn't want to say what he'd already said to her, too many times. In truth, he wasn't entirely sure how he was going to fight a battle and think only of his own safety when he knew she was somewhere nearby, dealing with the results of that horror. Men who had been maimed and punctured would be coming under her care, her sweet and wonderful care, and that was so much to ask of a woman. Any woman, much less "his" woman.

But there was no use butting heads with her. He didn't want their last few hours together to be those of conflict.

"Shall I wait for you in the common room while you wash?" he asked.

Corisande looked at him, seeing that he wouldn't look at her. He was looking at his feet. He sounded subdued, an unusual mood for him, and she knew it was because they'd ventured onto the subject of battle again. It was the only thing that dampened the man's emotions when it came to her. She was about to say something to him, but the tavernkeeper's wife rushed in with a copper pot and a stool. She was followed by two serving women lugging buckets of steaming water. Corisande stood back as the woman set the copper pot next to the hearth and put the stool in it as the serving women dumped the water into it.

"I'm sorry that I can't offer ye a proper bath," the woman said as the water splashed in. "All we have is the smaller bath that ye sit in."

Corisande smiled. "That is perfectly fine," she said. "Thank you for bringing it."

The woman nodded nervously, eyeing Cole as she shooed the serving women out of the chamber. Water dripped from their spent buckets as they fled, leaving a drippy path behind them. Cole continued to stand in the doorway, still looking at his feet, and Corisande put her hands on her hips.

"Well?" she said.

He looked up at her. "Well *what*?"

"Are you going to let me wash with the door open?"

He looked around as if to realize what she was saying before pushing himself off the doorjamb.

"I will leave you to your bath," he said. "I do not mean to

rush you, but my father will soon be joining us."

Without a word, Corisande went to him, pulled him into the chamber, and shut the door. She then directed him over to a table next to the hearth, pushing him down into a chair.

"Sit," she said. "You can keep me company while I bathe."

He frowned. "I will do no such thing," he said indignantly, standing up. "I did not procure this chamber so that I could participate in clandestine activities with you, so I will see you down in the common room."

He was already moving for the door, but her soft voice stopped him.

"Stay with me," she begged softly. "Cole… I do not wish to be morbid, but you are facing battle tomorrow. If… if something terrible happens, at least give me a memory of tonight to reflect on. At least give me the illusion of something sweet and simple, just for tonight, to keep with me always. I would be… grateful."

He paused with his hand on the door latch before turning to look at her. It was against his better judgment because he knew that once he looked at her, he would not be able to leave. And he needed to leave.

He lifted his eyebrows.

"If your brothers catch me here while you are bathing, I will have worse things than a battle to worry about," he said sternly. "Four seasoned knights doing battle against each other is like nothing you've ever seen, Cori. They will try to kill me and I will have to defend myself."

"They will *not* try to kill you."

"I will be forced to seriously disable all of them and we need them for tomorrow."

"Then go," she said, turning her back on him and going to the corner of the room where a privacy screen was propped against the wall. It was worn, three lightweight panels of wood that had once been painted vibrant colors, and she pulled it away from the wall. "Go down to the common room while I spend this time alone. You must do what you feel is right, of course."

He rolled his eyes. "I do not want to go, but…"

"I *want* you to go. Get out."

He shook his head faintly, trying not to chuckle because she was becoming petulant and dramatic. "Confound it, Woman, stop being so cantankerous," he said, stepping back into the chamber and shutting the door. "There. I am here. I am starting to think this is a plot for your brothers to murder me."

"If there was a plot, you would already be dead," she said crisply.

"Says you."

Corisande made a face at him as she propped up the privacy screen between the tub and the rest of the chamber. It started to fall over but Cole grabbed it swiftly, setting it up properly as she turned for her satchel behind her. She pulled out soap that smelled of lavender, a comb, and a sleeping shift. On the other side of the screen, Cole sat down again, removing his gloves and removing the belt that held his broadsword. Both ended up on the bed as he propped his feet up.

A sigh of relaxation escaped his lips.

"Well?" he said. "What do you wish to speak of now that I am here, in this very dangerous position?"

Corisande fought off a grin as she began to pull off her clothing. The apron and broadcloth dress went up and over the privacy screen, hanging there.

"We can speak of many things," she said. "For example, where shall we live once we are married?"

"Foulburn Castle," he said promptly, looking around to see if there was anything to drink in the chamber. "It is my garrison, a property my father has given to me, as his heir. My father is Baron Blackadder, you know. The king gave him that title. There is a courtesy title that comes with it of Lord Lambden, which is mine, though I do not use it. But if you like, I shall start using it and you can be Lady Lambden."

"Lady Lambden," she said, rolling it over on her tongue. "That sounds very nice. Tell me of Foulburn. Is it large?"

"Large enough," he said, realizing that he could see her silhouette through the screen because the wood was so thin. With the fire behind her, he could see every move. "It sits on a rise overlooking a small river called Foulburn, hence the name. My father keeps about a hundred men there, as a garrison, so the Scots will not try to take it over."

"Odd that you should not remain there since it is your property," she said. "Does your father demand you remain with him at Pelinom?"

"Nay," Cole said. "I have the freedom to choose where I serve."

"So you live and serve at Pelinom and leave your own property vacant?"

He didn't say anything for a moment. He knew she wasn't being nosy, simply asking normal and natural questions of a man she would marry, but the subject of what he actually did with his time had come up. She still didn't know that he served The Marshal, so he thought that now was perhaps the time for total truth.

As Lady de Velt, or Lady Lambden, it would be her right to know.

"There is a reason for that, love," he said, lowering his voice. "What I am to tell you must not leave this room."

He could see her through the screen as she sat on the stool and began to pour water on herself. "Of course, Cole," she said. "I would never repeat what you tell me in confidence."

"Good," he said. "It is important you do not. Ever. If you

do, my very life could be in danger, but as my wife, you have a right to know."

"Know what?"

"I am an agent for William Marshal."

She stopped pouring. He could see her outline as she sat there, pondering what he'd said and trying to make sense of it. "What does that mean, exactly?" she finally asked.

He leaned back against the wall, watching her as she resumed her bath. "Simply put, it means I am a spy," he said. "I have spent two years in the Scottish royal court, as a personal guard of William the Rough. That is why I do not live at Foulburn. I go where The Marshal sends me and on the rare occasion that I am home, I stay at Pelinom."

Slowly, she resumed her bath. She set down the pitcher she'd been pouring water with and picked up the soap. "A spy?" she repeated. "Cole, are you serious? You are a spy for William Marshal?"

"Aye."

She resumed scrubbing her arms. He could smell the scent of the lavender soap as she rubbed it all over her skin. "Oh," she said simply. "This is quite… surprising."

"I know."

"How long have you been a spy?"

"For ten years."

She didn't say anything for a moment and he watched her figure as she rinsed off her arms and torso. "That is a long time," she said. "But ten years of serving The Marshal as a spy? And the past two years in Scotland? You're not even Scottish."

He smirked. "*Chan fheum mi a bhith Albannach airson seirbheis ann an Alba.*"

"What in the world did you just say?"

"I said that I do not need to be Scottish to serve in Scotland," he said. "My Gaelic is perfect. I speak without an English inflection, so no one suspects that I am not Scots. Had it not been for me and Addax and Essien, we would have never known about The Rough's plans to invade England with the help of the Earls of Orkney. This entire army is because of me and a few brave men, doing our duty for our country. My work is important to the safety of England and I do not take it lightly."

"I should think not," she said, washing her torso and legs. "It does seem very important."

"It is."

"And you like this work?"

"I do."

She didn't say anything for a moment, rubbing her hands over her wet legs. "And… and this is something you intend to do forever?" she asked. "Even after we are married? It is very prestigious work, I think."

He moved his chair so he could lean against the wall. "It is only prestigious to those who know about it," he said. "But there are very few, which is why you must never tell anyone. If it becomes known, my service with him would be ended. A spy is no good if everyone knows he is a spy."

She rinsed off her torso and body. When she sat straight, he could see the silhouette of her breasts, full and round and firm, and it was far more of a show than he had been anticipating. The gentlemanly thing to do would have been to tell her she was casting shadows on the thin wood, or leave the room altogether, but he couldn't seem to bring himself to do it. It was the experience of a lifetime as far as he was concerned, and given what was going to happen tomorrow, possibly his last. He wasn't one for morbid thoughts, but Corisande had been right when she had said *at least give me this memory to reflect on.*

He needed that memory, too.

Of her.

But watching her breasts against the screen was arousing him, so he looked away, trying to think of something other than her silky, nude form.

"I would never tell anyone, I swear it," she said, breaking into his thoughts. "I think what you are doing is a fine and honorable thing. You are protecting all of us from those who would see us come to harm. But you did not answer me."

"Answer what?"

"Will you continue serving The Marshal after we are married?"

He paused a moment before answering. "Serving the man as I do, it is well and good because I have no dependents," he said. "Spying is not for married men. Take my mission to Scotland, in fact – I was there for two years, only coming home on rare occasions. I do not think I could be away from you for two years, Cori. I do not think I could be away from you at all."

"I do not think I could be, either," she admitted. "What you do is very dangerous."

"No more dangerous than being in an unmarried lady's chamber while she is bathing and her brothers are nearby."

He heard her giggle. "I shall not be unmarried for long," she said. "When this battle is over, promise me you will speak to your father about Lady Audrie. Tell him that he must tell the Earl of Teviot that you do not wish to marry his daughter."

"Nay, I do not wish to marry her," Cole muttered, watching her stand up in the bath and collect a piece of linen to dry off with. He couldn't look away any longer. "I wish to marry you and I shall, no matter what."

He could see her drying off her legs, her arms. "Cole, this may be a strange thing to say, but it is how I feel," she said. "I am rather old to be married, you know."

"How old are you?"

"Twenty years and three."

"Christ, an old maid," he said. "Is that what you wanted to tell me? That you're old for a bride? I am twenty years and eight, so we are not so far apart in age, you know. I suppose that makes me an old maid, too."

He was snorting, but she found no humor in it. "That is not what I wanted to tell you," she said. "What I wanted to say is this – ever since Auden left me, I truly never thought I would marry anyone else. I did not look for anyone and the suitors who did approach my father were turned away. I simply wasn't interested until I met you, but if you leave me tomorrow, there will be no one else. I have given my whole self to you, Cole. There is nothing left to give to another."

He wasn't smiling anymore. She came out from behind the screen, her hair wet and her body wrapped in the drying linen, and Cole could see that there were tears in her eyes. He stood up and went to her, putting his enormous hands on her shoulders, but the moment he touched her, the tears spilled over and he pulled her into a crushing embrace.

"You have made me the happiest man in the world," he whispered into her wet hair. "The gift of your love is more than I deserve, Cori, but I swear to you that I shall never take it for granted. I will strive every day of my life to show you just how greatly I appreciate it. And you."

She pressed herself against him, damp from her bath, but wanting desperately to be close to him.

"This may be the one and only time I feel such things," she murmured tightly. "I have seen battle, Cole. I know what can happen. I know that by this time tomorrow, I may have lost the man I love because I have seen men die before my eyes. I know how precious life is and I know how precious love is. Love me, Cole. Love me as if tomorrow will never come."

His face was pressed into the top of her head. "I will always love you," he whispered. "You need not even ask."

Sniffling, she stood back and looked up at him. She was looking him in the eyes when she let the towel go and it fell in a pile at her feet, leaving her nude and soft and clean. Reaching out, she grabbed his hands and pressed them to her breasts.

"This way, Cole," she whispered. "Love me this way."

Cole's control left him. Her soft breasts against the palms of his heated hands undid him. He didn't think about her brothers or father, or his father, or anyone else. He didn't think about the rightness or wrongness of it.

All he thought of was Corisande.

With a groan, he mouth slanted over her hers, licking and stroking her until she was gasping for air. His hands on her breasts fondled them, pinching the nipples until they were hard pellets. Corisande's gasps were muted against his fevered lips, moaning softly into the still night air as his mouth moved hungrily over her breasts and he took possession of a taut nipple. He suckled her hard, from one breast to the other, and Corisande's hands were in his long hair, tugging. The harder she pulled, the more he liked it.

In a flash, he lifted her up and lay her upon the bed, carefully setting her down to avoid his gloves and broadsword. He removed the items and tossed them to the floor. Unfortunately, he was still in full protection, so he fell to his knees beside the bed, his mouth on her breasts and belly as he feverishly worked his way out of his tunics and protection. Pieces were coming off, being flung across the room or onto the floor in the heat of passion. He tossed his de Velt tunic partially into the hearth, singeing the wool before he smelled the burned fabric and took the time to yank it out of the flames.

When he was finished batting the flames out, he looked at Corisande sheepishly and she started to laugh. He grinned, too, but the momentary humor gave him time to yank off his boots and his breeches. Everything came off, his body taut and aroused and powerful, and he came down on top of her as she lay upon the mattress.

His kisses were sweet and tender now, his hands roaming her soft body. He returned to her breasts, caressing them, because they had aroused him through the privacy screen. Corisande writhed beneath him, her legs instinctively parting to make way for his substantial weight, and as she did so, Cole moved to touch the unfurling flower between her legs.

He simply couldn't help himself.

Love me as if tomorrow will never come.

He fully intended to.

Corisande gasped with surprise when his fingers delicately touched the thick outer lips, matted with a fine fluff of dark hair. He was gently tugging on a nipple as he fondled her with the utmost gentleness, allowing her to become accustomed to his touch. Corisande groaned with pleasure as she gradually became accustomed to his careful fingers. Only when her body loosened beneath his restrained touch did he attempt to part her pink, quivering petals.

She was unbelievably hot and wet. He slipped a finger into her sheath, so incredibly tight that he very nearly released himself at that moment. But he fought his reaction, nibbling on her neck and her ear, whispering words of beauty and adoration. Corisande's reaction was to spread her legs a little wider, bending her knees, willing to submit to anything he wanted to do to her. Cole could feel her tight passage contracting about his slick finger, pulling at him.

Settling between her legs, he rubbed his manhood against her Venus mound, stroking the outer lips as he had done with his fingers. She was glistening with wet heat, spilling down onto the linens, and he continued to rub himself against her as she watched his face without fear.

Their eyes met.

"Are you certain this is what you want?" he whispered. "I can stop at this moment and there is no harm done."

Her answer was to pull him down to her, her mouth latching on to his, and Cole's restraint was gone.

He tried to move slowly. God knows, he did, but he found himself fighting against his natural instinct to drive into her like a rutting bull. He worked carefully, gaining headway slowly and feeling her tightness draw him in. She was so slick that it would have been easy to simply thrust into her and be done with her maidenhood quickly, but he held back. She was being bold, willing to know him on a deep and intimate level, but he wanted it to be a good experience for her.

He wanted her to love it as much as he was.

Corisande was calm beneath him, her hands on his enormous biceps for support as he forged ahead into virgin territory. Beneath her hands, she could feel his heated body trembling as he struggled to maintain control, but that didn't last.

His desire overwhelmed him.

Drawing her knees up, he thrust into her tender body and Corisande gasped loudly with the sting of possession. Cole was seated to the hilt and he pulled her into an embrace as he began to move gently within her. Slowly at first, relishing the feel of his erection embedded within her tender body as Corisande clutched him, wrapping her legs about his hips to hold him fast.

Cole's pace increased, quickening his thrusts into her. His strokes were measured and long; enjoying the moment, the closeness to her, experiencing an outlet for the emotions he was feeling for her. Against him, Corisande's gasps of passion told him that she was beginning to experience the same pleasure that had so easily consumed them both.

It was passion on an entirely new plane.

But it was passion that was building to a climax faster than

Cole had wanted. He had hoped to draw out their experience, to savor every move, every taste, but his body had other ideas. He was so highly aroused that his climax came like a tidal wave. It washed over him and he growled low in his throat as he spilled himself deep into her body, feeling every last spasm with the greatest of pleasure. But his release never stopped his movement; he continued to stroke in and out of her even after he spent himself, wanting Corisande to experience the same delirium that he was.

He shifted his weight, gazing down at her flushed face as he continued to roll his pelvis against hers. Her eyes were closed, her head thrown back, and he found his gaze drawn to her magnificent breasts as they bounced every time their bodies came together. One hand trailed down her neck, encircling a breast before moving towards the junction where their bodies were joined.

Seeking her hard little nub, he stroked her a few times before Corisande's eyes flew open with surprise. In the next moment, she bit off a loud shriek against his shoulder, muffled against his heated flesh. The last thing they wanted was to tip anyone off to their activities, so Corisande kept her mouth against his shoulder until the ripples faded and she was reduced to a quivering shell.

"Breathe, love," he whispered. "Just breathe."

Corisande pulled away from his shoulder, gasping for air. "What… what *was* that?"

He buried his face in her neck, chuckling. "*That* is why men and women risk everything to do what we have just done," he said. "Are you well? I did not hurt you, did I?"

Corisande swallowed hard as she caught her breath. "Not at all," she said, looking at him as he loomed over her. "That was… miraculous."

He smiled tenderly. "Are you sure you are well?"

"I am," she said. "I promise, I am. Oh, Cole… swear to me that it will always be like this. That this moment will come again."

He brushed a bit of stray hair off her forehead as he looked at her. "If it is within my power, it will always be like this," he murmured. "Forever and ever, I swear it."

She smiled faintly, gazing into his unique eyes. "Thank you."

"My pleasure, my lady."

He said it seductively and she realized that he didn't understand her. "I did not mean for that," she said. "I meant for coming to The Keld in the first place. For seeing something in me that I have never seen in myself."

"What's that?"

She lifted her slender shoulders. "Love, I suppose," she said. "You saw a woman you would marry. You saw love. No matter what happens tomorrow, I am yours until the end of time, Cole. There is no one in this world or in any other that could ever take your place in my heart or soul."

He put a massive hand on her face, dwarfing it. "I *will* see you tomorrow at the end of the day," he assured her softly. "I will return to you, Cori. The only thing that can keep us apart is death and I am not even sure that is strong enough to keep me from your side. I will always be with you, no matter what comes."

She reached up and cupped his big face with her two hands, stroking his cheeks with her thumbs. "I am not entirely sure I will have a chance to speak with you tomorrow before you go into battle, so I will speak to you now," she said. "I am so proud of you, Cole. I've never known pride like this. I pray God keeps you safe during the trials you must face in the coming battle, but whatever comes, know that I will be waiting for you in the end."

"Thank you, my queen. That means everything."

"And then we are going to get married!"

He laughed softly. "We are, indeed," he said. "Which reminds me – my father is probably down in the common room, wondering where I am. So as much as I hate to leave you, I must."

She sighed unhappily. "I know," she said. "And I must dress and come with you."

He scowled. "We cannot go into the common room *together*, you silly wench," he said. "We shall both be coming down from the upper floor? Do you have any idea how that will look?"

"Suspicious, I would imagine."

He grunted, kissing her swiftly before pushing himself off the bed and going in search of his clothing.

"Suspicious, indeed," he said. "I would have a hell of a lot of explaining to do, and I do not wish to get into a row with my father the night before a battle. Let me go first and you will give us about a half-hour before coming down yourself. I must tell him about us and I want to do it alone. In fact, I think I will climb out the window and come in through the front door just to be safe."

With a twinkle of mirth in her eyes, Corisande sat up, pulling the coverlet over her chest to protect her modesty as Cole pulled on his breeches. She'd seen men half-dressed before, as patients she had tended in the course of her duties, but this was different. Cole was absolutely magnificent, muscular and powerful. It made her heart thump against her ribs simply to look upon him, to know that he was hers.

Truly hers.

She'd never felt so content or happy in her entire life.

She must have been gazing at him rather dreamily because he kept looking at her as he dressed, pulling on tunics and boots.

"What are you thinking?" he asked.

She shook herself out of her reflections. "I'm thinking how happy I am," she said. "I'm sorry – I should offer to help you. Do you need help?"

He shook his head, able to pull on his mail coat. "Nay," he said. "What I'm wearing now is simple. Tomorrow, however, it will be considerably more complicated."

He may have been armed to the teeth, but he wasn't wearing what he would normally wear on the field of battle as far as protection on his forearms, shoulders, and legs. As he'd said, he'd be carrying much more tomorrow. Corisande swung her legs over the side of the bed, still holding the coverlet up to shield her nakedness.

"Are you really going to jump out the window?" she asked.

In response, he went over to the window and peered out. They were on the side of the tavern, with a yard down below. It wasn't too terribly high and he flung open the shutters wide.

"I am," he said, going back over to the bed and giving her one last kiss. "Hurry and dress, please. Do not delay."

"I won't."

He gave her a wink. "Good lass."

He scooted back over to the window and sat on the sill, slinging his legs over the side. Wrapped up in the coverlet, Corisande stood up and started to come over to the window, but he hissed at her and waved her away.

"Are you mad?" he whispered loudly. "Do you want someone to see you?"

Stopped in her tracks, she shook her head, wide-eyed. Carefully, he lowered himself out of the window until he was dangling and then he let himself fall to the yard below. Throwing caution to the wind, Corisande scooted over to the window, closing the shutters, but not before she peeked out to see Cole brushing off his knees and straightening his tunic.

As he began to head out of the yard, she quickly bolted the shutters, tossed the coverlet on the bed, and began rushing around for her clothing. The moment she lifted her hands, however, she realized that she could smell Cole on her flesh. Sniffing her arms and hands, his scent was everywhere and her heart fluttered wildly.

His sweet, delicious musk.

For a moment, she stood there, nude, looking down at her body and remembering all of the delicious and wicked things he'd done to her. She was an inexperienced virgin, or at least she had been only a short while ago, but that didn't stop lustful thoughts from claiming her as she thought of Cole's body upon hers. Timidly, she touched her breasts, the nipples he'd seemed so fond of, and a jolt ran through her when she touched herself.

A jolt that ran right down through her loins.

Hesitantly, she put a hand down there, feeling the fluff of curls. It was also damp and sticky from their lovemaking. As much as she hated to wash away his scent, she also didn't want to smell like a man because she didn't want anyone to catch wind of a scent that did not belong to her. Therefore, she turned towards the cool bath water and quickly washed up.

She had a father to meet and she didn't want to meet the man smelling of his son.

A son she loved with all her heart.

CHAPTER SEVENTEEN

"I WAS WONDERING where you were," Jax said as Cole came towards the table he had commandeered in the crowded common room of the tavern. "I hope you do not mind that I've brought Julian. It is rare when I have two of my sons together, especially on a night before the battle."

Cole eyed his younger brother as he sat at the table. He loved Julian, but he wasn't happy to see the man. He had wanted to see his father alone.

"Nay, I do not mind that he is here," he said, though he didn't sound sincere. "But I have something I must speak with you about, Papa. I was hoping to do it in private."

Jax's smile faded. "That's a coincidence," he said. "I have something to tell you, too. Julian will hear of it, eventually, so I suppose it does not matter if he is here."

Julian had a big cup of warmed wine, glancing between his father and brother, who were looking at him. His features twisted with frustration. "I will not speak," he said. "I will not repeat anything I hear, I swear it. I think you know me better than that."

It was true. Julian was most trustworthy. Cole finally shrugged and looked at his father. "What did you wish to tell me?"

Jax cleared his throat softly. "Do you not wish for wine and food first?"

"Nay," he said. "Why? Is it terrible?"

Jax shrugged. "I suppose it will be disappointing, but it is not the end of the world."

"*What* is it?"

Jax looked at him. "I saw Teviot tonight," he said. "He spoke to me of Audrie."

Cole put a hand up quickly. "Stop right there," he said, interrupting his father. "That is exactly what I wanted to speak to you about."

"What about her?"

"I do not want to marry her, Papa."

Jax stared at him a moment before sitting back in his chair. "Interesting," he said. "Because she does not wish to marry you, either."

Cole's eyes widened. "She doesn't?" he gasped. "Why?"

"She's evidently fallen in love with a son of Sunderland," Jax said. "She wishes to marry another man and Teviot was very concerned that you would be upset by it."

Cole quickly got over his shock and shook his head emphatically. "I am not upset at all," he said, "because I wish to marry another woman."

"*You?*" Julian piped up. "Get *married*?"

Jax shushed his younger son. "Seal your lips," he hissed before looking seriously at Cole. "What's this? You truly wish to marry, Cole?"

Cole nodded, a glimmer of mirth in his eyes. "I do," he said. "I wish to marry Lady Corisande de Bourne, Alastor's eldest daughter. I do not quite know where to start with this… one day, I met her and in the next, I was in love with her. She loves me, too, and we wish to be married."

Both Jax and Julian were looking at Cole in shock. Julian's mouth was actually hanging open. He looked at Jax, who was having difficulty processing everything – his career-oriented, emotional eldest son wanted to *marry*?

He could hardly believe it.

"But… when?" he finally said. "How? Is *that* why you went back to Castle Keld after I sent you to Alnwick?"

Cole nodded. "I went back to see her," he said. "I know this all sounds very strange coming from me, but I assure you, it is the truth. I have Alastor's permission, but I needed to settle the situation with Audrie first. But now it looks as if there is nothing to settle. Corisande is a wonderful woman, Papa. I know you will love her as I do."

Across the table, Julian grinned and held out a hand to his brother. "Congratulations, Cole," he said, grasping his arm and giving him a shake. "I could not be more pleased for you, truly. Is she beautiful with big breasts?"

Jax side-eyed his lewd son. "You told us you were going to keep silent, Julian," he said. "Shut your lips or leave the table. Your brother and I are speaking."

Julian picked up his cup and put it to his mouth, contrite. "If you are nasty to me, I shall tell Mother."

"If your threat is a real one, I will find the Northmen tomorrow and sell you to them," Jax said, lifting an eyebrow. "You can spend the rest of your life rowing one of those longships as they throw fishbones at you."

Cole started laughing. "Leave him alone, Papa," he said. "He is a foolish whelp, but he is our foolish whelp. Aye, she is beautiful, Julian. The most beautiful thing you've ever seen."

As Julian looked pleased, Jax seemed to be more contemplative. He was still quite surprised by everything. As the serving wench came and brought more food and drink, his gaze lingered on Cole as the man gulped his wine and took a helping of bread.

"Are you sure about this, lad?" Jax finally asked. "This seems rather sudden."

Cole shoved bread into his mouth. "I met her when we brought Canmore to The Keld," he said. "Papa, she exhibited such courage that day. Canmore took her hostage and she was calm and composed… I suppose that was when I realized I was interested in her. She impressed me greatly and that admiration has only grown. She is also de Bourne's surgeon and I have asked her to join us this evening for the meal."

Jax's brow furrowed. "A surgeon?" he repeated. "A woman surgeon? She's *here*?"

Cole nodded. "She is," he said. But he could see the disapproval in his father's expression. "I know what you are thinking. I, too, am grossly opposed to a woman surgeon, but it was not my right to make her stay behind at The Keld. Alastor is her father and he wished for her to come. Evidently, her mother was also a surgeon. It seems to be a family tradition."

Jax clearly didn't approve. "A woman surgeon," he muttered. "It is reckless and irresponsible to bring a woman to battle."

Cole wasn't sure what more to say about it, but he was saved when the door to the tavern lurched open and Atreus appeared. He came to the table in his usual congenial fashion and hugged Cole before sitting down next to the man. Julian shoved a cup of wine at him, but Cole was concerned now that they had yet another body at the table when he very much wanted the introduction between Corisande and his father to be something personal and intimate. With Atreus and Julian at the table, it was going to be baptism by fire for Corisande into the world of de Velt. Either she would accept the family or she'd run away screaming.

The thought made Cole inwardly chuckle.

More food and drink were brought to the table and the conversation moved to the battle on the morrow. More knights entered the tavern – Christopher and David de Lohr, Alexander, Kress and Achilles, Bric and Dashiell, all of them lumbering into the tavern in a big group. When they saw Jax, they kicked men out of a nearby table and pulled it up to Jax's table, joining in so now there were at least eleven knights at the table, all of them talking over each and calling for food.

Cole saw his opportunity for a nice, private introduction between his father and Corisande fly out the window. The Executioner Knights were now part of the de Velt party. The insults and laughter were coming fast and furious. He loved these men like brothers, but he very much wanted his nice little quiet supper with his father and Corisande to just be the three of them.

But that wasn't going to happen.

Catching his father's attention, he stood up and crooked his finger to the man.

Curious, Jax obliged and followed his son up the stairs to the second floor of the tavern. There were five doors on the landing and Cole went to the one furthest from the stairs and rapped on the door. Jax started to speak but Cole held up a hand, begging him for patience, as the door finally opened.

An exquisite blonde stood in the opening.

"Papa," Cole said, his eyes glimmering with warmth. "This is Lady Corisande. I do not think I want to introduce her to a table full of knights. It might be a little overwhelming for her, but I very much wanted you to meet her. Cori, this is my father, Ajax de Velt."

Corisande appeared a little startled by the surprise introduction, but she quickly dipped into a curtsy. "My lord," she said. "It is an honor to meet you. My father has always spoken most highly of you."

Jax didn't say anything for a moment. His gaze was lingering on Corisande and, after a moment, he reached out to gently take her hand.

"You remind me of my wife when she was your age," he said. "You have that same strong and lovely look about you."

"Thank you, my lord."

"My son tells me that you are a surgeon."

Corisande nodded. "I learned from my mother, who is no longer with us," she said. "I have been my father's surgeon for a few years now."

"And he always brings you on a battle march?"

"The men have a better chance of surviving if I come, my lord. I am not afraid."

Jax just stood there and held her hand, his gaze studying her. "I can see that," he said after a moment. "Cole tells me that he wishes to marry you."

That brought some surprise from Corisande, who looked at Cole before replying. "I… I wish to marry him, too," she said. "My father will give his permission if the situation with Audrie de Longley is settled, my lord. Cole told me about it and as I explained to him, I have no wish to build my happiness on someone else's sorrow. The situation must be resolved before I will marry him."

Jax fought off a grin as he kissed her hand and let it go. "Very noble, my lady. Most women do not care for another woman's feelings when it comes to a husband."

Corisande shrugged. "I am not heartless," she said. "A knight I was fond of left me for another lady years ago, too, and I will not do the same thing to someone else. It is a cruel thing to do."

"And if Lady Audrie insists on marrying Cole?"

Corisande tried not to falter at the mere thought; Jax could see it. She took a deep breath and steeled herself. "I would be the heartbroken one," she said steadily. "But I would understand. She had a claim with him long before he knew me."

Cole looked at his father, distressed that Jax would say such a thing to her when they both knew Audrie was already set to marry another man. But Jax had asked the question for a reason – Corisande's answer would speak volumes of her character.

He wanted to see what kind of woman wanted to marry his son.

"A reasonable attitude," he said after a moment. "But an unnecessary one. Lady Audrie's father, the Earl of Teviot, is in the encampment with his men. He has sought me out this evening to tell me that his daughter wishes to marry another man, something I just told Cole without even knowing he wanted to marry you. But now, I shall tell you, too. Lady Audrie is no longer an obstacle to this union."

Corisande's eyes widened. There was even a little glisten of tears as she looked at Cole, utter joy on her face. "Oh… my lord," she breathed. "That is most welcome news."

Jax could see, as she looked at Cole, how much adoration she had for his son. That glowing expression told him a great deal about this woman his son wanted to marry. As a father, it touched him, for every parent wanted their child to have the love and admiration of a wife or a husband. It looked like Cole was going to be so blessed.

Jax put a hand on Cole's shoulder.

"She is perfect for you," he said. "You have my permission to marry her if she will have you."

A smile spread across Cole's face. "Truly, Papa?"

"Truly," Jax said, looking between the pair. "In fact, I will go tell Alastor that the de Longley obstacle is removed and we may have a wedding as soon as he wishes."

With that, he turned and walked away, heading back down the stairs as Cole swept Corisande into a powerful embrace, one of joy and delight.

The last Jax saw of them as he descended the stairs, they were locked in a passionate kiss.

Jax grinned all the way back to the table.

CHAPTER EIGHTEEN

T HE SCOTS WERE waiting for them.

The battle for Berwick started at sunrise when the enormous English army, flying the standards of several powerful warring houses, approached Berwick from the southwest, over the fields slick with morning dew as a frosty mist hovered over them.

Earl of Pembroke...

Baron Blackadder...

Earl of Hereford and Worcester...

Earl of Teviot...

Descendants of Bloodaxe, Lords of Bernicia...

Earl of Savernake...

Earl of Canterbury...

House of de Winter...

Great warring houses who brought hell and fire with them, unleashed just after dawn as the archers let loose and rained flaming bolts onto the Scots who had set up a defensive perimeter to prevent them from coming close to Berwick.

The bolts flew before the siege engines began to let loose.

Jax and Teviot brought two siege engines each, meaning there were four big catapults to use against the Scots, who had dug trenches. Not deep ones, unfortunately for them, but they'd been given enough notice of an approaching army that they'd been able to give themselves some protection from the coming storm.

Until the siege engines began flinging rocks and boulders at them. The land around Berwick was rocky, so there was no shortage of projectiles to load into the buckets and sling at the Scots. Even a small rock could do damage hitting a man in the skull, so after a morning of bombardment, the Scots were forced to pull back or risk being pummeled to death.

The English moved closer.

"We need to take the bridge," The Marshal said to the commanders around him. "Once we control that, we can control this battle, so we must move forward to secure the bridge."

The men listening in were Christopher, David, Alexander, and Jax. Everyone else was spread out with the armies, including Cole. He was in charge of loading up his father's catapults, which were still doing spectacular damage. Next to The Marshal, Christopher was wrestling with a warhorse who was eager to chomp down on some Scots flesh.

"There is another bridge upriver about a mile to the west," Christopher said. "They call it the Ord Crossing. Our support wagons have been gathered near it, away from the heart of the fighting."

"I know," The Marshal said. "I do not see the Scots using it to counter us at this time but, at some point, we must control that bridge, too."

Christopher nodded his head. "I would say we should control it now," he said. "If this is the beginning of our three-pronged attack, then we must evaluate this situation carefully."

The Marshal looked at him. "What do you mean?"

Christopher gestured to the ridge north of the town. "Let us start with that," he said. "It seems to me that not all of the army is between us and the bridge into Berwick."

The Marshal knew that. He was looking to the north, too, where hills overlooked Berwick, and they could see smoke rising in those hills. Where there was smoke, there was an army.

They were lingering up there, waiting and watching.

"The army before us is *not* all of the men The Rough has to offer," he said, pointing to the hills. "If I know William, he is lying in wait, up there where the smoke is. Therefore, I will keep the Scots at this bridge busy while you take your army and de Velt and cross the other bridge. You are right; we should control it now. You can come around to the rear of the Scots to the north and keep them from reinforcing the ranks in the city."

Christopher was looking around. "I will," he said. "But I will take Teviot and de Bourne with me. You keep de Velt with you and put him on that castle. That is what the man does best. If we want to take Berwick Castle, he is our best chance. Jax, do you have anything to say to that?"

Jax was looking across to the castle, a behemoth structure that was one of the more impenetrable bastions in England and Scotland. He was listening to the conversation between The Marshal and Christopher, but all the while, his mind was working.

"Nay," he said. "But I will take the castle my way."

Everyone looked at him. "What do you mean?" The Marshal asked. "Honestly, Jax, I am afraid to even ask that question. Of course you can do it your way, but do you mean in the same fashion you took Fountainhall?"

Jax simply looked at him, those dual-colored eyes making the hair on the back of The Marshal's neck stand up. Understanding his silent meaning, he put up a hand.

"Jax, I am in full support of whatever you wish to do with the occupants of Berwick but leave the castle intact," he said. "I want it. Can you do this?"

The corner of Jax's mouth twitched. "I can do anything," he said. "But you are taking all of the fun out of it."

Christopher started to chuckle. "Ah, Jax, my good and true friend," he said. "Everyone wants to spoil your good time. I'm so sorry."

Jax's grin broke through as he looked over at the castle again. "Especially the Scots," he said. "And they are going to pay, just like their brethren at Fountainhall did."

The Marshal could see there was no use in holding him back. Jax was the warlord they all feared, brutality personified.

He was going to put that to good use.

"Do your worst, de Velt," he said. "I will get you across the bridge, but you must be prepared to act once I do."

"I will be ready."

As Jax spun his black warhorse around and headed towards his army, The Marshal turned to Christopher.

"God help us all if I do not get him across that bridge in a reasonable amount of time," he muttered. "He may start taking his frustrations out on the rest of us."

Christopher snorted. "Then that is prime incentive to take that bridge," he said. "If we do not want to be the focus of his aggression, then we had better do what we say we are going to do. Now, may I make a suggestion?"

"Please do."

Christopher pointed to the bridge. "Put de Winter and Savernake on driving the Scots across the bridge and away from the town while de Velt attacks the castle," he said. "De Winter and Savernake are your best war machines right now, so use them. Have East Anglia watch your flank and rear. We are close to the border and there could be a flanking maneuver, just as we are about to do."

It was the truth and William knew it. Their plans of splitting the army still held true, as those were their original plans, but now that they had a better look at the topography and the position of the Scots, those plans had to be flexible.

"Very well," he said. "Take Teviot and de Bourne and root them out of those hills. How far behind is Richmond?"

Christopher looked at him. "At least a day," he said. "We received word from Maxton last night. They're moving as quickly as they can, but Richmond is a big army."

William digested that. "When Cai and Maxton arrive, direct them to the mouth of the river," he said. "Tell Cai to put a line of archers with flaming arrows around the mouth and then in the sand to the north. As soon as they see those ships, launch the arrows. Burn those bastards at sea."

"I will tell them," Alexander said. "I am keeping a watch on any armies arriving from the south, so once they are sighted, I will move them towards the river's mouth."

"Excellent," The Marshal said, turning to Alexander. "And everyone else? What does your gut tell you, Sherry? How far behind us are they?"

Alexander sighed faintly. "It is difficult to know," he said. "The messengers I sent out last night have yet to return, so they are not close in any case. The last I heard, Gart and Pembroke were at least a week behind us, so that would put him at possibly five days or more. I would assume everyone else is still the same – Canterbury, de Lara, de Nerra."

That wasn't exactly what William wanted to hear, but that's what he'd known all along. Perhaps he was hoping for Alexander to tell him something different and come up with a miracle. He motioned to the soldier next to him, the man who always carried The Marshal's standards.

"Send for the commanders now," he said. "Bric, Dash, Kress, Achilles, Peter, Alastor and Ares, Addax and Essien… send them to me. Quickly."

The man was gone, yelling to other Marshal soldiers to seek out the Executioner Knights, who were now leading their armies. Spies who worked in small groups, or sometimes alone, were in truth seasoned knights with vast command experience. Like Dashiell and Bric, they commanded massive war machines.

Those war machines were about to get down and dirty.

"THEY'VE NO' TAKEN the Ord Crossing yet," a breathless Scotsman said. "We can use it tae flank their position, yer grace. Their entire north flank is open and that includes the provisions and surgeons tae the rear."

William was on a rise overlooking Berwick on this cold, misty morning. He'd just watched the English destroy the defensive line he'd had set up between the English and Berwick with their siege engines. His eyesight wasn't very good, but he had excellent intelligence. They told him exactly what he needed to know so he could form a larger picture.

"My old friend, William Marshal, has arrived," he muttered, sounding oddly satisfied. "The Scarlet Lion is once again in action for the English. Tell me the other standards ye see."

MacDuff was next to him astride his big, copper-colored steed. "'Tis difficult tae see from here," he said. "I'm told de Lohr has arrived along with de Winter and Savernake. Big and powerful houses, yer grace."

William was smiling, an odd gesture. "The Marshal has brought his most important warlords and if I know William, this is no' the end of it," he said. "There are more on the way. They will take Berwick unless our Northman allies arrive here in the next day or two. Where are they?"

"Sighted near St. Abbs," MacDuff said. "They'll be here by the morning."

"How many?"

"I'm told at least a dozen."

William calmly mulled over the information. "Then we must hold Berwick until they arrive," he said simply. "If we canna flank them or push them back, then we must weaken them."

MacDuff looked at him. "But how?" he asked. "They're too big tae flank, but we must hold the bridges. I've men at the Ord Crossing now, but no' enough if they try tae cross."

"But they havena yet," William pointed out. "The more we talk, the more chance of them trying tae come across that bridge. We need tae cross it first."

"Cross it tae where? Tae attack them?"

William shook his head. "Ye said that provisions wagons are exposed."

MacDuff nodded. "Aye, yer grace."

William looked at him. "Capture them," he said. "We want tae weaken them in a way that willna cost us many men, so capture their provisions. Bring them back across the bridge and hold that bridge until the Northmen arrive. After that…"

MacDuff was catching on. "After that, they'll be busy with the Northmen as well as the Scots," he said. "And we'll hold what's precious tae them."

"Indeed, we will. Go, now."

MacDuff was off, shouting to men as he went. He collected hundreds of them in short order, all of them racing for the bridge known as the Ord Crossing.

The battle for Berwick was about to become more interesting.

"CAN YOU SEE anything?"

Corisande was asking Gaia, who stood on the wagon bed, shielding her eyes from the morning sun as she watched the distant battle. Or, at least she was trying to.

"Nay," she said. "Too many trees and hills. I cannot see anything!"

Now, she was jumping up and down, as if that few inches of height advantage would help her see clearly.

But for Corisande, it was a nerve-wracking waiting game.

Men had already started to trickle in to camp, being tended to by their own surgeons. There were just a few of them, really, men who had tripped and broken an arm, or one man who had been singed by his own flaming arrow. No one from the de Bourne army had come to them for medical care, so Corisande paced around, wringing her hands, wondering what in the world was happening. As far as she knew, the battle had commenced just after sunrise, but they were far enough away that they really couldn't see it.

"Mayhap we are too far away," she said. "How can men find assistance if we are too far to the rear to help them?"

There were a few de Bourne soldiers with them, about twenty of them, men who usually helped Corisande in the case of a battle. They were either too old or too crippled to fight, really only good for helping out those who could.

Their encampment was only half-set up, just a couple of tents to receive the wounded at this point. Because the battle was fluid and they would be presumably moving closer to Berwick, they hadn't set everything up. Like the other surgeon's wagons, they were waiting for the order to move forward, which was why Corisande was so edgy. Since they couldn't even see the battle from where they were, she had no idea what was going on.

Or how Cole was.

That was her trouble, really. Thinking of Cole in the midst of that battle was driving her mad. Her brothers and father were in the midst of it, too, but she was accustomed to that. She was accustomed to them fighting. But Cole was a new element in this battle, an unanticipated concern that she had no control over.

It was a waiting game.

The position of the encampment was in a marshy meadow near the River Tweed. Behind them was an old stone bridge, spanning a narrow point in the river. They could see the bridge and its big, rock arches. It was a bright day and the fields and hills around were shades of green once the morning mist lifted but, in general, the area was heavily forested.

And it all seemed eerily quiet.

As Corisande milled around aimlessly, a rider appeared over the hill, heading in their direction. The men from the other encampments began to shout and everyone took notice. The soldier drew closer and they could see that he was wearing a de Lohr tunic.

He drew his frothing steed to an unsteady halt.

"The armies are on the move," he shouted. "Prepare to move forward!"

Everyone began to scramble, including Corisande. She ordered the men to break down the tents and put the horses back in the harnesses, and the soldiers moved quickly to do her bidding. Other wagons for other armies weren't as broken down as de Bourne was and they were able to move out more swiftly. De Winter was one, followed by Savernake. Those wagons were already on the road, moving towards Berwick.

Corisande didn't want to be the last one in a line of surgeon's and provisions wagons, so she urged the men to hurry. There were six de Bourne provisions wagons and the drivers were quickly hitching up the horses. Their encampment was closest to the river with Teviot positioned next to them. De Velt didn't even seem to have much by way of provisions, so they moved out quickly enough. Teviot and de Lohr, who seemed to be the largest, were moving more slowly, preventing those behind them from moving forward quickly.

And that was to be their undoing.

Corisande didn't even realize what was happening until it was too late. Her men had just finished loading the tents into their wagons and securing the horses when the trees around them suddenly came alive. Men in long *leine* tunics, with their faces smeared with mud and clubs or pikes in their hands, began to pour from the trees. Corisande watched in horror as Gaia was grabbed by a man who leapt onto the wagon bed.

But Gaia wasn't his target. The wagon was. He threw Gaia down onto the bed of the wagon and leapt onto the wagon bench. The old soldier who was already sitting there tried to fight him, but he brutally clubbed the old man and as the man fell off the wagon, Corisande jumped into the bed. The Scotsman was screaming and whistling to the horses and the terrified animals bolted. Corisande clung to the wagon bed as it took off through the trees.

"Gaia!" she screamed. "Jump! Jump out!"

Gaia was hysterical. She was clinging to the back of the wagon bench, refusing to listen, refusing to release it. Corisande couldn't let go of the side of the wagon for fear of being pitched off and she wasn't going to leave her sister, so she begged Gaia to let go and jump, but her sister wouldn't do it. She simply held on and screamed. The Scotsman drove the horses at a frantic pace onto a road which led straight to the old, stone bridge.

Corisande could see it in the distance.

"Gaia!" she cried. "Please listen to me! Jump out!"

Gaia wailed. Corisande dared to let go of the side of the wagon, creeping over to her sister, but being forced to grab on to the young woman when the wagon bumped over the terrible road. No matter how hard Corisande tried, she couldn't force Gaia to release the wagon bench. She was incoherent with terror. Corisande managed to look behind them and she could see several other wagons following them, driven by Scots.

So many English wagons, heading for Scotland.

Corisande had to do something.

The Scotsman driving the wagon was inches from her. Looking around for a weapon, there wasn't anything other than sewing kits and medicament bags. Fortunately, they were strapped securely to the wagon bed for travel, and they contained knives and bone saws. If she could get to them, she could use them as weapons, but the way the wagon was bouncing around made the process of retrieval extremely difficult. She'd have to get over to the bags, retrieve the weapons, and make it back to the bench without the Scotsman seeing her. That would prove impossible.

But she did have a kerchief on her.

Maybe she could strangle the man.

The stone bridge was looming closer. Corisande knew that once they crossed that bridge, it would be very difficult for them to return to England safely. They had to break free while they were still in England. Removing the kerchief from her head, she wound it up, took hold of both ends of it, and tried to stand up.

The Scotsman wasn't paying any attention to her as she managed to get her knees behind him. It was enough fabric to get the kerchief over his head and around his neck, but the moment she tried to do it, the wagon lurched and she ended up falling sideways. The Scotsman, realizing she was trying to attack him in some fashion, kept one hand on the reins and grabbed her by the hair with the other. In one swift move, he slammed her head against the side of the wagon, hard enough to knock her senseless.

One more blow and everything went black.

CHAPTER NINETEEN

Berwick

T HEY MADE IT across the bridge.

Nearing sunset on the first day of the siege on Berwick, the English had managed to make it across the bridge and into the town. De Winter, led by Bric, and Savernake, led by Dashiell, had breached the city walls and cleared the town of any hostile Scots for the moment, leaving the berg quiet except for pockets of fighting. Now, it was the de Velt army sizing up Berwick Castle, which seemed to be an impenetrable fortress. However, as everyone knew, that rule didn't apply to Jax de Velt.

But it was definitely going to be a challenge.

The gatehouse was a fairly small but fortified structure that protected a bridge that spanned a wide moat. That bridge led into a second gatehouse built into the wall of Berwick, which was substantial. There was also part of the wall that went down to the river and, it seemed, was perhaps the weakest part of the wall of protection. A barbican from the river protected stairs that led up into one of the towers.

Cole and Julian, helped by Addax and Essien, had brought the siege engines across the bridge and they now faced the castle. What they couldn't see, however, were many men on the battlements, watching them. There seemed to be very few. For a garrison, that didn't make sense. Either there were two thousand Scotsmen in the bailey, waiting to be unleashed, or the garrison commander had believed in his fortification so much that he'd sent his army out of the walls to fight the English with the rest of William the Rough's army.

Neither Jax nor anyone else were quite sure which it was.

"What do you think, Papa?" Cole asked his father. "How do you want to approach this?"

They were standing on the road into the village, looking up at the mighty bastion of Berwick Castle. Dark granite walls faced them, impressing upon them just how powerful the castle was. Cole and Julian stood with Addax and Essien, all of them gazing up at those terrible walls, waiting for an answer from The Dark Lord himself. Jax had faced some defiant castles in his lifetime and he was impressed by Berwick, but he liked a challenge. There hadn't been a castle built yet that could best him.

Berwick wasn't going to be the first.

"I noticed as we crossed the bridge that they've let the gate down by the river to fall into disrepair," he said. "The rest of the walls look solid enough and we can't get across the moat without the existing bridge. If they burn it, that may create a bit of an obstacle."

Cole looked at him. "If the river gate is compromised, we can go in that way," he said. "Mayhap you create a ruse with the siege engines while we try."

Jax was nodding even as he was speaking. "That is what I was thinking," he said. "If I can keep their attention, then you can select a group of men to go with you and breach the river gate. I suspect it is more fortified than we have seen, but it is worth a try. Otherwise, I'll have to put you and your brother in the baskets of the siege engines and fling you over the walls."

Cole grinned, looking at Julian. Jax made the comment because when they were young boys, they'd nearly done precisely that. The siege engines at Pelinom were stored in the stable yard and when Cole had been about six years of age, he'd talked one of the less-than-intelligent stable servants into launching him and Julian into an enormous pile of hay that had just been brought in from the fields.

Fortunately, the siege engines, which were catapults, needed some prep work before the boys could be launched and, in that time, Atreus had noticed what was happening and stopped what would have surely been a deadly event. Jax had calmly explained to his sons why it was foolish to try such a thing, but Kellington had simply spanked them.

Jax could still hear their cries as she pummeled their backsides.

Cole remembered it, too, which was why he was laughing at his brother, who hadn't learned his lesson the first time and had gotten into trouble with it again about a year later. But Julian put up his hands in surrender.

"I am *not* going to fly over the walls," he said. "Mother would only find out and beat me again. I am finished trying to fly through the air."

Both Cole and Jax were chuckling now, joined by Addax and Essien. In fact, Addax pointed to his younger brother.

"Es will volunteer, then," he said. "When we were lads, before we came to The Levant, we had heard of a story of a magic carpet that flew through the air. Es tried to take a hide off a roof one day when our caravan was stopped in the town of Ismailia. He fell into a fountain."

Jax eyed the youngest al-Kort brother. "It is a wonder any of you survived your childhood," he said, returning his attention to the castle. "Unfortunately, I do not think using the siege engines are an option to send men over the walls. The river's entrance may be our only solution."

Cole was thinking on the gate down by the river's edge. "Gates near water are usually secured with iron only because the wood will swell and warp with the moisture," he said. "I can bring a hammer and chisel and mayhap we can unseat the hinges of any iron gate we may come across. Or, if we can mount the wall itself, we can go right to the castle wall walk."

Jax looked at him. "Go," he said. "Take your brother and Addax and Essien. Atreus and I will create a diversion by concentrating on the gatehouse while you find a way in."

The young knights nodded and moved out. Julian and Cole plunged into the de Velt army, at a standstill several yards away, and pulled out one hundred men, younger soldiers they knew were swift and strong, and motioned for them to follow. They did, bringing ropes and iron grappling hooks, spurred on by Cole and his commands. If they were going to breach an iron gate, they needed the proper tools, but if they were going to mount the walls, then they needed the ropes and grappling hooks.

The men were moving quickly.

Night was beginning to fall, which would work to their advantage. They could use the cover of darkness to mask their movements down by the river because once they reached the water, Cole made them get into it. They were going to have to swim around the wall in order to get to the landing on the other side. The wall only went as far as the river, perhaps extended into it by about ten feet.

They were prepared to get around it.

Unfortunately, they were slowed down because only about half of the men could actually swim. The others were tethered with the ropes and pulled along, trying to keep their heads above water, and this included Addax and Essien. They came from arid lands and had never learned to swim properly, so Cole and Julian pulled them along, keeping their heads above water as they swam from the recently captured bridge all the way to the water wall of Berwick.

The water was freezing and the current was strong, but they managed to make it within sight of the wall. Only their heads were visible on top of the water and as they came within view of the shoreline inside the wall, they could see a group of Scots there, waiting. Cole came to a stop, allowing Addax and Essien and Julian to catch up to him.

"Look," he whispered. "There is a line of Scots there. See them?"

Their mouths were in the water so that they had the lowest profile possible. Julian motioned for the men behind them to stay silent and low as the knights assessed the situation.

They hadn't expected a welcoming committee.

"You know why they are there, don't you?" Addax said, shivering. "They are waiting for the Northmen. They must be closer than we thought."

Cole watched the silhouettes of men move around on the shore. "That was my thought as well," he muttered. "But it also means the gates to the castle are open from the river, or at the very least, accessible. Julian, if I can give the Scots a moment of confusion, can you and Essien run onto shore and keep those gates open for the rest of us?"

Julian was peering at the two short, stumpy towers near the water's edge. "Aye," he said. "But we will have to prevent those men from reaching the castle and alerting the garrison."

"Do what you must. You are a de Velt and we do not fail."

Julian nodded firmly. "I will not be the first to do so."

"Good," Cole muttered. "Gather the men close. Those on ropes need to be pulled forward so they can touch the ground. I am going to distract these Scots as much as I can, but we must all rise from the river in a group and charge them. No survivors, no witnesses. Is that understood?"

The men nearest him nodded, passing the word back. When the men on ropes were being pulled onto the shore where they could stand, Cole turned his attention back to the Scots in the distance.

"We move," he said. "Julian, you and Es get to that gate. Don't even try to fight any Scots trying to stop you. Leap over them if you have to. Just get to the gate."

Julian and Essien were laying low, moving closer to the shoreline, as Cole finally stood up and started walking towards the shore.

"Bhràithrean!" he called, lifting a hand. "Tha sinn air teicheadh às na Sasannaich. An urrainn dhut mo chuideachadh?"

Brothers, we've survived the English. Can you help us?

The Scots saw him coming out of the water, a dark silhouette against the night, and instantly moved into a defensive position, but his words were purely Gaelic. He sounded very much like a Scotsman. It was enough of a pause for Julian and Essien to gain their footing and bolt, running straight at the group of Scots. The sun was mostly set, and there were a few torches lit, so they had enough light to see by. They could see the shocked faces of the Scots, having no idea why men were charging out of the water towards them.

"Bhràithrean, an cuidich thu sinn?" Cole said again.

Brothers, will you please help us?

The words, the actions, were confusing, enough to stump the Scots. Julian and Essien barreled through a group of them, seeing an open iron grate in the wall of one of the stumpy towers. As Julian rushed through it, he realized that it led to a barbican that protected a staircase all the way to the castle.

And there was no one between them and the castle.

"Cole!" he cried. "We're clear!"

That was all Cole needed to hear. Unsheathing his broadsword, it was the signal to his men to charge, and charge they did. One hundred Englishmen rushed the shore where about forty Scots were standing and they never had a chance. The problem was not letting anyone from the castle see what was going on, so they shoved them back against the walls at an angle that made it difficult to see from the castle. More importantly, they had to eliminate their ability to shout, so throats were cut from the outset.

Bodies were falling in groups.

Almost as quickly as it started, it was over.

"The castle, Cole," Addax said, his dagger dripping with blood. "We must breach the castle now."

Cole knew that. There were still some Scotsmen alive, but Cole gave the order to kill every last man and throw their bodies in the river. He left ten men down on the river's edge to accomplish this and watch the river gate while he took the rest of his men and began to charge up the steep staircase towards the castle. With Julian at his side, and Addax and Essien behind them, they were prepared to do battle.

The sons of Jax de Velt were on a rampage.

Once inside the castle, they encountered far more resistance. A few hundred Scots were caught by surprise, but once they realized they were being infiltrated by the English, the swords and axes came out.

The fight for Berwick Castle began in earnest.

"WHAT HAPPENED?"

The question came from Christopher to a wounded soldier. There were several more wounded soldiers littering the area, most of them old men who had been stationed to the rear with the provisions and surgeon's wagons. Several of them were badly injured and there were even a few dead.

It was clear that something bad had happened.

This was the scene that Christopher and Alastor and Teviot came across as they moved their armies towards the Ord Crossing – the encampment they'd left behind in shambles. Those men that were able to walk were heading in Christopher's direction like the walking wounded.

It was a shocking sight.

"The Scots," the wounded soldier said. He was being propped up by Peter, who had leapt off his warhorse to help the man stand. "The Scots came over the bridge and out of the trees and took what they could. They drove several wagons back over the bridge."

Alastor turned white as he started to look around. "De Bourne," he managed to say. "Where are the de Bourne wagons."

"They were the first ones taken," the wounded soldier said, looking at Alastor with great sadness. "These dead are mostly de Bourne. They drove off with the wagons and took Teviot and some Savernake wagons, too. They came so quickly, out of the trees, and started jumping on wagons and driving them off. Those closest to the bridge were the first to be hit and de Bourne was the closest."

Alastor thought he might vomit. Ares, next to him, suddenly charged out towards an area where several men were laying dead in the grass and began calling for his sisters. He was followed by Atlas and Anteaus, who began shouting for their sisters as well, begging for a reply.

"My God," Alastor breathed as Christopher grabbed him

for support. "My daughters… Cori and Gaia… where are they? God help me, *where are they*?"

Adam, whose own Teviot wagons were taken, sent his son to look for their men, but Christopher passed a concerned glance at Peter, who let go of the wounded soldier and jumped onto his charger. He followed Ares in the search for the de Bourne daughters, but Christopher turned to his brother, next to him.

"Search the trees for them," he hissed. "Hurry!"

David thundered off with about thirty men behind him. They plunged into the woods and began searching all around the road that led to the bridge. All the while, Alastor sounded as if he were gasping.

"Not my daughters," he breathed, trying not to panic. "God, please. Not my daughters."

"We will find them," Christopher reassured him. "The Scots would not take them simply to kill them. They make valuable hostages and hostages are not treated poorly. Remember that, Alastor. I am sure they are quite well, if not a little scared."

But Alastor found no comfort in that. He put a gloved hand over his face, trying very hard not to weep. He could hear his sons calling for their sisters, and the guilt and terror he felt was overwhelming.

"She did not want to come," he whispered tightly. "My youngest, Gaia. She did not want to come. She wanted to stay at home, but I forced her to come with her sister. Dear God, what have I done?"

Christopher had his hand on the man's shoulder in a supportive gesture, watching as men rushed about the scene, looking for the wounded and searching for the women.

It was a chaotic situation, but one that couldn't take priority. He knew that. The Scots were watching them, closely enough to use the Ord Crossing to capture some of their wagons and women along with them, which changed the dynamics of the situation.

Now, the Scots had English hostages.

That changed things considerably.

Christopher waited a few minutes, watching the de Bourne brothers search in vain for their sisters. Some of his men, including his brother, were already helping the wounded, while still others were dragging the dead into an organized pile.

He sighed faintly.

"Your daughters are not here, Alastor," he said quietly. "Recall your sons."

Alastor was leaning forward on his saddle horn as if he had no strength left. Grief threatened to overwhelm him. He nodded, but he didn't make any effort to call to his sons, so Christopher sent men to round everyone up. He would leave a few men behind to collect the dead and attend the wounded, but The Marshal had to know what had happened. He turned to Adam, riding off to his left.

"You are missing wagons, too, are you not?" he asked.

Adam nodded seriously. "It seems so," he said. "But I also saw wagons belonging to me with the group that we just passed, the one moving up to follow the rest of the army at Berwick, so I did not lose all of them. At least I did not lose my daughters..."

He trailed off, an expression of pain across his face. He was feeling greatly for Alastor, who was weeping silently and trying not to show it. The knights began returning to the main body of the army and Christopher raised a fist to gain their attention.

"This situation changes our objective," he said. "Our original intention was to decimate the Scots army, but now they evidently hold the de Bourne sisters as hostages. Mayhap that was their intention all along, so it seems to me that we must reconsider our orders. I do not want to go rushing headlong into the Scots only to have them hurt the women."

That was a very real possibility and they were all quite aware. David reined his horse next to his brother.

"They could use those woman to keep us at bay, Chris," he said, hoping Alastor wouldn't hear him. "We cannot let this entire battle be dictated by two women hostages. You know this. There is too much at stake. Hell, they could use them to keep us off the Northmen when they come, too."

"I've considered that."

"Mayhap they'll threaten to kill them if we advance against them."

Christopher held up a hand to quiet his brother. David had a point – they couldn't let two women dictate their actions, as unfortunate as it was. But they also couldn't let the women be harmed.

He looked around to the men surrounding him – David, Peter, the three de Bourne brothers, Alastor, Adam and John de Longley. Fine men and fine knights. But his gaze mostly moved to Peter.

An Executioner Knight.

That gave him an idea.

"Come," he said. "We retreat back to our original encampment from this morning, where we first stopped and mobilized. But first, we secure this bridge with three hundred men. David, break out enough men from all three armies. Those men will remain here and hold this bridge at all costs. The rest of us – we return. Plans have changed and we must discuss the situation with The Marshal before proceeding."

It seemed reasonable enough. Alastor wasn't too keen to leave that very spot, the last place his daughters were, but Christopher and Ares managed to convince him that they needed to retreat in order to plan the rescue of his daughters. Everyone was acutely aware that the hostage situation wasn't a good one.

They needed to figure out how to get the women out alive.

CHAPTER TWENTY

H ER HEAD WAS killing her.

Corisande had awoken beneath a big oak tree, the last shades of day turning the landscape dark and eerie. She had no idea where she was but the moment she started to move, Gaia stilled her. She begged her to remain silent and unmoving.

That only confused Corisande further.

"What happened?" she asked.

Gaia was pressed up against her and Corisande could see her eyes darting about nervously.

"The Scots took us," she said, trembling. "Don't you remember? The man hit you on the head!"

"What man?"

"The man who stole the wagon with us inside it!"

Corisande lay there a moment, digesting what her sister was telling her. It took her a moment to remember the raid on the encampment, with Scots pouring out of the trees and stealing the wagons. She remembered leaping into the wagon where Gaia was clutching the bench, unable to convince her to let go.

And then… nothing.

Slowly, she started to sit up.

"Nay," Gaia hissed, pushing her down. "They keep asking

who we are, but I start crying and will not answer. They are waiting for you to awaken so they can ask you."

Corisande shoved her sister's hands aside, pushing at her because Gaia was trying to keep her down.

"Cease, Gaia," she said irritably, finally sitting up and regaining her balance. She groaned softly, a hand to her head. "I feel terrible."

Gaia looked at her anxiously. "What are they going to do to us?" she asked, tearing up. "Are they going to kill us?"

Corisande could see an encampment in front of them, with cooking fires spitting sparks into the night sky. A fog was rolling in from the sea, however. She could see it creeping in over the eastern hills.

"Where are we?" she asked.

Gaia huddled against her. "I do not know," she said. "I think we are near Berwick. I could see a big city down that way."

She was pointing to the south, but Corisande couldn't see anything. It was too dark and there were hills in the way. Her head was killing her, she was confused and cold and hungry, and her patience was at an end. She stood up, with Gaia trying to pull her down again.

"Nay, Cori!" she gasped. "Where are you going?"

Corisande yanked her arm away from her sister. "Stay here if you want to," she said. "I am going to find out what is going on."

Determined, she marched across the mashed grass towards the encampment of Scots. Gaia ran after her, clinging to her, and she found herself dragging her sister along. Gaia was so much dead weight as Corisande approached a group of Scots huddled around the nearest fire.

"Who is in command?" she demanded. "I want to speak with him."

The Scots looked at her in surprise. One of them stood up, setting his meal aside to face her. His eyes grazed her from top to bottom, lingering on her breasts before returning to her face.

"Sit with us, lassie," he said. "None of us have had the privilege of speaking with a proper English lass before."

Corisande didn't like the way he was looking at her. He made her skin crawl.

"If you do not take me to your commander, I will scream as if you are driving dirks into my heart," she said. "I'll scream loud enough to bring the English from Berwick. Will you take me your commander or should I start screaming?"

The man frowned, putting up his hands. "No need tae…"

Corisande started screaming. She screamed as loud as she could and when the Scots moved closer to her to shush her, she screamed louder and encouraged Gaia to scream, too. Soon, both of them were screaming their heads off and the Scots around the fire looked on with shock. Their screaming brought more Scots, however, running from all directions.

They were attracting quite a crowd, standing there and screaming as they were. It was quite unsettling and Corisande was coming to wonder if the screaming tactic had been a good idea. She brought attention, of course, but not the right kind. Finally, a tall, slender man with dark hair and a dark beard arrived, looking at the woman and the men surrounding them as if something terrible surely must have happened.

"What is the trouble here?" he demanded, looking to the men who had been huddling around the fire, minding their own business until the English woman approached them and started screaming. "What did ye do? Why is she screaming like that?"

The man Corisande spoke to looked a little ill. "The lassie wanted tae speak with our commander," he said. "I asked her tae sit and…"

Corisande cut him off. "And I started screaming," she said, angry and hoarse. "I demand to speak with the man in command, do you hear? I want to know why we have been brought here. Are you the man in command?"

The man with the dark hair nodded, his gaze lingering on her. "I'm Alexander MacDuff," he said. "I am at yer service, m'lady."

Corisande marched up to him, looking him over. "Mac-Duff," she repeated. The name sounded familiar, but she couldn't place it. "*Why* have you brought us here? I demand you release us immediately."

She was holding on to Gaia, who was clinging to her sister and weeping. MacDuff looked between the two women, both of them exceptionally lovely, but the older one... she was something spectacular.

"Ye're sisters?" he asked.

"Aye," Corisande replied. "Now that I have answered your question, it would be polite of you to answer one of mine."

MacDuff wasn't going to do it in front of his men. In fact, he had a good deal he wanted to ask of the sisters, women who had been with the auxiliary group to the rear of the English army. He wanted to know why.

And he wanted to know what they knew about the English positions.

"Will ye please come with me?" he asked, sweeping his right arm towards the center of the encampment. "Let me take ye someplace more comfortable. Surely ye must be hungry."

Corisande didn't answer. She was too angry and, truth be told, too scared. But she agreed to go with him, following the man through the encampment that smelled like a thousand filthy animals had gathered. There were men leering at her and she passed by dozens who looked as if they either wanted to kill her or molest her. With Gaia whimpering against her, it was a distressing trek all the way to a larger tent with lion standards flying over it.

But Corisande had no idea what that meant.

She followed MacDuff into the tent only to be met by a host of curious faces. There were men all over the tent, in smaller groups, a couple standing over a table with vellum upon it, and then one elderly man sitting in a chair next to a brazier.

"Yer grace," MacDuff said to the man with a cup of something steaming in his hand. He had dirty gray hair and gnarled fingers, but the eyes were sharp. "The lady wishes tae speak tae the man in command."

The old man set his cup down. "Greetings," he said with a speech inflection that sounded like a cross between Gaelic and French. "My name is William. Will ye tell me yers?"

Corisande's gaze moved from the old man to the men around the tent. The structure was full of heavily armed Scots, but more than that, it was a small armory in and of itself. There were hides on the ground against the dampness and a fine bed with curtains was against one wall.

Yer grace.

That was what MacDuff had called him.

A hint of suspicion came to her mind.

"William," she repeated. "Do you have a title, my lord?"

The old man nodded. "Aye," he said without hesitation. "I am King of the Scots. May I have yer name, lass?"

Corisande couldn't help but react from both surprise and fear. Perhaps his identity had been in the back of her mind, but now it was confirmed. The man Cole had spied upon, the King of the Scots, was sitting before her.

She proceeded carefully.

"My name is Corisande," she said, sounding breathless. "I did not mean to sound rude, your grace, but these circumstances… I am understandably distressed."

"Lady Corisande," William said, motioning for MacDuff to bring over another chair. "And who is the lass stuck tae ye?"

"My sister, Gaia, your grace."

MacDuff brought the chair and William motioned to it. "Please," he said. "Sit down. Ye must be weary. I'll have food and drink brought tae ye."

Corisande sat down, but she shook her head to the rest of it. "You do not need to bring us anything to eat or drink, your grace," she said. "I want to know why we are here. We have done nothing to warrant this. Please let us leave."

William looked at the pair. Corisande sat down and Gaia knelt next to her, still pressed against her sister's torso. "Ye were with the provisions wagons?" he clarified.

"The surgeon's wagon," she said. "I am a healer."

"I see," William said, nodding. "What is yer family name, m'lady?"

Corisande wasn't sure she should tell him. She remembered what Cole had told her when they'd first met about William the Lion sending missives to her father through Alpin Canmore. She wasn't sure she wanted to tell the King of Scotland that her father was the one who refused to join him.

She wasn't entirely certain how he would react.

"I… I am not certain that is relevant, your grace," she said evasively. "There are many English houses that are fighting your men right now, but I was not among those fighting. I heal – that is what I do. That is the only reason I am here."

"Papa says she is the best healer in England," Gaia suddenly piped up. "She learned from Mama, but I have not learned. I was only here because Papa forced me to come and I want to go home."

William focused on the very young woman with the quivering voice. "Who is yer papa?"

Corisande wanted to stop her from answering, but short of

slapping a hand over her mouth, she wasn't sure what more she could do. In a panic, she ended up pinching Gaia to shut her up just as the girl answered.

"Alastor de Bourne," she said, wincing as she looked at her sister. "*Ouch!*"

Corisande looked at her sister with a great deal of disappointment and sorrow, but Gaia had no idea why. With a heavy sigh, Corisande returned her attention to William only to see that the man was looking at her most strangely.

Surprised, even.

"De Bourne," he repeated quietly. "The descendants of Eric Bloodaxe."

Corisande met his gaze without displaying the fear she was feeling inwardly. Her silly little sister had just put the nail in the coffin that was going to drag them both into the abyss now that William knew who their father was. What she didn't know, or realize, was that MacDuff had heard the same thing.

The man who had come to The Keld those weeks ago to force her father to join the rebellion.

"We cannot choose our family or our siblings," she said, releasing her sister and shoving her onto her bottom. "Believe me, I would have chosen more wisely had that been the case."

William grinned, looking at Gaia, who was whimpering and grabbing at her sister. "Dunna be too hard on her," he said. "It was the polite thing tae answer my question, since I asked. I dunna know yer father personally but, of course, I know of him. Yer family has a long and distinguished family history."

Corisande wasn't sure where he was going with that line of conversation, but she didn't want to say anything more than was absolutely necessary, afraid she might say too much.

"It is not like being in the Scottish royal family," she said. "You have great expectations and obligations. Our family lineage has no such expectations. Kingdoms do not depend on us."

"But they did, once," William said. "Yer family were the Kings of Northumbria."

"Hundreds of years ago, your grace," Corisande reminded him. "It has no bearing on our lives today. We are simply Englishmen."

William's gaze lingered on her for a moment, suspecting why Alastor de Bourne hadn't agreed to an alliance. If that was the daughter's view of their family, then she must have gotten it from someone. It must have been Alastor's view, too. He didn't see himself as a man who had a kingdom taken away from him.

He simply saw himself as English.

But there was one way to find out for sure.

"Did ye know I asked yer father tae join me?" he asked. "In this push intae England, I mean. I asked yer father tae join me and my allies. Did he tell ye that?"

Corisande knew more than she wanted to let on. She was afraid of what would happen if she did.

"He does not confide in me, your grace," she said. "Why would he? I am only his daughter, not his wife."

"Then ye dinna know about the alliance proposal?"

She caught sight of movement in her periphery, turning to look at MacDuff, who was watching her very carefully. She sensed hostility from him where she did not sense it from William. Or perhaps he was simply better at hiding it.

"I only found out about your proposal when the Scots attacked our village last month," she said. "I was told they came to The Keld to force my father into joining the Scots rebellion but when he declined, they tried to burn our village."

"That's no' true!" MacDuff spat, realizing he had just been caught in a lie. "They attacked *us*."

Corisande turned to him angrily. "The Scots burned our village," she countered. "My father and his men rode from the castle to defend the village and for no other reason. They did not attack anyone."

MacDuff was turning red in the cheeks but William held up a hand to him. "Enough," he said. "It is over with. M'lady, how many men did yer father bring with him?"

Corisande was ready to go to fisticuffs with MacDuff when she suddenly realized that William was asking her pointed questions about the English strength. They were at war and she was a possible source of information, as he saw it.

Her apprehension grew.

"I do not know and that is the truth," she said. "I am the surgeon. I am not consulted on military issues. I do know that my father has almost fifteen hundred men and he brought most of them north."

"Who else came with him?"

She thought on that question. It wasn't like it was a secret with the way the English armies flew their standards high. "De Lohr, de Winter, Savernake, de Velt," she said. "William Marshal, too, but I do not know how many men have come. Thousands, at least."

"Anyone else?

"I remember hearing there were more to come, but they are far away."

William sat back in his chair, mulling that over. After a moment, he collected his steaming cup again.

"Tomorrow morning, I am expecting a dozen Northmen longships," he said. "Thousands of Northmen will be here and will more than likely destroy yer father. I'm told that the English have managed tae capture the city of Berwick, but that willna last. We have the castle and 'tis all we need, truthfully. With the Northmen, we can take back the north of England. Had yer father joined us, he could have kept his lands."

Corisande didn't sense gloating from him, merely the truth

as he saw it. She looked down at Gaia, who was gazing up at her fearfully. She put her arm around her sister again as she faced William.

"If anyone understands loyalty to one's country, it is you," she said. "You understand why men feel compelled to be loyal to the home of their birth. My father is simply loyal to the home of his birth, come what may."

William nodded faintly. "Ye're a reasonable young lass," he said. "Alastor did well with ye."

"Thank you, your grace."

"Will ye join me for a meal?"

Corisande shook her head. "You are kind, but I must decline," she said. "Please, your grace... may we return? We cannot possibly be of any value to you."

William's gaze rested on her for a moment before setting his cup down yet again and rising wearily. He moved away from the women, pulling MacDuff with him, until they were over by his traveling bed. When he was certain they were out of earshot, he faced MacDuff.

"What were the men able tae get when they raided the provisions wagons?" William asked quietly.

MacDuff was reluctant to tell him, but he had little choice. "Seven wagons of provisions and two surgeon's wagons," he said. "The men grabbed what they could."

"Were the provisions plentiful?"

"Nay, because the armies took what they needed as they advanced on Berwick."

"So ye took empty wagons?"

"No' empty, but no' as full as we had hoped."

"And ye abducted two women along with those wagons?"

MacDuff looked over at the blondes in the middle of the tent, embracing one another. "'Tis a grand opportunity, yer grace," he said. "Those are the daughters of Alastor de Bourne.

Do ye no' see, yer grace? God has put them in our hands."

"He has?"

MacDuff's gaze was intense. "We can use the daughters against their father," he said. "We can force him tae join our fight."

That was very true. William knew it was a prime opportunity to force Alastor de Bourne to his will. Once the younger daughter gave away her family name, that very thing popped into his mind. His gaze moved to the women, huddle together, as he pondered MacDuff's suggestion.

"What man wouldna do anything he could tae save his daughters?" he murmured. "As a father, I'd do anything within my power."

"Then we send the man word tonight?"

William shook his head. "Nay," he said. "And I'll tell ye why. De Bourne has sons and fifteen hundred men tae think about. He has a legacy tae think about. If he turns against The Marshal, he'll spend the rest of his lifetime, and probably his sons' lifetimes, being an enemy in the heart of Northumberland. He'll be destroyed. Men who were formerly his allies will make it so. Is that legacy worth the safety of his daughters?"

MacDuff wasn't following him. "Ye said yerself he'd do anything tae save them."

"But the family is greater than the children," William said. "Alexander, a man can stand losing children, but he canna stand losing his entire family or his legacy, and that's what this would cost him. Nay, he'd no' side with us, no' even if we hold his daughters, but I have something better in mind."

MacDuff thought the man was going soft in the head. "What is that, yer grace?"

William's yellowed eyes glimmered in the weak light. "Send them back tae The Marshal with a message," he said. "The mercy we show upon those lasses will indebt The Marshal tae me. It will indebt de Bourne tae me. Let them see our mercy because the next time we require such a thing from them, they'll be obligated tae give it."

MacDuff was starting to follow now. "Ye want them tae be indebted tae ye?"

"Exactly."

It wasn't madness. It actually made good political sense as far as politics went. But MacDuff was grossly unhappy that William wasn't going to make de Bourne pay for the debacle at Castle Keld, the same debacle that MacDuff had lied about. He'd told William that de Bourne had attacked him when the man's daughter had contradicted that.

No, he wasn't happy with de Bourne in the least.

Or his daughter.

"Is that yer command, yer grace?" he finally asked, jaw ticking with disapproval. "Tae send them back with a message?"

William nodded. "Tell the eldest one tae tell The Marshal that I spared their lives and expect the same courtesy in the future should I call upon him," he said. "Let the man see that I am merciful."

"Anything else, yer grace?"

William looked over at the women one last time. "'Tis too dark and dangerous tae release the lasses now, but ye'll return both of them tae the Ord Crossing at first light," he said. "Take them personally, Alexander."

"Aye, yer grace."

"If they willna sup with me, then find them a comfortable place tae sleep for the night."

With that, he turned away, heading back to his chair next to the brazier and a hot drink that was no longer hot.

MacDuff, however, had other plans for the eldest de Bourne daughter.

And he intended to carry them out no matter what William had said.

Berwick Castle

THE FIGHT HAD been a bloody one but, in the end, Cole and Julian, Addax and Essien had prevailed.

Focused on the gatehouse and making more noise than actually doing any damage, Jax wasn't surprised when Cole suddenly appeared at the inner gatehouse, fighting Scots like a madman, tossing them into the deep moat that surrounded the castle. He had watched, fascinated, while his sons did battle at the gatehouse until Julian broke free and raced over the bridge to the smaller gatehouse where his father was standing. There were Scots there, manning the gatehouse, so there was a fight before Julian managed to open the man-gate in the larger gates that were bolted and sealed. With the smaller gate open, Jax and his men poured in.

The fight was over in a relatively short amount of time.

In fact, from the time Cole left Jax and Atreus at the smaller gatehouse until Jax's men subdued the Scots in the castle, about an hour and a half had elapsed. The first thing Jax did was rip down the banner of MacHeth that had been flying over the battlements and raise the black and red de Velt standard.

He swore he could hear the men cheering in the distance.

With Berwick Castle in the hands of Jax de Velt, his men went about securing the castle against any counterattack. Berwick was a massive place, but they left no chamber unexplored, even down to the vault and the tunnels beneath the bedrock that led out to the river.

Everything was explored and the Scots were rounded up.

By that time, it was well into the night. The Scots manning

the castle, and they counted forty-three, were put on poles that had been cut down in the heavily wooded areas to the west of Berwick. Jax had told The Marshal he intended to take Berwick his own way and take it he did. The poles started going up on the road leading to the bridge like a macabre forest of dead bodies for all the world to see. MacHeth's son, the garrison commander, had the distinction of being nailed to a cross which was then hung from the castle walls.

All of it meant to terrorize the Scots.

Even as the castle itself was secured, the fighting continued with de Winter and Savernake taking the bulk of the casualties until de Lohr, Teviot, and de Bourne returned from the Ord Crossing. It was a premature return, which concerned The Marshal. After a brief conference with Christopher, he called back his forces to the city and the bridge only, allowing the Scots to leave the city and run north to their encampment.

Jax, of course, had been watching it all from the battlements of Berwick. He'd done his job and captured the castle, and he had no intention of leaving it as he watched the English and the Scots do battle. But when the English seemed to withdraw prematurely and the Scots flee, his curiosity was piqued.

It was piqued even more when he saw knights riding for the castle with banners flying.

Jax's army had every aspect of Berwick secure, including the double-gatehouses, which were opened for the incoming English. Torches were lit because a mist was rolling in from the sea, greatly diminishing visibility, and the effect of the torches against the fog was eerie. So were the bodies of the dead Scots lining the bridge and the street leading to the castle, as The Marshal and others discovered.

They had the distinct feeling of riding into hell.

Jax was there to greet them when they thundered into the bailey.

"Excellent work, Jax," The Marshal said as he drew his horse to a halt. "You managed to capture Berwick when I was fairly certain it was going to take you much longer. How did you do it?"

"Cole and Julian went by way of the river and managed to gain access through the river gate," he said proudly. "There were only forty-three Scots manning the castle, so it was a short-lived battle once we breached the walls."

William had been looking around the vast bailey of Berwick, but turned to look at Jax when he mentioned the short-lived battle. "I saw the results of that battle as we rode here," he said. "You do realize that is going to infuriate the Scots."

Jax smiled faintly, but it was not a pleasant gesture. "I hope so."

The Marshal snorted, finally slapping Jax on the arm. "I would laugh with you but, unfortunately, what you have done may work terribly against us," he said. "We have a problem. Where are Cole and the Kitara princes?"

Jax glanced at Christopher, who looked more solemn than usual. So did Teviot and David, who were with him. Alastor looked positively ashen, as did his sons. They all appeared sick.

Jax frowned. "They are securing the river gate," he said. "I will send for them. What has happened?"

The Marshal waved him off. "Not yet," he said. "Bring Cole here. We've something to do and we need him."

Jax had no idea what was going on. Beyond Christopher and Teviot and David, he could see Peter and Alexander, Kress and Achilles, Bric and Dashiell. They were away from their armies.

That puzzled Jax greatly.

He turned to The Marshal.

"*What* is happening?" he hissed.

Alastor couldn't keep his mouth shut. Before The Marshal

could reply, he pushed forward, shoving men out of the way until he came to within a few inches of Jax.

"The Scots captured some of our ancillary wagons, including my surgeon's wagon," he said, close to tears. "My daughters were in that wagon and now they are prisoners of the Scots. And you put their soldiers on poles for them to see? If the Scots see what you have done to their men, they will put my daughters on poles in retaliation!"

Jax scowled at the man in disbelief. "They *what*?" he hissed. "They have… Christ, they have Corisande?"

Alastor was white with fury, with despair. "They do," he said, his entire body trembling. "I do not think the Scots will take kindly to what you have done to their men. If they punish my daughters for your actions, I will blame *you* for their deaths. Damn you to hell, de Velt!"

Christopher had to pull Alastor away from Jax, shoving him back towards his sons, who gripped their father tightly. They were all upset, saying things they didn't mean. Alastor began weeping, low and mournful, adding to the already horrific situation.

But Jax understood. A month ago, he didn't give a second thought to putting men and women on poles when it came to the collapse of Fountainhall. He'd done what he had always done. He did it at Berwick, too.

But now that the Scots held Cole's intended, all of that changed.

He grabbed the nearest de Velt soldier.

"The bodies of the Scots," he hissed. "Get them down. Get them down *now*. And remove the garrison commander from the wall. Get them down and bring them in here, out of sight of the Scots. *Go!*"

The soldier, startled and confused, nonetheless took off running.

"They'll be down in an hour," he said, speaking to Alastor. "With the mist rolling in, chances are no one has seen them yet. De Bourne… I did not know. Please know I would never knowingly cause danger to your daughters or your family. Not like this."

Alastor was still weeping, but Ares was looking at Jax. He could see that the man was sincerely distressed.

"We know, my lord," he said hoarsely. "This not your fault. But the removal of the dead is appreciated."

Alastor was nodding as his son spoke, unable to articulate what Ares was putting into words. Wiping at his face, he struggled to compose himself as he turned to Jax and went to the man. He only meant to shake his hand but ended up putting his arms around him.

"Forgive me, old friend," he whispered. "I did not mean it. I did not mean any of it. I adore Cole and he will soon marry my daughter. I am proud to have him. Please… forgive me."

Jax put an arm around him, hugging him tightly. "There is nothing to forgive," he said. "I have three daughters of my own and not long ago, I was in this very position with one of them. A man who wanted to kill me took her hostage, so I understand your pain very well. Have faith; everything will be well again. You shall see them returned safely."

"Who returned safely?"

The question came from Cole.

Having seen the gathering of knights ride into the bailey of Berwick as he'd returned from the river gate, he wanted to be part of the celebration of the conquest of the castle. It was his celebration, after all. Julian, Addax, and Essien were with him, expecting a celebration but seeing something quite different. What they came upon didn't look like a celebration at all. Cole's father was embracing Alastor, who had clearly been weeping.

Cole frowned.

"Who will be returned safely?" he repeated, looking to his father. "What has happened?"

The only people who really knew about Cole and Corisande were their fathers and Corisande's brothers, and Addax and Essien. At least, that was the general belief among those in the know. But what they didn't know was that servants at The Keld had seen Corisande and Cole together, and the rumors had started. Gossip abound, so much so that all of the Executioner Knights had heard some version of the truth, so as they stood in the bailey of Berwick, there was a good deal of sympathy in their expressions as they looked at Cole.

They knew something he didn't, something that was going to affect him.

It was The Marshal, of all people, who finally spoke.

"Several hours ago, the Scots used the Ord Crossing to attack our rear," he said steadily. "Some of the wagons were stolen, including de Bourne's surgeon's wagon. De Bourne's daughters are now prisoners of the Scots and we must get them back. Cole, I need you for this task."

Cole stared at him for a moment. He blinked, wiped his chin, and then spoke in a strangely tight voice. "Corisande is a prisoner of the Scots?"

"Aye."

He blinked again as the news was confirmed a second time. Then, he looked to his father, to Alastor, and finally to Ares and the de Bourne brothers. They all looked as if they were grieving a death.

The realization hit him in the gut like a hammer.

"God," he grunted, teetering when he did so. "What in the hell happened? How were the Scots able to get to her?"

Jax put a hand out, steadying him. "The bridge is not being watched, at least not by the English," he said. "It was an oversight, Cole. Certainly no one expected the Scots to come by way of that bridge."

Cole's face was flushed red. "But they did," he said, feeling rage and grief and anger as he looked at Alastor. "She should not have come to battle. What fool brings women to battle? And now you see what has happened!"

He was shouting by the time he was done, causing Alastor to recoil. Ares was about to get in Cole's face, but Atlas pulled him back. Emotions were volatile.

No one wanted a fight.

"Easy, Cole," Jax said, his hands on his son to prevent him from charging the group of de Bourne men. "It is no one's fault. Mayhap measures should have been taken to…"

Cole cut him off. "Of course measures should have been taken to protect the women," he barked. "Are you telling me there were no guards on the provisions wagons?"

"There were about twenty soldiers with the wagons," Alastor said. "They help with the wounded, but they are fully armed. They were there, Cole. I would have never let my daughters remain with the wagons unprotected."

Cole opened his mouth to shout at him again but Jax shook him, breaking his concentration. "Nay, Cole," he said quietly, firmly. "He feels badly enough. Do not punish the man. We must focus on a solution now."

Cole was genuinely trying to keep his composure, but he was having a devil of a time. "I must go," he said, trying to pull away from his father. "I will go and retrieve her."

Jax was on him in a flash, grabbing him by the arms. "Cole, *listen*," he said. "You cannot go alone."

"Nay, you cannot," The Marshal said, coming to help Jax corral his son. "You cannot go it alone. This is a mission for a small group of men or a large army, but not for only one man. You would get yourself killed."

Cole didn't like being restrained. "I am *going*."

The Marshal had him by the arm. "You are going with your fellow knights," he said. "You, Addax, Essien, Bric, Dash, Peter, Sherry, Kress, and Achilles will enter the camp in stealth, find the women, and bring them back. Are you listening to me, Cole? I need your level head now, not your rage. Your rage will get everyone killed."

Cole knew that, but he was still verging on hysteria. The thought of Corisande in the midst of a gang of Scots had every fiber of his body in knots. His stomach was lurching, his hands contracting into fists as if to punch his way straight into Scotland.

But his heart was in the biggest knot of all.

It was slowly dying of grief.

God, no, he thought. *Not Corisande.*

Realizing he was about to go mad with anguish and fury, he did the only thing he could do. He took a long, deep breath and doubled over, fighting against everything that was straining to let loose.

"God," he groaned, squeezing his eyes tightly before standing up to focus on The Marshal. "I am calm. I swear I am. You have my level head. You have all of me. But so does Corisande. I am going to marry the woman, so I cannot simply stand here."

The Marshal put a hand on his shoulder. "I know," he said quietly. "I have heard the rumors. The knights in my stable may be able to keep the most precious secrets of state, but they tend to talk about one another. You know we have no secrets."

Cole looked to the men behind him, men that he knew and loved. He could see the sympathy, the support. He didn't know if that made it better or worse. "There has been no time to speak of it to anyone, personally," he said. "In fact, I have barely told my own father. I had hoped to speak of it to the rest of you when the battle was over and there was a wedding to attend."

The Marshal gave him a supportive squeeze on the shoulder. "There still will be a wedding to attend, I am certain," he said. "But until then, you must face this rationally. You are a knight, Cole. You know that you must contain your emotions. Especially now."

He was right. Cole was trying to keep his breathing steady, knowing that an unrestrained man would get himself killed. He struggled to focus on what needed to be done, not the danger Corisande was facing. If he focused on that, he would lose what was left of his control.

"Then I will take command of the rescue mission," he said, though his voice was quivering. "Do we know where they were taken?"

The Marshal glanced towards the north. "I believe William is in the hills north of Berwick," he said. "The Scots who took the de Bourne sisters came over the Ord Crossing. If you return to that bridge, mayhap you can follow their trail."

Cole thought on that. He looked up into what was presumably the sky, but he couldn't see it through the fog.

"In the night and in this mist, it will be difficult to see," he said. "My instinct is to go at this very moment and use the fog to our advantage, but that would be foolish. North of Berwick is unknown to me and in a mist like this, we could get lost."

By this time, Addax and Essien had moved forward to listen, as had Peter, Bric, Dashiell, Alexander, Kress, and Achilles. All of them seasoned agents, all of them listening to Cole try to reason out the situation. But he wasn't in complete control, terrified for Corisande, and that was something they could all sympathize with.

It was Alexander who finally stepped forward.

Out of the entire group, Alexander was the most natural commander. The Marshal had used him often for missions because Sherry, beloved by all of The Marshal's men, had the ability to see everything from all angles. He had never made a mistake that The Marshal had been aware of, so when the group of Executioner Knights stepped in to listen to Cole speak, The

Marshal discreetly motioned Alexander forward. Cole wanted to command the mission to retrieve the woman he was going to marry, but The Marshal wanted someone who was driven by logic and not emotion.

Alexander cleared his throat softly.

"Cole," he said quietly, smiling at the man when their eyes met. "Let me do this for you, my friend. Let me take charge of seeing your lady safely returned. Will you let me do this? You cannot go charging in there with your heart and not your head. That would jeopardize your safety as well as ours, so let me do this for you. Will you trust me?"

Cole looked at the man who had brought him into The Marshal's ring to begin with. He adored him. He also knew that everything Alexander said was right.

But, God, it was difficult for him to relinquish control where Corisande was concerned.

"We must get her out of there, Sherry," he insisted softly.

Alexander smiled at him, patting him on the cheek. "I know," he said. "We will. But we cannot do anything at this moment and I must have time to plan a well-timed incursion. With this mist, we have little choice but to wait it out. You know this."

Cole's heart was pounding against his ribs, painfully, and for the first time in his adult life, he felt the sting of tears. "I know," he said. "I know all of that. But give me something to do, something to plan, something to keep myself occupied or I swear I will go running into Scotland and kill every Scots bastard I can get my hands on."

Jax went to him, turning him for the gatehouse where his men were already starting to bring in the bodies that had been posted on poles.

"Take charge of the removal of the bodies," he said. "If the Scots see this, it could reflect badly on Corisande, so we do not want them to see this. Make sure the bodies are removed as quickly as possible and brought into the bailey so the Scots cannot see them."

That realization spurred Cole. "You're right," he said, turning to Julian and Addax and Essien. "Help me, please."

They surged forward, following Cole as he ran through the gatehouse, out to help the army remove the bodies on poles. Once Cole was occupied and focused on something other than his grief, Jax turned to Alexander.

"I do not know the landscape north of Berwick," he said. "If William believes the Scots are somewhere in those hills, then we must know something more specific. It occurs to me that we must find someone who knows those hills."

Alexander was listening. "Like who?"

"Like a Scotsman who is part of The Rough's army," he said. "Surely not all of them have fled. I would wager to say there may be one or more of them hiding in the city, mayhap in a tavern or two down by the river's edge where the boats throw anchor."

Alexander was following his train of thought. "And if there is not, I would imagine there is a villager who has lived in this town all his life and who knows the landscape around us."

"Find one. And find out what you are facing in those hills."

It was an excellent idea. Alexander turned to the Executioner Knights behind him and sent Kress and Achilles into the town, off to find someone who could tell them about the hills north of Berwick where the Scots army was located.

Someone to help them realize what they would be up against.

But whatever they were, or were not, to discover, Alexander and Cole would be leading the charge come the morning.

They could only pray the women could hold out that long.

CHAPTER TWENTY-ONE

MACDUFF HAD ESCORTED Corisande and Gaia to a smaller tent that was near the edge of the encampment, but it was surrounded by several fires, all of them with men huddling near the flame to stave off the mist that had rolled in from the sea. It was heavy now, blanketing the land, and wet to the touch.

It was like being covered with sea spray.

The smaller tent had a brazier, a pallet, and little more. It was quite spartan when compared to the grand tent of William. Corisande and Gaia stood near the door as MacDuff went to add fuel to the brazier, watching it spark up and flame. Holding his hands over the heat, he turned to the women by the door.

"Come in," he said. "Sit."

Corisande didn't like the feel of the situation. Something about the way MacDuff was looking at her made her feel vastly uneasy.

"I would rather not," she said. "When we were brought here, it was in a wagon. Where is that wagon?"

MacDuff left the brazier and went to the entry, sticking his head out into the misty night. "It is over where we left ye," he said. "Did ye no' see it?"

Corisande eyed him before peering out into the misty night.

She knew the general direction she had come from, so she looked off in that area. Oddly, the fog was heavier the higher it went, but not so heavy near the ground, so the visibility closer to the grass was better. She bent low, looking off towards the spot she remembered, and she could see the bottom of two wagons. The bottom of their wheels, anyway.

She stood back and looked at the man.

"We would rather sleep in the wagon," she said. "When are we to be released?"

MacDuff looked her over, remembering William's words. He wanted the women released with a message to William Marshal, but they didn't know that. They hadn't heard the directive, which would work in his favor, and they weren't going to know of it if he had anything to say about it.

They were only going to know *his* terms.

It was time to get to it.

"Sit yer sister down," he said. "I would speak with ye alone."

Corisande was feeling more uneasy the longer he looked at her, but she did as he asked and forced Gaia to sit down on the pallet. The young woman hugged her knees, fearfully, her gaze on Corisande as she went back over to MacDuff.

"Well?" she said. "What is it?"

His focus lingered on her. "Ye're no' very friendly, are ye?"

"Please tell me what you wish to speak with me about."

Her resistance only seemed to harden him. He stepped a few feet away, motioning to her, clearly putting distance between them and Gaia. What he had to say was for Corisande's ears only and she followed, but warily.

"Have ye no' heard my name?" he asked quietly.

Corisande had from the outset, though she couldn't place it. "I do not know," she said. "Why? Who are you?"

"The Earl of Fife," he said. "Did yer father no' mention me?"

"Nay. Why?"

"Because I came to The Keld those weeks ago tae speak with yer father about an alliance with Scotland," he said. "Yer father refused."

Her brow furrowed. "Then you were the one who attacked our village?"

That only made him harden. "Yer father was unreasonable and offensive," he said. "I came with a just offer. Alpin Canmore came with a just offer. We dunna know where Canmore is, but I can guess."

That was one thing Corisande did know about, but she wasn't going to say a word. She was afraid to tell him that Alpin Canmore was dead, afraid that she might be punished for it. Somehow, she was getting sucked into the politics of two countries and she was absolutely terrified.

She didn't belong here.

"I do not know what are speaking of," she said. "My sister and I will sleep in our wagon tonight and, tomorrow, I want to speak to the king again and ask him when he intends to release us."

She started to turn away, but he grasped her by the arm and forced her to remain. "Ye want tae know when ye'll be released?" he asked, frustration in his voice. "I'll tell ye. Why do ye think I brought ye here? There are terms tae yer release, my fine lady, and ye can thank yer father for them. He shamed me with his refusal, but I'll do the shaming now. I have his daughters in my control."

Corisande sensed something horrible coming. "What does that mean?"

His hand was still on her arm and he yanked her closer, eliciting a gasp of surprise and fear from her lips. His stinking breath was in her face as he hissed at her.

"Ye want yer freedom?" he said. "It will cost ye. One night

with me is the price for that freedom. Ye can return tae yer father and tell him the punishment for no' allying with the Scots was his daughter's innocence. It's his punishment for shaming me. Ye're going tae pay for all of yer father's sins, lassie, if ye want yer freedom."

Shocked and sickened, Corisande tried to yank her arm away. "How dare you say such a thing to me," she said through clenched teeth. "What a vile, despicable man you are!"

She continued to pull away, but he grabbed her with both hands, pulling her against his body. Corisande put her hands up against his chest as he sneered at her.

"One night," he muttered. "Warm my bed for one night and I will release ye and yer sister, and all of the men we captured. Agree and they shall be safe. Refuse and I shall take my frustrations out on yer sister and force ye tae watch. If you want tae save yer sister and the rest of the Sassenach captives, ye'll do as ye're told."

Terrified, Corisande lifted a hand and tried to slap him, but he pulled back and she only managed to rake her nails across his face. Infuriated, he shoved her to the ground and marched in Gaia's direction.

"Nay!" Corisande shouted, grabbing at his ankle and nearly tripping him. "Leave her alone!"

Gaia started to wail as MacDuff grabbed for her, but he slapped a hand over her mouth to silence her as he looked at Corisande.

"Ye know what ye must do," he said, his face red with fury. He removed his hand from Gaia's mouth and reached down, pulling Corisande off the ground. "Ye can return tae yer wagon and think about it. When ye make the proper decision, I'll be here waiting for ye. Make the wrong decision and I'll come for yer sister in the morning."

By this time, he was dragging them out of his tent and heading towards the two wagons that were parked on the perimeter of the encampment. There were men patrolling the perimeter with torches; they could see them through the mist. MacDuff dragged and pulled, hauling them all the way over to the wagons before lifting Gaia into one of them and then practically tossing Corisande in behind her.

"There," he snarled at Corisande. "Make yer choice and make it fast. I'll be waiting for ye."

With that, he whirled on his heel and stormed back through the mist. When he faded from sight, Gaia looked to her sister in horror.

"What choice?" she sobbed. "I heard him say something about Papa's sins. What did he mean? What is he going to do to me?"

Corisande looked at her little sister with horror and disbelief. Gaia may have been spoiled and annoying, but she was still her sister. She had to protect her.

She couldn't let anything happen to her.

She pulled Gaia into a frightened embrace.

"Oh, God," she breathed, fighting off tears. "He's not going to do anything to you. I will not let him."

Gaia didn't want to be hugged, at least not at the moment. She pulled back to look her sister in the eyes. "*What* was he speaking of?" she asked. "Cori, I know you think I am silly and lazy, and mayhap I am, but I have seen ten years and eight. I am educated, like you, and I am not stupid. I am not a child."

Corisande looked at her, seeing the young woman, but also still seeing the little girl she knew. "I know," she said. "It is difficult for me to realize how grown up you are. I will always want to protect you."

Gaia was surprisingly serious in the midst of their turmoil. "I understand," she said. "And although we have had our differences since I returned home, you are still my older sister and I love you. I know I am naughty and silly, but I do love you. Won't you please be honest with me and tell me what he said?"

Corisande wasn't entirely sure she should, but the more she looked at Gaia, the more she could feel herself relent. Perhaps if Gaia knew what was going on, she could protect herself should it come to that. All Corisande knew was that she was backed into a corner and she didn't see any way out.

The reality of it was starting to tear at her.

"You remember the battle at The Keld a few weeks ago?" she finally said.

Gaia nodded. "Aye."

"That man, MacDuff, was responsible for it."

Gaia's eyes widened. "What does he want from you?"

Corisande closed her eyes tightly before averting her gaze. "Oh, Gaia," she whispered, feeling the horror and pain to her very bones. "For the first time in my life, I am happy. So happy. Cole and I are to be married. Did you know that? Papa gave his permission."

Gaia appeared surprised for a moment but, just as quickly, her expression relaxed. "I suppose I knew it would happen," she said. "Oh, I pretended I did not, but I knew he was fond of you. I could see it in the way he looked at you. And I saw the way you looked at him. I… I am sorry for pinching him. I should not have done that."

Corisande looked at her and grinned, a moment of levity in the midst of a dire situation. "Not to worry," she said. "Cole told me that his hand slipped onto your buttocks."

Gaia grinned. "He spanked me!"

"You deserved it."

Gaia's expression of outrage held out for a mere second longer before she giggled. "I suppose I did," she said, but quickly sobered. "I am glad you are happy, Cori. I'm very glad Cole makes you happy. But what does that have to do with what the man said to you?"

Corisande lost her humor almost immediately. Heavily, she sighed. "He gave me his terms for our release," she said, struggling to get the words out. "He told me… he told me that one night with him would gain our release and the release of the English soldiers they captured with us. He'll free all of us."

Gaia's eyes widened when she realized what she meant. "You mean…?"

Corisande nodded. "He wants to bed me."

"And then he'll let us free?"

Corisande nodded again. Then, she burst into tears. "My God," she wept softly. "What will Cole say when he finds out? He will not want me after another man has touched me. But if I do not agree, MacDuff said that he will force himself upon you and make me watch. I have no choice if I am to protect you. Protect *everyone*."

She buried her face in her hands, sobbing, as Gaia sat there in shock. It was true that she was young and silly, and flirted with men most inappropriately, but she was an intelligent girl. She understood what her sister was telling her and she further understood what such a terrible proposal meant to her sister's happiness. Corisande, who was sweet and kind, who had suffered terrible luck with the knight from Hexham those years ago, and now had finally found love with Cole de Velt.

A happy future awaited her.

And now this.

Gaia had never done anything worthwhile in her life. She was vain and petty, and shallow if she was honest with herself. She wasn't worth her sister losing her happiness over and that was exactly what it would come to. Corisande was right – what man would want her after another had touched her?

Gaia could feel her sister's desperation, a horrible position to be in.

But there was something Corisande didn't know.

Gaia's promiscuousness wasn't something she simply acquired when she returned home from Prudhoe. It was something that had been part of her for the past couple of years, ever since she'd cornered one of the squires at Prudhoe and coerced the young man into kissing her. She had been curious and nothing more, but she discovered that she liked it. Kissing became fondling, and fondling had turned into coupling.

Gaia wasn't virgin.

In fact, she liked coupling a great deal. She liked the feel of a man between her legs. As she watched her sister weep over what would surely be a life-ruining event, Gaia knew she couldn't let her sister go through with it. Corisande had tried so hard to protect her, to be a good sister. She was everything Gaia wanted to be but couldn't. She didn't have it in her.

Corisande didn't deserve what the Scots bastard had heaped upon her.

Gaia knew she had to do something.

"Do not fret," she said after a moment, stroking Corisande's head. "Please do not fret. Mayhap it is not as bad as you think."

Corisande had tears and mucus running down her face. "He was plain with his demand," she said. "I did not misunderstand him."

She continued to weep into her apron now, bunched up around her face. Corisande was usually much more in control of herself, but the battle march and the stress of the situation had her in its grasp. Gaia listened to her weep, feeling heartbroken and sad.

"Lay down," she said, pushing her sister over onto the wagon bed. "Just… lay here for a while, Cori. Nothing is going to happen at this moment. You are tired. We are both tired. Lie down for a moment."

But Corisande struggled against her. "I cannot," she said. "If

I must do this, then I'd better get it over with. God, if there was only another way. To think of that man… doing things that only Cole should do…"

She was off sobbing again and, this time, Gaia pushed her all the way down onto the wagon bed.

"Shush," she said softly, stroking her sister's head. "Rest, Cori. Just rest for now. There is still time… time to do what needs to be done. Just rest."

Corisande stayed down this time. Lying on the cold planks of the wagon bed, she wept into her apron. She grieved for the situation, for the fact that, by choice, she would damage something solid and beautiful for the greater good. Not her greater good, but for her sister and the other English who had been captured.

For the greater good.

The ultimate sacrifice.

But her life, as she had hoped for, would be ended. As the mist grew denser and a think layer of water covered everything, Corisande wept herself into a fitful, exhausted sleep.

Gaia stayed with her sister as the woman slept, stroking her hair, trying to be of some comfort. But when it became clear that Corisande was in a deep sleep, Gaia stopped stroking. Carefully, she moved away from her sister and climbed down off the wagon bed.

The mist had grown heavier, but it wasn't so heavy that she didn't remember which direction MacDuff's tent was in. With a final glance to the wagon to make sure Corisande was still asleep, Gaia headed off through the mist.

She was nervous and shivering, terrified someone was going to grab her before she could make it to the tent. One of her failings, among others, was her complete lack of bravery, but that didn't stop her from going forth. Something deep inside her had stirred with her sister's situation, something buried and dormant. But Corisande's tears had awakened it.

Perhaps she wasn't completely lacking in courage, after all.

She just had to have a catalyst.

This was her moment to do something good.

MacDuff's tent was in front of her and she took a deep breath before entering. It was dark and smelly, but she caught sight of MacDuff lying on his pallet by the brazier.

She cleared her throat softly.

"I'm Gaia," she said. "I know what you said to my sister. I want to speak with you about it."

MacDuff sat up so fast that he nearly pitched himself off his pallet. He peered at her through the darkness of the tent for a moment. Once he was over his surprise, his manner cooled.

"What do ye want?" he asked. "Yer sister is supposed tae come tae me, no' ye."

Gaia stepped into the tent. "She is asleep," she said. "She does not know I have come and I want to keep it that way. You want something from her, but I am here in her stead."

"Why?"

"Because I will do what you asked of her."

That had him up off the pallet. "Ye?" he asked with suspicion. "Is this some kind of trick?"

"Nay. I am quite serious."

He eyed her as if he weren't convinced. She was young and pretty enough, and he looked her up and down in an appraising manner.

"If ye came tae talk me out of it, it willna work," he finally said. "Those are the terms. One night with me and I'll let all of ye go free."

Gaia didn't back away from him when he came close. "I did not come to convince you to change your mind," she said. She was wearing a simple but durable frock, like her sister was, something that laced at the neckline and down one side.

Meeting the man's eyes, she reached up and tugged on the tie at her neck. "I came to give you what you want. My sister is older and frigid. But I'm younger and need a good teacher. Will you teach me, my lord?"

As MacDuff watched, Gaia pulled loose the tie at her neck, revealing the tantalizing swell of her cleavage. He licked his lips, for the peek of her flesh was enough to arouse him. In truth, he supposed it didn't matter which sister he took, so long as he took one of them. This one seemed more compliant than the older one. When he took a woman to his bed, he wanted her to respond to him, not fight him. He couldn't be certain that even if the older one came to him of her own free will, that she wouldn't resist the whole thing.

But the younger one…

Nay, she wasn't resistant at all.

The more he looked at the younger sister, the more aroused he became.

"I can teach ye, lass," he said after a moment. "But will ye be a good student?"

Gaia smiled seductively. "More than likely your best student," she said confidently. "But just so we are clear on the terms – it was one night with one sister, correct?"

"Aye. And ye *will* speak of this tae yer father. I want him tae know."

"I will tell him," she said. "And you'll not touch my sister?"

He hesitated, so she reached out and put a hand on his crotch, feeling his arousal through the fabric. As she fondled him, MacDuff let out a hiss of pure lust.

"Aye," he said, groaning as she stroked him. "Give yerself over tae me and I'll no' touch yer sister."

"Swear it?" she said as she squeezed slightly.

He quivered. "Aye," he said. "I swear it. One sister is as good as the other."

Gaia's response was to reach underneath his tunic and put her hot hands on his swollen member. As she dropped to her knees and put her mouth on it, MacDuff lost all sense of vengeance and drive against Alastor de Bourne or his family. At the moment, the youngest daughter had him under her spell and he was willingly compliant.

And enjoying every minute of it.

He never did give her the message William had meant for The Marshal that night.

The only message that concerned him was his own.

CHAPTER TWENTY-TWO

CORISANDE WAS CONFUSED.

She'd awoken just before dawn to the wagon being jostled, rising to see that the horses were being put back into their harness. The English soldiers and wagons that had been taken captive the day before were being rounded up as several Scots, MacDuff included, began to organize them into a line.

Wiping the sleep from her eyes, Corisande couldn't believe her what she was witnessing.

The mist was still heavy, but there was a hint of sunlight overhead as dawn approached. However, it was dark and cold all around, and the Scots had torches to pierce the mist. She could hear gulls calling, as they usually did in Berwick, scavenger birds looking for a morning meal. Around her, it looked to her as if the captives were all being moved, her included.

Gaia was sitting next to her in the wagon, her legs hanging over the back. She was wrapped up in a blanket, watching the activity, as Corisande sat up beside her.

"What is happening?" she asked, sounding hoarse. "Where are we going?"

Gaia had circles under her eyes as she looked out over the

mist. "We are leaving."

"Leaving for where?"

"Back to England."

Corisande didn't quite understand her at first. Then, her eyes widened. "Back to England?" she asked, looking around rather frantically. "What do you mean? They're taking us back to Papa?"

Gaia looked at her, then. "We are going home," she said plainly. "They are releasing us, Cori."

Corisande stared at her sister. "But…" she sputtered. Then, she grabbed her sister by the arm and lowered her voice. "But how is this possible? MacDuff told me… I was to come to him last night and he would release us, but I must have fallen asleep. Why did you not wake me? You *knew* what had to happen."

Gaia's gaze lingered on her for a moment before returning it to the misty landscape and the men moving about.

"We are being released and that is all that should matter," she said. "Be joyful, Cori. We are returning to England and you can return to Cole with a clear conscience and a clean body. You needn't worry anymore. Cole will still love you."

Corisande stared at her. She may have been groggy, but she wasn't senseless. Something was amiss because Gaia was being far too casual about the entire situation. Her usually weeping, skittish sister was as hard as a rock. It was then that Corisande noticed that she didn't recognize the blanket Gaia was wrapped in.

It wasn't one of theirs.

"Where did you get this?" she asked, pulling at the fabric.

Gaia pulled it right around her. "It was cold."

"*Who* gave you the blanket, Gaia?"

Gaia stared at her a moment. Corisande was only now noticing the dark-circled eyes and she was greatly concerned, but before she could voice those concerns, Gaia spoke softly.

"Is it not enough that we are leaving?" she asked. "Please stop asking so many questions. If you misbehave, they may change their mind, so just... be quiet. Let us leave this place before you start pestering me."

Corisande had no idea what Gaia was talking about, nor did she recognize the attitude her sister was conveying. She peered at her closely, trying to figure out what was happening.

"Gaia," she whispered calmly. "What do you know about all of this? Won't you tell me?"

The wagon suddenly lurched, throwing them both off-balance as it began to make its way through the grass, heading towards the trees. On the other side of the trees was the road that they had traveled upon when they'd been brought into Scotland, but Corisande didn't know that and Gaia didn't remember. All they knew was that the wagons were heading into the trees with a Scots escort, including MacDuff himself.

Heading for England.

The mist was becoming lighter as the sun began to rise. They could see soldiers walking around them through the mist, a few of them leaning on colleagues for support. They were English soldiers and Corisande caught sight of a few de Bourne men up ahead.

Everyone was leaving, just as MacDuff had promised if she...

...if she...?

"Tell me what you know, Gaia," she turned to her sister and hissed. "If you do not tell me, I will start screaming and possibly they will stop this caravan to discover what is the matter. And I shall tell them that my sister is ill and they will..."

Gaia cut her off. "Shush!"

She put a hand over Corisande's mouth, but it was only a temporary measure. Gaia knew Corisande was serious. In fact, she knew she should probably tell her before someone else did.

When she'd returned to the wagon, wrapped in MacDuff's blanket, several English soldiers had seen her, including the de Bourne soldiers. They had seen her coming from the direction of MacDuff's tent.

But they'd also seen Corisande and Gaia coming from his tent the night before, which could have also meant something lascivious. Two women coming from the Earl of Fife's tent, unchaperoned, and then the captives being released at daybreak could start a myriad of dark rumors.

It had to be addressed.

But that was more terrifying than the actual deed for Gaia. Now that it was over with, she wondered if she was brave enough to face what she had done. Perhaps she had hoped to keep it from Corisande, but the truth was that it simply wasn't realistic. Corisande had to know. Last night, Gaia had been courageous, but this morning…

Not so much.

"Please, Cori," she said softly, pulling her hand away from her sister's mouth. "Please be quiet. I will tell you want you want to know, but you must be quiet."

Corisande's gaze was intense. "What do you know?" she demanded. "What *happened*?"

Reaching out, Gaia took her hand and squeezed it tightly. "Let me do this for you, Cori," she whispered. "I had to do it."

"Had to do what?"

Gaia took a deep breath. "It did not matter which sister warmed his bed, only that one did," she murmured. "I could not let it be you. Not when you have a future with Cole. You wanted to protect me, but not this time. Not like that."

Corisande's eyes widened when she realized what her sister was telling her. Then, she slapped her own hand over her mouth to keep from crying out. As she looked at her little sister, her eyes filled with tears.

"Nay," she breathed. "Oh, Gaia… nay. Tell me that you did not."

Gaia squeezed her hand again. "It is not the end of the world," she said. "Look at me. I am uninjured. You are uninjured. We are going home and you will marry Cole. Everything will be as it should be. That is all we should be concerned with."

The wagon bumped over the ground as they entered the trees, dripping wet from the mist. Water fell on their faces, but Corisande didn't even bother to wipe it away.

She was far too devastated.

"But you…" she wept softly. "You should not have done that. It is my duty, as your sister, to…"

Gaia cut her off. "You have always protected me," she said. "I have been a silly, worthless fool, but you have always protected me. It is my turn to protect *you*."

Corisande didn't know what to say. It was the most selfless, brave act she'd ever heard of. From Gaia, no less. She had no idea her little sister was capable of such things. She pulled Gaia into an embrace, holding her tightly and feeling like a failure. She was horribly torn. She loved Cole, but she loved Gaia, too. Now, Gaia had done something no woman should ever have to do, all to protect her sister.

It was shattering to realize that.

But that grief, that deep agony, was Corisande's last coherent through before the forest around her exploded.

THEY'D FOUND AN old man who knew the land around Berwick extremely well.

While chaos was going on in the town of Berwick and Scots were being captured or killed by the dozens, a very old man who lived in a hovel to the north of the town had been sitting in the tavern called *Blankenship* and drinking to his heart's content. When the English had come looking for someone to tell them about the hills north of Berwick, he'd been more than willing to come out with the information for the price of another drink. Three drinks later, Kress and Achilles had what they needed to know.

When the Scots began to move through the mist at dawn, the Executioner Knights were ready.

The old man had told them about a portion of the hills that was rocky and protected by a ring of trees, trees that would protect the Scots from English eyes or bombardment. He even drew a crude map for them in the dirt floor of the tavern, describing a stream that dumped into the river from the northeast, leading straight into the area where the Scots were most likely gathered. All the Executioner Knights had to do was find that stream that fed into the River Tweed.

It wasn't that difficult.

Heading out of Berwick city in the mist, they crossed the bridge and came to a road that led to the Ord Crossing. All they had to do was follow it. Once they made it to the bridge, they crossed over and began to search the bank on the other side where the old man had said the stream was located. They found it, though it was disguised in a marshy area, but the stream itself headed northeast, right into a forested area.

As they approached, they could smell the smoke from the cooking fires.

They knew they'd found the encampment.

At that point, the sun was rising further and there was more light to work by. And be seen by. They stashed the horses near the edge of the trees and made their way inside the forest, picking through the wet undergrowth, until they finally began to see signs of human habitation. An entire Scots encampment was beginning to awaken.

They spread out inside the tree line to see if they could find the women.

That proved to be a little more difficult and they hunted and hunted until, finally, Essien spied Gaia heading for a wagon. She was all wrapped up in a blanket, shuffling through the muddy, smelly camp. He passed the word to Cole, who came running. In fact, all of them came running. Where there was Gaia, there had to be Corisande, but they hadn't spotted her yet and Cole's heart was in his throat. He'd done a thousand dangerous missions, but not one as nerve-wracking at this one.

Then, the Scots started coming.

They were heading over to the wagon where Gaia was now sitting. There were other wagons around and they realized that they were looking at the wagons that had been stolen in the raid on the English. There were also English soldiers milling about, most of them wounded, all of the looking haggard and beaten. A man with a dark beard and expensive clothing began directing them to hitch the horses to the wagons.

Something was happening.

But their unimpeded view of the situation was disturbed by Scots patrols, who were prowling through the undergrowth with torches. It was that spot of light that gave them away, so the Executioner Knights had to hide until the patrol passed and then they'd go right back to spying.

Cole saw, very clearly, when Corisande sat up from the wagon bed. Evidently, she'd been there all along and he simply hadn't seen her. She and Gaia sat in the rear of the wagon bed as activity went on around them and the man with the dark beard directed men to drive the wagons into the trees.

Suddenly, they were coming in their direction.

With that, Alexander took charge. Using hand signals, he sent Cole, Addax, and Essien into trees to the south. Kress and Achilles weren't too far from them. Alexander took Peter, Bric, and Dashiell with him to the north as they hid out on the opposite sides of what was a clear wagon trail through the forest. That was where the Scots were heading.

As the Executioner Knights lay in wait, the Scots entered the forest.

From what Cole could see, there were only five or six Scots walking along with the wagons. The man with the dark beard was walking with them, unfortunately for him, close to the wagon containing Corisande and Gaia. Cole looked at Addax and Essien and indicated that he would be the one to take out the man with the beard and silently instructing Essien to jump onto the wagon bench of Corisande and Gaia's wagon. When the attack started and the alarm was raised, he wanted that wagon to be charging out of the trees and far away from any fighting that would occur.

Essien understood that.

The anticipation grew.

The wagons traveled deeper into the forest, including the one carrying Corisande and Gaia. Cole watched with concern because the women were embracing. He thought that Corisande might even be weeping, but he couldn't be sure. Nearly frantic to get to her, his gaze sought out Alexander's, back behind a rather large tree, and Alexander finally gave the signal to move out.

Everybody swept in.

Cole moved fast for a big man. He ran up behind the man with the dark beard before the man could even turn to look at him. Grabbing him by the hair, he dragged his dagger across the man's throat, slitting it so deeply that he nearly decapitated him. Kress and Achilles were on top of two Scotsmen who tried to put up a fight, but they could hardly get their swords up before they were having their throats cut. Everyone was going for the throat to prevent the men from crying out and alerting the thousands of Scots in the encampment.

No sound, no witnesses.

As the bodies were already falling away, Essien leapt onto the wagon bench. The wagon was being driven by a de Bourne soldier, but Essien yanked away the reins and frightened the horses into a run. The wagon zinged past Cole, who didn't even have time to say a word to Corisande. He watched her as the wagon headed towards the main road that would take them to the Ord Crossing, but all he could do was watch. She was being taken to safety and that was all he cared about.

Behind him, Addax had taken care of another Scotsman while Alexander and Bric had managed to take care of the rest. Peter and Dashiell were urging the English who were walking to jump into the wagons, which were then driven off in a rush.

As quickly as the ambush started, it was over.

Miraculously, the Scots encampment hadn't been alerted yet. The ambush had taken place deeper in the trees so that any odd sounds were muffled, and there wasn't an onslaught of angry Scots rushing them now. Cole and the others raced back to the horses and, quickly mounting, followed the wagons as they thundered from the trees.

Finally, they were free.

Cole was able to catch up with the wagon that held Corisande and Gaia. The women were holding on to the sides of the wagon for dear life, but Corisande caught sight of Cole and her features crumpled. He could see the tears. They couldn't stop until they were over the bridge and back with the English encampment to the south, so all he could do was blow kisses at her as she wept.

It was absolutely heartbreaking.

He desperately wanted to hold her.

Over the bridge, the wagons roared, finally into England. It wasn't a short ride, by any means, and took a couple of hours to reach their destination south of Berwick. They did slow the pace once they got into England, however, but they still wanted to reach the bulk of the army quickly, purely for safety reasons. They followed the road that curved around, following the bend in the River Tweed, and headed south where the armies had set up an encampment.

What they found when they came into sight of the encampment, however, was more armies than ever before.

Richmond had arrived.

The Richmond Castle garrison was the largest Marshal garrison in the north and there were at least three thousand men, all of them moving to the east towards the mouth of the River Tweed. The fog was lifting, burning off as the sun rose, and the landscape was laid open. The main encampment was visible in the fields to the south, with smoke from dozens of cooking fires spiraling into the air.

Since the pace was slower now and Alexander had called the wagons to a walk for the rest of the way, Cole directed his steed next to Corisande and plucked her right out of the wagon.

They came together in a clash of warmth and fabric, mail and hair. Her hair was all over him as she squeezed him around the neck, so tightly that she was nearly strangling him, but he'd never been so happy to be strangled. It was relief beyond measure for them both. Cole could hear her weeping softly against him and he let go of the reins so he could hold her with both arms. As Drago plodded along, weary from the run to and from Scotland, Cole pulled Corisande away from him so he could get a close look at her.

"Let me see you," he said, his voice tight with emotion. "Are you well, love? Did they hurt you?"

Corisande shook her head. "They did not hurt me," she said. "I am well."

He was looking her over carefully – her face, her neck, her head – as if he didn't believe her. He was touching, stroking, to make sure she was real. "Are you certain?"

"I am certain."

He let out a sigh that nearly deflated his entire body. "Thank God," he muttered. "Cori, I was so terrified that… it does not matter. Thank God you are well. That is all I care about."

Corisande nodded again, kissing him as he returned her kisses furiously. He was just so grateful that he ended up glancing up to the sky in a silent prayer of thanks as she buried her face in his neck. Finally, she was safe, exactly where he wanted her. But as he held her and gave thanks, he noticed a little, blonde head in the wagon bed.

He found himself looking down at Gaia.

"And you, my lady?" he asked, lifting his voice. "Are you well?"

Gaia had been watching their reunion very carefully, studying every movement, every kiss. There was something wistful in her eyes.

But she nodded her head.

"I am well," she said. "I am not injured."

He smiled faintly at her. "That is excellent news," he said. "God be praised that you are both safe."

Gaia smiled weakly, watching Cole and Corisande a moment longer before looking away. She seemed sad, and dazed, and Cole attributed that to the situation they had just been rescued from. He didn't give it another thought. He was just so grateful that he had Corisande in his arms that he really didn't think about anything else. They rode the rest of the way to the encampment where Alastor, Ares, Atlas, and Anteaus were waiting.

Alastor scooped Gaia out of the wagon bed, hugging his youngest child tightly. Though Cole was reluctant to let her go, for necessity's sake, he had to lower Corisande into Ares' waiting arms. Dismounting, he handed Drago over to a squire and immediately took Corisande back into his embrace in front of her brothers and father. He didn't even care that they were present with his unbridled display of relief and affection.

If they had a problem with it, then he invited them to say so.

He had an answer ready.

"Are you well, Cori?" Alastor asked her, Gaia still in his arms. "Did they hurt you, lass?"

Corisande shook her head. "Nay," she said. "I am not injured."

"Are you certain?"

"I am certain."

"What happened?" he asked. "Can you at least tell us that?"

Corisande wasn't sure what to say, at first. There were so many answers to that question, but she truthfully didn't feel like reliving any of it. She was still in the grips of the guilt over Gaia's sacrifice.

But for her father's sake, she answered.

"It is difficult to know where to start," she said. "We were taken as we waited to move forward with the armies yesterday. They took us to their encampment where we spoke with the king."

Alastor's eyebrows lifted. "The king?" he repeated. "William?"

Corisande nodded. "He was in the encampment with his men."

Alastor couldn't help the expression of shock that crossed his face. "I see," he said, setting Gaia to her feet. "What did he say to you?"

"He asked my name," she said. "He wanted to know who was fighting in Berwick. Since every English army flies a standard, I saw no harm in telling him."

Alastor regarded her a moment. "Did he know you were my daughter?"

Corisande looked at Gaia, the one who had divulged that particularly detail. "He knew," she said. "Papa, may we sit and rest? I am so very tired."

Alastor nodded. "Of course," he said. "Forgive me. I am just so glad to see you that I did not stop to think of your comfort. Please, come; the tents are warm. Are you hungry? There is food."

Corisande took Gaia by the hand, but not before she ripped the blanket off of her. She cast it to the ground. "Burn that," she told her brothers. Collecting Gaia's hand once more, she looked to Cole before she moved. "Are you coming?"

He nodded. "I will be along directly," he said. "Go ahead."

Wearily, Corisande moved in the direction of the largest de Bourne tent, finding her way through de Bourne soldiers with cooking fires of their own. Cole, Alastor, Ares, Atlas, and Anteaus watched them go.

"Well?" Alastor turned to Cole. "What happened? Where did you find them?"

Cole sighed heavily. "In the hills where The Marshal believed the Scots to be hiding," he said. "They are camped up in those hills north of the river."

"And how did you find my daughters?"

"We were very fortunate."

The answer came not from Cole, but from Alexander, who was walking up behind them with Addax, Essien, Kress, and Achilles.

They turned to him.

"Fortunate, Sherry?" Alastor said. "Explain."

Alexander pulled off one glove so he could scratch his scalp. "The Scots were moving them," he said. "I do not know where, but they were on the move. We caught them just in time."

Alastor looked stricken. "My God," he breathed. "They were going to take them somewhere safe, to use as hostages."

"Probably."

The mere thought horrified Alastor. "Then you have my deepest gratitude," he said, looking around at the Executioner Knights gathering. A couple of them, Bric and Achilles, had bloodstains all over them as a testament to the brutality of the rescue. "I am in your debt, truly."

Alexander held up a hand to ease the excited, relieved father. "We are glad we were able to find your daughters," he said. But his gaze moved over Alastor's head to the massive army moving in the distance, heading north to the mouth of the River Tweed. "It looks as if Richmond has arrived."

Alastor turned to look at the mass movement of troops. "Aye," he said. "Richmond and de Royans, apparently. They were able to bring troops from Bowes Castle. Well over four thousand men, now moving to the mouth of the River Tweed because the longships were sighted about an hour ago, heading south against a stiff breeze. The progress is slow, but that is working in our favor. The Marshal is calling all armies to Berwick and to the mouth of the river. It seems we take our stand today because as soon as the Northmen come closer, the Scots will try to join with them."

Everyone was watching the movement. In fact, they could see Savernake and de Winter moving out with them, too, armies that Dashiell and Bric were in command of.

"I suppose I shall join my men," Bric said what they were all thinking. "They cannot make a move without me."

The Irish brogue was thick with the jest, but the point was taken. Both Bric and Dashiell mounted their steeds, heading off to rejoin their armies. Achilles tapped Kress.

"We should join Richmond," he said. "Max and Caius will be expecting us."

Kress nodded, turning to Alastor and Cole. "We must take our leave," he said, his gaze lingering on Cole. "It was good to see you in action today, Cole. It has been a while since we have had such an adventure."

Cole smiled. "I have missed it."

Flashing a grin, Kress joined Achilles and the two of them headed off to join Richmond and de Royans. That left Peter, Alexander, Addax, and Essien, and it was Peter who bowed out next.

"My father will be looking for me," he said. "I must join the de Lohr war machine and so must Sherry. My father will come looking for him if he does not comply."

Alexander grunted. "The success of the entire de Lohr army has been up to me," he said sarcastically, eyeing Peter. "You are just another pretty blond de Lohr face, Peter. You can fight like the devil himself, but you haven't a brain in your head, I am sorry to say."

Peter started laughing. "That's not what your mother said last night."

"I do not have a mother."

"Not after I was finished with her, you don't!"

Alexander swatted him and Peter roared with laughter, heading off to find the de Lohr army as Alexander mounted his stallion.

"I swear to you that my sword will slip someday and cut off something vital of his," he said. Then, he snorted. "He's a fool, but I'm rather fond of him. And you, Cole – well done today. I am glad your lady is safe."

Cole went to him, taking his hand and holding it for a moment. "I owe you everything," he said. "I will see you after the battle."

"Indeed, you will."

As Alexander headed off, Cole returned his attention to Alastor.

"Does my father still hold the castle?" he asked.

Alastor nodded. "Still," he said. "He has his entire army positioned inside of it, prepared to fend off the Scots and the Northmen along with the Earls of Orkney should they break through the line of English."

Cole looked off to the northeast, to the city with the castle crouched like a panther over the dark blue ribbon of the River Tweed.

"Addax and Essien and I must join him," he said. "With your permission, I will bid Cori farewell."

Alastor nodded, but as Cole moved past him, he reached out and grasped the man's arm. "Your father told me about Teviot and Lady Audrie marrying another," he said. "I told you when that situation was settled, you would have my permission to marry my daughter. That is still true. You have my blessing."

Cole smiled broadly. "I had hoped you would say that," he said. "I promised you once that I would love her for the rest of my life, my lord. That has not changed."

"Good," Alastor said. "Go, now. Bid her farewell. We have a busy day ahead of us."

That was an understatement. Cole headed over to the big de Bourne tent, quietly calling to Corisande until the tent flap moved aside and she appeared.

The smile on her face filled him with comfort and contentment and joy such as he'd never known. He could look at that smile until the end of his days and never, ever grow weary of it.

"Gaia is already asleep," she said softly. "Poor dear. She is exhausted."

He reached up, moving a stray piece of hair from her face.

"And you?"

She shrugged. "Weary, of course," she said. "But I am thankful for my life. I am very thankful for your life. It was heroic of you to come and save us."

"And you think that I would not?"

"I did not mean it that way. I simply meant that you are a brave and bold man."

Reaching out, he took her hand in his big mitt, bring it to his lips for a tender kiss. "I am a brave and bold man who loves you more with each passing moment," he said. "I would do anything for you, Cori. Anything in the world."

"As I would do the same for you."

"Then go home. Take Gaia and leave this field of battle so I know that you are safe."

Her smile faded. "You know I cannot leave," she said. "As you have obligations, so do I. I know you do not like that, but you cannot change it. Not now, at least."

He didn't want to get into a tussle with her when he had only just gotten her back, so he backed off. He didn't want to ruin this moment by being belligerent.

"You may as well know that I am selfish," he said. "I only want you to be safe, my queen. You know that. And that makes me selfish because it is for my peace of mind."

Corisande relented a little. "It does not make you selfish," she said. "It makes you sweet and wonderful and thoughtful. But right now, I will not leave. My father needs me and so do my brothers. I must be here to see this through, but once we are married… if you do not want me to go on any de Velt battle marches as your surgeon, then I suppose I shall have to obey you."

A smile tugged at his lips. "Your father just told me that I have his permission without reservation to marry you," he said. "When this battle is over, I intend to do precisely that."

She broke out into a big smile. "There is nothing I want more," she said. "I am looking forward to it more than you know."

"As am I," he said. But then, he turned his attention in the direction of the mobilizing army, moving towards the river. "But first, we have a city to hold and Northmen to chase away. I am going to have to leave you for a while."

Her smile faded. "Where are you going?"

He looked over his shoulder, towards the castle in the distance. "To Berwick Castle," he said. "I must help my father hold the fortress. Our suspicion is that the Scots will try to take it back with the help of the Northmen, so I must be there to defend it to the last man if that is the case."

She reached out her hands, clutching his big fingers. "You will be careful," she said softly. "You are a great and noble knight and I should like you to father my children. And we are going to have a lot of children, so I will need you around for some time to come."

He chuckled. "How many children?"

She lifted her shoulders. "A dozen, at least," she said. "Mayhap more. I've not yet decided."

He wriggled his eyebrows. "That is a lot."

"Complaining?"

He shook his head, pulling her into an embrace. "Nay," he murmured in her ear. "Because the fun will be in the practice."

She giggled as he hugged her tightly, lifting her off the ground so that her feet were dangling. Her arms were around his neck, her hands in his hair, as they simply held one another. It was a big day and they both knew it, but Corisande couldn't even entertain the thought that this would be the last time she would ever hold him. To her, he was big and strong and indestructible.

She had to have faith.

"Until I hold you again in my arms, I will see you in my dreams," she murmured. "I love you, my darling. Be safe."

He kissed her head, her cheek, and finally her lips before setting her on her feet. "And I love you," he murmured, releasing her. Then, he pointed at her. "And stay away from Scots."

She grinned. "I will try."

"No trying. *Do.*"

"I will do my best."

"You are not giving me any confidence, Woman."

She laughed at him and he grinned, waving a hand at her as if he were finished with her foolery. But her smile faded and she blew a kiss at him. He gave her a wink and headed for his horse.

Corisande stood there and watched as Cole mounted Drago. Addax and Essien were already on their steeds and the three of them took off, heading for Berwick Castle.

Heading into the belly of the beast.

It was all she could do not to break down in tears.

"He will be fine, you know."

Blinking away the tears that stung, she turned to see Ares standing a few feet away. She nodded, trying very hard to be brave.

"He is a de Velt," she said. "They are unbreakable. I know he will be fine."

Ares' gaze lingered on her. "I thought, at first, that he was fortunate to have you, but now I think you are fortunate to have him," he said. "You know he serves William Marshal, don't you?"

She nodded. "He told me," she said. "How did you know?"

Ares gave her a wry smile. "It did not take a genius to figure it out when he assimilated into The Marshal's men," he said. "Spies and assassins and cutthroats, they are. But admirable knights. There are none finer."

Corisande smiled at her eldest brother, a surprisingly wise man when the mood struck him. "And you?" she said. "The great Sheriff of Westmorland? I think you're a fine knight, too. I'm very proud to be your sister."

He reached out, stroking her cheek affectionately. "I'm glad you're back from your Scots adventure," he said. "When you feel like telling me what really happened, I will listen."

Her smile faded. "What do you mean?"

"I mean that what you told Father wasn't the entire truth, was it?"

He was very astute. Years of dealing with criminals and liars in his line of work had made him so, but Corisande wasn't going to divulge something she wasn't even sure she could ever verbalize. Even as she thought on it, guilt consumed her like a flame consumes kindling.

She could feel it burning into her very soul.

"There is really nothing more to tell," she said, avoiding giving him an exact answer. "They captured us when we were waiting for wounded with the surgeon's and provisions wagons, they took us to their encampment, and Cole and his men rescued us this morning. It is not as if they had us in chains, Ares. They were not… unkind to us, given the situation."

He was looking at her as if he didn't believe her, but had the courtesy not to press her. "We can speak more of it when you are rested," he said. "As for Cole – he will be well. You will see him when this is over."

Corisande appreciated the encouragement. She also appreciated the change in subject. "I want to see you, too, when this is all over."

Ares flashed her a grin. "That is my intention, also."

"God go with you, Ares."

Corisande watched him head off into the de Bourne encampment where men were mobilizing. She could hear her father and brothers shouting at them. It seemed apparent that everyone was heading towards the city of Berwick and the mouth of the river, to both fight off the Northmen and repel the Scots that were determined to join forces with them. No matter what, they had to keep the Northmen out of the river.

Something told Corisande there were going to be a lot of wounded to tend to. Weary as she was, she had come on the battle march for a specific task. As she'd told Cole, she had no intention of shirking that duty.

Squaring her shoulders, Corisande went about preparing for what was to come and praying she still had a reason to live when it was all over.

God keep you, Cole...

CHAPTER TWENTY-THREE

Seven days later

"BERWICK HELD," COLE muttered, looking over the battered walls. "I will admit, I had my moments of doubt. But it held. We have the castle and the town."

He was speaking to Julian, Addax and Essien as they stood down by the river's gate of Berwick Castle. They were on the rocky shore of the river itself, gazing up at the walls that had taken a beating from the Scots.

But the river itself was even worse.

Burned-out hulls, three of them, littered the shoreline. Those were the unlucky longships belonging to the Earls of Orkney that had managed to break the line at the mouth of the River Tweed the day of their arrival, only to get close to the castle so Jax could unload his war machines on them.

They fired flaming barrels of fatty oil down onto the ships, barrels they'd confiscated from a couple of the taverns in town and tallow they'd taken from several residences. They'd raided the town in order to get enough fuel to launch at the longships that were trying to come ashore, but once the flaming barrels hit the decks and spread the burning oil, the ships went up in flames.

Those who escaped to shore found a line of de Velt men, led by Cole, waiting for them.

Bodies littered the rocky ground, the shallows of the river, and even up the sides of the hill upon which the castle was perched, not only from the Northmen, but from the Scots who tried to use the river to re-take the castle in the same fashion Cole had.

Only they'd been unsuccessful at it.

After seven long days of fighting, the worst was over. Berwick was still standing and the English still had control of it. But the mess of the battle, and the far-reaching implications, would last for months and probably years to come.

William the Rough had already taken what remained of his army back towards Edinburgh, and that included the remnants that belonged to the Earls of Orkney. They had been decimated. Of thirteen longships that had tried to come ashore, all of them had been burned in some fashion. Only one was remotely seaworthy, and Caius had control of that one. They were using it to keep the captives, like a floating prison, and there were plenty of prisoners this time around. There was talk of setting it on fire and sending it out to sea like a good Viking funeral.

Jax was in favor of that, and so was Caius and many of the other commanders, but The Marshal thought that might be a little too barbaric. However, when dealing with Executioner Knights and The Dark Lord, there were no limits to their barbaric ideals.

Even The Marshal knew that.

On the sixth day of the battle, the reinforcements had arrived with armies headed by Gart Forbes, Cullen de Nerra, and Kevin de Lara from the Marches. The bulk of David de Lohr's army from Canterbury was just a few days behind. New, fresh troops relieved those who had been fighting for six long days, which is why the battle wound up so quickly by the seventh day.

The Scots were exhausted, but they didn't have the reinforcements that the English did, so on this seventh day, nearly every part of what had been a nasty and prolonged fight was subdued.

Finally, the dawn of a new day signaled the end of the Scots and Northmen invasion.

For now.

"And what does the future hold for us all?" Addax asked in reply to Cole's statement. "Now that Berwick has held and it is in the hands of the English, what now?"

Cole looked at his friend, a man he'd been close to for two years. "What do you mean?"

Addax lifted his shoulders. "Just that," he said, looking around at the utter mess surrounding them. "Your mission is over, Cole. So is mine and my brother's. What do we do now? Return to your father's service along with Julian? Or do we find our adventure elsewhere?"

Cole smiled faintly. "I'll have plenty of adventure here," he said. "I am going to take a new wife and become the garrison commander for Berwick, as it now belongs to my father. Well, The Marshal thinks it belongs to him, but my father is not going to relinquish this prize, so I will be entrusted with it as a neutral party since I serve them both. The castle is mine. Julian is to go to Foulburn, my outpost, and assume command. With the Scots active, my father wants to make sure it is a fortified position."

Addax grinned at Julian for what was largely a promotion before slapping Cole on the shoulder. "I am proud of you, my friend," he said. "Garrison commander of this mighty bastion is a proud thing, indeed. Do you need a second in command?"

He meant him and Cole laughed softly. "I would not have it any other way," he said. "Will you join me here? Es, too. If we can stand him."

Essien was standing several feet away, listening to the chatter, but he didn't seem very attentive to it. In fact, he seemed weary and morose, which was not like him at all. Essien was always the life of any gathering, even if it was just a couple of men speaking of the future. But not today.

Both Cole and Addax looked at him.

"Why so gloomy?" Addax asked. "You have been perfectly fine all morning until you went off to run missives for The Marshal. What in the world did the man say to you that has you so woeful?"

Essien shook his head, trying to perk himself up. "Nothing," he said. "I am simply weary, like everyone else. It has been a long few days."

Addax nodded firmly. "Long days of killing the Scots," he said. "Truly, the bombardment of the longships that tried to reach the castle was a masterful stroke. I've never seen such skill, Cole. You are to be commended."

Cole was modest. "It was not easy, that is for certain," he said. "None of it would have happened had Julian not raided the entire town for barrels and oil. But the calculations of launching those barrels from the catapults so they could land on the ships was terribly difficult. I missed a few times."

"But you hit when it mattered," Addax reminded him, pointing to the burned-out hulls. "Here are the results of your skill. You are brilliant."

Cole lifted his eyebrows. "Aye, I am," he said. "And Lady Corisande is a very fortunate woman."

"Indeed, she is," Addax agreed. "When is the wedding?"

Cole shrugged. "I told her when this battle was over, so as soon as possible, I should think," he said. "When the Scots backed away from Berwick two days ago, I was able to break away to see her, but I've not seen her since and as much as I love the three of you, I love her more, so I am going to find my betrothed and spend some much-needed time with her."

Julian slapped him on the arm. "Go," he said. "Meanwhile, we'll start organizing men to clean up this shoreline, so we need to find some men to help. Everyone has been concentrated at the mouth of the river, but we need to start cleaning up this area, too."

Cole started to move towards the stumpy tower that led to the stairs up the wall. "You'll have to ask Sherry where he can spare men," he said. "He is in command of the clean-up after the battle. He'll assign some men to help."

Julian followed him, as did Addax. "And you will not help us?" Julian asked. "When you are done with your lady-love, that is."

Cole turned to glare at his brother. "Nay," he said flatly. "I have done enough, making sure these ships were burned to the waterline. The least you can do is clean up my mess while I go on to more relaxing pursuits. Like Cori."

Julian chuckled. "She will be very glad to see you."

Cole could only smile. Anything that had to do with Corisande had him smiling. It had indeed been a long seven days, and he'd only been able to see her once for a very short time during that period, so he was anxious to go to her. It was all he'd been dreaming of. He was just heading up the stairs when he noticed that Essien was still down on the shore. He was moving, but not very quickly.

Cole paused.

"Es!" he shouted. "What are you doing? Are you coming with us?"

Essien nodded and ran to catch up with them. But the moment his foot hit the bottom step, he came to a stop.

"Cole, wait," he said.

Cole came to a halt with Julian and Addax behind him, all of them turning to Essien. "What is it?" Cole asked.

Essien took a deep breath and peered up at him. "I… I need

to speak with you."

"What about?"

"Something I heard when I was running missives for The Marshal earlier today."

"What did you hear?"

Essien sighed heavily and hung his head for a moment, trying to find the right words. "Come... come down here, please," he said. "I do not want to shout at you."

Cole, Julian, and Addax looked at each other, shrugged, and came back down the stairs so they were standing next to Essien at the very bottom.

"I am here," Cole said. "What is so important?"

Essien scratched his head. "You know I would never lie to you, Cole."

"I know."

"And what I am about to tell you is the truth, as I heard it."

"And?"

"*And* I heard something today that I think you must know," he said. "Even if it is only malicious gossip, it must be addressed."

"What is it?"

Essien took a deep breath and looked him in the eyes. "You know I'd never say something unless I felt it was important," he said, clearly hesitant. "But... well, the soldiers who were captured along with Lady Corisande and Lady Gaia have been... talking. I have heard that they have been telling others that we did not save the ladies. They said that the English captives were already being returned to England when we ambushed the Scots and killed them."

Cole didn't seem to see anything shattering about that. "I do not see that as a concern," he said. "In fact, it would make sense because when we found them, they were moving south. We thought they were moving the women to another location to keep them hostage, but it is equally possible they were taking them back to England. But my question would be why? *Why* would they do that?"

Essien closed his eyes a moment before looking at him. "The soldiers are saying because Lady Corisande traded favors with the Scots commander for their freedom," he said quietly. "That is why they were being released."

Cole didn't quite understand. "Traded favors?" he said. "What favors?"

"Cole, she gave herself over to the commander," Essien said quietly, making it clear. "She let the man bed her as a condition for their release. She was seen going into his tent, alone, and the next morning, they were released."

Cole's eyes flew open wide when he finally realized what he was saying. "Those men are saying *that*?" he hissed.

Essien nodded, disgusted with the entire situation. "They are," he said miserably. "The rumors have been going around camp for several days, evidently, only we heard nothing about it because we've been sealed up at Berwick Castle. But I heard it today when I was running missives."

Cole stared at him a moment and they could see that his cheeks were turning a dull shade of red. "It's not true," he said hoarsely. "It is not possibly true."

Essien lifted his shoulders. "True or not, that is what they are saying, Cole. Surely there has to be another explanation other than the idle gossip of vicious tongues."

Cole continued to stare at him, processing what he'd been told. Something was building in him, something explosive. Perhaps even something uncontrollable. Those two-colored eyes took on a terrifying gleam. Without another word, he turned back to the stairwell and began racing up the steep stairs. After a split second, Julian followed.

Essien called after them.

"I am sorry, Cole!" he shouted. "I thought you should know!"

Cole didn't answer. He just kept running. Distraught, Essien turned to Addax, who simply shook his head with pure, unadulterated disgust.

"I had to tell him," Essien insisted. "He had to know."

Addax nodded. "I know," he said, greatly disheartened by the whole situation. "Come on. Let's follow him to make sure he does not kill anyone."

The brothers followed.

CORISANDE WAS STIRRING a giant iron pot filled with boiling water as Gaia gingerly tossed bloodied and soiled linen bandages into it.

It was not her favorite task.

"Gaia, watch what you are doing," Corisande scolded. "We do not want to toss the bandages into the fire."

Gaia was absolutely disgusted. She held up a linen bandage by the very edge, soiled with something green, and shrieked.

"It smells!" she cried.

"Then do not smell it," Corisande said impatiently. "Just put it in the pot."

Making a terrible face, she tossed the bandage into the pot as Corisande stirred. "This is awful work," she said unhappily. "Why can't someone else do this?"

"Because *you* are doing it. I have asked this of you."

Gaia was pouting. Looking around their encampment, she was trying to think of something that wasn't disgusting, smelly, or awful. She eyed her sister unhappily.

"Then let *me* stir the pot," she said. "You can toss in the soiled linen."

"Gladly," Corisande said, rolling her eyes as Gaia took over with the big stick. "That's right; stir it boldly. You have to make sure that all of the poison on the bandages comes off."

Gaia was trying to stir and stand back from the flames at the same time. "It's hot!"

Corisande grunted unhappily at her sister's complaining. Everything she did was something to complain about and it was becoming frustrating. "*Stir*," she commanded. "Keep stirring. I will go check on the men and bring back more soiled bandages."

While Gaia whimpered and whined, Corisande headed off to check on her sick and injured men.

Behind the de Bourne encampment, she had a large tent set up and several lesser shelters, with canvas strung up over poles to create shelter from the sky and the elements. The more badly wounded men were in the tent while the lesser wounded were under the canvas, carefully tended to by Corisande and several of the old soldiers who had been captured at the same time she and Gaia had been. At least, the ones that hadn't been too badly injured in that event.

It made for an efficient hospital.

In fact, Corisande had the most organized hospital out of all of the armies. She had even taken in men who were too badly wounded from other armies because she seemed to know what to do. She'd done some horrifying battlefield surgery on several men, but due to her skill, she'd only lost two of them. The rest were in various stages of healing, although a few of them were still bad off.

She was keeping a close eye on them.

Her first stop was the tent to check on those with the more terrible wounds. They were stable and she was grateful. One man was missing the lower part of his right leg and poison threatened, so she was bandaging him with clean linen every couple of hours. She went to him to check up on him, pleased to see that he seemed a little stronger. She had one of her helpers remove the bandages and she took them away as her helper wrapped the stump with fresh boiled linen.

As Corisande came out of the tent and headed over to the pot where Gaia was stirring, she happened to see Cole and Julian entering the de Bourne encampment. A smile came to her face at the sight of Cole. It had been two days since she'd last seen him and the mere sight did her heart good. He was still safe, and whole, and that was all she cared about. She dumped the dirty bandages into the pot as he entered the wounded area.

"Greetings, my lord," she said sweetly. "It is good to see you on this fine day. I've heard the battle is mostly over. How is the castle holding?"

He marched up on her with the strangest look in his eyes. Not only did he not greet her, he also didn't make any move to touch her. Not a hug or a kiss.

Nothing.

He just stood there, looking at her.

"I am going to ask you a question and you will tell me the absolute truth," he finally said, sounding strangely tight. "Do you understand?"

Julian, right beside him, put a hand on his brother's arm. "Cole, please," he muttered. "Be calm. Be…"

Cole roughly shook off his brother's hand. "Get away from me, Julian," he growled. "This does not concern you."

Julian knew that tone. He knew better than to argue. With a heavy sigh, he wandered away, leaving Corisande greatly confused by Cole's manner.

Her smile faded.

"I would not lie to you," she said. "What is the matter?"

"When we ambushed the wagons as the Scots led them out of the encampment, where were you going?"

She cocked her head. "Back to England, I was told."

"So they were releasing you."

She nodded, still confused with the line of questioning. "That was my understanding," she said. "Why? Does it matter?"

It was apparent that he was trying very hard to keep his composure and she truly had no idea why. "*Why* were they releasing you?" he asked.

Corisande was greatly puzzled. "What do you mean?" she asked. "Cole, what is the matter? Has something happened?"

His jaw flexed dangerously. "Answer me," he said, lowering his voice. "Why were they releasing you?"

She shook her head. "What else do you do with prisoners?" she said. "If you do not need them or want them, you release them, I suppose. We were of no value to them any longer, so…"

He cut her off. "Did you make a deal with them?"

"A deal? What *deal*?"

He was starting to breath heavily, his chest heaving with emotion. Corisande had never seen him in such a state and, frankly, it was frightening. He looked as if he were coiled, ready to strike, and she took a step back from him.

He took a step forward.

"Did you warm some Scotsman's bed in exchange for your release?"

Corisande felt as if she'd been slapped. All of the color drained from her face and, in a panic, she went on the defensive.

"Who told you such things?" she hissed.

"Do you mean to tell me that it is not true?"

Corisande backed up again, but he was on top of her. For every inch she put between them, he closed the gap and then some. She finally put her hands out to push him back because he was starting to overwhelm her.

"I am not telling you anything," she seethed. "But by the tone of your voice, you clearly believe it is true, so anything I tell you will not matter."

"Tell me the truth."

"Would you believe me if I did?"

His jaw continued to work, infuriated and shattered. "Do you mean to tell me you do not know anything about the rumors flying fast and furious that you exchanged your body for your release?" He sounded like he was growling. "When we found your caravan, you were heading south. I want to know *why* they released you, so you will answer my question. And do not tell me that they released you because they no longer had need of you. In war, one does not simply release hostages. One uses them."

Corisande stared at him. She could hardly believe what she was hearing. She was shocked and horrified, everything she could possibly feel, but there were two things whirling through her mind that she could grasp above all else. The first was that Cole already believed whatever rumors he had heard and that cut her to the bone. Did the man have so little faith in her?

The second was that she had to protect Gaia.

There she was, back in the position of protector again. Her little sister had made the ultimate sacrifice and, horribly, there were rumors about it. Or, they were about Corisande. She wasn't going to ask Cole because whatever the rumors were, he believed them.

She wasn't going to tell him the truth and destroy her sister's sacrifice in the same stroke.

Let them think it was her.

Let Gaia keep the dignity she sacrificed to free them.

"You believe the rumors already, Cole," she said coldly. "There is nothing more I can say."

"You can tell me the truth."

"You have your truth as you believe it. Your lack of faith in me is clear and I will not dignify the question with a response."

"*Did* you let the Scots commander bed you in exchange for your freedom?"

It was a direct question. Looking up at Cole, Corisande couldn't have felt more grief had he ripped her heart out of her chest. The pain was beyond anguish. It entered the realm of becoming something that filled her as surely as blood filled her veins. The man she loved thought the worst of her without giving her a chance to tell him the truth. He had asked her for it, but he really didn't want it. He already believed what he'd heard.

He wanted a confession.

She wasn't going to give it to him.

Leaning forward, she looked him in the eyes.

"Go to hell," she hissed. "And don't come back."

Cole's head snapped back. That hadn't been the answer he had been expecting. He didn't know what he'd been expecting, but that wasn't it. Overwhelmed, and overcome with grief and rage, he spun on his heel and marched off, heading out of the encampment.

Corisande stood there and trembled.

Standing behind Cole, several feet back, were Julian and al-Kort brothers. All three of them appeared extremely grieved by what had happened and when Cole pushed through them, Julian and Addax turned to follow.

But Essien just stood there with tears in his eyes.

Corisande saw him but she kept her chin up, defiantly. She wasn't going to let them know how badly she was crumbling. If they wanted to believe she had let a Scotsman take advantage of her, then so be it. She didn't care.

Better they think it of her than of Gaia.

"Cori?"

She heard a soft voice off to her right and she turned to see Gaia standing there, weeping. She had heard the entire conversation and she had seen what her sister had done to protect her, once again. She wasn't going to let men know what Gaia had done and she'd let the love of her life walk away because of it.

It was Cole or Gaia.

She'd chosen Gaia.

"Cori, go after him," she sobbed. "Do not let him leave."

Corisande held up a hand to her sister to silence her. "Not a word," she said, her voice tight with emotion. "You will not say another word about this, ever."

Fearful of her sister's reaction if she did not obey, Gaia did as she was told. She returned to stirring the soiled linen as Corisande went to the smaller tent that she and Gaia shared and collapsed.

She could hear her sister's sobs all across the encampment.

When she saw Ares moving for the tent, hearing the sobs also, Gaia left the linen boiling and ran to him. If the truth was to be known, then it needed to come from her and she needed to tell someone who had a reputation for being fair and just.

Big brother had just become Father Confessor.

Gaia didn't want her sacrifice with Alexander MacDuff to be in vain.

CHAPTER TWENTY-FOUR

"**W**HAT HAPPENED TO him?"

It was Jax asking the question. It was nearing sunset on the seventh day and the fog was beginning to form along the coast, preparing to roll in, but from the battlements of Berwick, he could see Cole down by the river's edge where the burned shells of longships were still lingering in the shallows.

Cole was standing in the water to his knees. Simply standing there as the frigid water rushed over his lower legs as Julian and Addax stood about a dozen feet behind him on the shore, simply watching. They were all just standing there, looking out onto the river.

Atreus was on the battlements with Jax, as was Essien. In fact, it was Essien who had found Jax on the parapet to tell him that Cole was in distress.

Now, Jax wanted to know what that distress was.

Essien had the unhappy duty of telling him.

"My lord, I was running missives for William Marshal this morning and I began to hear some disturbing rumors," he said. "I told Cole about them because they had to do with Lady Corisande."

Jax turned to look at him. "What rumors?"

Essien hesitated before continuing. "There are rumors amongst the armies, my lord," he said. "The men who were captured with Lady Corisande and Lady Gaia say that Lady Corisande went to the tent of a Scots commander, unchaperoned, and the next morning, all of the captives were released. The rumors are that she traded favors for the release of the captives. Cole has only just heard the rumors and when he confronted the lady with them, it was… ugly. Very ugly. Julian and my brother are standing there in case Cole tries to drown himself in the river."

Jax stared at Essien in shock before returning his attention to his son, standing amongst the ravages of battle on the edge of the river.

"God," Jax finally muttered. "I'd not heard those rumors. But, then again, we've all been locked up in this castle. I haven't heard anything. The men are really saying that?"

"Aye, my lord."

"*Which* men?"

"I heard it from Teviot's men, but I'm sure it's all over. You know how men talk."

Jax just shook his head, appalled to hear such a thing. But not surprised. "They gossip like fishwives," he muttered, looking at Atreus. "Did you hear any of this?"

Atreus shook his head. "Nay," he said. "But I have been with you the entire time. We've lived isolated, like hermits for the past week."

Jax sighed heavily and looked out at his son again. "And you say he asked Lady Corisande about the rumors?"

He was addressing Essien. "Aye, my lord."

"What did she say?"

Essien was willing to tell Jax about the rumors, but revealing a conversation between Cole and Corisande felt invasive. Like he was gossiping himself. But if Jax knew what was said, perhaps he'd understand the seriousness of the situation.

"Cole was… upset, my lord," he said. "He asked her if the rumors were true and she told him that by the way he had asked her, he must have believed them already. They argued and she finally told him to go to hell and not return."

Jax closed his eyes, shaking his head regretfully. "He could not have taken that well," he said. "I will go and speak to him."

That was what Essien wanted to hear. He looked to Atreus, hoping that meant everything would be well again, but Atreus' expression didn't seem too encouraging.

As Essien waited on the battlements, Jax made his way down to the riverside where Cole was still standing in the water. He walked up beside Julian and Addax, standing there a moment and looking at Cole, before quietly asking Julian and Addax to step away and give them some privacy. They complied, backing off, as Jax walked to the edge of the river.

"Cole," he said. "I was told what happened. Come out of the water and let us discuss this calmly. Surely it is not as bad as it seems."

Cole didn't move. He remained in the same position, looking out over the dark blue waters of the River Tweed.

"Go away, Papa," he said. "I do not want to discuss it."

Jax folded his big arms across his chest. "You know I will not go anywhere and you cannot make me, so you may as well accept my presence," he said. "Tell me what happened with you and Lady Corisande. I want to hear it from you."

He heard Cole sigh heavily, a pent-up sigh that seemed to come from his toes. "I do not wish to discuss it."

"Then we are going to stand here a very long time. Do you not trust me with such matters?"

Even in his state of turmoil, Cole was not going to insult his father. Of course he trusted him. But it was more that he didn't trust himself to speak, afraid he would lose control and never get it back.

He was hanging by a thread.

And that thread was unraveling.

"I… I feel like I did when Mary and Lucy died," he finally said. "Grief… loss… but this is different. When they died, it was the will of God. That's what everyone told me, anyway. It was something I could not control. But this… this cuts deeper, but in a different way."

"What way?"

"Because I let myself be happy again. I was not prepared for the fall from grace."

Jax hated to hear that come out of his son's mouth. "Tell me what happened so that I may understand."

Cole shifted on his undoubtedly frozen legs. "There is nothing to tell," he said. "She gave herself over to her captor in order to secure the release of the English captives. I asked her and she did not deny it."

"So you believe the rumors."

"As I said, I asked her and she would not answer me."

"You just told me she did not deny it. Now you tell me she would not answer you. Which is it?"

Cole did turn to look at him, then. "Both," he said. "She would not give me a straight answer. That is the same thing as not denying the rumors."

Jax looked at his boy. He loved all of his sons, but Cole was his firstborn. He was the child who made Jax grow from a soulless barbarian to a man with feeling. Cole was the light of his life. But he was also stubborn, ridiculously so, and he had a temper. Jax could see that both of those things had come into play in the situation. Cole was seeing it the way he wanted to see it.

He wasn't seeing it from any other perspective.

"So she did not deny them," he said. "And now you hate

her."

Cole shook his head. "That is the problem," he said. "I don't. I never could. Papa, I love her. How could she do such a thing? How could she violate everything we have between us?"

Jax cocked his head. "Let me understand this situation as you see it," he said. "She violated your bond, your trusts, in exchange for the release of captives. That means she does not love you?"

"After our most recent conversation, probably not."

"The woman is so shallow that she could not love you after an argument. Is that what you're telling me?"

"Nay, that is not what I'm telling you," Cole said, growing frustrated. "I don't know what I'm telling you."

He turned back around, facing the river, and Jax walked in next to him. The water was so cold that he started to lose feeling in his toes almost immediately.

But he had a point to make.

"You thought she was honorable enough and wonderful enough to fall in love with," he said. "Has that changed so drastically?"

Cole's jaw was ticking again. "She gave herself over to another man."

"Do you think she did it happily?"

That forced Cole to think. It forced him to be honest. "Nay."

"Do you think she wanted to?"

Cole paused. "Nay, she did not want to. I would never believe that. But she did."

"Did you ever think that mayhap she was forced to?"

Cole's head snapped to him. "Raped?"

Jax looked him in the eyes. "If the woman loves you and she is honorable and loyal, what other circumstance could there be if, in fact, she did this?" he asked. "Did you ever stop to think about the fact that mayhap she was assaulted and too ashamed to tell you? Did you even give her a chance to tell you, lad, before you were demanding to know the truth?"

Jax could see the color drain from Cole's face. "Oh… my God," he breathed. "Do you think that is what happened?"

"I do not know. But did you give her the chance to tell you?"

Cole started twitching, his eyes glazing oddly, as he suddenly slogged out of the water. "Nay," he said. "I… I asked her, but I was upset… I was distraught. I asked her but… nay, I did not ask her. I accused her. I demanded… I don't even know what I demanded. God, Papa, what have I done?"

Jax put his hands on the man because he was coming apart at the seams. The thread that was keeping his control had finally snapped. "Breathe, Cole," he said. "*Breathe.* Calm yourself. You've always been an emotional man but, in this case, you must not be. If that is what happened, Corisande needs your love and understanding, not your rage. This happened to her, not to you. It is not your right to go to pieces. You must be her rock. Think of her and not yourself for once."

Cole drew in several long breaths through his nose, like he was trying not to hyperventilate. As he bent over, trying not to get sick, he caught sight of something over near the stairwell leading up to the castle. Standing tall, he could see Ares coming from the stairs, heading towards him.

And Gaia was with him.

Jax, too, caught sight of them and he stood next to Cole as they approached. He thought that perhaps Ares had come to pick a fight with Cole for his argument with Corisande, but it wouldn't have made sense to bring Gaia along if that was the case.

In fact, he was most curious about their appearance.

Ares, unusually pale and serious, looked straight at Cole.

"I heard what happened," he said. "Gaia has something she wants to say to you. She asked me to bring her to you."

With that, Ares grasped his little sister by the arm and pulled her front and center. Gaia looked at Cole fearfully, but she was looking even more fearfully at Jax, the legendary and terrifying warlord.

She swallowed hard.

"May I… may I speak with you privately, Cole?" she asked.

Her voice was trembling. Jax graciously bowed out, but he didn't go far. He went to stand next to Ares and they were easily within earshot of Gaia and Cole, but they were behind Gaia so she couldn't see them.

It was a good thing, too, because Gaia was very nervous. She'd just been through a soul-baring confession with Ares, who hadn't been pleased, but at least he hadn't exploded. He'd been surprisingly sympathetic, even more so when he realized why Gaia had done such a thing. He'd taken her straight to Cole because he was the one who really needed to hear her confession.

She could hardly look at him.

"I… I want to first say that I am sorry I pinched you," she said as tears stung her eyes. "I knew you were fond of my sister, and she was fond of you, and I should not have pinched you. I am very sorry I did that."

Out of all the things Cole expected to hear, that wasn't on his mind. Moreover, he had no idea what Gaia could possibly say to him and, frankly, he wasn't in the mood to hear anything from her. He was desperate to find Corisande and apologize more fervently than he'd ever apologized for anything in his life.

If she'd listen to him.

Therefore, he struggled to stay patient with Gaia.

"No harm done," he said. "But your apology is noted."

Gaia nodded, wiping at her eyes because tears were starting to trickle through. "I wanted to tell you that I know my sister loves you," she said. "She's a wonderful, loving sister and I love her very much. She was so excited to marry you so I knew I had to help her. I had to protect her, so when MacDuff told her that he would release everyone if she warmed his bed for the night, I knew I could not let that happen."

Now, she had Cole's attention. Brow furrowed, he bent over so he could hear her better because she was speaking so softly, she was barely audible.

"Is *that* what happened?" he said, struggling with his emotions again. "It was Alexander MacDuff who captured you? The same man who came to The Keld and demanded your father's loyalty last month?"

Ares heard him. "Aye," he said, answering for Gaia. "The same man, the Justiciar of Scotia. He's a powerful man, Cole."

Cole began to put the pieces of the puzzle together. "So MacDuff was your captor," he said. "Being beaten back from The Keld must have been a humiliating experience for him, so when he realized he had Alastor's daughters as captives, he must have seen an opportunity to get back at Alastor. Is that true?"

Ares shrugged. "It is very possible. But that is not what Gaia came to tell you."

Cole refocused on Gaia. "Gaia, did he offer to release everyone if Corisande would… surrender to him?"

Gaia nodded. "She was so sad," she said, starting to weep a little. "She was devastated. She kept saying that you would never want her if another man had her. When she finally found happiness, it was about to be taken away, so I went to MacDuff in her stead. It was me, Cole. Corisande never warmed his bed. *I* did."

Cole was thunderstruck. Eyes wide, he grasped Gaia with

both hands, forcing her to look at him. "Then why didn't she deny it?" he demanded, his voice cracking. "I asked her and she would not deny it."

Gaia began to sob. "Because she was still protecting me," she wept. "She has always protected me. She did not want anyone to know that I made the sacrifice so that she would not have to, even at the cost of her own happiness. Even at the cost of you. But it wasn't her. It was *me*."

She was off on a crying jag by that time and Cole wasn't much better. Tears filled his eyes and he pulled the young woman into an embrace, hugging her because she needed the comfort. She'd shown astounding bravery to spare her sister and he'd been a monster about it.

So much bravery from two small woman.

It was incomprehensible.

"I must go to her," he said hoarsely, releasing her. "I must go to her and apologize for my…"

"Nay!" Gaia said, grabbing him as he tried to walk away. "She must not know that you know the truth. She has tried to protect me and you must let her continue to do so. It would be terrible if she knew I told you the truth. Don't you see? If you apologize to her because I told you the truth, it would mean that it was the *only* reason you apologized. It would be a worthless apology. It wouldn't be because you love her unconditionally, no matter what she did to save a group of captives."

"She's right," Jax said softly. He'd been listening to the entire thing, feeling such sorrow for Gaia, for Cole, for Corisande. It was such a bitterly beautiful thing that Gaia had done and he looked at the young woman through new eyes. "Gaia has made a tremendous sacrifice, Cole. And so has Corisande for letting everyone think she was the one who did the unspeakable thing in order to protect her sister. You will diminish both of their acts of bravery if you let Corisande know that you know. Let her continue to be brave and love her because of it."

Cole could see all that, very clearly now. Odd how the confession of one young woman suddenly righted everything in his world. He looked at Gaia, who was still so vastly upset, and put his hand underneath her chin, tipping it up so she was looking at him. He smiled at her, wearily.

"I have seen many men in battle," he said quietly, "but I've not seen any man who has come close to the courage you showed in the face of the enemy. You have my deepest admiration and thanks, Lady Gaia."

Gaia sniffled, her tears fading with Cole's words. He made her feel better about herself with that gentle praise. He made her feel as if she were actually worth something. Instead of looking at her with disdain, he was looking at her with respect.

She hadn't expected that.

Cole winked at her and dropped his hand, looking to Ares.

"Where is your sister?" he asked.

Ares tipped his head in the direction of the encampment. "When I saw her last, she was in her tent," he said. "I assume she's still there."

Cole nodded, heading for the stairs, but he put his hand on Ares' arm as he walked by.

"Thank you," he muttered. "For everything… thank you."

Ares, Jax, and Gaia watched him run up the stairs, heading back to Corisande where he belonged.

If she would have him.

Jax found himself praying the young woman had the capacity for forgiveness where his son was concerned.

CHAPTER TWENTY-FIVE

THE WOUNDED NEEDED her.

After her breakdown, Corisande was back with the sick and injured, tending men because that's what she was good at. It gave her something to focus on other than Cole, someone she would now have to forget.

But she wasn't sure she could.

Still, she would have to. She would have to force herself. After what had happened between them, there was no going back. Cole would move on with his life and she would move on with hers, but it would not be as one.

Somehow, she'd have to find the will to go on.

She wasn't sure she could.

Corisande was coming to think that God simply didn't want her to wed. He didn't want to see her happy. Spinsters or widows or unmarried women often devoted themselves to the cloister by way of a livelihood, but Corisande wouldn't consider it. Why would she serve a God who didn't want to see her happy?

But she also knew she couldn't stay at The Keld.

Odd how it had been her home since birth but, somehow, returning to such a place would remind her of Cole. In the grand scheme of things, he'd hardly spent any time there, yet his mark was upon it, indelibly. She couldn't go back there and remember those wonderful memories.

Corisande didn't know what she was going to do, but she did know one thing – she would never recover from this.

She would never be the same again.

But her focus, for now, had to be on the sick and wounded. She couldn't let her personal issues get in the way of making sure men lived. It was easier to function if she had something to focus on, something to chase away the crippling thoughts of Cole. But try as she might, she couldn't keep him from her mind. She couldn't get his accusing eyes out of her head. That he would not even give her the opportunity to explain cut her to shreds but, in hindsight, she would have only told him what he suspected.

Perhaps it was better this way.

Evening was starting to fall and the torches around the hospital area were lit, weak light to stave off the mist that was now starting to roll in from the sea. It smelled strongly of salt. Corisande moved among the men, making sure those not in the tent were well-covered against the dampness.

The cooks of de Bourne's army had prepared a meal, including a big pot of beef broth from the bones of the beef they'd been cooking for the regular army. It was a rich broth, salty, and some of Corisande's helpers began giving it to the wounded. The hospital area, in fact, was surrounded by the regular army, with Teviot's army immediately adjacent, so they could smell food from all sides as the evening meal commenced for the weary men. Corisande was kneeling beside a man who had taken an ax to the shoulder, helping him lift his head to drink the beef broth, when she heard someone lifting his voice behind her.

"It has come to my attention that there have been some

rumors spreading amongst the armies." It was Cole, standing right in the middle of the hospital area. "I have heard of these rumors myself, cruel and vicious rumors regarding the release of captives from the Scots several days ago. You know who you are, men spreading these rumors, and when I find you, I will make you pay."

He had the loudest, most terrifying voice possible and with the fog, it carried. Hundreds of men were hearing him. Corisande sat there, frozen, having no idea what he was going to do. He'd run off earlier and now he was back, perhaps to do greater harm to her and her reputation.

Or perhaps he was having some kind of tantrum.

Frantically, she looked around for her brothers, but the mist made it difficult to see if they were around. She didn't want them to charge Cole because a spectacular fight would result that she didn't want to witness. No matter what she was feeling, or what he'd done, she didn't want Cole injured by her angry brothers. But she couldn't seem to make herself move, frightened into inactivity, as Cole began to pace around near the enormous iron pot that was boiling soiled bandages.

He looked as angry and terrifying as she had ever seen him.

"I want all of you who can hear my voice to listen to me and listen well," he said. "These rumors that Alastor de Bourne's daughter has traded her innocence in exchange for the release of the English captives is false. It is a lie perpetuated by small and feeble minds. I want to be perfectly clear about this, so any rumors you now spread will be countered with the truth. Nothing lascivious or untoward happened. But a great sacrifice did. It had to be explained to me before I understood it, so I tell you now that any man I find speaking against the daughters of Alastor de Bourne will meet my wrath. I do not care who you are or where you are – I will find you and I will cut out your offensive tongue."

Shocked, Corisande began to tremble. She set the broth down on the ground and stood up, having no idea what to make of any of this. Cole was shouting loud enough for the Scots in Edinburgh to hear him, laying open a situation that had, since it happened, been whispered and sneered about.

But he was bringing it all to the forefront.

Corisande made her way out of the shelter, looking at Cole with surprise and apprehension. When he caught sight of her, he turned in her direction, his eyes locking with hers. A thousand unspoken words passed between them, words of sorrow and longing, fear and love, but he didn't move for her.

Not yet.

He wasn't finished.

"I have fought in many battles in my lifetime," he said. "I come from a family of warriors and you all know that. The name de Velt is synonymous with battle. I have seen bravery that has impressed me and I have seen men sacrifice themselves for a cause, but I have never in my life seen more courage than I have seen from Corisande de Bourne. She is a lady of great character and bravery I could only hope to have, and I shamed her greatly by allowing myself to be sucked up into the filth that was being spread about her. But no more. She does not deserve what your dirty minds have cast upon her."

His voice was echoing off the tents. Men were coming into view now, from all armies, listening to Cole as he bared his soul for all to hear. Corisande would have seen her brothers and father come into view had she not been so focused on Cole.

Here he was, making sure everyone heard him.

Making sure everyone, including Corisande, knew what was on his mind.

Making sure everyone knew what the just and right cause was.

"I will tell you now that it does not matter to me what Lady

Corisande did or did not do," he said. "Those with polluted mind will think what they will, but even if the rumors are true, one must look at the situation as a great and noble sacrifice. In battle, men sacrifice themselves for others. Men die for others. But with women… sometimes, their sacrifices go deeper even than that and they should be commended for it, not scorned. Being a captive of the Scots was a battle – make no mistake – and a woman fought back with whatever she had in order to save others. Be ashamed that any of you thought such a sacrifice was dirty or ruinous. Be ashamed if you looked upon the woman involved as less than noble, for I assure you, she is more noble than you could ever hope to be. I was wrong; anyone spreading such rumors was wrong. We were *all* wrong. We do not know the meaning of the word sacrifice or honor. But Corisande de Bourne does. She has lived it."

Tears were pouring down Corisande's face by the time he was finished. Cole had laid himself bare in the most brutal, beautiful way possible. His guard was down, his pride was gone. He was letting her know, and everyone else, that he had been wrong. That it didn't matter what Corisande had done or hadn't done. He loved her still.

And always would.

It was incredibly quiet when he stopped talking as thousands of men stood still, listening to Cole de Velt scold them. For those who spread the rumors, or spoke ill of Lady Corisande, they deserved it.

But for Cole, it was the public apology he needed to make.

Seeing Corisande standing on the other side of the boiling linen pot, several feet beyond it, Cole came around the fire, his eyes riveted to her. He could see the tears streaming down her face. As he looked at her, his eyes filled with tears also.

He didn't try to stop them.

"Love is a funny thing," he said, his voice softer now. "It can be the strongest of motivators, like the love between sisters or between husband and wife. But it can also be the cruelest of emotions when abused. I am sorry I abused it, Cori. Although I do not expect you to forgive me, know that I am sorry just the same. I was wrong. I do not care what has happened because my love is not limited to a woman who only does what I think she should do. It is unconditional when it comes to you and I am sorry that my actions, for a short time, proved otherwise."

Corisande sobbed into her hand. "There is nothing to forgive, Cole," she said. "But you did not have to champion me in front of the entire army."

"Aye, I did," he said, coming closer and lowering his voice even more. "I had to make sure they understood the truth. Surrendering my pride is my penitence for being so selfish and blind that I did not understand that true love is absolute. It knows no limitations, no boundaries. And this *is* true love, Cori. I will love you, just as I do now, until the end of all things. You are my queen, as you always have been, and I worship you. But I want to know one thing. May I ask?"

Corisande nodded. "Anything."

"*Where* is Alexander MacDuff? I understand he was part of the contingent that captured you."

There was hazard in his tone. Corisande sniffled, finally wiping at her face. "I do not know," she said honestly. "He was accompanying the wagons as we headed out of camp. He was with us when you ambushed us."

Cole reflected back to that short, violent event. "We did not leave anyone alive."

"Then he must be dead."

Somehow, that eased Cole's mind considerably. The bastard who had forced that horrible situation upon Corisande and Gaia was dead at the hands of the Executioner Knights.

Perhaps there was a God, after all.

He smiled faintly.

"Now," he said, "as I was saying, the battle is over and we have a wedding to attend to. I hope. Is this still true?"

She nodded so eagerly that her hair lashed her face. "It is."

His smile grew. "Would you be opposed to being married in front of thousands of soldiers and about a dozen knights who would dearly like to witness the ceremony, your father and my father included?"

Corisande broke into a radiant smile. "I cannot think of anything more appropriate," she said. "But are you certain? What about your mother and sisters? Will they not want to attend?"

He shrugged. "We will marry again at Pelinom for their benefit," he said. "And my mother can throw a wild, lavish party for it. But right now… right now, I want to take you as my wife. I will not wait another moment to begin the rest of my life. With you."

Corisande threw herself at him, her arms around his neck, her lips against his. Cole kissed her deeply and gratefully, so very thankful for this moment. It was the best thing he'd ever done, the happiest event he'd ever known, and even as he kissed Corisande, he could hear cheers and whistles.

He knew it was his brothers, the Executioner Knights, cheering him on.

Every last one of them.

For The Dark Spawn, the son of the most feared knight in the realm, and the strong, noble daughter of the hereditary King of Northumbria, that moment at the end of a battle was the beginning of their lives together. The start of a tide of blessings to come.

The genesis of a love that would last until the end of time.

Two souls that were finally one.

And they were the better for it.

EPILOGUE

Berwick
Two years later

THE STANDARD FOR The Black Dragon was flying high over the tournament field.

So was the standard for the God of Vengeance.

It was the greatest tournament that the north had yet seen, sponsored by the House of de Velt, Baron Blackadder, and his son, Lord Lambden, commander of Berwick Castle. Everyone who was anyone showed up for the games, something that had been promoted for an entire year.

Now, the day was here.

On the fields south of the city, where the armies for William Marshal had gathered two years earlier, now stood a newly built tournament arena. Great houses were encamped all over the field and there was an entire area dedicated to trades – smithies and the like – and another area dedicated to food.

That was where Cole and Corisande found themselves now.

They were with Jax and his wife and Cole's mother, Kellington, who was carrying Cole and Corisande's year-old son, Atlas. He wasn't necessarily named for Corisande's brother, but more that they simply both liked the name, but Uncle Atlas told anyone who would listen that the green-and-brown-eyed baby with the dark hair was indeed named for him.

Atlas the Younger, as he was known in the family, was smart and feisty, and just learning to walk, which made carrying him difficult for Kellington. She'd had six children of her own, but wrestling with a baby took a particular talent.

Atlas wanted to run.

They were walking with the crowds in the section that held the food vendors because Corisande, seven months pregnant with her second child, had smelled all of the wonderful smells from the ramparts of Berwick Castle and had asked her husband if they could procure some food. Being that she was with child, and at this stage eating anything she could get her hands on, Cole agreed and took his entire family down into the masses.

But what fun it had been, so far.

Corisande's first selection of the day was a hollowed-out bowl of bread that contained beef and gravy. Cole, Jax, and Julian thought that was rather tasty-sounding, so they bought some as well. Addington and Effington, Cole's younger sisters, weren't interested in the food, but Addington in particular was interested in all of the handsome young knights who had come to the games, the joust of which was to begin shortly. So was Gaia, who had found a fast and true friend in Addington. The had been as thick as thieves since they were introduced two years ago. Everyone was purchasing their food before taking it into the lists.

"Papa, can we *please* go into the arena now?" Addington begged, holding Gaia's hand as they leaned heavily in the direction of the lists. "We are going to miss the joust!"

Jax had a mouthful of beef. "We will not miss anything," he said. "If you are not going to eat, hold the baby so your mother can eat."

Addington looked at her nephew, as adorable as he was, and shook her head. "Nay," she said flatly. "He likes to kick and I do not want to be kicked in the face. He kicked Gaia yesterday."

Gaia pointed to her face where there was a tiny little red mark on her chin. "Look at what he did!" she said dramatically.

Jax tried not to grin at Gaia's genuine outrage. "Terrible," he said, but it sounded insincere. "But I can hardly see it. I think you are safe."

Gaia was displeased with that answer and so was Addington. She pointed to her sister. "And Effie said he bit her yesterday."

"He *chewed* on her," Kellington clarified as she tried to distract the fussy baby by swinging him gently. "His teeth are sprouting. He did not bite her."

Incensed, Effington held up a finger. "It is swollen, Mama," she insisted. "Look how lumpy my finger is!"

Julian, well-entrenched in his food, snorted. "Lumpy," he said. "You'd better not let your glorious beloved see that finger. He will cast you aside like a piece of moldy bread."

Effington frowned. "At least I have an intended, which is more than can be said for you."

The insults were starting to fly. That was usual with the de Velt brood. Three brothers against three lively sisters were normal, the chaos Jax and Kellington had brought into the world but chaos he lived for. Before he could put up a hand to prevent a fight, he heard someone calling his name.

"Papa! Mother!"

They all turned to the sound of the shouting to see Cassian, the youngest de Velt brother, rushing in their direction. Kellington gasped and handed the baby to the nearest person, who happened to be Jax. He grabbed his grandson around the torso as Kellington ran to the son she hadn't seen in over a year. Tall, dark, and handsome, Cassian swept his mother into an embrace.

"Mama!" he said, kissing her cheek. "I went to the castle to find you, but they said you had come to the games."

Kellington squeezed her baby boy. "Let me look at you," she said, pulling back to study him. Unlike his brothers and father with their straight, dark hair, Cassian had been born with dark, curly hair, which he kept cropped. He had his father's coloring and eye-color trait, but his features were all his mother's. "You have grown inches since I last saw you. I did not know the House of de Lohr was coming."

Cassian grinned, looking very much like her. "I did not send word because I wanted to surprise you," he said. "Everyone came, even Sherry, although after marrying Christopher's daughter last year, he wanted to remain with her at Lioncross because she is due to give birth soon. He does not want to miss it, but Christin insisted that he come, so he is here."

Kellington smiled. "I am happy to hear it," she said. "It has turned out to be a great event, bigger than we expected."

It was clear that Cassian was excited about it. "Every great house is here, from what I've seen – the Earls of Teviot, the House of de Bourne, de Royans, the garrison at Richmond Castle, the Earl of Wolverhampton, and so many more. I could go on and on. What I did not see was William Marshal's standard."

"He'll be here," Jax said, coming up to his son with the baby in one arm. He hugged his son with the other. "He told me that he would attend. And speaking of attending his first tournament, you've not yet your nephew, Atlas."

Cassian looked at the baby, who looked very much like his brother. But he would never let the man hear that from his lips. "He looks like his mother, thank God," he said. "A strong little lad. That is a proud thing, Cole."

Cole had finished his food so he took the baby from his

father so Jax could finish his. "He'll be on a horse next year, jousting with rest of us," he said. "'Tis good to see you, little brother. It has been a long time."

Cassian looked to the brother he admired deeply. "I've missed you," he said, looking around at his family as Julian came up to embrace him. "I've missed you all. It feels good to be home in the north again."

"You can always come home, Cass," Julian said, a glimmer in his eyes.

Cassian shrugged as if to concede the point. "I know," he said. "And I will, someday, but right now, Peter and I are having grand adventures. I like it on the Marches."

"And you like a certain young lady, too," Jax said.

Cassian looked at his father sheepishly. "Brielle is on my mind, I admit it."

He was speaking of Christopher's second eldest daughter, a young lady he'd had his eye on since he first went to serve at Lioncross Abbey. That was the worst kept secret in both families.

"Get her out of your mind and into your bed, Cass," Julian said as his mother hissed her disapproval. "I mean marry the woman. What are you waiting for?"

Jax put up a hand. "A conversation for another time," he said. "Right now, we have games to attend or Addie and Gaia will have fits. Come with us, Cass."

"I will," he said. "But I must tell Lord Christopher that I will be with you this afternoon so he will not go searching for me. May… may I bring Brielle?"

Kellington latched on to his arm. "If you do not, I shall be very disappointed," she said. "Tell Chris that I demand his daughter's company this afternoon."

Cassian grinned. "I was hoping you would say that," he said, kissing her cheek swiftly. "I will find you in the lists!"

With that, he bolted off. Kellington watched him go, her eyes alight with the joy of seeing the son she seldom saw.

"He has grown so much," she said, turning to Jax. "They are all growing up. Jax, I must have more grandchildren or I shall shrivel away."

Jax started laughing. He pointed to Cole, Atlas, and, finally, Corisande with her enormously pregnant belly. "*I* am doing the best *I* can," he said. "I cannot force them to have children any faster, you know."

Kellington laughed softly, hugging her husband, the man her entire world revolved around, even to this day. That had never changed since the moment they'd fallen in love. Theirs was an unusual but powerful love story. But once she was finished squeezing Jax, she took Atlas from his father and hugged the baby, but Atlas didn't want anything to do with her. He kicked so much that she had to set him on his feet, holding his little hands to help him balance.

"I'm finished with that dish," Corisande said, rubbing her back because it pained her these days with the belly she had to balance. "I want something sweet, Cole."

She'd barely gotten the words out of her mouth when Atlas broke free of his grandmother and started tearing down the avenue as only a toddler can. Kellington and Jax went in pursuit, chasing him down as he screamed. That disinterested Addington, Gaia, and Effington, who were already heading for the lists, and Julian was due to compete in the afternoon, so he turned for the castle to prepare.

That left Cole and Corisande watching Cole's parents hunt down a skittish toddler. Cole put his arm around his wife's shoulders as she leaned into him, drawing strength from his warmth and power as she always had.

"You know that he runs like that because of the way my father chases him," she said, grinning when Jax finally grabbed the baby and swung him into the air. "And my brothers. Do you remember their last visit when they pretended that he was a wild boar and chased him all through the bailey, hunting him?"

Cole laughed at a particularly silly memory. Alastor and the three de Bourne brothers had come for a visit last month, but they'd turned into giddy fools around a baby who only wanted to run. It had been hilarious and shameful at the same time to watch grown men behave like that, but Cole had to admit he was guilty of it, too.

"I know," he said. "But given how smart Atlas is, he will be escaping them in little time."

"True," Corisande said as she watched Jax kiss the cheek of the screaming baby. "Moments like this… they seem so surreal to me."

He looked down at her. "Why?"

She shook her head, trying to put her feelings into words. "I don't know, exactly," she said. "I just feel like this is a dream. I'm living a dream I wasn't sure I'd ever have."

He smiled, kissing her on the top of the head. "You *are* the dream," he murmured. "The best and richest dream a man could ever have, my queen."

She met his smile, gazing up at the man she adored with her entire being. Cole de Velt had proven himself a wonderful husband, and exceptional father, and a fine and noble human being. He was everything she could have hoped for and more.

Their life at Berwick was magical. They were raising their family among the very fields and beaches that had seen turmoil from time to time, and would see again for centuries to come. Cole no longer went on missions for William Marshal, but The Marshal knew he could call upon him and his particular set of skills should he ever need him.

Once an Executioner Knight, always an Executioner Knight.

He would always be part of the brotherhood.

Even now, at this very tournament, he was surrounded by his Executioner Knight brethren – Maxton had come up from Gloucester with Christopher and David de Lohr, Achilles had come up from Hampshire, and Dashiell and Bric had arrived together. As the crowd in the lists roared, Addax and Essien beat down the competition, a fiery return of The Black Dragon and the God of Vengeance from their days of tournaments past. It was a joyful thing to watch, but there was change on the horizon. After this tournament, the Princes of Kitara would be heading to Lioncross Abbey to serve the man who had made it all possible for them, Christopher de Lohr.

Cole was sorry to see them go, but he understood.

Life was a constantly evolving thing.

At this moment, all that mattered to him was his family and the vast and compelling love story between him and his wife that continued to grow. Two people who had once been unlucky in relationships and had suffered through their own private heartbreak finally found a love for the ages in each other.

It had been a journey, though. Cole had learned that women were often far braver than men were, in ways he could have never imagined. Corisande never knew that he was aware of Gaia's sacrifice because that was the way Gaia wanted it, and it gave Cole such a deep and abiding respect for his wife's sister even though she never did learn *not* to pinch. She lived with them at Berwick these days, but he didn't mind.

Anything she wanted to do was fine by him.

For her part, Corisande had learned that not all men broke their word. Faith was something that she had in Cole, something that would never waver. It was faith and love that only multiplied when their beautiful son, Ajax, was born healthy two months later.

The circle of life continued and from time to time, Cole

thought on Mary and Lucy. He knew that wherever they were, they were smiling down upon him because they'd been his first lesson in unconditional love.

It was a lesson he'd learned well.

I did not understand that true love is absolute. It knows no limitations, no boundaries. And this is true love.

For Cole and Corisande, it was.

❦ THE END ❧

Author's Afterword: Berwick Castle

I hope you enjoyed Cole and Corisande's story. Boy, I love a story with a lot of battles and fights in it, and this one had several. Always so much fun to write.

So let's talk a little about Berwick Castle.

Berwick plays a big role in the de Wolfe Pack series, as William de Wolfe's son, Patrick, is the garrison commander. That's well established. Now, about fifty years prior to Patrick taking it over, it belongs to Cole. That means that somewhere during that fifty years, custody of the castle switched from de Velt to de Wolfe, which is fine because they're allies. We'll just assumed Jax, or Cole, passed the torch.

Berwick Castle was really a prize to both the Scots and the English in real life. The reality was that Richard the Lionheart actually did sell it to the Scots to raise funds for his crusade to The Levant, and it was in Scots hands for the entire 13th century when I have it belonging to both de Velt and de Wolfe. The truth of that "possession" is that the castle really did go back and forth between the Scots and the English during that time but, technically, it always belonged to the Scots. Berwick did indeed guard the mouth to the River Tweed, coveted by both countries. There were some even bigger battles there in the 14th century, one of which is depicted in my novel, *The Savage Curtain*. In that book, the hero – Stephen of Pembury – becomes the garrison commander of it when the English take it. Yet another hero who is a commander of Berwick Castle (about 1333), which means the House of de Wolfe had to lose it in the early part of that century. Since I'm not prepared to address how they lost it, we'll just say that they did – for now – and leave it at that. I don't want to think about Patrick losing anything, to be honest. Love my Patrick de Wolfe!

So – just some fun tidbits about Berwick, but it makes for really interesting reading if you have the time. Simply Google Berwick Castle and see what pops up.

Hugs,

Kathryn Le Veque Novels

Medieval Romance:

De Wolfe Pack Series:
Warwolfe
The Wolfe
Nighthawk
ShadowWolfe
DarkWolfe
A Joyous de Wolfe Christmas
BlackWolfe
Serpent
A Wolfe Among Dragons
Scorpion
StormWolfe
Dark Destroyer
The Lion of the North
Walls of Babylon
The Best Is Yet To Be

De Wolfe Pack Generations:
WolfeHeart
WolfeStrike
WolfeSword
WolfeBlade

The de Russe Legacy:
The Falls of Erith
Lord of War: Black Angel
The Iron Knight
Beast
The Dark One: Dark Knight
The White Lord of Wellesbourne
Dark Moon
Dark Steel
A de Russe Christmas Miracle
Dark Warrior

The de Lohr Dynasty:
While Angels Slept
Rise of the Defender
Steelheart
Shadowmoor
Silversword
Spectre of the Sword
Unending Love
Archangel
A Blessed de Lohr Christmas

The Brothers de Lohr:
The Earl in Winter

Lords of East Anglia:
While Angels Slept
Godspeed

Great Lords of le Bec:
Great Protector

House of de Royans:
Lord of Winter
To the Lady Born
The Centurion

Lords of Eire:
Echoes of Ancient Dreams
Blacksword
The Darkland

Ancient Kings of Anglecynn:
The Whispering Night
Netherworld

Battle Lords of de Velt:
The Dark Lord

Devil's Dominion
Bay of Fear
The Dark Lord's First Christmas
The Dark Spawn

Reign of the House of de Winter:
Lespada
Swords and Shields

De Reyne Domination:
Guardian of Darkness
With Dreams
The Fallen One

House of d'Vant:
Tender is the Knight (House of
d'Vant)
The Red Fury (House of d'Vant)

The Dragonblade Series:
Fragments of Grace
Dragonblade
Island of Glass
The Savage Curtain
The Fallen One

Great Marcher Lords of de Lara
Dragonblade

House of St. Hever
Fragments of Grace
Island of Glass
Queen of Lost Stars

Lords of Pembury:
The Savage Curtain

**Lords of Thunder: The de Shera
Brotherhood Trilogy**
The Thunder Lord
The Thunder Warrior
The Thunder Knight

The Great Knights of de Moray:

Shield of Kronos
The Gorgon

The House of De Nerra:
The Promise
The Falls of Erith
Vestiges of Valor
Realm of Angels

Highland Warriors of Munro:
The Red Lion
Deep Into Darkness

The House of de Garr:
Lord of Light
Realm of Angels

Saxon Lords of Hage:
The Crusader
Kingdom Come

High Warriors of Rohan:
High Warrior

The House of Ashbourne:
Upon a Midnight Dream

The House of D'Aurilliac:
Valiant Chaos

The House of De Dere:
Of Love and Legend

St. John and de Gare Clans:
The Warrior Poet

The House of de Bretagne:
The Questing

The House of Summerlin:
The Legend

The Kingdom of Hendocia:
Kingdom by the Sea

The Executioner Knights:
By the Unholy Hand
The Mountain Dark
Starless
The Promise (also Noble Knights of
de Nerra)
A Time of End
Winter of Solace
Lord of the Shadows
Lord of the Sky
Splendid Hour

Gothic Regency Romance:
Emma

Contemporary Romance:

**Kathlyn Trent/Marcus Burton
Series:**
Valley of the Shadow
The Eden Factor
Canyon of the Sphinx

**The American Heroes Anthology
Series:**
The Lucius Robe

Fires of Autumn
Evenshade
Sea of Dreams
Purgatory

**Other non-connected
Contemporary Romance:**
Lady of Heaven
Darkling, I Listen
In the Dreaming Hour
River's End
The Fountain

Sons of Poseidon:
The Immortal Sea

**Pirates of Britannia Series (with
Eliza Knight):**
Savage of the Sea by Eliza Knight
Leader of Titans by Kathryn Le
Veque
The Sea Devil by Eliza Knight
Sea Wolfe by Kathryn Le Veque

Note: All Kathryn's novels are designed to be read as stand-alones, although many have cross-over characters or cross-over family groups. Novels that are grouped together have related characters or family groups. You will notice that some series have the same books; that is because they are cross-overs. A hero in one book may be the secondary character in another.

There is NO reading order except by chronology, but even in that case, you can still read the books as stand-alones. No novel is connected to another by a cliff hanger, and every book has an HEA.

Series are clearly marked. All series contain the same characters or family groups except the American Heroes Series, which is an anthology with unrelated characters.

For more information, find it in **A Reader's Guide to the Medieval World of Le Veque**.

About Kathryn Le Veque

Bringing the Medieval to Romance

KATHRYN LE VEQUE is a critically acclaimed, multiple USA TODAY Bestselling author, an Indie Reader bestseller, a charter Amazon All-Star author, and a #1 bestselling, award-winning, multi-published author in Medieval Historical Romance with over 100 published novels.

Kathryn is a multiple award nominee and winner, including the winner of Uncaged Book Reviews Magazine 2017 and 2018 "Raven Award" for Favorite Medieval Romance. Kathryn is also a multiple RONE nominee (InD'Tale Magazine), holding a record for the number of nominations. In 2018, her novel WARWOLFE was the winner in the Romance category of the Book Excellence Award and in 2019, her novel A WOLFE AMONG DRAGONS won the prestigious RONE award for best pre-16th century romance.

Kathryn is considered one of the top Indie authors in the world with over 2M copies in circulation, and her novels have been translated into several languages. Kathryn recently signed with Sourcebooks Casablanca for a Medieval Fight Club series, first published in 2020.

In addition to her own published works, Kathryn is also the President/CEO of Dragonblade Publishing, a boutique publishing house specializing in Historical Romance. Dragonblade's success has seen it rise in the ranks to become Amazon's #1 e-book publisher of Historical Romance (K-Lytics report July 2020).

Kathryn loves to hear from her readers. Please find Kathryn on Facebook at Kathryn Le Veque, Author, or join her on Twitter @kathrynleveque. Sign up for Kathryn's blog at www.kathrynleveque.com for the latest news and sales.